10440683

A dark, gothic novel with interesting characters and a strong Christian thread woven through it. *Gatehaven* is a wonderful read for lovers of gothic novels, and I am one. Thank you, Molly Noble Bull, for this page-turner.

—Lena Nelson Dooley is the multi-award-winning author of the McKenna's Daughters Series and *Love Finds You in Golden, New Mexico*

I never read fiction…until I read *Gatehaven*. I invite you to take the journey of this adventure. You will go places and even learn something along the way. It is enjoyable reading, and I especially liked the adventurous settings and spiritually enlightening plot. A definite hit and one book you will want to read!

—Jeff Harshbarger is the founder of Refuge Ministries and helped occultists come to Jesus Christ for over a decade. As a former Satanist, he authored *Dancing with the Devil* (Charisma House) and *From Darkness to Light* (Bridge Logos). Harshbarger has appeared on TBN, Daystar Network, *The 700 Club*, and The Miracle Channel. His website is www.refugeministries.cc

Molly Noble Bull certainly knows how to grab the reader right from the start. While her previous books were directed mostly at Christian women, her plot line in *Gatehaven* seeks a broader audience through arcane mysteries, spiritual intrigue, along with her telltale use of romance to satisfy her fans. New readers, as well as old, will be fascinated by her relatable characters and well-conceived plotline where a young Christian girl, caught within Europe's nobility, must face down "the wiles of the devil"—advanced through centuries-old occult rituals, crystal ball gazing, and amidst gothic imagery of medieval castles with the hidden secrets of the Knights Templar lurking about. Well done, Molly!

—S. Douglas Woodward is the author of *Power Quest: America's Obsession with the Paranormal*, and six other books on eschatology, alternate history, and spiritual warfare

Gatehaven by Molly Noble Bull is a dark and scary Gothic novel set in Europe and the state of South Carolina in 1784. *Gatehaven* will keep you reading to the very end, and yes, Molly is a distant cousin. But I would have read her exciting book anyway.

—PHIL NOBLE IS A FAMILY HISTORIAN AND AUTHOR OF ARTICLES AND SPEECHES ON THE NOBLE AND CALHOUN FAMILIES FROM HIS HOME IN CHARLESTON, SOUTH CAROLINA.

Gatehaven is an award-winning book and it's not hard to figure out why—just read the first few chapters. It has a strong plot and strong characters, clean and tight writing, drama, suspense, and a style and drive that keeps the reader turning page after page after page. If this is your first introduction to Molly Noble Bull, you're in for a lot of good reading and a lot of excitement. Highly recommended.

—MURRAY PURA IS THE AUTHOR OF *THE WINGS OF MORNING AND ASHTON PARK*

MOLLY NOBLE BULL

GATEHAVEN

A NOVEL

GATEHAVEN by Molly Noble Bull
Published by Creation House
A Charisma Media Company
600 Rinehart Road
Lake Mary, Florida 32746
www.charismamedia.com

This book or parts thereof may not be reproduced in any form, stored in a retrieval system, or transmitted in any form by any means—electronic, mechanical, photocopy, recording, or otherwise—without prior written permission of the publisher, except as provided by United States of America copyright law.

All Scripture quotations are from the King James Version of the Bible.

Design Director: Bill Johnson
Cover design by Nathan Morgan

Copyright © 2014 by Molly Noble Bull
All rights reserved.

Visit the author's website: www.mollynoblebull.com.

Library of Congress Cataloging-in-Publication Data: 2013951544
International Standard Book Number: 978-1-62136-400-9
E-book International Standard Book Number: 978-1-62136-401-6

While the author has made every effort to provide accurate telephone numbers and Internet addresses at the time of publication, neither the publisher nor the author assumes any responsibility for errors or for changes that occur after publication.

14 15 16 17 18 — 9 8 7 6 5 4 3 2

Printed in the United States of America

Put on the whole armor of God, that ye may be able to stand against the wiles of the devil.

Ephesians 6:11

DEDICATION

This novel is dedicated to Charlie, Bret, Burt, Bren, Bethanny, Hailey, Dillard, Bryson, Grant, Grace, Jana, Linda, Angela, and Kathryn.

But to God give the glory.

TABLE OF CONTENTS

AUTHOR'S HISTORICAL NOTES

FRANCE WAS A traditional ally of the Scots, and some French Protestants, called Huguenots, resettled in Scotland, marrying into Scottish clans. Eventually they found themselves in the middle of an uprising between the Scots and their enemy, England.

After the union between England and Scotland, some Scots, called Jacobites, fought to undo what had already been done. However, their cause was finally lost on a moor at Culloden in 1746. Afterward, the Clans were forbidden to wear kilts and tartans. They were not allowed the playing of pipes or to own weapons of any kind. The Huguenots living in Scotland might have wondered what would be next, and it is not surprising that some searched for a new land where they could practice their religion in peace.

Some Huguenots settled in Luss, Scotland, and *Gatehaven* is set in Luss in 1784. In the heart of Loch Lomond country, Luss is a real place and quite ancient—perhaps a thousand years old. However, most of the novel takes place in a haunting mansion in northern England, and the story ends in America and the state of South Carolina.

Between 1754 and 1763 the English colonies, including South Carolina, were at war with the Indians and the French. The Long Cane Massacre of 1760 took place near present-day Troy, South Carolina, and it was mentioned briefly in *Gatehaven*.

CHAPTER ONE

A country estate in Northern England

Early January 1784

MONSIEUR ETIENNE GABEAU wasn't his *real* name.
His name was Leon Picard. But Etienne Gabeau was the only name he'd answered to since making England his home.

He stood at a window in his sitting room, smiling inwardly as he looked out. "The haunting presence that surrounds your mansion always amazes me, my lord."

The young earl made no reply.

"Christians who read the Bible might say the atmosphere at Gatehaven is quite the devil's doing. We both know why." Leon/Etienne's laugh had mocking overtones. He pulled his dark cape closer to his thin, shriveled body. "It's a bit chilly tonight. Surely you must have noticed."

"Of course I noticed." The earl laughed from across the room. "An icy rain was coming down when I arrived. You might have to put me in a spare bedroom for the night, Monsieur. And why did you mention the Bible? Who among *our* circle of friends pay any mind to it?"

"A point well taken." The Frenchman pushed back a curl from his eyes.

His thick mass of dark curly hair had more white strands than black, making Leon look older than his forty-five years. But twenty years ago, he was called handsome.

"Still," Leon continued, "to the local villagers your estate is quite mysterious. It reminds me of structures I saw in France, growing up. And who can forget the red gate which gave Gatehaven its name?"

"When did you learn of the red gate, Monsieur Gabeau?"

"I learned the secret when your late father was the earl. You were but a boy then."

Lightning cracked the night sky. Thunder boomed.

"I saw it again, my lord."

"Really?" The earl's weak smile indicated that he was mildly interested. "What did you see?"

"Gatehaven…during that flash of lightning."

Someday I will have Rachel and own Gatehaven as well, Leon vowed mentally.

The earl cleared his throat. "I've decided not to go to Scotland after all, Monsieur."

"Not go?" Leon turned around in order to face him. "You *must* go." Leon Picard limped to his high-backed leather chair near the fireplace, tapping his cane on the pine floor as he went. "You *will* go."

"I beg your pardon."

"I said that you *will* go." Leon hooked his cane on the arm of his chair. Then he sat down and reached for the portrait on the small table beside him. "I demand it." Leon's words, spoken with his usual French accent, hung heavy in the air.

The earl didn't answer.

Leon thought that Edward Wellesley, the Earl of Northon, looked stiff—as if he'd suddenly turned to stone. At last the earl gazed at Leon from a chair facing his.

"Demand?" The muscles around the young earl's mouth slowly relaxed. "You have crossed the line, sir. Besides, I cannot go to Scotland. I have pressing business here. However, a French gentleman like you should enjoy such a journey." His smile was edged in sarcasm. "Why not go yourself?"

"On these crippled legs? I think not. Besides, she would never receive me."

"I am sorry. But it would be impossible for me to leave the country at this time."

Leon turned, gazing at the fire flickering and popping in the hearth. "You want the money, do you not?" He looked back at the earl like a hungry cat that cornered a mouse.

"But of course. You know I need money to pay my gambling debts."

"Precisely." Leon didn't miss the fleeting expression of fear that crossed the younger man's face. "I recently bought all your debts. I will destroy them all, but only if you do exactly what I say. At dawn on the morrow, you will set out for Scotland. And do dress warmly, my young friend. It will be cold out."

The earl's forehead wrinkled. "You say her last name is Aimee, and she lives in the village of Luss. But how would an English earl meet a Frenchwoman living in Scotland?"

"I believe your family owns a hunting lodge near Luss, does it not?"

The earl shrugged. "Even if I saw her on the street or near the Loch, I would never recognize her. What is she called?"

Leon's quick laugh held a trace of mockery. "In France, she was called Rachel. I see no reason why that would not be her name today." Leon grabbed the pearl handle of his cane with his left hand, leaned forward, and handed the portrait to Edward. "Look at this portrait carefully. Burn it into your brain. When you have brought her to me, your debts will be paid in full—and not a moment sooner."

"But how can I convince her to come to England? I don't even know the woman."

"You are a fine-looking young man with your gold-colored locks and blue eyes. I am sure you will find a way." Leon rubbed his aching knee. "Romance her. That should meet with success. Tell her you love her and plan to marry her. Women like that. And my spies tell me that she is not wedded at the moment."

"You have known me long enough to know, sir, that I am not the marrying kind."

"Have you no wits about you?" Leon sent the earl a harsh glance. "I don't want you to actually marry her—only promise that you will."

"I cannot see how…"

"Tell her you want her to come to England to meet your family before the engagement is formally announced." He smiled. "Yes, that would be the thing. She is a peasant woman, but well educated. Apparently, at one time her father was a teacher and a historian of sorts; she will understand that you must have your mother and grandmother school her in the ways of the quality before she becomes a part of it. And do smile a lot, Lord Northon. Let her see those sparkling teeth of yours."

"I will do as you say. But I doubt it can possibly work."

"It *will* work. Or you could find yourself in debtor's prison." Leon sent the earl another smile—long and slow and filled with hidden meanings that only Leon and Lord Northon could know. "And on your way back to England, stop by the chapel near Edinburgh your grandmother told you about. Do you know the one I mean?"

"Of course."

"I should like to hear the latest news from there. One can never learn too much about the craft—as I am sure you would agree."

CHAPTER TWO

Luss, Scotland—four months later

"MAMA, PAPA." SHANNON Aimee stood with her back to the fireplace—barely able to hold in her desire to shout her good news from the housetops. "I have been offered a proposal of marriage, and I accepted. He is coming here on the morrow to ask for my hand."

"So, Rachel Shannon." A quick smile lighted her father's face. "Ian Colquhoun finally asked you to be his wife."

Why did her father always call her Rachel Shannon? Mama was Rachel, and he knew she liked to be called Shannon. And why did Papa assume she was marrying Ian?

"Tell Ian that your mother and I could not be more pleased."

"And about time, too." Her mother smiled. "Ian has loved you all your life."

"I have no wish to marry Ian. He plans to become a man of the cloth, and I would never make a pastor's wife." Shannon took a step toward her parents, seated side by side on a blue settee so faded with age its color had all but disappeared. "With your permission, I hope to marry the earl—the Earl of Northon—as soon as my baby sister or brother is born."

"The Earl of Northon? When did he ask you to be his wife?"

"Last night, Mama, after the service at our church. You saw me talking to him in plain sight. And I promised to travel to England with him to meet his family."

"No!" Her mother popped up, her hands trembling. "That is out of the question. I will not allow it."

"Will not allow it?" Shannon couldn't believe what she had just heard. What could have caused her mother to be so upset? "Why, Mama? I thought you and Papa liked the earl."

"I said the English earl was handsome. But Ian Colquhoun is handsome, too."

"Did you refuse to let me go to England because you want me to marry Ian? Is that the real reason?"

Her mother shook her head. "I cannot allow you to go to England because I cannot go along as your chaperone—even if the baby were not on the way. It is much too dangerous."

"Now Rachel." Her father reached out and took her mother's hand. "What happened in England was a long time ago." He gently pulled Mama back down to the settee. Then he put his arm around her. "I agree with your concerns. But England should be safe for any of us now."

"But Javier."

"Do not worry, my love. With the baby coming and all, it would not be good for your health."

Mama crossed her arms over her chest. "I cannot stop worrying."

Papa gazed at her mother with gentle, comforting eyes. "Have you forgotten that we are under the shadow of the Almighty and that one day we will enter the pearly gates of heaven?"

His voice sounded as kind as he was. But Shannon noted a wrinkle on his forehead above his dark eyebrows.

"We moved here because we thought Scotland was a safe place for Huguenots to live," her father said. "But Scotland is not fit for Scots or Huguenots since the British took over. Were it not for the fighting across the sea, we would have moved to Charles Towne years ago—where your Uncle Henri lives today. Henri thinks we should emigrate now, and I want us to leave as soon as possible."

But did anyone care what Shannon thought or wanted? She'd made it clear that she wished to marry the earl and move to his estate in England. But was anybody listening?

"In the colonies, we will practice our faith in peace." Her father hesitated before going on. "I have known some good Englishmen and some who are bad. Now I also know the earl.

"With a few exceptions, I have no love for the British or the earl you say you love, Rachel Shannon. He talks to you before and after church meetings but seldom speaks to us. But even if I approved of him, I would never allow my only daughter to make such a journey without a chaperone." He gazed down at her mother's large belly. "Obviously, your mother cannot travel now. Your grandmother would not be of much help either since she speaks mostly French. Besides, as I said, we plan to sail to the colonies as soon as the baby is able to travel. We expect you to go along with us."

"Papa, you know I would never consider going to England until after my baby brother or sister is born. I made that clear to the earl. His aunt, Miss Foster, lives with other members of his family at the earl's hunting lodge near here, and she has promised to serve as my chaperone. Miss Foster is coming with the earl when he comes to ask for my hand, and I know you will like her. She and her personal maid will ride along in the carriage with us. So as you can see, everything has been arranged."

"Why must you go to England?" her mother asked. "It seems to me that the proper thing would be for his family to come to Scotland—to meet us."

"The earl said that there are some things his mother and grandmother want to teach me."

"Teach you? You've had a wonderful education. What do they expect you to learn?"

"They want—" Shannon hesitated. "I think they hope to teach me the social graces."

"Social graces?" Her mother looked at her father, and they both frowned. "Perhaps you better explain."

"We are not rich and titled like the earl's family is. I would have thought you and Papa would be pleased that I will be marrying a wealthy and titled man."

Mrs. Rachel Aimee bit her bottom lip. "No doubt his mother and grandmother want to teach you the correct way to pour English tea into a cup. Is that not so?"

Shannon didn't answer because that probably was what the earl's family had in mind. Maybe they didn't approve of the match. Maybe her parents didn't either. But Edward Wellesley, the Earl of Northon, said he loved her. And she loved him. Nothing else mattered.

She thought of the tender words of love that the earl had whispered in her ear at the ball and again after church on Sunday. She'd never been kissed by anyone but her parents. But one afternoon the earl pulled her into a shadowy area right there in the churchyard, and when nobody was looking, he kissed her. Her parents would be outraged if they knew. Still, she would never forget the thrill of it—the excitement. She would marry the earl if she had to run away to do it.

Her father stared at her for a moment. "It appears to me that the earl and his family do not think you are good enough."

She blinked because she really hadn't been listening.

"In return," he went on, "I say that he is not good enough for you, and I intend to remind him of that when he comes here. Though we do not have a great deal of earthly wealth and do not even own the farm we live on, we are children of the King of the Universe, and we have a great deal of wealth stored where rust cannot change its value and thieves cannot steal it."

"Please, Papa. Promise me that you will not say anything like that to the earl. And please refrain from speaking French in front of him."

"And why not?"

Too late, Shannon realized that asking her father to make such a promise was not likely to soothe his ruffled feelings. He could feel insulted.

"Forgive me, Papa, for not showing you proper respect. But I wanted you to know that the earl and his family are acquainted with the French language but speak mostly English. They—they attend the Church of England every Lord's Day—just like we attend our church." Shannon wondered what to say next because the earl had implied that his family didn't think God was as important as hers did. "Well, maybe they aren't as devout as we are, but they do go to church. The earl has been attending our church since I met him at the ball, and he might take offense if we suggested that his family are not true believers."

"Your mama and I have worried for some time that you are not as close to the Lord as we think you should be, Rachel Shannon."

His words hit Shannon in the heart like a fiery dart. "Is it not true that I go to church every time you and Mama and Peter do?"

Her father slowly nodded.

"Yet you never once doubted that my brother is a good Christian. Only me." Shannon's voice quivered with hurt and embarrassment, and unless something was done, her watery eyes were sure to become encased in full-blown tears. "Why, Papa? Why is that so?"

"You must discover the answer to that question for yourself. In the meantime, your mother and I withhold our permission for you to go to England."

Shannon felt drained—as if all hope had been surgically removed from her body. If she didn't leave at once she might throw something across the room or disgrace herself in some other way.

"I have some thinking to do." Shannon glanced toward the door. "May I be excused from this conversation? I would like to go for a walk."

"Go. Your mother and I also have some thinking to do. But stay within the grounds of the farm. We would worry if you ventured out alone beyond the front gate."

Shannon hurried outside. On the verge of exploding with pent-up anger, she kicked a rock with the toe of her brown leather shoe. It sailed through the air and landed on the grass a short distance away.

Her childhood friend, Ian Colquhoun, hit the trunk of a tree with both fists when he was angry. She'd also seen other Scottish men fighting trees and their demons in such a way. But her father was a gentle man. It was unlikely that he would do such a thing.

Shannon fisted her hands and stared at them. They looked fair and soft—unthreatening. Still, if a tree was nearby, she might wham it to discover for herself the advantage of giving in to primitive urges. The longer she stood there, the more she wanted to hit something.

She would find a way to go to England. She simply must.

◆——◆——◆

Ian Colquhoun had heard some disturbing news. His sister, Kate, had said that Shannon Aimee planned to marry the Earl of Northon. Though Shannon begged Kate not to tell anyone, Kate told Ian the news right away.

He hurried down the road that led to the farm managed by Shannon's father.

Ian had intended to marry Shannon as soon as he saved a bit more money. In fact, he'd planned to make Shannon his wife since they were children. It never occurred to him that she would fall in love with an arrogant snob like the earl. But now…

Oh, Shannon was a beauty, all right, with that long auburn hair and green eyes. It was not surprising that the earl would want her.

Ian's father had said that Shannon looked exactly like her mother did on the day she and her father arrived in Luss, and that Mrs. Aimee was still a handsome woman. Ian agreed. Shannon's mother was a very pretty lady. However, in his eyes, Mrs. Rachel Aimee could never compare in beauty and charm to Shannon, her lovely and exciting daughter.

True, Ian had never kissed Shannon or discussed topics like love and marriage, but he'd assumed she knew how he felt. Then he saw Shannon and the earl dancing together at a ball given by Ian's rich uncle, and he'd wondered if his chances to win her were lost.

But why would an English earl marry a Scottish girl like Shannon?

She had no wealth, no title or connections, and her parents came from France. The earl could pick from any number of attractive young women of quality in his own country. If the earl's intentions were less than honorable, Ian intended to prove it.

In fact, he would stop this union before it took place. He just needed to figure out how to do it.

◆——◆——◆

Shannon had only planned to go as far as the road that lined the farm where they lived. When she reached the gate that fronted the property, she stood there a moment.

Apparently, her parents thought her brother was perfect; therefore,

Peter never had problems like this. He was three years older than Shannon, but if Peter had wanted to go to England when he was nineteen, he would have been given permission as soon as he asked.

"Peter is the sort of boy a man can be proud of," her father once said.

Then her mother had added, "And he takes his responsibilities seriously."

Her mother didn't actually say that Shannon never took her responsibilities seriously or that she acted like a child, but she might as well have. In Shannon's mind, her parents' true feelings were clear enough.

Peter wanted to immigrate to the colonies where Uncle Henri and his new wife lived, and he'd convinced Grandma and their parents to travel with him. Mama and Papa would insist that Shannon immigrate too. But how could she? If only she could convince them that her future was with the earl.

The early autumn air felt cool on her face. The bushes and grass that edged the road clung to the thin, rocky soil like a lifeline, and though there weren't many trees, the few she saw pointed upward to a clear and windless sky.

In the distance, heather bloomed sweetly, coloring the hillsides in shades of pale purple and gray. She took in a deep breath and released it slowly. Despite everything, she savored the moment.

The farm didn't front the loch like Ian's farm did. But sometimes when the wind was right, she smelled the faint odor of the sea.

Today, a mist slowly draped the landscape like it often did over the Loch.

Shannon shivered. There was something haunting about a mist—especially when it hung over the smooth yet deep waters of the loch like old lace. When they were children, Ian had often taken Shannon and her brother out on his small boat on sunny afternoons in summer when the sky was clear.

They picnicked on a nearby shore, and sometimes on their way home, she would lean over the side of the boat, dip her fingertips in the cold water, and gaze at the rocky shore. She never tired of studying her surroundings— green hills and a lake as big as the sky.

"Do not do that, lass," Ian would say. "Sit right in the boat. If ya lean over like that, you could upset the balance. We could go tumbling into the loch."

Ian was the tallest and handsomest young man in Luss. Everybody thought so. He watched after her like an older brother might, but Shannon already had a brother. She would love Ian forever, but he didn't make her heart beat faster. Just looking at the earl did.

The Earl, Edward.

Thoughts of her recent conversation with her parents blocked out everything else. She longed to see the earl—needed to see him—at once.

He was staying at his hunting lodge, but sometimes he came to church in town.

"To see you," he had said.

The village of Luss beckoned. She never went to the village unless Mama or her brother went with her. Today, she would. She would stroll down the country road until she reached the village and pay a visit to her grandmother. Grandma Aimee might be the very one to convince Papa to change his mind and let her go to England with the earl.

The earl had men working for him. Shannon called them his spies because whenever she entered the village, she found them watching her. Sometimes the earl would appear a few minutes later whether at church or at the shop where she and her mother bought bread. Maybe she would see him again today.

Her heart beat faster with the hope.

She was about to cross the bridge over a small stream when she noticed Ian strolling briskly at the water's edge. Ian's father was the second son of the Laird of the village, and though his family lived as modestly as hers, Ian's last name had always given him a certain prestige among the villagers that newcomers, like the Aimee family, had never known.

Ian didn't appear to have seen her yet.

The soles of her shoes tapped the wooden bridge. He probably couldn't have heard, but he looked up.

If only he'd smiled. His smile always warmed her—even on the coldest day in winter. Merely looking at him made her almost forget her troubles at home, and she'd always counted on Ian in her time of need. Maybe he would be willing to talk to her father about the earl on Shannon's behalf.

"Good morning, Ian."

"Morning, lass. I am surprised to see you walking out here alone."

Normally, dimples dotted both his cheeks, and his wide smile lifted her spirits. Today, the sun hid behind the clouds, and she saw no smile at all. Today his hair looked as thick and dark brown as her father's. Yet on other mornings, the sun turned it almost as red as her own.

"Where is your brother?" Ian asked.

"You would have to ask Peter where he went this morning."

"What brings you to the village so early in the day?"

"I thought I would visit my grandmother. She has been feeling poorly of late. It was time I paid her a visit."

"Mind if I walk along?"

She turned. "Please do. I would appreciate the company."

"Maybe we should take the road nearest the Loch. We are less likely to be seen there this time of day, and we would not want to damage your good name."

Shannon looked up at him and smiled. Despite the tender sound of his words, the flesh around his lips tightened, and he didn't smile back.

Her head barely reached his shoulders, and he'd always walked with a long stride. Yet when they walked together, he often set his pace to fit hers. Today she had to practically run to keep up.

Obviously, his normal good humor had faded. She would need to find a way to revive it.

"Ian, I've known for a long time that you hope to go into the ministry. Have you found a mentor yet—now that our pastor will retire to his sister's home in the country soon?"

"Not yet, I am afraid."

"My father would be willing to teach you about the Bible. But that would never make you a man of the cloth. However, I know someone who might."

"And who would that be?"

"I am sure you know that the Earl of Northon has a hunting lodge near here. But you might not have heard that I agreed to marry him."

"Aye." He glanced away. "I saw you dancing with him at my uncle's ball."

Then he looked down at his feet like he always did when he didn't want to say more.

Shannon scolded herself internally for feeling obligated to rush into a long explanation. She had the right to marry whomever she pleased. At the same time, Ian was her oldest and dearest friend.

"I know it seems unlikely that a man of the quality would choose me—a young woman with no money or high station in life. But as amazing as it might sound, he loves me, Ian, and I love him. It would so please me if you told Papa you agree with the match."

"Apparently, congratulations are in order," Ian said, ignoring her request. "But what does any of that have to do with me?"

"I am getting to that." She was talking much too fast and probably telling more than he needed to know. "You see, the earl employs a vicar to tend to the spiritual needs of his family and those who live in the village nearby, and every few years they select a young man to come and live at the vicarage and learn from the vicar. They are looking for such a young man right now. All I would need to do is say the word, and I am sure the earl would choose you."

Shannon had tried to fill her voice with the promise of great things to come. However, Ian's cold glance indicated that he hadn't received her suggestion with interest and excitement as she'd hoped.

"Like your parents, I am a member of the reformed church," he replied. "What benefit would learning the ways of the Church of England be to me?"

She tried not to roll her eyes. "Is it not true that just last Sunday our pastor said that God is the same yesterday, today, and forever? So the earl's church must be more or less the same as ours."

He shook his head. "I disagree about all the churches being the same."

"Still, how could serving under an English vicar not help in your quest to become a pastor?" Shannon's lips turned up at the edges. "Besides, I would miss you terribly if you did not go to England with us."

"Would you now?"

"Most certainly. You are my oldest and dearest friend. Please say you will go."

"I cannot promise. But I will agree to think about it."

If Shannon were Ian's judge, she would say that he wasn't as happy about her good fortune as she had hoped. In fact, she didn't think Ian wanted her to go to England at all.

He gazed at her like a provoked parent might do. "To be completely honest, lass, I do not trust the earl. I feel it my duty to warn you. Continued association with this man could put you and perhaps your entire family in danger."

Shannon bit her lower lip to keep from saying something she might regret later. As much as she loved and trusted Ian, she was in love with the earl. Why didn't Ian understand?

Her grandmother wasn't home, and Shannon didn't see the earl or any of his servants, so they headed back to the farm. Ian bid her farewell at the gate of the family farm and went his own way.

"I must finish my chores," he said.

Before Shannon had reached the front stoop, her father rushed out the door to meet her. "Shannon." He seemed relieved to see her. "I thank the Lord that you are home."

Shannon halted. Tears moistened the edges of her father's dark eyes. He'd never looked so grave. Something was terribly wrong.

"Your mother was so worried about you, Rachel Shannon, after you ran away like you did. Now, she—she—"

"What is wrong, Papa? What happened?"

"The baby is coming. Hurry, she is in the bedroom. She will need you now."

Shannon raced into the house. Her mother groaned as Shannon hurried into her parents' bedroom.

CHAPTER THREE

IAN DECIDED TO visit his pastor at his home before turning in that evening. He hoped to learn Pastor Petit's opinion as to whether or not he should accept the position Shannon mentioned—if indeed it was offered. Like Shannon's father, his pastor, Rev. Isaac Petit, was a French Huguenot. Ian thought of him as a friend or family member—like a grandfather or a trusted uncle.

Pastor Petit and his wife settled in Scotland years before Ian was born. A widower now, the gentleman was getting on in years. Yet he won Ian's respect and devotion because of his gentleness, his charitable works, and his excellent Bible teachings.

The pastor's cottage was small but well kept, and located on a road not far from the church. Ian noticed a weak light glowing through a front window as he walked up. A light rain dotted his brown jacket as he stood on the stoop and knocked.

Ian waited. His pastor was hard of hearing. He knocked again.

The door opened. Pastor Petit held a lighted candle. "Mr. Colquhoun, it is good to see you this evening. Please, come in and sit by the fire. The spring season is still fairly young, and it's damp—far too chilly for my old bones. I was about to have tea. I will pour a cup for you, and we shall have a cozy talk."

Ian and his pastor met in the church office often, but he hadn't visited his home in a long time. While the pastor went to pour the tea, Ian brushed off his shoes and stepped inside.

Oak bookcases crammed with books framed the stone fireplace in the sitting room. He was about to sit down when he noticed that an English Bible lay opened on a table by the pastor's chair. The minister gave Ian an English Bible soon after he learned that Ian hoped to one day become a man of the cloth, and Ian loved and respected the old gentleman all the more for it.

He doubted that his pastor would advise him to become an assistant to a vicar in the English church. Still, he wanted to hear what he might say regarding the matter.

Pastor Petit handed Ian a cup of warmed tea and settled onto the high-backed armchair facing him. "You are well, I hope."

"Oh, yes sir. I am well indeed."

"And your family?"

"They are well, too."

The minister smiled. "Good." He took a sip of tea, setting his cup on the small table beside the Bible. "Did you know that we are told in the Holy Scriptures to present our bodies to God as a living sacrifice? I was reading about it shortly before you came in."

"No Pastor, I did not. But it sounds reasonable, considering all the Lord has done for us."

"You are exactly right, and that scripture is found in the Book of Romans—chapter twelve and verse one." He reached for his Bible, placing it on his lap. "I had a dream a night or two ago, Mr. Colquhoun, and in it, you were asking me questions—as you and other young people in the church often do. In the dream you said that when you give your body as a living sacrifice in prayer as Scripture says to do that a troubling thought often comes to your mind. You said that when you meant to say 'I give my body as a living sacrifice,' the words 'I give my body to be burned' comes to your mind instead."

"Yes, I've had troubling dreams like that." Ian leaned forward slightly in his chair. "How did you know?"

"I didn't."

"So what is the meaning of your dream, sir?" Ian asked.

"Only God knows the meaning of dreams. But if we wish to pray or do as God tells us to do and something like a voice or voices tells us to say or do something contrary to the Scriptures, we must assume that the devil is attempting to somehow hinder our Christian walk."

A shiver shot through him. "You mean Satan?"

"Yes. But don't take my word for it. I could be wrong. Read the Bible for yourself."

Ian gazed down at his cup without saying anything more. His pastor was a true man of God, and he'd given Ian something new and different to think about. But it might take time before the words took root in his mind. Pastor Petit had presented him with many deep teachings in the last year or so—teachings he'd never had the time to mediate on as he should. If he decided to go to England with Shannon and the earl, he would have many hours to think on these things during the long journey to the earl's estate.

"Thank you for that teaching, sir. You can be sure that I will think on your words again." Ian took a sip of tea, wondering if he should jump in with questions of his own or allow the minister to say more on the current topic. He'd allowed the old gentleman to control the conversation. Was it time to explain the reason for his visit?

After a moment, Ian said, "You know, Pastor, that I felt called to go into the ministry years before I told my family. And I wanted you to be the first to know that I might soon have the opportunity to travel to England and become the assistant to a minister there."

"What a wonderful opportunity for a young man like you, Mr. Colquhoun. Going to England will not only broaden your horizons, it will help you develop as a man of God. What is the name of the clergy you will be working under? It is possible I might have heard of him."

"I doubt you would have." Ian hesitated, sending up a quick prayer for the courage to continue. "You see, if I choose to take this assignment, I will be serving under a vicar in the British church."

"The British church? I am indeed surprised. How did this come to be? And you a loyal Scotsman."

"Miss Shannon Aimee hopes to pay a visit to the home of the Earl of Northon—well chaperoned of course, but I dare not trust the earl. Miss Aimee told of the possible opportunity for me to become the assistant to the earl's confessor, and I—"

"Say no more. I think I understand your motive here." The pastor lifted his cup to his lips and took a sip of tea. "You wish to protect Miss Aimee from what could be a dangerous situation."

"That is my hope. Otherwise, I would never consider traveling all the way to Gatehaven."

The pastor's eyes widened. "Gatehaven, did you say?"

"Yes. That is the name of the earl's estate."

The pastor grew pale. Before Ian could make a comment, the old man pulled a white cloth from the belt of his dark clothing and wiped his brow.

Ian rushed to his side. "Are you all right, sir?"

"I will be. Give me a moment."

Ian reached for his tea, pressing it to the pastor's lips. "Here, sir, drink this."

Pastor Petit swallowed a mouthful of tea. Then he closed his eyes and pressed his head against the back of his chair.

"Should I go for a physician?"

"No. I am not ill. Merely surprised." The pastor opened his eyes. "But this is all so peculiar."

"Peculiar? How is that so, sir?"

The pastor's smile looked weak. "Sometimes the Lord answers prayer in unusual ways." He shook his head as if he couldn't believe what he'd just heard. "My cousin was murdered in England some years ago."

"Murdered?"

"Yes. Her name was Magdalena Petit, and she was thirty-five years of age when she died. It was tragic for my late wife and me because Magdalena was always very special to us. We never had any children of our own, and when Magdalena's parents died, she lived with us for several years. Magdalena was also a Huguenot, and during her eighteenth year, she moved back to England to live with an older sister. However, we corresponded often. My wife and I were devastated to learn of her death—doubly so because her murderer was never found."

"Sure and that is a tragedy, Pastor Petit."

"Indeed. I'd been praying that the person who killed Magdalena would come to justice. Three years ago, I started corresponding with a vicar in England whose parish is near Gatehaven—the very estate you mentioned. I think the vicar there might know more about my cousin's death than he is willing to say in a letter. Perhaps he fears the letter might fall into unfriendly hands. The vicar has suggested several times that I journey to England and pay him a visit so we can discuss this crime face-to-face. However, I cannot leave my flock here in Scotland. I will soon leave the village for good and retire to the country in my old age. However, *you* could go as my ambassador, Mr. Colquhoun, if the position is offered to you and you go to England partly on my behalf."

"I am not a member of the Church in England, sir," Ian explained. "As you well know, I am a member of the Reformed Church. Of what benefit would becoming the assistant to an English vicar be to me?"

The pastor leaned forward. Ian noted that a bit of color had returned to his cheeks.

"Much good could come of this, Mr. Colquhoun. Not only would you be protecting a young woman's honor, you might also bring a criminal to justice, and you should gain much from working under my friend, the vicar. He is a true man of God, and he reads his Bible daily." The pastor motioned toward a desk by the door leading to the other room. "I have received many letters since the vicar penned a letter to me the first time, and I have kept them all. I keep them in the drawer of my desk, and I want you to have them."

"I cannot take your letters, sir."

"It would be a gift to you from me and my late cousin."

"But I am not sure I will be given the position in England that I mentioned."

"Take the letters and read them even if you are not selected. I beg you. You will please an old man if you do."

Ian opened the drawer that his pastor mentioned and found a stack of letters tied with a black ribbon and arranged by date. He felt a little uncomfortable taking them to his house and reading them, but at the same time, the idea intrigued him.

That night, Ian opened the first one.

Dear Pastor Petit,

My named is Mr. E.G. Steen, and I am a vicar serving at a parish in England near Gatehaven—an estate owned by the Earl of Northon. While on holiday in London recently, I met the son of another English earl at a church, and he told me about a terrible injustice. He said that a Frenchwoman living in England by the name of Magdalena Petit was murdered twenty years ago. Her house was burned to the ground, and her murderer was never found.

After I returned home, I could not forget what the gentleman told me—as if it had been nailed to my mind. A few days after that, I read a list of pastors living in Scotland in a post I received from a friend from another village. When I read your name on that list I thought of Magdalena Petit. I cannot help but wonder if you might be related to her.

It would be advantageous to both of us if we could discuss this mystery in more detail. But in any case, I hope to hear from you soon.

Respectfully,
E.G. Steen, Rector
Saint Thomas Church
Fairs, England

Seated at his father's desk in the small sitting room of his family home, Ian put the letter back on the stack. To think that God might use him to help bring a murderer to justice was more than he ever thought possible. He would need to pray now and read the Bible to learn God's will for his life. It seemed incredible that the Lord might use him in this way, and the fact that he might also be able to protect Shannon made going to England sound very appealing.

·———·

A frosty spring followed the winter the earl arrived in Scotland, and spring melted into early summer. Shannon spent her days and many nights helping her mother with the new baby—rarely seeing the earl except at church on Sunday mornings. He must have stayed away because he knew how her parents felt about him. Yet his loyalty to Shannon made her love him all the more, and he never failed to mention their approaching marriage each time they met.

But now it was mid-June. The arrangements for her journey to England were completed. Shannon sat by a window in the sitting room owned by Ian's parents, gazing out at the Loch. All that was left to do was say good-bye to her friends and loved ones.

On the morrow, she would be leaving for England, and though she still dreamed of going there, leaving those she loved made a part of her feel sad. Somehow, looking out at the Loch gave her the strength she needed to say good-bye to her best friend—Kate Colquhoun.

Kate leaned toward her. "Do you truly love the earl that much?"

Shannon heard a creaking sound nearby. "What was that?"

"Maybe it was the wind." Kate shrugged. "It is often windy here—probably because we live so near the Loch." She paused briefly. "You have yet to answer my question."

Seated on the settee with Kate beside her, Shannon whispered her reply in case Kate's younger sisters happened to be within earshot. She *had* heard something, and she didn't think it was the wind.

The younger Colquhoun girls often listened to conversations while hidden from view, and when she first came in, Shannon had thought she heard the creak of a wooden floor plank near where they sat now.

"Do you love the earl, Shannon, or not?"

Shannon blinked and nodded. "I love him as much as you love my brother, Peter. Maybe more."

"Well, if you are sure, that is all I really wanted to know." Kate smiled. "I want you to be happy. You are my oldest and dearest friend. I only want the best for you."

"Kate, I love you, too. You know that. I just hope my brother is the man you really want to spend the rest of your life with. He can be a little—"

"I know you and Peter have never gotten along," Kate said softly. "But I love him and always will."

"Then I am happy for you and glad that one day you will be my sister."

"I am honored to be your future sister as well as Peter's wife."

Shannon released a deep breath. "I wish I could stay longer, but I must go." She got up and glanced toward the door. "I promised to help Mama bathe my baby brother before she puts him down for his afternoon nap. Besides, I have last minute packing to do."

Kate smiled as she got up and stood beside Shannon.

"How is the baby doing?"

"Thriving. I think he's going to be as tall as Peter. Maybe even as tall as Ian." Shannon reached out and embraced her friend. "I'm going to miss you, Kate Colquhoun."

"As I will miss you and Ian. Please, Shannon, promise to write often. I know Ian will not, and I want to keep informed on the doings of my brother and my best friend."

Their good-bye was an emotional one—at least for Shannon. Afraid she might break down and weep if she said more, Shannon reached out and hugged Kate again.

Ian was the one who had been standing in the shadows listening, but he never meant to do it. He'd come in the back way about the time Shannon entered through the front door of the cottage.

He'd read all of Pastor Petit's letters and longed to share them with Shannon, but she was too devoted to the earl to listen to his concerns. He also had news for Kate.

He hadn't counted on Shannon coming over to visit his sister, and he hadn't wanted to spoil their emotional farewell. However, he was tired of standing there, waiting. If Shannon hadn't left when she did, he would have made himself known to them.

Peter was on his way over to speak to Kate. It was important that Shannon not know what Peter had to say.

Kate shut the door and crossed to the archway leading to the dining room. Ian stepped out from behind a large china cabinet and stood in her path.

"Well, Ian. How long have you been here?"

"Long enough. I came in to tell you that Peter is on his way over."

Kate smiled. "Peter is coming here?"

"Yes."

Kate pushed back a lock of her curly brown hair that had fallen across her forehead. "What is this all about, Ian?"

"That is what I planned to tell you. But when I saw that Shannon was here, I decided to wait until she left. I did not wish to interrupt your conversation, and if I had moved an inch, you would have known I was here."

"And all this time I thought our little sisters were the eavesdroppers in the family."

"I'm sorry, but it was necessary." He motioned toward the settee in the sitting room where Kate and Shannon were seated earlier. "Let us sit down, and I will explain."

Kate sat down stiffly, her arms across her chest. "Now, what is this all about?"

"Peter's parents do not feel comfortable having Shannon go to England with a group of strangers. They were pleased that I took the mentoring position Shannon mentioned and that I will be going to England. But they want a member of their family to go along as well. Therefore, Peter is also going."

"*My* Peter is going to England, and he never told me. I do not believe it."

"It is true, Kate. Peter will be here shortly to tell you himself."

"If Peter was going to England, Shannon would have told me."

"Shannon doesn't know."

"You mean his own sister was never told?"

"Her parents thought it best that she not know, and you must promise not to tell her."

"We share everything. Of course I will tell her."

"Peter and I believe that the earl is not the noble soul Shannon thinks he is, but we have no proof of that. Therefore, Peter will be trailing us to England—staying at inns near the earl's estate but out of sight. He will also be seeking temporary employment there, and together, we will continue our investigation of the earl Shannon is so fond of."

"Shannon is in love with the earl, Ian," Kate said softly. "You must face that truth before you are hurt more than you already are."

"I know she *thinks* she is in love with him. As our pastor would say, we will see how she feels once the scales are removed from her eyes."

———◆———

Early the next morning, Ian climbed in the second carriage behind the one that Shannon, the chaperone, and the earl would be riding in. The earl's valet and Miss Foster's maid sat stiffly, facing each other on the opposite side of the carriage.

The three of them met briefly a week ago, so there was no need for introductions. Ian greeted them cordially, sitting down beside Dickson, the valet, but close to the window. Dickson and Polly, the maid, were about Ian's age.

Polly looked scared to death until she and Dickson realized they came from the same village not far from Luss and that they knew each other as children. All at once the two of them were chattering between themselves like a couple of crows on a fencepost. But Ian probably wouldn't have known them when he was a child even if they were from Luss.

He'd attended a school for rich young gentleman in England when he was a boy—except he wasn't rich or English. Ian's father was the second son of the Laird of the village, meaning his uncle got the title, the family home, and all monies the family had. Ian's father got nothing. Perhaps Uncle George paid for Ian's schooling in England to mute a guilty conscious.

Ian had several conferences with his pastor since the one he had on the

day Shannon told him of her plans to marry the earl. In each meeting he
learned something new about the Bible he'd never known previously. But
some of the things they discussed were about the dark forces of this world
and how to combat them. His chores on the farm and other family duties
kept his mind and body occupied, and the long journey ahead would give
him time to think on the things he'd learned and how to apply them in
his daily life.

For now, he would sit here and wait. Shannon and her chaperone
would be arriving soon, and he hoped to watch as she and the earl entered
the head carriage in front of them.

◆——◆——◆

At daybreak on that same morning—before the cock crowed—Peter
Aimee had mounted his brown-colored horse and galloped to the edge of
the village. He hid behind an abandoned mill and watched as his younger
sister climbed into the carriage with the Earl of Northon and his maiden
aunt, Miss Foster.

Their little brother, Andre, was born on the day Shannon told Mama
and Papa that she wanted to go to England. Later that same day, as
Shannon helped their mother with the baby, Peter sat with his father in
the sitting room of their small cottage.

"Your sister is a strong-willed young woman, Peter, just like your mama
was at her age, and that can be a good thing. It can also be dangerous. I
know my daughter. We will not be able to talk Shannon out of going to
England to meet the earl's family—no matter how hard we might try. She
will run away if we refuse to give our permission, and we will lose her forever. Therefore, your mother and I devised a plan. We want you to follow
your sister to England without being noticed. And you must promise
not to tell *anyone* of our plan—even Kate. You will eat in out-of-the-way
places—sleep on the ground in mild weather. I have a little money saved
which I will give you to pay for your keep until you find employment."

"No, Papa, I cannot take your money. You planned to use it to pay for
passage to the land across the sea and to buy a farm once we arrive."

"We will worry about money for boat passages and a farm when the
time comes. Now we must protect your sister from a dangerous young
earl who thinks she is as beautiful as her mother."

Peter had no intentions of spending all of his father's hard-earned
money. He would take any job he could get once he reached the village
near the earl's estate in England.

At the time he made that decision, he'd thought he would be the only
one going to England other than those in the earl's party and the only one
with Shannon's best interest at heart. But after his friend Ian accepted

the position Shannon found for him, Peter realized that he would have a comrade in his quest to protect his sister from the British earl.

Still, he regretted having to say good-bye to Kate.

They had walked down to the Loch. Kate wore a blue dress that matched her eyes. A summer breeze whipped her long brown hair in all directions, and he'd kissed her before he told her he was leaving. But she already knew.

"It's all right, Dear One," she had said. "Go. I love your sister, too. And I will be waiting here at the Loch when you return."

If he hadn't already planned to make her his wife, he would have known Kate was the one when she said those words.

CHAPTER FOUR

S HANNON ALREADY MISSED Andre, her baby brother, and they had only been gone a little over an hour. Andre had looked a bit small for a newborn on the day he was born, and Shannon was the first to hold him. Ever since, she'd felt guilty that she might have caused the baby to arrive too soon. Nevertheless, Andre thrived on his mother's breast milk, and Mama predicted that one day Andre would be as tall as his father and his brother, Peter—and as handsome, too.

At least Ian finally agreed to study under the vicar at Saint Thomas Church. He was traveling with them, which made leaving home for the first time easier.

Shannon still didn't know why her mother was so afraid for her to go to England. The English were certainly different from the French and the Scots, but not *that* different.

The middle-aged spinster, Miss Foster, had been living in the family's hunting lodge in Scotland since her parents moved there when she was a child. Miss Foster claimed to enjoy visiting the earl's family in England and said she could hardly wait to get there.

Shannon confessed to Miss Foster in whispers that she loved the earl. However, he hadn't said much to Shannon or to his aunt since they left her village. He hadn't seemed especially interested in the few comments Shannon made during the long ride in his expensive-looking carriage.

Like the earl, Ian never talked much. However, he was always willing to listen. Shannon was glad that Ian and Polly, Miss Foster's maid, and

Dickson, the earl's valet, were traveling in the carriage right behind them and that she would be seeing Ian often once they arrived in England.

Nevertheless, she missed hearing the sound of the earl's deep baritone voice. Maybe he kept quiet because he would rather that Miss Foster not hear what he had to say. Still, he looked at Shannon longingly now and again. For the present, she would have to settle for that.

She'd hoped to discuss marriage plans with the man she loved during the long trip. But his aunt kept discussing other topics—dark, disturbing ones—that would probably cause Shannon to have bad dreams at the end of her first day of traveling.

Stranger still, her father had made an odd comment shortly before she climbed up in the carriage beside her chaperone.

He'd hugged her real close and said, "Do you know the meaning of the word *wiles*, Rachel Shannon?"

"Wiles? No, Papa, I do not."

"I was told it means beguiled. Your brother thinks the earl has beguiled you." Her father handed her a sheet of parchment folded in half. "I have written a scripture from the Bible regarding this matter, and I want you to set it to memory. Will you promise to do that?"

"I will read the scripture verse, Papa."

But she refused to promise to remember it.

"I love you." Her father kissed her on the forehead. "Godspeed. And may the Lord go with you."

"And go with you and Mama, too."

She'd put the parchment in the sack her mother had fashioned to match the gold material in her dress. She loosened the gold string and pulled out the message, written at her father's desk with pen and ink.

Put on the whole armor of God, she read, *that you may stand against the wiles of the devil. Book of Ephesians, chapter six and verse eleven.*

Shannon shook her head. The message held no meaning for her. How could someone put on the whole armor of God? Where would she find such a garment? The earl had told her of metal clothing that men once wore into battle and that he kept such an item of clothing at his hunting lodge. He'd urged her to come to his hunting lodge and see it for herself, but she never had.

She folded the parchment and put it back in her carrying sack.

They traveled through what appeared to be a hilly wilderness where trees were seldom seen. Everything she saw looked new and fresh. Shannon couldn't get enough of merely gazing out the windows on first one side of the carriage and then the other.

But she missed Ian and looked forward to visiting with him when they stopped for the night. He knew a lot about the Bible. Maybe he would tell her the meaning of the scripture verse.

Miss Foster began a discourse on the merits of owning a crystal ball and the insights she'd gain from hers. Shannon hadn't known what a crystal ball was or its use until her chaperone volunteered to tell her. However, the explanation sounded odd to say the least, and a bit unsettling. Shannon turned her thoughts to a different kind of ball—the ball in Luss held on the day she met the earl for the first time.

She was standing with her father and mother, waiting for Ian Colquhoun to claim his dance. However, she'd thought of nothing but the handsome Earl of Northon since he entered the hall. She found herself dreaming of meeting him, but at first, he neither sought her out nor glanced in her direction.

The young earl appeared to be searching for someone. Obviously, Shannon wasn't that person.

All at once he walked right in front of them.

Shannon sucked in her breath.

He wore a long, black coat over the finest white shirt and dark breeches she'd ever seen. What looked like a diamond glittered from his frothy cravat.

"Rachel Shannon," her father said.

"Yes, Papa."

The earl had started to walk off, but he turned and looked right at her.

"We will be leaving the ball soon," her father added in French. "Dance with Ian once. And then we will go."

Shannon's eyes seemed to connect with the young earl's sky blue ones, and his with hers. He looked at her as if she was the only woman in the room, and then he disappeared into the crowd. She never expected to see him again, and when Ian returned to collect his dance, she gladly accepted.

"This will be my last dance of the evening," Shannon explained as Ian escorted her back to her parents. "Papa said we would be going home now."

But as soon as Ian walked away, the earl and Laird Colquhoun, the leader of the Clan, walked up and joined them. Laird Colquhoun introduced Shannon and her parents to the earl, and he managed to convince Shannon's father that it was much too early to consider leaving the ball.

All eyes turned to Shannon Aimee when the earl led her out for a country dance. Their eyes probably opened even wider when he asked her to be his partner a second time.

"I wish to dance every dance with you," he whispered in a breathy tone.

"But this is the second time you called me out, my lord. It would be unthinkable for us to dance again."

His wide grin warmed her heart. "I know a bench where we can sit and talk. I am eager to learn all about you, and the bench is very private, indeed. Nobody will be able to hear us. Yet your parents can watch us from afar—as you would expect them to do."

Shannon never expected her father to agree to such an arrangement. However, Laird Colquhoun convinced him to accept. And her father's attention never moved from that bench during the time that she and the earl sat there talking.

"Miss Aimee," Miss Foster said, cutting in on her recollections. "Are you enjoying your journey thus far?"

"Oh yes, ma'am—very much so." Shannon returned her chaperone's brief smile and gazed at the earl, hoping he would make some sort of comment. When he glanced her way, she continued. "Lord Northon, where will we be spending the night?"

"At an inn your father mentioned. But on the morrow, we will stay at an inn near a chapel I would like for us to visit. I am sure you will find it as interesting as I do."

"Then we will be attending church?"

"Church?" He laughed. "I said we will be visiting a chapel—not attending services there."

Shannon turned her head at an angle. "If we will be visiting a chapel, why not attend services? I am sure my parents would like that very much."

"I would not," he retorted. "We will tour the building—inspect the carvings and other objects of interest there—and then we will leave. I will take you and my aunt back to the inn, and I will attend an important meeting with friends from the village."

Shannon nodded. "I see."

But she didn't.

The earl had seemed so aloof since they left Luss—almost as if he was a different person. It had to be because Miss Foster hung on their every word. Things would return to normal once they arrived at his estate.

Shannon had thought—hoped—that she would be having her supper that evening with the earl. She'd dreamed that they would share a table for two—that he would whisper sweet love words as he had done in Luss. But that did not happen.

The earl left the inn as soon as they checked in.

Later, Shannon sat at a table below stairs long after Miss Foster turned in for the night, hoping the earl would return. Ian sat with her.

"To keep you from being lonely," Ian said.

During the long evening, Shannon told Ian of the message with the scripture verse in it and asked if he knew its meaning. He confessed that he did not.

Then Ian reminded her of their happy childhood in Luss and told a funny story or two—perhaps to cheer her up. Soon she felt a lot better, and when she actually laughed at some of his remarks, she realized that a merry heart really was like a medicine.

◆———◆———◆

Peter Aimee stood just outside the circle of light coming from lamps— lamps that hung from a tree and from the eves of the Lion's Inn. His sister, Shannon, as well as the earl and his party were staying the night at the inn. Peter would be sleeping in a field nearby on a blanket he'd brought from home.

He'd followed the earl after he left the inn to another establishment further on where he heard loud music coming from inside. He peeked in a window and saw a lot of men drinking from large mugs. The earl was one of them. And young women showed their ankles as they danced on a lighted stage.

Peter saw enough to know that the earl was up to no good. He'd mounted his brown horse and headed back to the inn. He wanted to check the time when the earl returned and the condition he was in when he staggered inside.

The entry door to the inn opened. Ian Colquhoun stepped onto the stoop out front.

"Ian," Peter said from the darkness. "I'm over here."

"Peter?"

"Yes. Over here."

Peter watched as Ian moved toward him.

"It's awfully dark out here, my friend," Ian said, "and the dim light coming from the inn helps but a little. Will you join me at a table inside? You must be starving."

"True, I am hungry. But it's too risky for me to be seen at an inn where my sister is sleeping. She would be furious if she knew I followed her here. I have no wish that the earl find me here either."

"Shannon was very tired and went up to bed." Ian shrugged. "I cannot say where the earl might be."

"I can. I followed him, and the earl went out for a night of drinking. I doubt he will return until the early hours of the morning."

"Then I see no reason why you cannot come inside." Ian motioned toward a path at the side of inn. "There is a back door to the eating area. Go around to the back, knock, and I will open the door. We will take a table near the door. And while we talk, you can eat your supper."

Peter nodded. "I might regret this, but I am too tired and hungry to argue. I will knock on the back door shortly."

"And I will open it as soon as you do."

Ian went back inside.

The plump, middle-aged woman who had served their supper stood just inside the door. She sent him a toothless smile.

"Lass," Ian said as if he thought he was talking to a much younger woman, "please send someone to the table in the back a bit later. I will be likin' to eat another bowl of stew."

The woman laughed. "Eatin' again, are ya?"

He nodded and grinned.

"You're a handsome, lad, you know. But if you keep eating two suppers a night, you'll soon be lookin' like me husband." She motioned toward the rotund little man with the bald head standing behind the counter.

Ian couldn't keep from laughing. "Wait a few minutes before bringing my order. As I said, I'll be hungrier by then."

The woman's loud giggle echoed all around him as Ian hurried to the back of the eating area. After a moment, he heard a knock and opened the door.

"Come in while nobody is watching." Ian motioned to the table nearest the door. "We will sit there."

Ian pulled out a chair and sat down. Then Peter did.

"The mutton stew is good here." Ian grinned. "In fact, it is the only meal they serve."

"Then I feel sure I will be having stew."

They both laughed.

"We will not be traveling all the way to Edinburgh on the morrow as I would have thought," Ian said. "We will only be going as far as the village of Rosslyn. The wife of the innkeeper here is a talker, and she told me a little about strange doings in that village."

"Strange doings?" Peter leaned forward in his chair. "I am eager to hear what she said."

"Well, the innkeeper's wife claims that Rosslyn is known as a place where the wee people live—as well as ghosts and goblins. And she says that she knows for a fact that a Black Mass was held there once."

"A Black Mass, did you say?"

"You heard right."

Peter's forehead wrinkled. "So why would the earl be stopping there on his way to England?"

Ian shrugged. "I have not one idea in my mind."

"I will travel to Rosslyn before ya—if I can," Peter said. "I want to find out what business the earl might have in Rosslyn and more about the village. I don't believe in the existence of fairies and the like, but the Black

Mass concerns me. I have heard of odd happenings around here, and I want to know more about all of this."

That night before blowing out the light in his room, Ian read his pastor's second letter again—the one from the vicar in England.

Dear Pastor Petit,

I was delighted to hear from you. However, I was sorry to learn that you are related to the murdered woman. Please accept my belated condolences. Most of what I know is hearsay, and as men of God, we cannot condemn a person to prison without two witnesses. I have none. Here are the facts I do know to be true.

The murder of your cousin, Magdalena Petit, took place in the English village of Cert. A well-dressed Frenchman, a man in the clothes of a monk, and two or three other men spent the night of the murder at an inn in the village.

A young barmaid employed at the inn told the innkeeper that the handsome young Frenchman she found so interesting said he was born in England of French parents. However, the monk told someone else in the village that they had only recently arrived in England from France. Another witness stated that he saw a monk and two other men walking away from the area where Magdalena lived after the fire started, but nobody saw who started the fire or who killed Miss Petit.

The next morning after the murder, the Frenchman and the other strangers moved on. They were never seen again.

You said in your letter that your late cousin was a French Protestant or what you would call a Huguenot. Could that have been the motive for your cousin's death? Or was it perhaps for reasons unrelated to religion?

Some in my parish are telling tales of witchcraft in our midst and of young girls disappearing and never being seen again. I am sure it is merely idle talk started by gossips with little to keep them busy at home. Still, I do wonder. Do some members of your congregation report such mischief as well? Or is this unique to my parish?

Ian shook his head, folding the letter in half. He'd tried to convince Shannon's parents not to let her go to England. But after they met Miss Foster, they gave their permission.

Apparently, the earl's aunt made a good first impression. Ian could only hope Shannon's parents were right about the woman, but he had doubts. He put the letter with the others and tried not to think about the missing young women the vicar mentioned.

Each time he read one of the letters, he became more convinced that he was a part of an important mission. The letters were keys that fit unknown

locks. Doors needed to be opened if he hoped to save Shannon and find
a murderer. Somehow, he knew he must act as a watchman on the wall
until his mission was complete—no matter how long it took.

For now, he would read and study the Bible, and then he would go to
sleep.

◆——◆——◆

Dickson had told Ian that after they broke the fast the next morning, the
earl's party would set out for the village of Rosslyn and stay the night.
The valet had seemed untroubled by that agenda. Ian found it disturbing.
Pastor Petit had warned Ian to beware of that particular town and especially a certain chapel there, and so had the innkeeper's wife.

Ian hadn't liked sitting in the carriage on the previous day with nothing
to do and nobody to talk to but a skinny valet and a skinnier maid who
barely appeared to notice him, and he would have many more such days
before they reached the earl's estate in England. The thought of spending
his days with Dickson and Polly gave him no joy.

As they rolled on toward Rosslyn the next morning, Ian's thoughts
returned to conversations he had with his minister shortly before he left
Luss. The churchman had informed Ian of scriptures about binding Satan
and that the devil was sometimes called the strong man. Ian had listened
carefully but didn't ask questions on that topic until a later visit and after
he'd had time to think about it.

"How would a Christian bind the devil if ever he needed to do that?"
Ian had asked.

"I would ask the Lord in prayer to bind up Satan and his demons and
fallen angels in heaven as I bind them on earth—in the name of our Lord,
Jesus Christ," his pastor had replied. "But don't take my word. Read the
Bible for yourself.

"In the Book of Mark," the minister went on, "chapter three and verse
twenty-seven, Jesus said, 'No man can enter into a strong man's house,
and spoil his goods, except he will first bind the strong man; and then he
will spoil the house.'"

"And the strong man is the devil?" Ian asked.

"I believe in this scripture, the strong man is indeed the devil." The minister nodded as if to confirm it. "Jesus also talks about binding and loosing
in the Book of Matthew, chapter sixteen and verse nineteen. And I must
remind you to always test the spirits—whether human or angelic—to see
if they are of the Lord."

Ian blinked and shook his head. None of this was clear in his mind.

"In the Book of 1 John," the pastor continued, "chapter four and verse
one, the Bible says, 'Beloved, believe not every spirit, but try the spirits

whether they are of God: because many false prophets are gone out into the world.'"

Ian recalled being totally confused. "Forgive me for interrupting, sir," he'd said. "But what does that verse mean in plain language?"

The pastor had smiled. "God knows the deeper meaning of Scripture. I can only tell you what I think it means." He cleared his throat. "I once knew two women that attended services at our church, and both have moved away since the telling. One of these women was a former witch that once read tealeaves for money and claimed to know the future. The other had always been a member of our church."

"A witch? Surely you jest."

"I am telling the truth. As I said, both these women were members of our church, and both women heard voices in their heads they claimed came from God. Neither one bothered to test the spirits to see if what they heard came from God or from the spirit of antichrist. Perhaps they didn't know how to test the spirits or even that they should do it."

Ian leaned forward. "So what did you do?"

"I told them to test the spirits."

"But don't take my word," Ian finished for him. "Read the Bible for yourself."

"I say 'don't take my word' often, do I not?" The pastor laughed. "The Bible explains how to test the spirits in verses two, three, and four of that same chapter—1 John chapter four."

"What happened then?" Ian asked.

"One did nothing. She just kept hearing voices she claimed came from God. But the other did as the Scriptures said to do. When a voice spoke to her, she said, 'Has Jesus come in the flesh?' The voice stopped—didn't speak another word—at least on that day. She'd done exactly as the Bible said to do by testing the spirits. God does speak to the hearts of believers. But the voice she heard failed the test. Humans can deceive us, too. We should always beware."

"Incredible." Ian released a deep breath of air. "And I guess the one who tested the spirits was the one who had always been a member of our church. Am I right?"

"As it turned out, you are wrong, Mr. Colquhoun. The one who was once a witch was also a new Christian; so she did as the Bible said. She had never read the Bible or said a single prayer until she visited our church and found the Lord. Afterward, she was so glad that she'd repented of her sins and accepted Jesus as Savior that she wanted to do all she could to show her love and thankfulness by keeping the commandments. So she tested the spirits."

"And the other woman? What happened to her?"

"She was convinced she was right and that the voice she heard came from the Lord. As a result, she refused to test the spirits. I can only hope that she has changed her mind now and is doing God's will—wherever she might be." He stared at Ian for a moment. "Don't be merely a hearer of the Word, Mr. Colquhoun; be a doer of the Word also."

◆ —◆— ◆

As soon as the earl's party arrived at the inn in the village of Rosslyn where they would stay the night, a maid led the women to their rooms while a man showed the men to theirs. Shannon walked in step with the maid, who was about her age. Miss Foster trudged along a few steps behind them.

They had only gone a short way when the maid told Shannon of a chapel in Rosslyn that she had visited many times, and that the chapel was becoming quite famous—that people came from as far away as the north of England to visit the mysterious chapel. According to the maid, many spent the night at the very inn where the earl and his party were staying.

Shannon knew her papa would be pleased that so many people were visiting the village in order to go to church. Some pastors were quite talented when delivering scriptural messages. The pastor at the chapel in Rosslyn had to be a skilled speaker in order to attract such a wide audience, and she so wished that she could hear his message and tell Papa about it when she got home. Perhaps the earl would change his mind and allow them to stay for the service once they arrived.

She could only hope that it would be so.

After breaking the fast the next morning, the earl and his party drove a short distance to the chapel. The earl took her arm as Shannon got out of the carriage, nodding toward the chapel. Then the horses and carriages were parked in a field across the way.

She wore her best dress, a soft tan colored one, and when she looked up at the earl, smiling from under her new bonnet with its bows and yellow ribbons, she expected him to return her smile. But he'd focused his attention on the church just ahead.

They strolled down the rock walkway that led to the church on maybe the warmest morning in the history of Scotland. Yet a chill shot down her spine—perhaps a grim warning of things to come.

Shannon studied the chapel as they moved closer. She didn't know what happened to Ian, but Miss Foster was right behind them.

She noticed the pointed peaks, the arches, and the elaborate carvings that decorated the outer walls of the stone structure. Her father had told stories of gargoyles and grotesque images like this that were carved on the walls of churches in Paris, France, and how frightening they had looked the first time he saw them. But nothing compared to the disturbing carvings she was seeing now.

They had almost reached the heavy front doors of the chapel.

"Be careful," the earl warned. "It will be dark inside. I would regret it if you fell and hurt yourself."

Shannon gazed inside. It was dark, all right. Only a handful of candles lighted their way.

"Close your eyes, Miss Aimee. Then open them slowly. It will make it easier to see inside."

Shannon shut her eyes, hoping the disturbing feelings she'd been having would go away. Instead, she felt as if a kind of evil engulfed her—covered her like a blanket—pushing her inside the door. But how could that be? This was a church. Wasn't it?

"Come." The earl pulled her forward. "I want to see the Pillar. I have heard so much about it." He smiled. "That must be it." He pointed to a huge pillar with carvings all over it. "Is not the Pillar wonderful?"

Shannon's heart pounded as if it was about to jump out of her chest. She couldn't have answered if she'd wanted to. In fact, she didn't want to say anything.

"Look at the base of it, my dear," the earl said. "I was told I would find eight dragons carved there with vines growing out of their mouths. Notice how the vines wind around the pillar itself. Have you ever seen anything so exquisite?"

She had to agree that the workmanship was excellent; it was the subject matter that bothered her. She didn't know much about the Bible, but she knew that the dragon was the symbol of Satan. So what were images of the devil doing in a church?

The oppressive atmosphere made her feel sick to her stomach. She had to get out of there before she spilled her breakfast all over the floor. Without a word, Shannon headed for the door.

"Shannon," the earl shouted. "Wait!"

She raced out the door and down the rock walkway. A large tree towered off to one side. She ran for it as if she thought it was some kind of refuge.

CHAPTER FIVE

✦

Ian must have been waiting behind that tree because all at once he stood beside her.

"Are you feeling ill?"

Shannon nodded.

He reached out and took her hand in his. "I've seen that look too many times not to know it when I see it. I went into the chapel before you came. It made me sick, too. Sit down," he said as if she were a child, "under the tree. I will go for water."

Shannon did as she was told. She was too sick to do otherwise.

"I'm leaving now."

She glanced at his strong back as he walked away. Extreme nausea flooded her. Shannon leaned forward and heaved, spilling her first meal of the day on the grassy lawn.

A few minutes later, he returned with a cup of water and a damp cloth. He handed them to her and sat down beside her.

Shannon drank the water. Then she squeezed drops of water from the cloth into the palm of her left hand, rubbing it on her face. The damp and cooling cloth had helped somewhat. Still, she felt dirty. She doubted that even an all-over bath would make her feel clean again.

She longed to go back to the inn and climb in bed, but the horses and carriages wouldn't be leaving until the earl was ready to go. Shannon felt too ill to walk the distance. They would have no choice but to wait for the earl and Miss Foster to finish their tour of the chapel.

The earl and his aunt lingered inside. In fact, they didn't come out for several hours. After a while, Shannon realized that she hadn't missed them at all.

At first, the earl had seemed upset that Shannon left the chapel so abruptly, but after she explained that she'd become suddenly ill and had no choice but to leave the building, he seemed to understand. He even sent her one of his dazzling smiles.

But when they returned to the inn, the earl left them for that meeting he mentioned. Shannon didn't see him again until the next morning.

They spent their days traveling and their nights in various inns along the way. Shannon and the earl still hadn't found a private moment. His aunt never left Shannon's side. Shannon never spent time with Ian either, and that worried her even more. Ian seemed anxious about something, and she was eager to learn what it might be.

One day Shannon was especially bored. Nobody in the carriage had spoken more than a few words since they broke the fast that morning. Shannon fidgeted in the seat beside Miss Foster, curling a lock of long hair around her forefinger.

"What gave Gatehaven its name?" Shannon glanced at the earl, hoping he'd reply, but he appeared to be sleeping. She turned to her chaperone. "Please tell me, Miss Foster. I would really like to know."

"Gatehaven was named for the red gate."

"Red gate? Would that be the gate one enters when a person first arrives at Gatehaven?"

"No." Miss Foster shook her head with such vigor her glasses slipped to the end of her long, pointed nose. "The red gate I am talking about is inside the house, not out. You will find it soon enough whether you are looking for it or not, and that is all I have to say on the subject." The woman stretched and yawned. "I am tired, and the earl is sleeping. I think I shall go to sleep, too."

Miss Foster leaned back and closed her eyes, ending the conversation before it had really gotten started. Shannon closed her eyes, too, but instead of sleeping she kept thinking about the red gate—wondering what Miss Foster's words could possibly mean.

Mid-afternoon on that same day, the carriage slowed at a fork in the road. A sign pointed to the right. A bird flashed by, finally perching atop a rustic gate, reminding her again of the red gate Miss Foster mentioned.

The carriage took the road to the left, and the earl opened his eyes.

"Oh, you're awake." Shannon sent him her sweetest smile. "Was your long nap restful?"

"No, but tolerable."

"My lord." Shannon leaned forward. "I have wanted to ask you about the red gate Miss Foster mentioned—the one that gave Gatehaven its name. I find it quite intriguing. Please, can you tell me a little about it?"

The earl shook his head and glanced down at his black boots. "People tell fables about old mansions. Gatehaven is no exception."

He lifted his head and gazed at Shannon. "Some see a shadow and think it is a ghost. They see a red line connecting one side of a corridor with the other and call it a red gate." His gaze intensified. "Wash these tales of demons and red gates from your mind, Miss Aimee. They are illusions. Perhaps you didn't know that such nonsense is not in fashion among the quality." He turned and looked out a window.

"Look." The earl pointed his forefinger toward something he must have seen in the distance. Then he glanced back at Shannon. "You can see Gatehaven, if you look through those trees."

She looked. The mansion was more like an ancient fortress than a home for the earl and his family. They must be richer than she thought possible. Yet even from that distance, there was something dark and mysterious about Gatehaven.

And what of the red gate? Did deeper secrets wait behind the rock walls? Were dangers her mother only hinted at lurking there as well? Shannon tossed back her curls as if she thought it would push away the doubts.

The earl would say that I am imagining things that do not exist. Still, Gatehaven is huge—even bigger than I expected.

But the closer they got to the mansion, the more foreboding it became—at least in her mind.

* —+— *

Leon Picard was about to take the rock path to the double doors of the mansion when he happened to glance toward the road. An impressive black carriage followed by smaller ones and men on horses loomed in the distance.

Fine carriages didn't arrive at Gatehaven every day. As far as he knew, the earl's mother and grandmother weren't expecting anyone. Ladies Catherine and Victoria might not appreciate his company with visitors on the way. He turned around and headed back to his carriage, located nearby. Then he stopped to reconsider.

He needed to know the identity of those visitors. Maybe he would hide in the shadow of the trees to watch—see who came to call. Leon tapped his cane on the hard ground, hobbling over to a nest of closely spaced oaks a few yards away.

His leg hurt, but that was nothing new. His body had ached every day for over twenty years—every day of his life since Rachel pushed him into that well. His jaw tightened.

So what if he tripped and fell instead of being pushed. Either way, it was Rachel's fault. He hated her for making him a cripple and for other reasons. Yet he still wanted her.

It made no sense.

Rachel was a young Huguenot woman living in his village in France the first time he saw her as an adult. He'd wanted her instantly, but she seemed shy, refusing even to talk to him—especially after she learned that he was married. She wouldn't even tell him her name until he cornered her one day down by the seashore. She said her name was Magdalena Petit, and that she planned to marry a French Huguenot name Javier Aimee—a young man that wasn't rich or as well educated as Leon. He wanted her anyway—pursuing her relentlessly.

Not long after that, Leon was waiting for her behind a tree near an old mill when she crossed the glen near the church. She'd taken that path many times, walking right by the old mill, and he knew he'd find her there—if not on that day, soon. He stepped out from behind the tree, and she started running. He raced after her.

In his rush to catch her, he forgot all about the abandoned well near the mill. Someone had put a thin covering of wooden planks over it to keep the schoolchildren from falling in. But when his feet hit the planks with such force, the covering broke. He fell in.

He must have lost consciousness for a moment. Blinding pain in his right leg awoke him with a start. Rachel sat on the edge of the well, looking down at him. She must have been on her way home from the butcher shop because the odor of sausages coming from inside the bag she held floated down to him.

She heard him beg for help from the bottom of that well. Nobody had the right to live after hearing Leon plead for mercy. She told him about the Lord, and then she left.

Not long after that, a priest arrived with several other men from the village. He would always remember the pain he felt as they pulled him from the well.

"A pretty young girl told us to look for you here," the priest had said. "But she never told us her name."

Leon knew he was talking about Magdalena. A year later, he learned the truth. Magdalena wasn't her name at all. Her name was Rachel.

Rachel deserved to die for making him love her—then marrying Javier Aimee and leaving France with the man. Leon deserted his young wife in order to follow them to England only to find them briefly and then lose them again. He had enough money left from his inheritance to travel the world searching for them, but he hadn't counted on being a cripple for the rest of his life. Without a doubt, Rachel caused all the miseries he suffered now.

He thought of how Rachel had looked that day in France, gazing down at him from the top of the well. Her long auburn mane fell about slender shoulders. Strands of her hair had tumbled forward like a rust-colored waterfall against her milk-white skin.

He couldn't have seen her eyes from that distance. Yet he remembered well their emerald-like brilliance and the way her long, black lashes framed them.

Rachel could hardly have been more than nineteen years old on the day Leon fell in the well. Yet his mental vision of her was forever young. It seemed impossible that by now Rachel must be over forty.

Had he told the earl how old Rachel would be today before sending him to Scotland? He hesitated in order to give himself time to think—perhaps not. To be honest, he couldn't recall.

But what did it matter? The earl would not have a hard time finding her. How many Rachel Aimees could there be in a little Scottish village like Luss?

In the years since leaving France and settling in England, he'd learned to hate to an extent he never thought possible. Leon had always hated Jews and Huguenots. Now he hated all Christians. In fact, he hated religion in all its forms—except the craft, of course.

Rachel and her husband, Javier Aimee, were Huguenots. But in England, they were called Protestants.

The earl was a Protestant, as was the vicar, and everybody else Leon knew. All his so-called English "friends" were Protestants, and they all thought he liked and respected them.

A smile that started in his mind melted into an audible laugh that echoed all around him.

If his English friends knew how he really felt, they would be appalled.

* —————— *

The first carriage pulled to a stop in front of the mansion. Shannon thought she could make out someone standing in a room on the top floor.

"My lord, who is that?" Shannon pointed to the room in question.

"What are you talking about?" the earl said. "I see no one."

"That woman with the long black hair—standing at the window. Surely you can see her."

"Perhaps you are imagining things, my dear. I would suggest you put it out of your mind. We will emerge from the carriage at any moment. You will need to prepare to exit it as soon as possible."

A woman with black hair stood at the window whether the earl noticed her or not. Shannon continued to gaze at the window.

Another woman with yellow-colored hair joined the first woman at the window. Shannon glanced at the earl. He was studying his mansion with great intensity. Were they looking at the same window? If so, the earl knew that neither of the women were figments of Shannon's imagination.

+ —•— +

The earl stepped out. But instead of going inside, he offered his hand as if to help someone down.

Rachel. Excitement at the thought of seeing her again filled Leon's mind. He thought of kissing her. But for now, he must stay hidden.

A dainty hand reached out. The earl covered her hand with his.

Leon saw a mass of auburn hair. All doubts vanished. She was Rachel.

The woman who stepped down from the carriage looked young, shapely and beautiful. Leon released an audible sigh. The years hadn't changed her.

She wore a lavender dress and a bonnet of the same color. He would know her anywhere. But why hadn't she aged in over twenty years?

Thirsty for answers, he wanted to rush right over. But his sense of caution together with his physical condition made that desire impossible.

Leon would wait until they went inside—until they had greeted the earl's mother and grandmother. His heart pounded. Perhaps then he would pay the family a visit and see Rachel again. The earl had promised to send a letter telling when they would arrive. Yet Leon had received no such letter. As far as he knew, the earl's family wasn't notified either.

+ —•— +

Shannon stopped for a moment before moving down the rock path, staring at the stone mansion the earl called Gatehaven. The women were no longer standing at the window. Perhaps she had imagined them. Still, she didn't think so.

The sun hid behind the clouds when she studied Gatehaven the first time. Suddenly the sun beamed down on the mansion as if directing her to it—pointing the way. What a difference a bit of sunshine made, and how wonderful to have finally reached their destination.

Other than the castles she'd observed from a distance on the journey from Scotland, she'd never seen a dwelling more magnificent. She hoped to remember every inch of it.

Miss Foster, her chaperone, stood beside her. The woman cupped her hands like Shannon did when she planned to whisper something in someone's ear. "I must relieve myself before going in to greet Lady Catherine and her mother. I will join you shortly inside."

Shannon nodded and forced a smile. She was eager to meet the earl's mother, Lady Catherine, and his grandmother, Lady Victoria.

She liked her chaperone well enough. Still, the woman's strange behavior troubled Shannon. Miss Foster constantly discussed disturbing topics—like crystal balls and haunted castles, hinting that ghosts roamed the halls of Gatehaven as well. Shannon refused to believe such nonsense, of course, but the thought of it played on her mind.

The earl touched her arm. "Are you ready to go inside?"

Shannon looked up, and his warm smile engulfed her. "Yes, my lord, I most certainly am."

He loves me. How could I ever doubt it?

She would remember that moment forever, the earl's blue eyes and how his blond hair curled around the edges of his black hat. He offered her his arm in a gentlemanly fashion, and she took it.

Shannon felt like a queen as he whisked her up the stone steps to a foyer that looked almost as large as her entire house. She glimpsed a white marble stairway before they entered a huge drawing room with its gold cornices above the windows and its flowing purple drapes. The earl had promised to write to his mother and his grandmother to announce their arrival, but from the astonished looks on the faces of the two women glaring at her, Shannon presumed that neither of them knew who she was nor why she came.

The earl made some rather stiff introductions. Then he said, "Miss Aimee lives near our hunting lodge in Scotland, Mum, and she is here as my—my guest." He gazed at her and smiled in that special way again. "I know having her here will brighten my days."

Two pairs of blue eyes stared at Shannon—the earl's mother and grandmother, she assumed. A white cat purred at the feet of the older of the two, and the women looked astounded.

Shannon needed Ian. Why didn't he come inside when she did? And what was keeping her chaperone, Miss Foster? She should have tended to her private matters by now.

The earl's mother got up out of her chair. "I will ring for Millie and have her take Miss—Miss Aimee to her room. I am sure she will want to freshen up after her long journey." She pulled a gold-colored cord that hung from the ceiling. Then she pulled it two more times.

A young woman in a white maid's cap rushed into the room.

"You rang, ma'am?"

"Yes. Please take Miss Aimee here to the room across from Maude's and help her settle in."

With her flushed face and shaky hands, Shannon thought the maid looked as uncomfortable as she felt. Perhaps Millie had never been in the drawing room previously.

"Sure and I will do as you say, ma'am," Millie said with a Scottish accent. "But—"

"But what? Speak up, girl."

"Are you sure you will be wantin' me to take her to the room across from Maude's—that being the maid's quarters and all. I just thought—"

"Yes. Take her to the room across from Maude's. She will be comfortable there, and do hurry. I think the poor girl looks exhausted."

Shannon swallowed. *She thinks the earl hired me as a maid.* She glanced back at the earl, hoping he would explain her reason for being there. He started toward her.

"No, Edward," the older of the two women said. "You stay here. Your mother and I want to speak with you."

Shannon had no choice but to follow Millie out of the room.

CHAPTER SIX

SHANNON WENT OUT the door and turned toward the massive stairway she noticed when they came in.

"No," Millie said, "not that way." She smiled. "Follow me. I'll show ya where to go."

Shannon forced a smile. "Thank you. You are very kind. But what about my boxes and other belongings?"

"Someone will be bringin' them down to ya later."

Down? Down where?

Doubts had been building since she entered the huge double doors of the mansion. Now a lump lodged in her throat, and she found it difficult to breathe. She would have screamed if she'd thought it would do any good.

Millie led her through a maze of long halls to a huge kitchen. Servants were preparing a meal. Still, they took the time to smile when she came in.

"Everybody be busy right now, miss, preparing for Tea Time," Millie explained. "I'll introduce you later." She pointed to a corner of the room near a brick wall. "The stairs be right over there."

The stairwell looked dark. Shannon had always hated the unknown—now more than ever. She hesitated at the head of the stairs before going down. Obviously, it led to the basement of the mansion. This might be a good time to let out that scream she'd been holding in.

"Have ya been working as a maid long?" Millie asked.

Shannon stood at the top of the stairs, trembling internally and unable to move physically. Clearly, a terrible mistake was made. The earl would set things right. She merely needed to try to relax until he did. Nevertheless, she was beginning to wish she'd never left Scotland.

"Well, have ya?" Millie said again in a friendly tone.

"Have I what?"

"Been working as a maid long."

"No. No, I have not. I—I came from Scotland, and I have never worked as a maid."

"Well, don't let it worry ya none." Millie motioned toward the dark stairwell as if she expected Shannon to go on down. "Maude and I be helping ya all we can. You can be sure of that, and I am so glad to hear ya came from Scotland. My family came from Scotland, too."

Shannon forced a smile and descended the stairs.

Millie moved ahead and opened a door at the end of the long hall. "This room belongs to you now, Miss Aimee." Millie motioned for Shannon to go in. "Your key, I believe." Smiling, she handed her the key.

The room looked extremely small—bare white walls, a narrow bed, and a chest of drawers. In one corner, she saw a table with a candle on it. Besides the candle, a high window over the bed gave the room its only light.

Shannon went over and sat down on the edge of the bed. Then she looked away to keep from allowing her disappointment to show in her face.

"Sure and I would like to stay and visit with ya for a while." Millie leaned forward and ran the palm of her hand over the stiff quilt that covered the bed. "But I must be going now. Like I said, someone will bring your bags to your room soon." She closed the door.

"No, wait!"

Shannon got up, opened the door, and peered down the hall. But Millie had disappeared—probably down one of the other long halls.

She went back inside, slamming the door behind her. She'd wanted to tell Millie not to send her boxes and bags because she would be moving to another room. And she had so many questions she wanted answered. It would seem that it was too late to have Millie answer them —at least for now.

Well, her belongings would simply have to be moved a second time.

She sat back down on the small bed, crossing her arms across her chest.

Where was the earl? He should have come to her rescue by now. She reached down with nervous fingers and smoothed the wrinkles from her skirt, pulling the pale gold material tight against her knees.

Maybe the earl couldn't find her. She was in the basement. Shannon had no choice but to wait until he finally came for her no matter how long it took.

Ian shifted his weight from one leg to the other as a middle-aged gentleman with a limp made his way to the door of the mansion. Since they arrived, Ian had been standing behind the carriage that Shannon and the earl had traveled in, waiting to be told where to go. He still didn't know a thing.

He'd expected to stay in the vicar's cottage. But where was it located? The earl had said that someone on his staff would direct him there. A tall and thin footman in a dark blue uniform stood a short distance away. Ian went over to speak to him.

"I am a guest here and in need of a place to stay the night. Can you direct me to the vicar's cottage? I was told that I would be staying there."

"I can direct you, all right, but Pastor Steen—he is gone."

"Gone? Where?"

The footman shrugged his shoulders. "He got some bad news, I wager, and left the next day. I don't expect him to return for at least a fortnight."

Now what should Ian do? Where should he go?

The vicar wasn't home, and Ian had never even met the man. To stay in the vicarage under those circumstances was unacceptable—at least as far as Ian was concerned.

He'd promised his pastor before he left Scotland that he would try to solve the murder of his cousin, Magdalena Petit. But how could he keep that promise now? The vicar was away from the village of Fairs, and Ian had given his word that he would not discuss the murder with anyone but Pastor Steen.

The footman cleared his throat, interrupting Ian's thoughts. "I suppose it would be all right for you to stay in the guardhouse with the other guards." Then he walked off before Ian learned the location of the guardhouse.

He was beginning to wonder why he agreed to come to England in the first place. And where was Shannon's brother? Shortly before they left Rosslyn, Peter had informed him that he planned to do a little investigating before leaving that village. He was especially interested in learning more about the chapel. But Ian had expected him to catch up with the caravan before they reached the earl's estate. So far, he hadn't.

Leon Picard was led into the library instead of the drawing room as he'd expected.

"The earl and his family are having a private conversation at the moment," the butler had explained. "Please, wait here."

"Wait?" Leon's jaw tightened.

"Yes, sir. But the Earl of Northon should be with you shortly."

Outrageous! The earl owed him money, and Leon was in no mood to be put off.

"Would you care for some tea, sir?" the butler asked.

"No. That will not be necessary."

Leon glared at the butler as he turned and left the room.

He settled into the earl's favorite chair with its cushioned back and brown leather arms. The earl could sit in the chair facing him. He knew from experience that it wasn't as comfortable. He grinned internally. It served him right.

◆———◆———◆

Peter Aimee guided his brown gelding to a slow trot and then to a full stop, exhausted physically and emotionally. If what he'd been told at the fork in the road was true, the earl's estate was beyond the rise just ahead, and he'd pushed his horse hard to get there. He was eager to reach his destination, but he would never require an animal to go beyond its normal capabilities—a human either, for that matter.

Peter had traveled a long way since leaving Rosslyn, Scotland, and he'd learned a lot while he was there—information that he still didn't want to believe. If true, some from Rosslyn were devil worshippers, and he'd seen the earl enter their meeting place with his own eyes.

Still, the earl could have gone in by mistake. Peter almost went inside as well in order to see what went on there. But if his suspicions were true, Shannon could be in danger. He would have to tell Ian before it was too late.

◆———◆———◆

Leon had been reading from a book of poems for half an hour when the earl was finally announced. He put the book back on the shelf by his chair without looking up.

"Sorry to have kept you waiting."

Leon sent the younger man a cold glance. "You should be."

The earl sat down. "It could not be avoided."

"So, what have you done to deserve the money I have been sending you for your journey to Scotland? The package I requested is in good condition, I presume."

"Excellent." The earl reached for the snuffbox by his chair. "The young woman is in good spirits—and quite beautiful, I might add." He opened the gold box and dabbed a bit of the white powder under his nose. "She thinks I love her and plan to marry her."

"She is certainly beautiful. But I would never call her young."

"She is nineteen, sir."

Leon froze. "What?" A sudden chest pain made it difficult for Leon to breathe. He covered the pain with his left hand, gripping the arm of the chair with his right.

The earl shot out of his chair, reaching him in two steps. "Are you all right, Monsieur?"

Leon swallowed. "I will be."

"Let me ring for my butler."

"That will not be necessary. I have had this previously." Leon licked his dry lips. "If you would be so good as to hand me a glass of water."

"Of course." He glanced around. "Oh, my. The water pitcher is empty. The butler will—"

"Please retrieve the small box of pills in my vest pocket."

"At once." The earl reached in Leon's vest pocket, retrieved the box, and opened it. "How foolish of me. I should have rang for the butler—with the water."

"Are you an idiot? Forget the water! Just put the pill on my tongue."

The earl did as he was told. Then he pulled the gold-colored cord that hung from the ceiling by Leon's chair. "The butler should be here shortly. Now, let me help you to the settee." The earl reached out and tried to take Leon's arm. "In this instance, it might be wise if you lie down and put your feet up."

Leon pushed his hand away. "Stop treating me like an old man. I will be as good as new long before the water arrives. Besides, I fear you brought the wrong woman from Scotland. Where is she?"

"In her room, of course."

"I must go and see her for myself."

"Are you sure you are feeling well enough?"

"Would I have suggested it, if I thought otherwise? Besides, I am already feeling better. I wish to meet the woman you brought at once."

The earl hesitated. "That might not be possible, sir. She is tired from her long journey and went to her room. Until she is feeling more rested, why not investigate our gardens? We have some new plants, and the fresh air will do you good. I will invite my mother and grandmother to go with us. I am sure they would enjoy an outing, and they always delight in visiting with you."

"I am very displeased." Leon glared at the earl. "Have one of your servants tell the woman to join us as soon as she is able."

◆——◆——◆

Still standing near where the carriages were parked, Ian watched an attractive young woman in a white maid's cap as she stepped out a side door of the mansion. She poured water from a bucket—probably dishwater—onto the grass by the small porch.

Ian moved toward her. Maybe she could provide him with information.

A footman started across the grass straight for her as well. He wore a gray uniform that was nothing like the blue ones worn by the earl's footmen, and he was quite plump. In fact, he looked as if he might pop out of his jacket at any moment. Ian waited a moment before moving forward as the maid and the rotund footman talked in whispers. Then they started toward a group of men in blue uniforms.

"Wait!" Ian hurried to catch up with them. "I need directions."

The couple stopped and turned.

"Might I help you?" the young maid asked.

"Yes. I need for someone to direct me to the guardhouse."

"I'll help you if you'll first help me." The portly footman had a heavy Scottish accent. "One of the earl's guards is sick and cannot deliver boxes to the servant's quarters below stairs. I promised to do it." He motioned toward Shannon's belongings on top of the second carriage.

"Are you sure those bags and boxes go to the servants' quarters?" Ian asked.

"Yes, sir," the woman said. "I took the pretty lady to her room meself."

"What does the pretty lady look like?"

The woman shrugged. "She is not tall—about my size—but a wee bit thinner. She has auburn hair and green eyes."

"And her name?"

"Miss Aimee."

What was Shannon doing in the servants' quarters? Ian planned to find out.

"I will be glad to help you with the boxes." Ian smiled at the attractive young maid. "And on the way, one of you can direct me to the guardhouse."

<hr />

Shannon heard a knock at the door. Had the earl come to her rescue? Or had someone arrived with her bags? She hoped it was the earl. She produced her prettiest smile and opened the door.

Ian stood in the hallway outside beside the large box where most of her belongings were stored. A plump man she didn't know in a gray uniform stood beside him.

Her smile fell away. "Ian, what are you doing here?"

"Helping deliver your box from home. May we come in?"

"Of course." She motioned for them to come inside.

"Where should we put this?" Ian asked.

Shannon looked around. "Against the wall next to the bed will do. It will have to be moved anyway."

"Why must it be moved?" Ian asked as he and the Scot dragged the heavy box inside.

"Look around you," Shannon said. "Obviously, I was assigned the wrong room."

"I see." Ian motioned toward the box. "So is this where you want it?"

"For now, yes. But you could have put it anywhere because as I said, I will not be staying here long." She tossed back her curls. "This is the servant's quarters, and I am the earl's future wife. He will have me in a better room upstairs soon enough."

"I will go and get the other bags, sir." The portly footman headed for the door.

"Yes, that is a good decision. Thank you."

"No, wait!" Shannon shouted.

She'd wanted to tell the footman not to bring in the rest of her bags. But the door was already closed.

"Why were you given a room in the servants' quarters, lass?"

She tossed her head with all the indignation she could muster. "The earl's mother and grandmother made a mistake. They must have thought I was hired as a maid. But I am sure the earl will clear it all up."

"Either that or they plan to make you their servant," he said under his breath.

Shannon heard what Ian said but didn't want to start an argument.

Ian glanced around the room. "It is a little stuffy in here, and I know how much you like flowers. Would you like to go outside and take a turn around the garden?"

"I would love to. But I have to be here in case the earl comes."

"Well, if you're looking for the earl, I can tell you where he is."

"Where?"

"Strolling in the garden with a distinguished-looking gentleman with a cane and two arrogant-looking women. I noticed them just before I came inside."

Shannon laughed. "The women are the earl's mother and grandmother. And we cannot know for sure that they are arrogant. Can we?"

"Maybe not. But considering what I have seen and heard so far, they are not two sweet little ladies. I can tell you that. In fact, the older one is anything but little. She is quite large."

Shannon laughed again. "Shame on you. You should never say such things."

"Then why are you laughing?"

"It was wrong of me to laugh." She felt her cheeks warm with embarrassment. "Let us go outdoors. I want to talk to the earl."

◆——◆——◆

Despite the foreboding tone of the rock mansion with its shadowy exterior and dark inner walls, Shannon thought the manicured garden in the front of the house looked green and lush. Lined with trimmed hedges and flowers in a variety of colors, the cobblestone walkway comforted her as well.

Papa put down walkways like this around our house at the farm.

Shannon heard a rustling in the trees nearby. She whirled around. Was someone watching them? She saw a black flash. A man in dark clothing went behind a tree.

The warmth she'd felt an instant before evaporated. "Who was that man?"

"What man?" Ian asked. "I see no one."

"Neither do I. Now. But someone was hiding behind that tree. I saw him."

"I agree that this mansion is rather morbid, lass. But please refrain from telling me you saw a ghost. I see no such thing."

"The man I saw was no ghost. Besides, he is gone now. Still, I know what I saw. Furthermore, I dislike it out here. I want to go back inside."

"We cannot go back." He motion toward three people standing on the opposite side of the yard. "I just saw the earl and the two women standing beyond those hedges. I think they might have seen us."

The earl stood with his mother and grandmother amidst a riot of pink and red flowers. As soon as Shannon saw him, all interest in going back inside disappeared.

"There he is. There is my beloved." She started toward the earl, sensing that Ian was right behind her. The earl looked right at them. But instead of rushing toward her as Shannon so wanted, he simply stood there—watching them.

"My lord." She waved.

He glanced back at the two women for a moment as if asking their permission, and then he strolled slowly toward her. When she hastened her steps, he moved a little faster.

"Miss Aimee." The earl stood in front of Shannon as if he was trying to keep his mother and grandmother from seeing her. "What are you doing here?"

"Looking for you. What else?"

"I thought you would be unpacking or something." He glanced at Ian. "Mr. Colquhoun, I hope you are settling in."

"Not yet, I am afraid."

"Really?"

Shannon thought the earl looked mildly surprised.

"You might not have heard but the vicar is on holiday," Ian said. "I have no place to stay."

"Sorry. I was unaware of your problem. But you need not worry. I am sure a bed can be found for you in the guardhouse until the vicar returns."

"That is exactly where I hope to stay."

The earl looked back at Shannon. "And you, Miss Aimee. Are you all settled in as well?"

"I am afraid not. My room is unsuitable."

"Your room does not meet your needs? I am sorry to hear that."

"My room, as you call it, is down in the basement, my lord, and it is miles from my chaperone. My parents will be very displeased should they learn that I am not situated near my chaperone."

Shannon didn't like the earl's attitude. He seemed cold and distant again. Where was the man she fell in love with back in Scotland?

She managed a weak smile. "You will find me a new room as soon as possible. Will you not, my lord?"

"Of course." The earl glanced toward the two women waiting near the maze of hedges. "But first, I must get back to my family. My mother and grandmother are discussing something important, and we have a guest." He glanced around. "I do not see him now, but he is here—somewhere in the garden. I must go at once."

Are not my needs important? Shannon wanted to say. Somehow, she knew that they weren't important—at least, not today.

"You and Mr. Colquhoun should take a long walk, Miss Aimee. Explore the grounds. And if you get hungry, there is food in the kitchen. Just tell Cook, and she will fill your plates."

"Later," the earl went on, "perhaps I will take you to your new room or have one of the servants do it."

The earl smiled. Shannon didn't.

"Until then, I hope you both will enjoy your walk." The earl turned back to his family and hurried away.

CHAPTER SEVEN

S HANNON WIPED MOISTURE from her right eye with a white linen
cloth. "Ian, why would the earl treat us as if we were servants? I don't
understand why he walked away."

"Remember, he said he had important business to discuss with his mother
and grandmother. Perhaps he did."

"But I am to be his wife."

"I know."

Ian nodded as if he understood how terrible she felt. Shannon felt very
close to him.

"I hate to worry you," Ian went on. "But you must consider the possibility
that the earl is not the man you think he is."

That did it.

Shannon tensed, glaring at Ian. It was one thing when *she* listed the earl's
shortcomings. But she refused to hear them from anyone else.

"Do not start on that topic again, Ian. It is disloyal to the man I love." She
crossed her arms over her chest. "I was looking for a reason for his strange
behavior—not condemnation."

"Your loyalty is to be commended, even if slightly misguided, and you are
certainly loyal."

She put her hands on her hips. "I have the feeling I have just been
insulted."

"Take my words any way you wish, lass."

"The earl is still the man I love," she insisted. "He is just—he is behaving
strangely because he failed to tell his family about me before I arrived. That

must be the reason. He needs time to explain who I am." She forced another smile. "Then everything with be splendid again—as it was in Scotland."

"For your sake, I hope you are right. Still, I think you should give some thought to my conclusions. Not all people are good, you know. Some only pretend to be good in order to achieve a particular goal."

Shannon put her hands over her ears. But it was too late. She'd already heard what he said.

She dropped her hands. "You are only three years older than I am, Ian. How did you become suspicious at such a young age?"

"Have you forgotten that I spent part of my growing up years at a school for boys in England?"

She hadn't forgotten about the time Ian spent in England. Those were the loneliest days of her girlhood.

"Was it very bad here—in England?"

"Not entirely. But there was one boy. We called him Eddie." Ian shook his head. "Until today, Eddie had not crossed my mind in years."

"And was Eddie unkind to you?"

"Yes, lass, he was. But not just to me. Eddie was cruel to several of the boys—especially those who were younger or not as rich as he."

"But surely you do not think that Edward—surely you cannot think the earl is—"

He shrugged. "I am not sure, but I have every intention of finding out. But for now, I need to check on my bags." He glanced toward the door. "I will meet you in the garden behind the mansion shortly. And then we will go inside the mansion and eat."

✦━━━✦

Unless somebody had moved it, Ian's luggage was still stacked on top of the carriage he arrived in. But before he would worry about that, he needed to find the guardhouse where he would store his bags and spend the night.

Certainly he couldn't count on the earl for help. He'd had suspicions about the British lord since the day he arrived in Luss, but never more than when he and Shannon talked with him earlier. It was the arrogant way the earl had cocked his head, as if looking down at them, and that had caused Ian to remember Eddie's blue eyes. He'd seen a flash of anger behind the earl's eyes, and he had a feeling that Eddie recognized him, too.

While helping the portly footman with Shannon's box, he'd learned the location of the guardhouse. Ian was determined to go there as soon as possible.

At the corner of the mansion, he was about to take the path to the left when his body slammed into something.

Ian froze. Then his jaw hung loose. He'd collided with a middle-aged gentleman. The man, dressed in black, fell back, landing in a bed of pink flowers that edged the north wall of the mansion.

"Pardon me, sir." Ian offered his right hand. "Let me help you up."

The man pressed his thumb and forefinger to his forehead. Ian thought he looked dazed—perhaps bewildered. He finally reached out and allowed Ian to help him to his feet.

The man must have dropped his cane as he fell. It lay on the walkway near the flowerbed. Ian brushed dust and dirt from the man's dark jacket and handed him his cane.

"Are you all right, sir?"

"I—I will be." The older man had a heavy French accent. "As—as soon as I have time to catch my breath." He peered up at Ian's face. "I am Monsieur Etienne Gabeau. And you are the young man in the carriage behind Rach— behind the earl's carriage. I saw you and the lady when you arrived—from Scotland, I believe."

"Yes." Ian took the man's free arm. "My name is Ian Colquhoun."

"Ca—"

"My surname has what some might call an unusual spelling, but it is pronounced Ca-hoon. Let me escort you to wherever it is you were planning to go."

"I had planned to inspect the earl's flower beds behind the mansion and then meet him and one of his guests there. But I've had some unfortunate outcomes today and would rather not try for a third. I think I shall get in my carriage and have my driver drive on home." A black carriage was parked on the road to the north of the mansion. "My estate is not far from here."

"Should we tell the earl what happened, sir? I could go and tell him. The earl might want to contact a physician before you leave."

"That will not be necessary. I have no need of a physician. And I visited briefly with the earl earlier. I had planned to leave soon anyway."

"Then please allow me to walk along with you to your carriage. It's a nice day, and I should like a stroll before eating my noon meal."

"I should enjoy the company," the Frenchman said.

Ian thought he looked a little shaky. Ian would walk the older man to his carriage, and he looked forward to inspecting it and the team of black horses he saw in the distance. The man dragged one of his feet as they trudged along. Ian couldn't help feeling sorry for him.

"Sorry we met under such unfortunate circumstances," Ian said, "but I'm glad to make your acquaintance. I would offer my hand in friendship, but it might be best if we put that off until we reach your carriage."

The older man nodded, and then he looked up at Ian. "And where were you going in such a hurry, Mr. Colquhoun?"

"To the guardhouse. I need to find a place to sleep tonight. I am to be the vicar's new assistant and will be residing at the vicarage. But I was told that he is currently on holiday. I hope to find lodging in the guardhouse until he returns."

The man with the French accent smiled. "So you are the one. I thought that might be the case. The vicar told me to keep an eye out for you. He didn't know exactly when you would arrive, and he hated to leave without knowing. But a close family member is gravely ill. He needed to be at her side immediately. So I told him I would look after you until he returned." He glanced at Ian's hand on his arm. "But it looks now as if you are taking care of me."

Ian laughed. "It is the least I could do after knocking you down as I did."

"You must stay with me until the vicar returns." The Frenchman nodded yet again as if to confirm it. "Yes, I insist. The vicar would be put out with me if I allowed you to stay anywhere else, and I have many extra bedrooms. Not only that, but I live near the vicar's cottage.

"I have been lonely since the vicar went away and would appreciate the company. Besides the earl and his family, the vicar is my oldest friend since moving here from France."

"I appreciate your kind offer, sir. But I cannot put you out like that by accepting."

"Nonsense. You will accept and stay with me until the vicar returns. I refuse to take no for an answer."

Ian didn't like being forced to do something he might not want to do. At the same time, he needed a place to stay, and the gentleman's dwelling seemed like the perfect solution. He was about to accept when the earl stepped out from behind a stone wall and strode toward them.

"Oh, here you are, Monsieur Gabeau." The earl smiled at the older gentleman, but when he turned to Ian, his smile vanished. "Mr. Colquhoun." He sent Ian a sharp look and gazed back at the older man. "My mother and my grandmother told me to tell you that the upcoming meeting we have all been waiting for will be held here at Gatehaven as planned. We would like for you to help us decide the time and the exact date before an announcement is sent out."

The muscles around the Frenchman's face tightened, and his thick lips turned down. Ian imagined sparks shoot out of the older man's eyes, and those sparks were aimed at the earl.

"As I told you in the library, my lord. I am not feeling my best today and have much to do at home. Mr. Colquhoun has promised to reside with me until the vicar returns."

Reside with him?

Ian had fully intended to accept the Frenchman's offer, but he hadn't put that conclusion into words yet. It bothered him that Monsieur Gabeau spoke as if he had. Edward looked shocked. "Monsieur Gabeau, you cannot mean that Mr. Colquhoun will be staying at your estate as your guest."

"Yes, but only until the vicar returns. He will keep me from feeling so lonely in that big old house. I want to get Mr. Colquhoun settled in as soon as possible."

"I can see that you are eager to be on your way," the earl said. "But if you would be so kind as to put off leaving for—for a say an hour—and share a meal with us, I would appreciate it. I wish to speak to you alone on matters of utmost importance."

The Frenchman's jaw tightened. "I am a busy man, my lord, and not feeling my best. I will agree to delay my trip home for one hour—no more."

"One hour should be plenty of time, Monsieur."

He turned to Ian. "If you will show McGregor, my driver, where your bags and boxes are located, he will help you load them onto my carriage. I will join you shortly."

"I will help him load my belongings into your carriage as you suggested, sir, and then I will visit that garden you mentioned. I also understand that a meal is waiting for me in the kitchen, and I am looking forward to that as well."

"Excellent." The Frenchman motioned to the portly guard that Ian had talked to earlier. "McGregor, help this gentleman load his bags into my carriage. I should be back in about an hour, and then you will drive us home."

"Very good, Monsieur."

As he limped away with the earl at his side, Ian shook his head. Apparently, some sort of hostility was going on between the earl and Monsieur Gabeau.

Not only that, the Frenchman had said his portly driver was named McGregor. The driver had seemed friendly enough when Ian saw him for the first time with the young maid at Gatehaven, but the Colquhoun and McGregor clans had never gotten along. Would his friendship with the driver continue if he knew that Ian was a member of the clan Colquhoun?

Ian had assumed that the Frenchman was a commoner. Normally, an earl would assume the dominant position in such cases. But the Frenchman took the high road—strange, to say the least. Ian didn't know what this was all about, but it would be interesting to find out.

+———+———+

Shannon and Ian strolled through the garden behind the mansion. Earlier, she'd been furious with him, but her anger faded like it always did. She gazed up at him.

It certainly took Ian a long time to secure his bags and find the location of the guardhouse. She'd wondered what kept him so long and if he intended to return at all.

He'd told her the names of several unusual flowers and other plants they found in the garden, but she hardly listened. Her heart ached because of all she'd seen and heard since leaving Scotland, and she longed to go inside. Ian kept asking her why she seemed so upset. Even a room alone in the servants' quarters would be better than trying to verbalize her biting disappointment.

At last, they entered the house through the back door and sat down at the kitchen table. The cook served them steaming bowls of mutton stew. Shannon didn't feel like eating.

When Ian took his last bite, Shannon got up and stood beside her chair. "I'm tired from the long journey. I think I'll go to my—my room. I have no doubt that I will soon be moved to another room. But in any case, I shall keep in touch with you."

"You do look tired, lass. Go to your room and get some rest. And I look forward to seeing you again very soon."

Shannon and Ian stacked their dishes on the table by the kitchen door, and she watched him go outside. Then she went to her room.

The rest of her bags waited at the door. She dragged them inside.

She really did feel tired. Shannon stretched out on the bed, and if she went to sleep, all the better. As her French grandmother often said, sleep will block out all your cares. You will not have to think about them again until you wake up.

* ———+——— *

Shannon awoke to the sound of someone knocking on her door. She got up and hurried across the room.

"Who is there?"

"The Earl of Northon."

Edward.

She put in the key and turned the latch. Then she opened the door with such force that it banged against the planked, white wall.

"Oh, my lord!" She reached up and grabbed him around the neck. "I knew you would come."

"Of course I came." He wrapped his arms around her and pulled her close. "You are the most beautiful creature I have ever seen." He lifted her into his arms, carried her inside the room and slammed the door. "I have been counting the minutes until we could be alone."

"Put me down this minute!"

CHAPTER EIGHT

✤

THE EARL SET her on her feet, and then he kissed her. Shannon responded.

But when one kiss melted into another, she pulled away. "We should not be alone like this." She tried to sound as if she meant it. "You know it is wrong—as do I. My parents would never forgive us if they knew."

"So." He grinned. "We will not tell them. Say that you like kissing me."

"Of course I like kissing you, my lord. But we must wait until we are married. Have you found me a room near my chaperone yet?"

"No, I have not. Why should I?" He sent her a mocking grin. "I like having you in this room where we can—can be alone whenever we want. I like it very much indeed."

"I do not! And unless you move me to another room at once, I will run away from Gatehaven, and you will never see me again."

The earl dropped his arms and took a step back. "You wound me deeply." He put his hand over his heart, and then he grinned.

A strand of his golden hair had fallen across his forehead. The earl looked adorable and extremely handsome standing there. Shannon knew she couldn't even pretend to be angry with him for long. At last, she smiled.

"It is about time—my little French darling." He took her hand and kissed it. "Lately I was beginning to think you favored Mr. Colquhoun instead of me."

"I have known Ian all my life, and we are just friends. I only love you, my lord. But unless you find me a room near my chaperone, I will run away— just like I said I would."

"I like the fire I see in your green eyes, Miss Aimee."

"Enough."

"All right," he said at last. "I will send someone to move you to another room—but perhaps not today. My mother and grandmother were not pleased that I failed to tell them you were coming here. It might take time to gain favor with them again."

Shannon stared at him. "You have yet to tell them of our upcoming marriage?"

He looked away briefly. "I will straighten this out soon enough." He turned back to her and smiled. "In the meantime, we can enjoy being together."

"There will be no *in the meantime*," she retorted. "I demand to be put in a room near my chaperone today."

The earl's smile fell away. "I want you, Shannon, and I intend to have you whether my family likes it or not."

He said he wanted her. But did that mean that he loved her and wanted to marry her? She watched as he turned and walked away.

• ——+—— •

The butler escorted Leon and the earl into the family dining room at the back of the mansion near the kitchen. It was one of several dining rooms in the mansion—each more spacious and better equipped than the one before it. Leon had visited all of them, including the huge banquet hall with its massive oak table.

However, this was one of his favorites. It had a large rock fireplace and walls planked in cedar, giving it a woodsy smell and flavor. His dark heart laughed, recalling how he'd introduced himself to the stranger as Etienne Gabeau. He was Leon Picard and always would be, but both the British and the Scots were too weak minded to know they were being deceived.

The earl nodded to his servant. "You may leave us now. I will ring when we are ready to be served."

"Very good, my lord."

Leon sat down at the head of the table. Under normal circumstances, an earl would never allow such an outrage—especially in his own home. But the earl would do nothing. Leon hated weakness in anyone. The earl was no exception.

He might have lost interest in the beautiful Rachel years ago if she hadn't proven to be such a worthy opponent. Leon loved the chase, and Rachel had kept him running after her for most of his life.

"I assume you are comfortable there—at the head of my table," the earl said with a trace of sarcasm.

"Quite comfortable." Leon's burst of laughter was filled with anger and contempt. "Thank you for inquiring."

The earl sat in the chair to Leon's right.

"I will sit here so we can talk in private," the earl said. "I believe there is a financial transaction we need to discuss."

"Before we discuss your gambling debt, my lord, I have a question."

"What might that be?"

"The last time we spoke, you mentioned that the woman you brought from Scotland was only nineteen years of age." He chuckled softly. "Surely you jest. She would have to be over forty now—no matter how well preserved she might appear to be."

"I do not jest, Monsieur. Miss Aimee is nineteen—barely out of the schoolroom."

Leon tensed—his chest tightening again. This time he would brave through it without saying anything.

Beads of perspiration popped out on his forehead. Moisture damped his upper lip as well. Leon rubbed his lip with his forefinger and took a deep breath. He would continue this discussion if it killed him.

"How do you know her current age?" Leon asked.

"She told me one day in front of her parents. I doubt she would lie with her mother and father standing by."

"Parents?" Leon leaned forward in his chair. "What parents?"

"Mr. and Mrs. Aimee. Who else?"

Leon pressed his hand against his chest as if he thought it would reduce the pain. "Tell me about Mr. and Mrs. Aimee."

"You look pale," the earl said. "Are you all right? I could hand you your pill like I did the last time."

"There will be time for pills later. Answer my question. Tell me about Mr. and Mrs. Aimee. Do you know their names?"

"The baker in Luss said that Mr. Aimee's mother calls him Javier."

Leon tensed. "And Mrs. Aimee? What is she called?"

"I believe he said that her mother-in-law called her Rachel."

"You fool!" Leon felt his face heat up. "You have brought the wrong woman!" The pain in his chest intensified. He reached for his cane and hit the table with it, causing a deep scratch in its polished surface. "Now get me my pills. And be quick about it."

✦━━◆━━✦

Seated in the Frenchman's carriage, Ian heard sounds coming from the woods nearby. He thought he heard someone whisper his name. He looked out the window on the left side of the carriage. A man stood in the shadow of the trees.

"Ian," Peter called out. "I am over here."

Peter Aimee moved into the light, motioning for Ian to join him under the trees. Then he stepped back into the shadows again.

Ian looked around to see if the Frenchman was coming, but didn't see anyone. He got out of the carriage, carrying his leather knapsack with him. McGregor, the portly carriage driver and footman, sat on his perch yawning. Ian wondered if the large man had been sleeping off and on since he arrived.

Ian looked up at McGregor. "I am going to find a big tree to stand behind. If Monsieur Gabeau returns before I get back, please tell him where I can be found."

McGregor nodded and yawned again.

Ian crept into the underbrush. Peter stood before him.

Ian smiled. "It was time you arrived."

"Fortunately, I was missed."

The two men embraced as a father and son might after not seeing each other in a while. They stepped back from each other.

"How is my sister?" Peter asked.

"Well enough." Ian pressed his hands to his sides and glanced down at the tops of his shoes so he wouldn't have to look at Peter. "I am keeping a close watch. I will continue to do so, of course." He hated to tell the location of Shannon's room, but he had to be honest. "She was given a room in the maid's quarters."

"What?"

"It was probably done by mistake. Apparently, the earl failed to tell his mother and grandmother that Shannon would be arriving with him. They must have thought he hired her to work as a housemaid."

"I hope that is all he hired her to do."

"Stop worrying." Ian nodded as if to assure him. "For the moment, I have the situation under control."

"And if that should change?"

"I will make the necessary adjustments. You have my word on it. Now—" Ian smiled. "Have you eaten?" He studied Peter for a moment. Then he pulled the leather knapsack from his shoulder. "Of course not." He handed the knapsack to Peter. "Your flesh is melting right off your bones."

"What is this you gave me?"

"Food from the earl's kitchen. You eat while we talk."

They sat down under a spreading oak. Peter opened the sack and pulled out a link of sausage.

"Now." Ian pressed his back against the trunk of the tree and tired to relax. "What did you learn after we left Rosslyn?"

Peter swallowed a mouthful of sausage. "I learned that those stories about goblins and witches and Black Masses are not far wrong."

"You are, of course, joking."

Peter sent Ian a long, thoughtful look. Then he shook his head. "I wish that were so."

Ian laughed. "I do not believe you. I have known you too long to think you believe in witches and goblins. The Peter I know would never accept such nonsense."

"I never said *I* believed it." Peter pulled out a knife and sliced another bite of the meat. "But apparently there are people who do."

"And who are these people you speak of?"

"People who are said to worship the devil."

"No, Peter, that cannot be true."

Peter nodded his head as he chewed. "I hope you are right. And I will not say more until I know more. But Shannon could be in danger."

"How could she be in more danger than coming to Gatehaven to begin with?"

"I do not know for sure, but the earl could be involved with these people. I will need to discover the truth. Let me explain."

"Please do," Ian said.

"Before I was born, my parents fled France for political reasons. An evil Frenchman followed them, but an English earl helped them escape. They eventually reached Scotland and safety, and they owe it all to the goodness of God and His servant, the Earl of Willowbrook. I promised my parents that I would visit the earl while I was in England.

"I have never trusted the Earl of Northon," Peter went on. "Yet the tales I heard in Rosslyn indicate that he might also be evil. I must know whether or not these stories are true. As I said, my sister could be in danger."

"Maybe the Earl of Willowbrook will tell you what he knows about the Earl of Northon *and* the Chapel at Rosslyn."

"That is my hope." Peter put down his knife. "But if my suspicions are true, I will need your help, Ian, in order to convince Shannon that the Earl of Northon is the wicked man we think he is."

"Aye." Ian nodded. "But convincing your sister of anything is never an easy task. As you know, I was educated in England, and as a schoolboy, one of my fellow students was a rich boy named Eddie. I cannot recall his last name, but I remember his cold blue eyes. I think the earl *is* Eddie, and I mentioned my assumptions to Shannon. She grew angry with me. And of course, I have no way of proving what I believe to be true."

"The Earl of Willowbrook might know." Peter got up and wiped his hands with a piece of white cloth. "The earl has lived among the quality all his life. When I see him, I will ask him." Peter offered Ian his hand in friendship. "I put Shannon's life in your hands, Ian, until I return. The Earl of Willowbrook might not know anything about Rosslyn or the Earl of Northon. However, he might know people who do."

Leon opened the carriage door and climbed inside. Ian's bags were tied to the back of the carriage. His overweight driver sat on his perch, looking sleepy. Leon grinned sheepishly. Perhaps his driver had paid a visit to one of the earl's housemaids last night. McGregor had seemed quite friendly with the pretty one they call Millie.

But where was Mr. Colquhoun? Leon had expected the Scotsman to be waiting inside his carriage when he arrived. He wasn't. He looked around but didn't see him. *Idiot.* Leon slammed the carriage door and considered fastening the lock. If he locked Colquhoun out of his carriage, that should teach him a lesson. But Leon wouldn't reach his goal if he did it.

Leon hated waiting and hadn't liked Colquhoun in the first place. But the young man from Scotland could be useful. He would discover just how useful once they reached his home on the outskirts of the village.

The earl had returned from Scotland with Rachel's beautiful daughter instead of bringing Rachel as he'd been hired to do. Leon had no intentions of settling the earl's gambling debts until the right package arrived.

The earl of Northon had promised to make the exchange—produce the right woman—but he doubted the young earl had the gumption to do it. Still, Leon had a few ideas of his own. Colquhoun might be able to help him reach his goal whether he knew it or not.

If Leon were a younger man and in better physical condition, he would have gone after Rachel himself. He rubbed his knee with both hands as if he thought it would lessen the pain. He'd overdone it that day, and he knew it. Nobody else would.

As he sat rubbing his knee, he thought of the beautiful young woman Edward brought back with him from Scotland. The earl swore that Shannon, Rachel's daughter, looked exactly like the girl in the portrait—the painting of Rachel that seldom left his side.

Shannon was no substitute for the real thing no matter how many times the earl praised her rare beauty. Leon smiled to himself. She would certainly make a nice before-dinner appetizer.

He'd tripped, fallen to the bottom of a near empty well, and broken his leg. The pain and humiliation he'd felt at the time had never left him. Yet even looking up at Rachel from the bottom of the well and being so mad he wanted to kill her, he'd wanted her. He still did. That was what amazed him the most. He still wanted Rachel after all these years.

He grounded his jaw teeth together.

He would have her—no matter what the cost or whom he hurt in the process.

The young lady with all that shiny auburn hair that the earl brought from Scotland wasn't Rachel but her daughter, Shannon Aimee. From what little he'd seen of Shannon, she was almost as lovely as her mother.

Shannon's parents were French Protestants called Huguenots. He'd always hated Jews and Huguenots, and they deserved to be punished. Shannon would get her just rewards for being their daughter, and Leon meant to destroy her—along with her friend, Ian Colquhoun.

Then another idea came into his head. What if he used Shannon to lure her parents to England? That way, he could get even with all of them at once. The earl had said that Shannon had an older brother, Peter, and an infant brother as well. Leon felt sure he could provide enough weapons to do away with all of them in one grand sweep.

Rachel married Javier Aimee and left France forever. He'd searched for her over the years but never thought to look in Scotland until ten months ago.

But the bumbling young earl had brought the wrong woman to England. Now as he sat there in the carriage and thought about it, he realized that Shannon was a very beautiful carrot on a stick—a shapely lump of bait on a line.

Leon's spies had informed him that after he abandoned his French wife and she moved back to Paris, she bore him a son and named him Leon Picard after his father. Later, she and the boy moved to the colonies. His son would be twenty-five years old by now. Perhaps he would search for him when all this was over.

Leon looked out the window by the carriage door. Ian Colquhoun was walking toward him. The younger man had probably stepped into the woods to relieve himself, making Leon wait in the carriage when he wished to move on.

His jaw firmed. Leon wanted revenge.

But it might not be in his best interest to scold Mr. Colquhoun just yet. He forced a smile and opened the door. "Come in, my good man."

Ian paused at the door of the carriage. The Frenchman's voice sounded kind and welcoming. Yet he heard something else, too. A ring of insincerity—perhaps mockery—shined through as well. He shook his head as if to wipe away his doubts and climbed inside.

The Frenchman motioned to him. "I had almost given up hope that you were coming."

"Forgive me, Monsieur Gabeau, for being late. I had personal matters that needed my attention." Ian sat down in the carriage seat across from his host.

The Frenchman nodded as if he understood. But for some reason, Ian still didn't trust the man. He forced a smile.

"Did you enjoy your dinner in the earl's kitchen?" the older man asked.

"Yes. We were served a wonderful meal."

"We? What *we* might you be talking about?" His deep voice contained a relaxed, conversational tone.

"Miss Shannon Aimee. Miss Aimee and I were childhood friends back in Scotland."

"Then you must know her parents."

"Of course."

It was certainly kind of the French gentleman to invite him to stay in his home. But for some reason, Ian didn't feel comfortable around the man any more than he trusted him. Did Monsieur Gabeau have a hidden agenda that had nothing to do with being kind and helpful?

"Miss Aimee's brother, Peter, and I are the best of friends," Ian explained. "I spent a lot of time visiting with the family on their farm."

"Then Monsieur Aimee is a farmer?"

"One of the best farmers in Luss."

"The earl mentioned that you and Miss Aimee were from Luss. So what can you tell me about Madam Aimee—the girl's mother? I understand she is very beautiful and that she had a child recently."

"She had a boy—Andre."

"A boy who looks like his father, I wager."

"It is hard to tell. The child is small. But I think he will look more like his mother."

"Ah yes. The beautiful Rachel."

"Then you know Mrs. Aimee?"

The Frenchman looked stunned for an instant as if he'd said more than he intended. "No. We have never met. But the earl speaks highly of the woman and her husband."

Why was Monsieur Gabeau asking him all these questions? Was he merely making polite conversation? Or was there another reason? Perhaps he should have refused his offer and stayed in the guardhouse after all.

Ian glanced out the window on his side of the carriage. There was something in the Frenchman's facial expression when he mentioned Shannon's mother that bothered him. Monsieur Gabeau called her beautiful. Briefly, a faraway, almost dreamy look had softened the older man's features. Had the earl's description of Mrs. Aimee brought back memories of a lost love? Was the Frenchman more of a romantic than Ian would have thought possible—or was he imagining things?

Maybe it was time to start asking questions. Certainly he was within his rights. He hardly knew this man, yet he could be spending a fortnight with him—or longer if the vicar delayed returning to his post at the church.

Shannon sat on the edge of her bed drumming her fingers on her knees. She'd just looked out the only window in her small bedroom, noting that the sun was lower in the western sky.

The earl should have returned by now or sent someone to move her to another room. She couldn't—wouldn't—sit here forever. She had to do something. *Now.*

She sprang to her feet. *Ping.* The room key she was holding in her lap dropped to the floor. She reached down and picked it up. Then she dusted it off with the hem of her green muslin dress. Shannon hurried to the door and stepped out into the hallway.

The hallway looked empty.

What if she simply climbed the stairs to the kitchen? She could sneak around to the front of the house and open the main door. No, the butler would never allow her to come inside. She would need to think of something else.

The young maid she met earlier turned a corner and started toward her.

Shannon smiled as an idea came to her. "Millie. I was hoping I would see you again. Can you come inside a minute? I need company."

Millie gazed down at the stack of clean linen she held in her arms. "I was on me way to deliver these, miss."

"Please," Shannon said in a pleading voice. "I am so lonely."

Millie shrugged her shoulders. "I dare not." She looked to her right and to her left. "Maude would send me on me way without paying me first— she would—if she knew."

"I really need help." Shannon opened the door all the way and motioned for Millie to go in first. "It should only take a moment. And I will never tell anyone you were here."

"Well—" Millie glanced down the hall again. "I guess I could come in— but only for a minute." The maid went inside and spread the stack of linen on the straight-backed chair by the bed. "Now, how can I be helping you? Are you sick, miss? You look a bit pale."

"I am well enough. Now, come and we will sit together on the edge of the bed and talk. I have questions to ask."

"You sit, miss. I will stand. It ain't fittin' that I should sit on a bed in the daytime. The housekeeper would let me go for sure, if she knew."

"Then I will stand as well." Shannon forced another smile. "I spoke with the earl a while ago, and I will soon be moving above stairs to a room near my chaperone, Miss Foster. But he forgot to tell me how to find the stairway the servants use."

"If that be all you're wanting, I can show ya the way." Millie scooped up

the stack of linen. "I am on me way to a room near the stairs right now."
She headed for the door. "Follow me."

"Thank you, Millie. I really appreciate your help."

Shannon had to practically run to keep up with Millie's fast pace. They
hurried to the opposite end of the long hall from the one that led to the
kitchen, made a few more turns and finally reached another stairway.

"I've been on the second floor only once, miss. But the housekeeper says
that these stairs go up and up and up."

"Has she ever mentioned who lives on the top floor?" Shannon asked.
"I saw a young woman with black hair standing at a window when I first
arrived."

"Oh no, miss." Millie shook her head and glanced down at the floor.
"The maids never talk about such things—not here. Maude would put a
switch to us if we did."

Shannon saw what she perceived as fear in Millie's eyes before the maid
developed a sudden interest in smoothing the stack of linen. Shannon
wanted to learn more but not now. She would interview Millie again
when they knew each other better.

"Thank you again, Millie, for all your help. And please never mention
our conversation to anyone. The earl might not have told the housekeeper
or anyone else down here about his plans to move me to another room. I
would never want to get you in trouble."

"I'll shut my mouth, miss. You have me word."

"Then my lips are shut as well. And thank you, Millie, for all your help."

Shannon glanced up the wooden stairway. She knew it would be dangerous. Nevertheless, she would climb to the very top the first chance she
got.

CHAPTER NINE

✿

SHANNON HID IN the linen closet Millie showed her, staying there for what seemed like hours. Her heart pounding, she glanced both ways and finally crept to the bottom of the stairs. She gripped the railing and looked up. After a moment, she climbed the stairs on tiptoes. Halfway up, she paused and looked around before going higher.

On the second floor, she looked around again to see if she was being followed. Then she headed down a long hall that she estimated to be at least fifteen feet wide. Heavy chandeliers hung at intervals from a high ceiling. Walls of stone were painted a soft white. Still the hallway was too dark to suit Shannon.

A table stood outside one of the tall oak doors. Piles of linen had been stacked on it. Millie had carried a stack of linen.

Shannon grabbed a stack from the pile and held it in her arms as she'd seen Millie doing. The earl's mother and grandmother thought she was a maid. Now she would pretend to be one.

The soft linen material seemed out of place against the homespun look of her muslin dress. Unlike Millie, she wasn't wearing a white apron and matching cap. But it would be easier to explain why she wasn't wearing a uniform than what she was doing on the second floor in the first place.

A door opened up ahead.

A middle-aged woman in a white cap and apron came out and headed straight toward her, carrying a silver teapot. The woman was looking off to her left as if she'd heard something. Perhaps she hadn't seen her.

Shannon pressed her body against one of the other doors and tried not to breathe. The doorframe was at least twelve inches wide. Maybe it was enough. If the round little maid turned and went in the opposite direction, she was saved. If not, she could be discovered.

The maid continued down the hall straight for her.

Still pressed against the door, Shannon sent up a quick prayer as she fumbled for the door latch. She reached out but found nothing. Apparently the door was wider than most.

The maid moved closer and closer.

Her father and mother had always told her to call out to the Lord when danger strikes. But she'd never really done that. Maybe now was the time to start.

She inched to the left. Her hand touched something hard and cold. It had to be the latch. She'd found it. But would the door be locked? She sent up another prayer.

Shannon tried to move the latch. It moved. A loud metallic click rang out. Her heart pounded. If the maid hadn't heard that click, she had a hearing problem.

She opened the door. *Creak. Another sound.* The maid would have to be deaf not to hear that one. She slipped inside the dark room and closed the door.

Nobody was inside; she could be thankful for that. But what if the maid happened to open the door to check on things? She trembled. Where would she hide?

Fear not.

Where had that thought come from? She looked around as if she thought she might find an answer. Then she remembered. It was a scripture verse she'd learned from her father. Was this a coincidence? Or had she received some sort of message from beyond her understanding? She was never much of a Christian, but her parents would say God was speaking to her through His Word—the Bible.

She didn't believe in miracles either. But a dash of courage couldn't hurt at a time like this.

Shannon laid the clean linen on a table by the door. She lifted her chin and straightened her back as she'd seen the earl's mother doing. Then she opened the door and stepped out into the hall.

The maid she'd seen earlier had passed on by, but she could still see her back. "Madam," Shannon called out.

The maid stopped and turned around. "Are you calling me, miss?"

"Yes. Would you mind coming here for a moment?"

"Sure and I will." The woman started toward her.

Shannon had no idea what she might say to her. She just hoped the right words would come out of her mouth at the proper time.

The maid had almost reached her. "What might you be needing?"

"Directions. I appear to be lost."

The teapot was centered on a silver tray. She also saw what looked like a bowl for holding sugar, a small pitcher for cream, and a white china saucer with an empty teacup on top of it.

"And where are you needing to go?" the maid finally asked.

Shannon smiled. "I am looking for a Miss Foster. She is about your age and a visitor here at Gatehaven."

The maid nodded. "Oh yes, miss, I know where Miss Foster is." She smiled. "They call me Maude, they do. I have to pass right by Miss Foster's room on me way to the kitchen. Follow me, and I will show ya."

So this is Maude, Shannon thought as she followed the woman down the long hall.

Lady Catherine had said that Shannon was to sleep in the maid's quarters in a room across from a Maude. Was the woman with the teapot *that* Maude? If so, Shannon could find herself back in the maid's quarters before she knew it.

They turned a corner.

"This is Miss Foster's room, miss." The older woman pointed to the corner room on their left. "I must return to the kitchen with the silver teapot. So, I will leave you now."

"Thank you, Maude, for helping me."

"Helping those of the quality is me job."

Shannon smiled and looked down at her muslin dress. *She thinks I am quality—even in these clothes.*

She knocked on the heavy oak door.

"Who is there?" she heard Miss Foster say.

"Miss Aimee."

"Well, are you going to just stand there? Come in."

Shannon opened the door but stood in the doorway a moment before going inside. While her room in the maid's quarters was small and somewhat dark with only one window, Miss Foster's room looked huge. A line of windows along one wall made Shannon feel as if she was outdoors in the sunshine instead of this dark and gloomy mansion.

Miss Foster reclined on a sort of couch by an enormous bed.

"It is about time you arrived," Miss Foster said. "Where have you been?"

Shannon hesitated, trying to think of the best way to explain her tardiness. "I was given the wrong room by mistake. My bags and boxes are in the maid's quarters."

"The maid's quarters? However did they find their way there?"

Shannon shrugged so she wouldn't have to reply.

"Your room must be the one connected to mine by a dressing room."

Miss Foster motioned to a door to her left. "Go in now. I will send for your belongings and have them sent to your room. Now I must dress quickly."

"Where are you going?" Shannon asked.

"I am expected downstairs for dinner in an hour. Polly will assist in unpacking your bags and boxes as soon as she has helped me with my toiletries."

"What about me? Where will I eat my dinner?"

"There was no mention of you going downstairs for dinner this evening, Miss Aimee. I will have my maid bring something up for you from the kitchen. Polly is always glad to help."

Shannon nodded and headed for the door the woman had mentioned. Apparently, she was not invited to Lady Catherine's dinner party that evening and doubted it was an oversight.

The earl's mother and grandmother didn't approve of the match and didn't want her near them—or the earl. Edward would need to explain that they were betrothed—and soon—or this problem would only get worse.

Shannon hurried through the dressing room and into what was to be her room.

The room was spacious but rather dark, and she only saw one large window. Still, it was a huge improvement over the tiny room in the maid quarters.

A bed as large as or larger than the one in Miss Foster's room centered the east wall. Shannon's eyes were instantly drawn to the bed's ornately carved headboard. She stepped across the pine floor for a closer look.

Two dragons were carved into the headboard. Like the carvings at the base of the pillar in Rosslyn, vines grew out of the dragons' mouths, forming a sort of frame for the entire headboard.

"According to the Bible," her father had said, "the dragon and the serpent are symbols for Satan—the devil."

A shiver ran down Shannon's spine.

The dragons faced each other—one on the right side of the bed and one on the left—and a small cross was carved between the towering dragons. Was it put there by mistake? Or was a subtle rebuke of Christians and Christianity posted deliberately? Shannon's father would say it was the latter.

Certainly, the contrast was staggering. Many if not most people would simply call it an inspiring work of art and scold her for reading a deeper, more sinister meaning into it. But Shannon wasn't reared as many or most people were. She was the daughter of Javier and Rachel Aimee—Huguenots who fled France for religious reasons.

Shannon disliked the carvings. They caused the same sick feeling she'd experienced in the chapel at Rosslyn, and she didn't want to have to look at the dragons or have them hanging over her bed while she slept.

The entire headboard sent chills racing through her. She would cover the headboard with a cloth before climbing into bed that night, and she would keep the headboard covered as long as she stayed in that room.

Ian expected to share a meal with his host before turning in for the night. The air was damp and a bit chilly. The Frenchman sat in a chair near a rock fireplace in the sitting room.

"I will sit here and rest while my housekeeper shows you to your room on the second floor. But I am afraid you will be dining alone. Some time ago, I accepted an invitation to dine with the earl and his family tonight, and I will return quite late."

Ian stood in the doorway, wondering how to respond.

"Mrs. Woodhouse is my cook and housekeeper; I call her Cook. She will serve your supper in the small dining room. And feel free to explore my library if you have a desire to read. I was born in France, and I am especially proud of my books on the history of that country. I think you will find them quite interesting."

"I am sure I will," Ian finally said, "and thank you for your kind hospitality."

"I am happy for your company, Mr. Colquhoun. In fact, it is my hope that you will stay here even after the vicar returns."

Ian nodded and followed a butler out of the room. He had no intentions of staying in Monsieur Gabeau's home any longer than absolutely necessary. But it wouldn't be polite to express that view. Besides, he was tired from his long journey and planned to request that he be served his evening meal early.

After a meal of mutton stew and vegetables, Ian went into the library. Since France had long been an ally of Scotland but an enemy of England, he'd concluded that he might find the history books in the Frenchman's collection interesting.

Floor to ceiling bookshelves filled the library on three sides. A rock fireplace dominated the wall at the far end of the large room. Tables and comfortable-looking chairs were scattered here and there. The housekeeper had equipped the library with extra candles as if she'd expected Ian to visit there that night.

He ran his fingertips along a line of books at eye level. Most of the titles were written in French, but he saw English titles as well. He pulled out a volume, read the cover and returned it to the shelf. On his third try, Ian pulled out a worn black book with an intriguing title, *The Secret Religious Movements of France.*

He flipped to the Table of Contents and noticed a chapter on the Huguenots and another on the Reform Movement. A black bookmark protruded from the center of the book. He opened to that page first.

The chapter was titled "Jacques DeMolay." Ian took the book, moved to a chair with a lighted candle beside it, and sat down. He had no idea who DeMolay might be, but since the chapter was marked, he decided to read it.

Jacques DeMolay was born in France in 1244, he read. *At the age of twenty-one, he joined the Order of Knights Templar.*

Ian frowned thoughtfully. *Knights Templar.* He'd never heard of that order and wanted to know more about it.

The Roman Catholic Church sanctioned members of the Knights Templar, and the knights participated in the Crusades where they were declared heroic men of valor. In 1298, Jacques DeMolay was given the title of Grand Master of the Knights Templar, and at that time, the knights were one of only two groups who still fought the Saracens. As a result, they gained wealth, and DeMolay also gained power and prestige.

This was a lot of information for Ian to swallow in one sitting. He would need time to digest it all. Still, he continued reading.

Phillip the Fair was the King of France in 1305. Some insist that he related wild stories about the heresies the knights performed behind closed doors.

Heresies? Ian could hardly wait to learn to what heresies the author referred.

On October 13, a Friday, all members of Knights Templar still living in France were arrested and accused of heresy. They were tortured in hopes that they would admit their heresies. Jacque DeMolay was burned at the stake.

Burned at the stake? Now that *was* shocking.

Ian froze. Someone was coming.

Ian started to put the book back on the shelf exactly where he'd found it. But why should he? He was invited to explore the library by its owner. He closed the book but continued holding it. He intended to finish reading the article as soon as possible.

The butler and carriage driver entered the library holding a tray with a bottle of wine perched on it. "Sir." The Scotsman's smile looked forced. "Monsieur Gabeau thought you might like a glass of port before turning in for the night."

"I appreciate his thoughtfulness," Ian said, "but I think not. I plan to go right up to bed."

After the plump butler nodded and left the room, Ian breathed a sign of relief. The Scottish servant hadn't realized that he and Ian were ancient enemies. But McGregor would soon know that Ian was a Colquhoun. Ian put the book under his arm and followed McGregor out. He was interested in reading about the heresies of which the Knights Templar were accused.

In his room above stairs, he sat down on a cushioned armchair that looked almost exactly like the one in the library. He opened his book to page 78 and began reading. The article told more about the life of Jacques DeMolay before his execution.

I have no interest in reading about the man's life, he thought. *I want to read about the heresies.*

Ian turned to the next page.

Startled, Ian froze. He couldn't believe his own eyes. The next twenty pages had been torn from the book.

Who would do this? And why?

Someone didn't want him or anyone to read those twenty pages. Now he was even more curious about the heresies of Jacques DeMolay.

———✦———

Leon arrived for dinner at Gatehaven that evening and was escorted into the library to wait for the earl. He came earlier than expected because he wanted to meet Miss Aimee, and he was in no mood for another of the earl's lame excuses.

Leon sat in the earl's chair by the fireplace. He was tapping his cane on the floor when the young earl finally entered the room.

"Sorry for the delay," the earl said with a trace of nervousness.

"I am sorry, too," Leon replied hotly. "You know how I hate to be kept waiting."

"It could not be helped."

"Why?" Leon asked.

"I have been looking for Miss Aimee, but I cannot find her."

"Cannot find her? Whatever do you mean?"

"Miss Aimee has disappeared." The earl shrugged and sat down in a chair across from the earl. "She simply vanished."

"Surely you jest." Leon's chuckle held sarcastic overtones. "It is highly unlikely that a lovely young lady such as Miss Aimee would simply vanish without a trace. Now where is she? I had hoped to speak with her before we went in to dinner."

"I am not jesting. I have my servants looking everywhere for her."

"I am not amused, my lord." Leon frowned. "I paid a good deal of money to have a certain package brought here from Scotland. You brought the wrong one. Now this?"

"Everything is being done to find her. My butler is questioning all the maids as well as the kitchen staff personally in hopes of finding her."

"Your kitchen staff? Why would you question them?"

"I failed to write my mother and grandmother ahead of time to let them know I was bringing Miss Aimee with me. They assumed I hired her as a maid and had sent her below stairs—to—to the maid's quarters."

"The maid's quarters? Have you lost your senses?"

"I had intended to tell my family the real reason I brought her here. They know that I bring young women to the estate from time to time and have come to expect it. But before I could explain anything, Miss Aimee disappeared. I would search for her myself," the earl went on, "but as you know, we are expected for dinner within the hour."

"And after dinner?" Leon prompted.

"We both have a meeting to attend—after dinner tonight."

Leon threw back his head and laughed mockingly. "Ah yes. The meeting." Then his smile vanished as suddenly as it appeared, and his mouth turned down. "I will be returning to Gatehaven for dinner again in one week. By then, I expect you to have found Miss Aimee, settled her down, and told Lady Catherine and Lady Victoria my plans for this young woman and her family. Of course, you cannot tell them everything, but enough to keep them quiet. We will need their help if we hope to achieve my goals. Is that understood?"

"Of course." The earl went to the window by the fireplace and looked out. "There is a full moon tonight. Had you noticed?"

"I noticed, my lord. Why else would we be having dinner on a meeting night? Has everything been prepared?"

"Everything."

"At least you can do something right."

◆——◆——◆

Shannon couldn't sleep. She kept hearing noises she could not identify. After all, she was staying in a strange room. She'd locked her door and covered the carvings of the two dragons as best she could, but she still didn't feel safe. And the white cloth she used didn't completely cover the carvings on the headboard. The tail of one of the dragons and some of the vines were still exposed.

She'd noticed a table with white linen stacked on it just across the hall from her room. Maybe she would snatch one of them and use it to cover the rest of the carvings.

Shannon stepped out into the darkened hall to retrieve the cloth. The only light she saw came from a lamp over the table. The cloths were stacked in neat piles. She crept across the hall on bare feet and grabbed a white cloth from the top of the stack nearest to her.

She heard footsteps coming closer. Shannon gasped and stepped back, pressing her body against the wooden door that led to her room as she had done previously.

She wore a white sleeping gown and robe over her chemise, and it wouldn't be proper for a young woman to be caught walking about the halls at night in her sleeping attire. Lady Catherine and Lady Victoria would be displeased if they knew.

Shannon sucked in her breath as ten or more dark figures walked one behind the other, and close to where she stood. They would surely have seen her if they had glanced her way. The dark figures wore identical robes with hoods that covered their faces, and they walked in step as soldiers might with their heads down.

She'd never felt so powerless in her entire life.

At the corner, they turned down a different hall and disappeared from view. Later, she would probably regret not following them. But at the moment, all she wanted to do was cover the headboard with the extra cloth she managed to grab, climb in bed, and hide under the covers until she stopped shivering.

CHAPTER TEN

I AN CREPT DOWNSTAIRS, gripping the book with both hands, and slipped into the library. All but one of the candles were extinguished, making the room much darker than when he came in earlier.

He intended to return the book to the proper slot on the shelf before Monsieur Gabeau or his housemaid came in and found it missing. He was given the right to read any book in the library, but he would rather the Frenchman not know the name of the one he found most interesting—just yet.

He reached up in order to put it on the proper shelf and stopped. Which two volumes was it placed between? Was it between the two books of poetry? Or the two on French history? He couldn't say which. To put it back in the wrong place might be more telling than to not return it to the shelf at all.

Ian tossed the book on the small table by Etienne Gabeau's chair. Tomorrow he would say that he took out the book and read a few pages but didn't know where it belonged on the shelf. Rather than put it in the wrong space, he left it out for McGregor or the housekeeper to return to the proper place.

The truth was always preferable to a lie—especially for Christians.

If the Frenchman asked him if he'd noticed the missing pages, he would simply tell the truth. His honesty might even lead to more information, and he certainly hoped to learn all he could about those heresies.

He closed the library door—*squeak*.

The Frenchman needs to have his housekeeper oil his hinges. From what he'd learned about the man, it might be a good idea to have his brain oiled as well.

Ian thought he heard sounds coming from outside the mansion. He paused—hoofbeats. Apparently the Frenchman had returned from his night at Gatehaven, and at a late hour. It was well past midnight.

Had Shannon attended the dinner at the mansion? Had Monsieur Gabeau met her? And would Ian ever know whether or not he did or didn't?

Ian yawned and turned toward the stairs. They could discuss the book he found in the library at another time. For now, he was going to bed.

✦———✦

The next morning Ian returned to the maid's quarters at Gatehaven and knocked on Shannon's door.

"Miss Aimee," he called. "Open the door, lass."

When nobody responded, he knocked again.

Shannon's bedroom door was partly open. He looked inside, but he didn't see Shannon or her belongings.

What happened? Where could she be? She couldn't have simply vanished. Ian raced back up the stairs—two at a time. He must speak to the maid he met on the previous day. Millie would know where Shannon was.

Millie stood with several other maids in the middle of the big kitchen, holding a stack of what looked like fresh laundry. The cook stood in front of a long table chopping vegetables, but she looked up when Ian came in.

"And what might you be doing here, sir?"

"I am looking for Miss Aimee, the young lady that arrived yesterday from Scotland."

He turned his attention to Millie. "I thought maybe Millie or someone else might know where I can find her."

Millie put down the stack of clothes on the table by the door, but when her gaze connected with Ian's, she shrugged and looked away as if she didn't want to look at him.

"Millie," the cook said louder than necessary. "Speak up, girl, and tell this young man what you know."

"I know nothing, mum, nothing at all."

"She must be telling the truth," the cook said. "The earl's personal valet came in here earlier this morning looking for Miss Aimee as well, and we all assured him that we knew nothing. If Millie knew anything, she would have told the earl's man. She knows she will lose her job if she ever lies to me."

Ian disagreed with the cook's conclusions. Millie knew something. He intended to find out what it was.

Millie gazed at the back kitchen door. "I will be going out now, mum, to bring in the rest of the clothes from the line of rope out back."

"Hurry then and go. We have a lot of work to do this morning."

"Yes, mum." Millie opened the door and went out.

Ian gazed at the cook. "It is such a lovely morning that I plan to explore the garden behind the mansion. So I will be leaving you now. But do let me know if Miss Aimee returns."

"If you come here again, I will tell you anything I know."

Ian went out the back door and stood on the stoop. Flowers in a variety of colors were planted on small plots of ground, and rock pathways surrounded each plot. But where was Millie? He looked for a long line of rope with clothes hanging from it. Millie was sure to be nearby.

A thick hedge outlined the entire garden, and a metal gate separated the garden from the barnyard beyond. Ian opened the gate and went into the barnyard.

He noticed a wooden cage where chickens were kept, and to the right of it he saw a line of white cloths blowing in a gentle breeze. Millie would have to be there.

Millie was leaning over a wicker basket, folding a white cloth. Her back was to him. He assumed she hadn't seen him yet.

"Miss Millie," he said.

She jerked around. Then she just stood there—staring at him.

"Sorry. I hope I didn't frighten you. But I must speak with you for a moment."

"I have nothing to say to ya, sir."

"I have plenty to say to you. You see, I think you like Miss Aimee almost as much as I do." He hesitated before saying more in hopes of getting her attention. "She could be in danger."

"Danger?"

"Aye. Someone might want to harm her. Miss Aimee must be warned. If you refuse to tell me all you know, how can I possibly help her?"

"I know nothing." Millie glanced off toward the mansion. "If I did know something, I could lose me job, if I spoke me thoughts where others could hear."

"Whatever you tell me will be in strict confidence. I will not tell the cook or anyone else anything you tell me." He smiled, hoping to gain her confidence. "Please tell me what you know. The longer you wait, the more danger Miss Aimee could be in."

Millie bit her bottom lip. "All right, I'll tell ya what little I know. But it's not much, mind ya."

"Anything you can tell will surely help."

He expected to hear her report. But she didn't say anything. "Well," he said and cleared his throat. "I'm waiting."

"Miss Aimee wanted to go up on the second floor. She said her room must be near her chaperone. She wanted me to show her the way to the servants' stairway. Well, sure and I showed her, all right. Then I went back to the kitchen. I went to see Miss Aimee later to see how she faired. Her room was empty. All her boxes were gone. I do not know where her things be taken or who took them. And I know no more than that, sir."

"I believe you. Now will you show me how to find those stairs?"

She nodded. "Follow me. I know another way to get to the back stairs, and we need not go through the kitchen to get there. Cook might ask questions if we go by way of the kitchen."

Ian followed Millie to another back entrance he hadn't noticed previously. "I also want to thank you for your help." Ian waited while Millie opened the door. "And your secret is safe with me, Miss Millie. But I do want to ask you one more question." Ian followed her inside.

"What question, sir?"

"Is the door we just entered ever locked?"

"Aye," she said. "At night."

"And the key. Where is it kept?"

She shook her head. "I dare not tell ya. I would be fired for sure if I did."

"Please, Millie." He followed her inside and down a long hall. "It is very important that I go up those stairs tonight. Miss Aimee's life might depend on it."

"The key can always be found under the straw mat in front of the door. If ya use it to go inside, you must promise to put the key back where ya found it."

They turned a corner, and Ian saw the stairway just ahead.

"As I told Miss Aimee," Millie said, "I never went up the stairs but once. But I heard that the stairs go up and up. Sure and I went in the main parlor for the first time the day Miss Aimee came. Maude said she had important doings that day. I took her place. But I'm not allowed to go in that part of the house anymore. Only Maude goes up those stairs to the second floor now."

"Why would she go upstairs?"

"Maude carries food trays to the rooms on the second floor or gives them to the butler to deliver to the bedrooms up and up."

"Up and up? What does that mean?"

"Maude told us of guest bedrooms on the top floor."

Ian followed Millie back down the long hall to the door they entered earlier, thinking about the risk he might be taking if he climbed the stairs to the second floor at night. If discovered, he would surely lose his position as the vicar's assistant, and Millie could lose her job as well. He could be forced to return to Scotland.

What help would he be to Shannon if he left Gatehaven forever?

Nevertheless, he would return to the stairway later that evening—when it was dark.

＋——＋——＋

Peter Aimee guided his horse to a slow walk near a country estate owned by another earl—a nobleman who happened to be an old friend of his parents. He'd heard about the Earl of Willowbrook all his life, but he'd never actually met him.

The journey had left his backside a bit numb. Other than that, he felt extremely fit, and he looked forward to meeting the earl for the first time.

His parents had said that after the earl became a Christian, he befriended them when they needed help the most, and that the two families had remained friends through the years, exchanging letters back and forth. However, the earl wasn't expecting a visit from Peter. To push his way to the front door of the mansion as if he belonged there seemed presumptuous for someone of Peter's station in life—regardless of the friendly connection.

From his location on a rise at the edge of the woods, he saw two men in green uniforms standing some distance away. He assumed they were footmen. He also saw someone tending the garden in front of the mansion. Perhaps the gardener would be willing to announce him to the earl's caretaker.

Maybe the Earl of Willowbrook would invite him inside—if so, well and good. If not, he would simply turn around and ride to the village of Fairs near the estate where his sister was staying. He hoped to find employment in Fairs so he could keep a watchful eye on Shannon and his friend, Ian Colquhoun.

Peter hesitated a moment longer. Then he reined his horse toward the man working in the garden. With any luck, he could be talking to the earl within the hour. He wanted to hear all there was to learn about the Earl of Northon, and he hoped the Earl of Willowbrook could provide him with the information he needed. He also wanted to discuss what he'd heard about the Chapel at Rosslyn with someone he could trust. His parents had assured him that the Earl of Willowbrook was such a man.

Less than an hour later, Peter sat in a huge parlor facing an elderly gentleman that he now knew to be the Earl of Willowbrook.

"It is such a pleasure to meet the son of my dear friends." The earl sent Peter a smile that would surely melt the snow off the top of the highest mountain in Switzerland. "At the moment, my son, Lord Wilburn, and daughter-in-law, Lady Juliet, are away on a short holiday with their two children. However, it is my hope that you can meet them before you return to Scotland."

"I would be honored to meet your family, my lord."

"I trust your parents and sister are well."

"Oh yes—very well indeed. In fact, I have a little brother now."

"Splendid."

"Andre was born a few months ago, and I think he looks just like Papa."

"I knew your father when he was about your age, Mr. Aimee, and you are so like him." He picked up a cup from the silver tray on the table before them and took a sip of tea. "And your sister is with your parents in Scotland, I presume."

"No, my lord. In fact, she is one of the reasons I came today."

The earl leaned forward in his chair. "Is something bothering you, young man?"

Peter felt it was wrong to tell stories about others unless he knew them to be true. At the same time, his sister could be in danger. If the earl knew something about the Earl of Northon that he was willing to share, Shannon might avoid a disaster.

Peter cleared his throat, and then he told the earl all that had happened since the Earl of Northon first arrived in Luss, Scotland.

"On my way to England, I heard some tales while visiting the Scottish village of Rosslyn," Peter went on. "I would not mention it now except that the Earl of Northon insisted on visiting a rather peculiar chapel near Rosslyn. Perhaps you have heard of it. As I said, I heard many stories about the goings on there before I left Scotland. Can you tell me anything about the chapel or the strange tales connected with it?"

The earl shook his head. "Until this moment, I had never heard of the chapel or the town of Rosslyn. However, Lord Wilburn visits London far more often than I do these days. He might know something. If he does, you can be sure that I will get back to you with that information as soon as I have it. And I am not in the least surprised that the Earl of Northon found the strange chapel intriguing. He has a reputation for disturbing and—and shall we say, *unwise* adventures. I should not be surprised at anything the young earl might say or do."

"You must know a great deal about the Earl of Northon, living here in England as you do," Peter said. "But I know nothing about the earl—nor do I trust him. Am I imagining problems that do not exist? Or should I worry about the situation my sister finds herself in?"

"Your worries are not groundless," the earl said. "To say the least, they are quite perceptive."

"Please, my lord, explain what you mean."

"Like you, I hate to be the teller of tales. But in this incidence, I think it is important." The earl set his empty cup back on the tray. "My son, Lord Wilburn, is some years older than the Earl of Northon. Still, he knows him well. And my son has always said that Eddie has a taste for beautiful women—especially those from a lower station in life than his own."

"Eddie?"

"The Earl of Northon was known as Eddie when he was a child. My son and I often refer to him by that name—even today."

I knew it. Wait until I tell Ian.

"Some say that the young women brought to the earl's estate are never seen again. But I have no proof of that. These stories could all be lies. But I am afraid that they could also be true."

Peter stood. "Thank you for your hospitality, my lord. But I must return to my sister at once."

"Of course, you must. But first, let us pray together. Your mother and father are great believers in the power of prayer—as am I. Is that also the case with you, Mr. Aimee?"

"Yes, my lord, it is. And I would be honored to pray with you."

As soon as the prayer ended, Peter said good-bye to the earl and sent for his horse. If he rode hard, he could be at Gatehaven on the morrow.

At dusk, Peter reined his horse into a dark forest. A few minutes later, he heard what sounded like hoofbeats. Startled, he glanced off to his left. He didn't see anything and looked back. A low branch of a tree was right in front of him. He threw his hands in front of his face...

Bam.

Everything went black.

* ——◆—— *

Peter opened his eyes. Pain engulfed him. He tried to move—*groan.*

"Oh look, Uncle," a woman said. "The man be awake."

Peter felt sure that the soft, melodious voice he'd heard belonged to his beloved, Kate Colquhoun. His head ached and his shoulder burned like hot metal. Still, he lifted his head in hopes of seeing her face. Daylight faded, and his body spun around and around. Everything went black again.

* ——◆—— *

On her second morning after arriving at Gatehaven, Shannon found a sweet love note from the earl tucked under her door. Until she got the letter, Shannon hadn't known that the earl knew she'd moved from the maid's quarters to a new room on the second floor. Apparently, he knew. Miss Foster must have told him.

The note convinced Shannon that the earl still loved her. However, she hadn't actually seen him since the day she arrived at his estate.

"Be diligent and understanding, my love," the earl had explained in the letter. "I must prepare my mother and grandmother for our eventual marriage. Such a task takes time."

Time? How long would it take for him to sit down with two women and tell them his marriage plans—five minutes—perhaps less? How much preparation would such a meeting require?

Shannon missed Ian and wanted to see him. But would he ever find her now that she'd moved to the second floor? Her chaperone had arranged to have all her meals served in her room, and she was encouraged to stay in her room as much as possible.

"It wouldn't be wise for you to stroll through the mansion alone," Miss Foster had said, "especially at night. Young girls have been known to get lost in big houses such as this."

If Shannon hadn't seen the robed nightwalkers with her own eyes as they marched down the dark hall outside her door, she might have ignored Miss Foster's warnings. Under the circumstances, she listened and intended to obey the warnings as much as possible.

Miss Foster wanted to read Shannon's palm, and Shannon promised to allow it. She didn't believe in crystal balls and palm reading, but if it pleased her chaperone to hold the palm of her hand and look at it, she could stand it for one night.

Shannon went into Miss Foster's room for the palm reading. She was not prepared for what she saw. The room was crammed with lighted candles. The fumes together with the intense heat made it difficult for Shannon to breathe. The sickeningly sweet odor reminded her of a million perfumes all mixed together.

Miss Foster sat at a table peering at what looked like a crystal ball. A black shawl was draped over her head and shoulders.

Was Miss Foster a gypsy—or slightly demented? Papa would say she was a witch. How had Miss Foster managed to so deceive her parents?

"Sit down, my dear, and show me your palm. The right one will do nicely."

Shannon wanted to retreat to her room and lock the door. But to be honest, Miss Foster was far kinder to her than anyone else at Gatehaven—except for Millie, of course. What could it hurt to humor the woman—do as she asked?

She opened the palm of her right hand and showed it to her chaperone. Miss Foster guided Shannon's hand to the lighted candle nearest the crystal ball. Then she studied her palm as if she expected to find something hidden there.

She would allow Miss Foster to read her palm, and then she would leave. But Miss Foster just kept peering at the palm of her hand as if she had entered another world—perhaps a very dark world at that.

Shannon wanted this nonsense to end. Instead, she said, "Is there love in my future?"

"Love, yes. But I also see danger."

"What kind of danger?"

"You must watch your back or you will be sorry."

Enough. Shannon jerked back her hand. "I am sorry, Miss Foster, but I am feeling ill." She rose from her chair. "I must return to my room at once."

"But I have yet to tell your future. And there is more to tell."

"Perhaps another time. I must go now."

Shannon ran through the dressing room and on to her own room and shut the door. She had left a candle burning by her bed. In the near darkness, she could see that the cloth had fallen or been removed from her headboard. The dragons appeared to be looking at her as if their wooden eyes were somehow alive.

She had to get out of that room. It wasn't merely that the room was dark and stuffy. She needed to breathe fresh air. Maybe she also needed to pray. Wasn't that what her parents would do if they were in a situation like this?

Despite the dangers she might find in the darkened hall, she opened the door and stepped out. Miss Foster had said that nobody was staying in the room across from hers and that it opened onto a balcony. If she crossed the hall to the vacant room and went out on the balcony, the fresh air might revive her spirits. She decided it was worth trying.

Shannon entered the darkened room. Moonlight streamed in from a door that must have been left open. She assumed that the door led to the balcony and headed straight for it.

The moon wasn't as full as it had been on the previous night. Yet it gave off enough light to turn the ground below into a garden edged in gold. She still felt weak and lightheaded and reached out for the banister for support. Then she gripped it with both hands.

She heard a sound. Shannon tensed. Was someone coming? She glanced back. But it was too dark to see anything.

Someone grabbed her from behind, putting a hand over her mouth. She wanted to scream but couldn't utter a sound.

CHAPTER ELEVEN

S HANNON STRUGGLED TO break free.

"Calm yourself, lass. It is only me. Ian."

She stiffened. The hand over her mouth disappeared. "How dare you, Ian Colquhoun—creeping up on me in the dark."

"I had to make sure you did not scream."

She slowly turned and faced him. "I would bite your fingers this minute if your hand was still over my mouth."

He chuckled softly. "Glad it is not."

"My mother told me that once my father played a similar trick on her shortly before they married."

"Who can say but that one day we will wed as well."

"That shall never happen," she insisted. "And you know it."

"Nevertheless, I would hate for my future wife to bite my fingers. The thought is most unpleasant—whoever she might be."

Shannon suddenly realized that having Ian nearby had removed all the fear and worry she'd felt earlier. "Now, Ian Colquhoun, what are you doing on the second floor in the middle of the night?"

"Looking for you, of course."

"It would be dangerous for you, if you were found here."

"It cannot be helped."

Ian took Shannon's hand and led her to a bench facing the night sky. "You might be in danger."

Shannon tensed. Miss Foster had said she was in danger, and she'd been thinking the same thing but didn't want to admit it.

"What danger?" she asked.

"I have been pondering something I learned while we were in Rosslyn. Sit down and we will discuss it."

They sat side-by-side on a bench on the balcony. Their only light was the moon that seemed to reach out to them with its light. He pushed back a lock of her hair that had fallen across her forehead. Shannon felt warm all over.

"I do not wish that you would worry," Ian went on. "But the tales we heard in Rosslyn about witches and goblins and Black Masses might be truer than we thought."

"What a horrible conclusion."

Ian nodded. "And if the Earl of Northon has a hand in any of those evil things, you could be in danger."

Shannon stiffened. She would not allow Ian or anyone to speak against the man she loved—a man who had tucked a sweet love note under her door.

She tossed back her hair. "Unless you have proof that the earl is a part of this nonsense, I will not stay here a moment longer and listen while you discredit him."

"I have no proof—only strong notions. I am merely giving an old friend a warning. And if you are as wise as I think you are, you will make yourself aware of the possible danger you might be in."

Shannon glared at him. "Either we discuss another topic this instant or I will get up from this bench and go back to my room."

"Very well." Ian paused before continuing. "Perhaps we should each tell the other all the events that have transpired since last we met. Does that topic suit you, lass?"

"It does. In fact, I would enjoy discussing recent events very much."

As Ian told about meeting the Frenchman and staying in his home until the vicar returned, Shannon thought about all that had happened since she arrived at Gatehaven. She knew she would love the earl until her dying day and didn't want to hear Ian or anyone say a word against him. Yet in her heart, she wondered. Did he truly love her as much as his love note suggested that he did?

At last Ian said, "The earl and Ladies Catherine and Victoria will be leaving for London in the morning at daybreak. They are not expected to return for days."

"How could you possible know something like that? If it were true, the earl would have told me."

"It is true. Believe me. Monsieur Gabeau told me, and he knows things."

"How would he know the earl's plans?"

"The Frenchman and the earl are good friends—perhaps partners in some endeavor."

"Then this is hearsay?" Shannon stood. "Ian, I do not believe that you would ever lie to me. It is not in you. At the same time, you have no proof that what the Frenchman told you is true. My father always said that to repeat a lie is almost as bad as creating one." She sniffed deliberately and with an indignant air. "So, I will leave you now."

"I will walk you to your door."

"No." She whirled around. "There is no need."

"There most certainly *is* a need if I say there is a need," Ian said. "I will accompany you to your door, or I will pick you up and carry you there. It is your choice. Which will it be?"

"Neither. I will walk on my own two feet—alone."

"Then I will walk on my own two feet as well—one step behind you."

⋅────⋅

When Shannon awoke the next morning, she saw that another note was pushed under the door during the night. Eager to read it, she got out of bed and reached down to retrieve it.

> My dear Miss Aimee,
>
> I had hoped that we might see each other today or soon. That is not to be. At first light, I will travel to London with Ladies Catherine and Victoria on urgent business. I love you so and long to kiss your sweet lips once more. I will contact you as soon as I return.
>
> Your Servant,
> Edward, The Earl of Northon.

Ian was right.

Shannon dropped the letter. It floated softly to the floor. The earl left Gatehaven without telling her in advance, just as Ian predicted. Yet he found time to inform that Frenchman of his plans.

Miss Foster cleared her throat. Until that instant, Shannon hadn't known she was standing in the doorway between her room and the connecting room.

"Dress quickly, Miss Aimee," Miss Foster said. "The earl and his family are away from Gatehaven at the moment, and we will be breaking the fast downstairs in the small dining room." Miss Foster turned sharply and went back to her own room.

So. Shannon bit her lower lip. Miss Foster also knew that the earl was leaving for London before Shannon did. Perhaps the entire household knew—if not everybody living in the nearby village of Fairs. She still loved Edward, but it was becoming harder and harder to trust him.

Ian sat at a table in the smallest of the Frenchman's dining rooms, breaking the fast.

Was Shannon still upset with him?

By now, she would know that the earl had indeed left for London. Would the earl's abrupt actions insure a reconciliation with Shannon? He doubted it would make a difference—at least not right away. But she would come around—eventually. She always did.

Ian looked up when Etienne Gabeau came in. He forced a smile. "Good morning, Monsieur. I hope you slept well."

He did not return Ian's smile. "My ability to fall asleep was retarded when you chose to go out last night without telling me in advance." The Frenchman took a plate from the stack and began filling it with food. "I heard your feet on the stairway long after midnight, Mr. Colquhoun. Wherever did you go—if I might ask?"

"I was unable to sleep as well, sir. So I went out for a walk. A stroll in the night air is very invigorating—do you not think?"

Gabeau held his plate in one hand and his cane in the other. "If you enjoy a good stroll in the open air so much, perhaps you would agree to give me a hand today."

"But of course. What would you have me do?'

Leon hooked his cane over the back on the chair at the head of the table and sat down. "My driver has been under the weather and unable to perform his normal duties. I promised the vicar that I would make sure his dog was fed each day until he returns. Would you be willing to go to his cottage and feed the beast? The dog is called Buster, and is a very pesky animal, in my opinion. Buster is kept in a pen behind the cottage. Cook will tell you where the animal's feed is kept and fill in all the other details."

"I have a fondness for dogs, sir. And I would be only too happy to see to Buster's needs."

Shannon only pretended to eat her porridge and dark bread. Instead she surveyed the dining room with its wooden walls painted white and its rectangular oak table. It was the first time she'd been allowed on the first floor since the day she arrived, and she traced her steps from the time she left her room on the second floor until she went in to break the fast. She intended to retain a picture in her mind of her surroundings in case that information was needed at a future date. She didn't want to get lost as those other young women had and not be able to find her way back to her bedroom.

"The earl and his family left for London rather unexpectedly," Miss Foster explained. "I only learned of their journey the morning after I arrived here."

Shannon nodded, hoping Miss Foster thought she'd heard the news ahead of time as well. It was a weak attempt to pretend she was a member of the inner circle when she wasn't. But it was the only thing she could think to do under the circumstances.

"There wasn't time for the Ladies Catherine and Victoria to cancel prior commitments," Miss Foster went on. "An all-day meeting of the Spiritualist Society is scheduled in three days—here at Gatehaven. I must host it now, and it is quite a responsibility. You are welcome to attend our meeting or go your own way."

Shannon had no wish to attend all-day meetings sponsored by the Spiritualist Society—whatever that was. But Miss Foster had been kind to her. It might hurt her chaperone's feelings if she refused to attend.

"How many people will be attending the meeting?" Shannon asked.

"I could not say—perhaps as many as twenty or twenty-five. I daresay carriages will be arriving all morning on the day of the first meeting. I hope the main parlor will hold them all. Will you be sitting in with us, Miss Aimee?"

"Yes, thank you. I believe I will."

Shannon smiled internally. Maybe it was a meeting of all crystal ball owners in the area.

"I tend to move around in my chair when I sit too long," Shannon continued. "If that should happen, I might have to get up and go outside."

"Go and come as you please. I will not be available to serve as your chaperone until the meetings end."

• ——◆—— •

As soon as Ian walked up to the dog's cage, the animal growled.

Ian frowned. "Steady, boy."

The dog's watering trough was dry—as if it hadn't held water in days. The feeding bowl was empty, too. Buster looked gaunt. From the evidence at hand, the animal hadn't been fed or watered in a long time.

"The Frenchman should be whipped for allowing this to happen," he muttered.

Ian put down the bucket of water. He set the bowl of food on top of it, and unlocking the animal's cage, he went inside. The gate slammed shut behind him. "I will have you eating and drinking like a Scotsman at a wedding feast in minutes."

The brown and white dog lapped up every bit of the water. Ian poured more into the trough while Buster wolfed down milk and bits of meat in his bowl.

Buster wouldn't be called attractive in some circles and didn't appear to be any special breed. But to a dog lover like Ian, the physical appearance of an animal didn't matter. He had a notion that it didn't matter to the vicar either.

It *would* matter to someone like Etienne Gabeau.

When Buster had his fill, he wagged his tail. Then he went over and licked Ian's hand.

"Good boy. Would you like to get out of that cage for a while and go for a walk? I have the time, if you do."

Ian opened the cage. The dog shot out like a flash of lightning.

"Come back here, Buster," Ian shouted. "You follow my rules. Or you go back in the cage."

The dog kept running. But instead of running away, he circled the vicar's garden as if it was something he was in the habit of doing.

"You want to play, do ya now?"

The dog sped by right in front of Ian and made another turn on the grounds.

"Very well, then. Run if you must. We can put off our walk for a bit." Ian noticed a stone bench under a tree. "In the meantime, I'll sit on this bench until you are ready."

As the dog slowed from a run to a fast walk, Ian thought about Peter. He should have returned from the home of that other earl by now. Then he thought about Shannon. All his thoughts began and ended with her.

With the earl away from Gatehaven for a few days, Shannon would be safe—for now.

At last, Buster ran up to Ian and put his paws on Ian's knees.

"Ready to go for a walk now, boy?"

The dog wagged his tail vigorously.

"You are?" Ian stood. "Then I guess it's time to go."

They hiked down a dusty road that Ian had never seen previously. As he walked along, Ian saw a wooded area that skirted green fields and meadows. He assumed the land belonged to the earl, but perhaps at least part of it belonged to the Frenchman.

At the edge of the woods near a pond he noticed a small cabin. It was located between the earl's mansion and the vicar's cottage. He couldn't see it clearly from that distance, but the dwelling seemed to be pulling him forward—inviting him to come closer and take a look.

The cabin in the woods was small but welcoming. His sister, Kate, would call it charming. Flowers he couldn't identify in a variety of colors lined a wooden fence. The walls of the house were made of native stone, and the thatched roof reminded him of his little sisters and their gold colored hair.

The dog barked. Then he charged forward playfully—straight for the cabin.

"So, Buster. You've been here before, have you?"

Ian stepped back—out of sight. He wasn't in the mood to meet strangers. And why did he have the feeling he was being followed?

Behind a cluster of trees he watched as the dog sat on the stoop and barked again. But nobody came to the door. Apparently, the people who lived there were not at home.

For a moment, Ian thought he saw a young woman standing at one of the windows. Then she was gone.

"Come on, boy. It's time to start back. But we will go walking again—very soon. I promise."

Shannon had always liked hiking in the woods. Maybe next time he would invite her to go along with them. With the earl in London, she might accept.

———

Peter opened his eyes again and shut them. The pain together with the light blinded him. He groaned. His mouth felt dry, and he was thirsty. He tried to speak. No words came.

"Come here, Uncle. The young man's eyes opened."

The woman still sounded like Kate. It must be her. But who was the uncle? Peter didn't know where he was or how he got there, but it was comforting to hear Kate's voice.

He swallowed. "Kate."

"I be not Kate, sir," the woman said. "I am called Millie. We wish to help ya. But my uncle must go to work soon. Let us feed you before ya go to sleep again."

Peter nodded. "How long have I been here?"

"Two nights—one day—so far. You have cuts on your head and shoulder," she said, "and bruises all over."

He wondered how she knew that.

"I am going to be lifting your head now," she said, "and givin' ya some water."

He opened his eyes. The pain shut them again.

"Be still and open your mouth, sir. I want to give you some water. And do not forget to swallow."

He smiled despite the pain.

———

The Frenchman kept Ian busy filling in for McGregor until the servant returned.

Three days later, his driver and butler finally returned to his job.

Ian planned to visit Shannon at Gatehaven. He'd sent her a letter telling her of his plans, and Monsieur Gabeau had said he would deliver the letter. But Ian had no idea whether or not she actually got it.

After he'd returned Buster to his pen that morning, Ian journeyed on to Gatehaven. Perhaps the earl's cook would prepare a picnic lunch for two. He'd never known Shannon to refuse the chance to go on a picnic.

Ian went in the back door of the kitchen and found the cooking staff at work in earnest. They hardly noticed when he came in. He looked around but didn't see Millie anywhere.

"Where is Miss Millie," he asked.

The main cook turned to him and frowned. "Millie does not work here anymore."

"If I might ask, why not?'

"We think she helped Miss Aimee move her things to the second floor without permission. I did not see her do it, mind you. But Maude thinks it was Millie what helped the girl escape—Millie and that fat uncle of hers."

"Monsieur Gabeau's driver?"

"The same."

Ian nodded. "The earl told the Monsieur that I was to have any available food I want from his kitchen as long as I am here. Today, I plan to explore the countryside while I have the chance. The vicar could return any day now."

"Tell me what you want, sir, and be quick about it. I must prepare a noon meal for over twenty-five people today. And I have much to do."

"I would like you to prepare a very large picnic lunch for me. I am hungry now and expect to be even more so by the time the sun is highest in the sky."

"Very well." She pointed to a straight-backed chair in the corner by the door. "Sit over there, please, out of our way. I will have someone bring your lunch to you when I have it ready."

◆—◆—◆

Shannon sat in a chair in the parlor, listening as the Spiritualist Society conducted their meeting. The members were made up of people of all ages, and they wore black, both men and women. A tall man talked about a frightening group of men called the Knights Templar.

Their gestures and speech patterns together with what they actually said was so bizarre Shannon barely listened. Still, she expected to be taken on a tour of the red gate or perhaps a cemetery at any moment. The earl said *the quality* didn't engage in gossip, illusions, or myths—perhaps because they were a part of the entire wretched mess.

Some of the women wore black lace head coverings as well as black clothing. But Shannon's head was bare. Her green muslin day dress and brown leather shoes looked as out of place as she felt.

"Miss Aimee is visiting here from Scotland," Miss Foster finally said.

Shannon had turned her pearl ring so many times the skin underneath it looked red. Everybody studied her even more. Nobody said anything.

She hadn't uttered a sound since the meeting began, but she felt her eyes widen. Her heart had skipped so many beats she lost count. She'd tried to make a mental list of all the new words she'd heard so far. But *divination* was the only one that stuck in her mind.

She'd heard that word previously. She couldn't recall when or where.

Miss Foster got up and stood in front of her chair. "We will go into the main dining room now." She smiled. "Tables were prepared. Feel free to sit at the grand table or wherever you like. Our noon meal will be served, and then we will welcome the spirits."

Everybody clapped. Shannon pretended to, and then she tensed. *Welcome the spirits?* What did that mean?

Shannon hadn't eaten a bite of her first meal of the day. She didn't feel like eating her noon meal either.

The second part of the meeting began as soon as the society members finished eating. They squeezed close together around the huge dining table and made strange noises that sounded almost like a prayer, but wasn't. They were saying something else entirely. Some looked dazed as if they had entered a world that Shannon was not a part of.

Miss Foster sat at the head of the table in a chair that the earl probably sat in on other occasions. She looked different somehow—like someone Shannon had never met. Even the muscles in her face had changed and in a very disturbing way.

"I will now attempt to reach Clem, my master," she said in a manly voice.

Shannon had heard enough. She got up from her chair.

Normally, she would have given her excuses before heading outside. In this case, nobody would have noticed if she stood on her head. She crept quietly to the door and went out.

CHAPTER TWELVE

As SOON AS her feet touched the stone path that surrounded the mansion, Shannon noticed Ian. He stood over by the fence but moved toward her as soon as their gazes connected. She was so glad to see him; she raced toward him. When she reached him, he embraced her within the circle of his arms.

"What is wrong, lass? You are trembling."

"I have much to tell you, but not here. Just hold me."

"Have you eaten?" He held up a straw basket so she could see it. "I have brought us a lunch."

"You eat, Ian. I cannot right now."

"Then I will not eat until later." He took her arm. "Where would all the visitors be now?"

"In the main dining room."

"Then we shall go into the earl's library. I doubt the visitors would go in there unless they were invited." He smiled. "Come. Monsieur Gabeau told me exactly how to find the library. It will be quiet there."

Shannon was still trembling when he ushered her inside and shut the door.

They sat side by side on the settee, and Ian held her for a minute.

At last he said, "Now, what happened inside the mansion that upset you so?"

She swallowed. "Evil."

"Evil? You mean because of the crystal ball and the people you told me about that wore hoods and walked the hallways at night?"

"That is part of it but not all." She swallowed again before saying anything more. "Gatehaven is filled with wicked people who do, say, and think evil things."

"Please Shannon, explain what you mean."

She turned slightly to the side in order to face him. "A meeting of the Spiritualist Society is being held at Gatehaven today and again on the morrow."

Ian nodded. "Monsieur Gabeau told me about it. What happened that frightened you so?"

"When I first arrived, someone gave a lecture on how Gatehaven got its name."

"That sounds like an interesting topic."

"No, Ian, it was not. The man giving the lecture said that Gatehaven was named for a red gate that people are able to see occasionally but not all the time. He said that it is really the gateway to the underworld. But the earl said the red gate was a deception, a trick of the eye."

"The eye can play tricks, all right. It has happened to me more than once."

"Yes, but the man who gave the lecture said he saw the red gate—only he called it Lucifer's gate. My father said that Lucifer is another word for the devil. Papa also said that the dragon is a symbol for Satan and the devil. As I think I told you, there are dragons carved into the headboard of my bed here. The people at that meeting attempted to call up spirits while I sat and watched, and they talked about something called divination."

Ian frowned. "Divination. I've heard that word somewhere."

"It sounds evil, Ian. Do you know what divination means?"

"No. But our pastor back in Luss talked about evil often. He also told me things to do to fight evil."

"Tell me what they are, Ian. I have to know."

"I'd forgotten about it until now, but he said that God lives in the praises of His people. When we thank the Lord and praise Him in the name of Jesus, we know God is near. What could be more comforting than to know the Lord is close at hand? The important thing is that we do as the Bible says to do if we expect to receive God's best for us. The battle is the Lord's. And if God is with us, who can be against us?"

"If God is for us, who can be against us?" Shannon repeated. "I find that scripture reassuring. Still, I have more to tell." She took a deep breath and released it slowly. "Just before I left, Miss Foster's face changed completely. She was seated at the head of the table, and she—and all at once she talked in a deep voice—like a man."

"You jest?"

"No, I do not. If only you'd heard her. If you had, you would think as I do. You would think that a man was speaking through her."

"Wait." He looked around. "There must be a Bible in here somewhere."

"I noticed a podium when we first came in." She motioned toward a wooden stand by the door. "A Bible might be there."

"Of course." Ian got up and went to the podium.

Shannon followed him. She wanted to be as close to Ian as possible.

A Bible lay on the podium as Shannon expected.

Ian thumbed through the pages. "I think the scriptures I want are found either in Leviticus or Deuteronomy. I cannot remember which." He turned to the next page. "Oh yes, here it is. Deuteronomy chapter eighteen verses nine to eleven." He looked down as if he was reading.

"Read the verses aloud, Ian," she ordered. "I want to hear them, too."

"Of course." He cleared his throat. "*When thou art come into the land which the Lord thy God giveth thee, thou shalt not learn to do after the abominations of those nations. There shall not be found among you any one that maketh his son or his daughter to pass through the fire, or that useth divination, or an observer of times . . . or a necromancer.*"

"What does that scripture mean, Ian?" she asked. "And necromancer, what does it mean?"

"I *da* not know the meaning of a lot of these words. But I intend to learn." He glanced at Shannon and smiled. "We need to find a volume that tells the meaning of words. Now, you search the shelves to our left. I will search those on the right. If you are able to find such a volume, let me know. Then we will sit at the table by the window there and study the book together."

They combed the shelves for almost an hour. At last it became clear that no such book existed—at least in the earl's library.

Ian shook his head. Then he moved away from the shelves and sat down at the table. "The information we need does not seem to be here." He hesitated and looked away like he always did when he was trying to find the answer to a puzzle. "But I think we might be able to find the kind of book we are looking for in Monsieur Gabeau's library. His library is even larger than this one, and I found a peculiar book there. I feel sure there are other strange volumes in his library as well. He might also have a book on the definition of words. We must wait and see.

"Perhaps Etienne Gabeau is also a member of the Spiritualist Society," Ian went on. "Time will tell. Regardless, I will have the best opportunity to survey his library tonight after the French gentleman goes to his bed."

Ian smiled. "For now, Shannon, I would like to take you on a picnic in the woods. An outing such as this is sure to cheer you up. And frankly, I am hungry." He snatched up the basket from the table by the door. "Will you agree to go on a picnic with me—or not?"

"Yes, Ian." Shannon returned his smile. "I should like a picnic—very much."

He chuckled softly. "See, the thought of a picnic in the woods is already cheering you up. Think how much better you will feel when we start eating."

Leon stood by his horse in the shadows near the entrance to Gatehaven. He'd intended to attend the meeting inside, but today he had more important matters on his mind. Since morning, he'd been following Ian Colquhoun to see where he went and to whom he spoke. So far, he hadn't been caught.

True, his leg ached. But it didn't hurt enough to cancel his quest.

He pulled a letter from his pocket and smiled.

Rachel. He opened it.

Dear Shannon,

Your father and I are well, and your baby brother is growing by the day. Javier did not want me to tell you this, but your brother is in England now and plans to find employment near the earl's estate. Say you are not angry. Your father is concerned for your safety, as am I.

Peter penned a letter to us that was mailed in Scotland before he reached England. The village of Rosslyn, I believe. Your father insists that the village is dangerous. We are glad you are well away from it now.

Peter said that he misses Kate. He said he also wrote her a letter and intends to marry her as soon as he returns. In fact, Kate and her mother are already preparing her wedding gown.

We hope you are well and that we will receive a letter from you very soon.

We love you,
Mama

Leon gazed at the letter a moment longer and put it back in the pocket of his vest.

The earl brought Shannon to England instead of her beautiful mother, and that was a huge mistake. Nevertheless, if his plan continued to work, he would see Rachel again—perhaps sooner than anyone would have thought possible.

The side door of the mansion opened. Someone came out. No, two people exited the mansion through the side door.

Leon sucked in his breath. Ian and Miss Aimee were moving around to
the front of the mansion. He wanted to rush forward and introduce himself to Rachel's lovely daughter, but it might not be a wise decision.

A new thought came to him. Leon slowly made his way to his horse and
put his left leg in the stirrup. He swung his other leg around. Thoughts
mixed with pain engulfed him.

Gone were the days when he mounted a horse like a champion and
rode like the wind. The simple act of mounting his black gelding had
become a huge task, and all because of Rachel Aimee.

Revenge. He had to welcome it—embrace it. Otherwise, he would
never be free of her.

◆——◆——◆

"Look, Ian." Shannon pointed to a window on the top floor of the mansion.

"Look at what?"

"That woman. Can you not see her? She is standing at a window."

Ian squinted in the direction she indicated. "I see nothing."

"She is gone now. But a woman with black hair was there, and this was
not the first time I saw her. She was standing at that same window on the
day I arrived at Gatehaven, and on *that* day, she was not alone."

"Who was with her?"

"A woman with long blond hair." Shannon shrugged her shoulders.
"The earl said I was imagining things. But I know what I saw."

They were standing in front of the mansion, and Shannon realized she
was trembling.

"Cold?" he asked.

Before she could answer, he removed his jacket and wrapped it around
her shoulders.

"The breeze is swift this afternoon," he added. "And this entire estate
is more than a little disturbing." He chuckled softly. "When I visit here, I
expect ghosts and goblins to come out and grab me at any moment."

She gazed up at him, hoping that somehow he would understand.
"Please believe me, Ian. I know it sounds absurd, but I did not see a ghost
or a goblin. I saw a real person."

He put his arm around her and gave her a quick hug. "As strange as
it may sound, I do believe you. A moment ago I had the strangest feeling
that somebody was watching us."

◆——◆——◆

Leon trotted his horse through the main gate of his estate and on toward
his stately home. He noticed McGregor carrying a bucket in the direction
of the horse barn. He assumed his driver was watering the horses.

It was about time. McGregor had been out sick for several days, and his work was of poor quality since he returned.

"McGregor, hitch up my carriage. I want to go for a ride."

"Very good, sir. I mean Monsieur."

He intended to follow Ian and Miss Shannon Aimee that very afternoon—see where they went. Perhaps he would invite them to take a ride in his carriage. His lips formed a mocking smile. Yes, that was exactly what he must do. Later, he would persuade them to join him for supper at his estate.

Ian and Shannon strolled hand-in-hand through a green pasture and into the woods beyond. They spread a blue cloth on the ground, put the basket of food in the middle, and sat down.

Ian watched Shannon as she removed the food from the basket, one item at a time, and placed them around the basket.

"That cheese looks good," he said. "I think I will try it first." Ian took his knife and chopped the cheese into slices.

He didn't want to push unpleasant topics down Shannon's throat, but he'd learned from his mother and sisters that sometimes women just needed to talk. If Shannon wanted to discuss what happened inside the mansion that morning, he was willing to listen.

At first, she didn't say anything.

Ian swallowed a bite of cheese. "The cheese tastes good, too." He smiled. "Have you heard from your family in Scotland yet?"

He thought she looked a little sad.

"No. I have not," Shannon said. "Have you heard from yours?"

"Yes. I am happy to say. Letters from Mama and Kate arrived yesterday. And apparently your family is well and hoping to hear from you very soon."

"Do you know if they received any of my letters?" Shannon asked.

"I do not."

"Strange. I posted letters to my family as soon as I arrived. And Mama promised to have a letter waiting for me as soon as I arrived at Gatehaven. But so far, none have reached me."

A blue ribbon circled her wrist, and a sack that matched her blue dress was attached to it. She opened her drawstring sack and peered inside.

"I wrote another letter to my family last night. I planned to give it to my chaperone tonight and ask her to mail it."

"Scotland is a long way from here, lass. Sometimes letters are delayed or lost during the journey."

But deep down, he didn't think that was the case. He couldn't stop wondering if the earl had allowed *any* of her letters to go out. And if she received letters from home, had he withheld them from her?

"I plan to go into the village on the morrow to see what I can see," he said. "If you will give me your letter, I will make sure it is posted."

She pulled her letter from the sack and handed it to him. "Thank you, Ian. I appreciate your willingness to help."

After they finished their meal, they started back to Gatehaven. They had some distance to walk in order to get there.

The path ahead was uneven and dotted with mudholes. One hole looked especially deep. Ian hadn't noticed it the last time he came that way. And Shannon was headed straight for it.

"Look out!"

Her ankle turned to the side at an awkward angle. He grabbed her arm to keep her from falling.

"Oh, Ian," she said. "My ankle is most painful!"

He swooped her up in his arms.

A carriage pulled out from behind a group of trees as if it had been parked there on purpose. Ian recognized McGregor. He sat up top, wearing his uniform. Monsieur Gabeau was sure to be inside.

"Who is that?" Shannon asked.

"Monsieur Gabeau, the Frenchman I've been telling you about."

The carriage pulled to stop directly in front of them. Gabeau got out and limped toward them, leaving the carriage door open.

"I see that you and the young lady are in a bit of trouble. May I assist you by driving you back in my carriage?"

Ian was prepared to refuse the offer. He mistrusted the Frenchman and didn't want him around Shannon.

He still held her in his arms. "Thank you for the offer, Monsieur. But Miss Aimee is as light as a child might be. I can carry her back."

"Nonsense. You must climb in my carriage. Miss Aimee needs to see a physician at once. I will have it no other way."

"He is right, Ian," Shannon put in. "I will not allow you to carry me all the way to Gatehaven. I wish to ride in the carriage."

Ian didn't move.

"Please Ian. My leg hurts. As the gentleman said, I need to be seen by a physician as soon as possible."

Ian placed Shannon inside the carriage as gently as he could manage. Then Gabeau climbed in and finally Ian.

"May I introduce myself? I am Monsieur Gabeau. And you are Miss Shannon Aimee, I believe."

"Yes. I am."

"It is an honor to make your acquaintance, Miss Aimee."

"I am pleased to meet you, sir. And thank you for your kindness."

The carriage moved slowly at first. Then in what seemed like an instant, the wheels turned faster. But instead of driving back to Gatehaven, the carriage sped off in the opposite direction.

"Where are we going?" Ian demanded. "Gatehaven is north of here. We are going south."

"Miss Aimee needs to be where she can rest immediately," Gabeau insisted. "And she needs medical attention. My estate is closer to the village where the physician lives. We will be going there, now."

Shannon sent Ian what he called a pleading look—as if she was begging him not to protest.

He released a deep breath. "Very well. We will go to your estate, but only for a short time. Miss Foster will worry if Miss Aimee does not return soon."

"Do not concern yourself, Mr. Colquhoun. I will send word so Miss Foster will know that Miss Aimee will be delayed. Then her chaperone will have no reason to worry."

Ian doubted that statement on several counts. Most of all, he was beginning to think the Frenchman was as wicked as the earl. In fact, he might be worse.

* ——✦—— *

The driver placed Shannon on an extremely long settee near Gabeau's chair by the fireplace, and he had McGregor push the settee closer still. Ian was allowed to sit in the chair across from them, and even that surprised him. Judging from the way Gabeau was studying Shannon's slender form, Ian had expected to be banished from the room, if not the entire estate.

The Frenchman hooked his cane on the arm of his chair and turned to his driver. "McGregor, fetch the physician from the village at once."

"Aye, sir. And shall I also inform the young lady's chaperone of her mishap?"

"Bring the physician here first. Then you can ride over to Gatehaven and tell Miss Foster what happened today."

"Very good, sir." McGregor turned and left the room.

"Are you still in pain, Miss Aimee," Gabeau asked, "or has it faded a bit?"

"I am feeling better, thank you. I appreciate your thoughtfulness."

Gabeau's smile held menacing overtones. "Splendid." He reached for a wooden frame by his chair.

Ian had seen Monsieur Gabeau holding that frame and fingering it tenderly many times, and he had wondered if it might be a favored painting or a portrait of someone dear to him. However, Ian never found the right time to ask that question.

"So, Miss Aimee." Gabeau smiled. "I understand you are visiting here from Scotland."

"Yes."

"The earl said you lived in the village of Luss near his hunting lodge."

"That is correct." She bit her lower lip.

Ian wondered if her leg hurt more than she was willing to admit.

"I visited Scotland some years ago, but not recently." The Frenchman gazed down at the painting and smiled. "Can you humor a lonely man and tell me a little about it?" He turned and looked at Shannon. "I believe you live on a farm with your parents. Am I right?"

"Yes."

"Please tell me about your family. The earl said that your parents were well thought of in the village and that your mother was extremely beautiful."

Ian wondered. *Why is he asking Shannon all these personal questions?*

"You are kind, sir, to say such nice things about my family. And my mother is very handsome." She smiled briefly. "My father thinks so, too."

For an instant Gabeau's dark eyes burned hot with what Ian deemed rage. Then his forehead wrinkled, and he looked away.

Ian had no idea what might have caused the Frenchman's emotional reaction to Shannon's statement.

Gabeau turned back and smiled again. But Ian thought his smile looked as if an artist had painted it on to cover a rather grim facial expression.

"Forgive me for staring, Miss Aimee," the Frenchman said. "But you remind me of someone who was once most dear to me."

Shannon blushed.

"I have no wish to embarrass you. But the similarity is too great to ignore. See for yourself." He reached over and handed the wooden frame to Shannon.

Shannon glanced down casually. All at once, her eyes widened. "Oh, my. The portrait *does* look like me. But how could that be?"

CHAPTER THIRTEEN

S TRANGER THINGS HAVE happened, I suppose," the Frenchman said.
"Ian," Shannon called, "come here and look at this portrait."

Ian didn't have to be invited to take a look. He'd already emerged from his chair and was halfway across the pine floor. He moved behind the settee, and, leaning over Shannon's shoulder, he gazed at the young woman in the small painting.

She wore a brown and yellow plaid dress, and she held a long-stemmed yellow flower in both hands. Her thick mass of long auburn hair fell across one shoulder. Yet the artist managed to capture the essence of the woman as if he knew her well.

Ian wondered if the Frenchman was a portrait painter. If so, he was very skilled.

The eyes of the girl in the painting were closed. Yet long black lashes edged her lowered lids. Was she perhaps in prayer? Somehow Ian knew that if her eyes opened, they would be sea green and sparkle like emeralds. No wonder Monsieur Gabeau kept the painting at his side at all times.

"Well, does the woman in the portrait look like me or not?" Shannon asked Ian.

"I think she looks a lot like you." Slowly, Ian nodded his head. "I am amazed."

Ian suddenly realized that the cook and a young woman he didn't know stood in the doorway leading to another part of the house. Cook motioned for Monsieur Gabeau to come forward.

The Frenchman grabbed his cane. Then he reached over, snatching the portrait from Shannon's hands without uttering so much as one word of explanation. The women were no longer standing in the doorway. Monsieur Gabeau stormed across the room on crippled legs, through that doorway and out of sight.

"Ian," Shannon said. "Do you think something is wrong?"

"Who knows with that man." He studied Shannon carefully. "Is there anything I can get you?"

"My throat is dry. I wish I'd asked the cook to bring me a cup of water."

"You wait right here. I will go and fetch it."

A pitcher of water and cups for drinking were always kept in the small dining room. Ian went down the hall, heading in that direction.

He was pouring water into a cup when he heard loud voices coming from the room next to the dining room. The door was slightly ajar. He couldn't help hearing what was being said.

A woman was sobbing, and he heard what sounded like a child say, "Papa! Don't hit my mama."

"I'm not your papa," the Frenchman shouted back. "At least in public, I'm not."

"But he's sick," one of the women said. "He needs to see the healer."

"Get him out of here!"

Ian tensed as anger and indignation boiled inside him. A woman and perhaps her child were being abused in that room. Maybe the cook was being harmed, too. He heard more screams and furniture being smashed around.

He couldn't hold his emotions in check a moment longer. He dropped the white cup, allowing the expensive-looking china object to crash to the floor, and moved to the connecting door. He yanked it open all the way. The door banged back against the paneled wall.

An exterior door was open in the main dining room. A young woman and a boy of six or seven raced through it and out into the yard. He didn't see the Frenchman's cook, but Mrs. Woodhouse must have exited too since she wasn't in the room. Maybe the young woman and the boy were related to Mrs. Woodhouse.

Only the Frenchman was in the main dining room. He stood in the middle of the floor with his skinny arms over his chest.

"I heard noises," Ian said. "Is everything all right?"

"But of course."

"Who was the young woman and the child I saw just now?"

"The young woman is Lela Woodhouse, the cook's daughter. She works for me now and again. There was no child here."

"I heard a child say 'Mama.'"

"You are mistaken. Cook is a widow. Lela has never married." Monsieur

Gabeau produced what Ian called a sardonic smile, filled with deception and every kind of hate. "I see you dropped a cup. I will have Cook clean up the mess when she comes back inside.

"The physician should be arriving soon. Let us go back and see how Miss Aimee is getting along. Shall we?"

Ian glanced out the window nearest to him. The woman, the cook, and the child were walking toward a small cabin beyond the kitchen house. He could only hope that they would be all right.

Maybe the physician would see about the child without letting the Frenchman know about it. Ian would certainly tell him what he saw, if he got the chance.

◆—◆—◆

Shannon bit down on a piece of wood. The pain devoured her. She wanted to scream. At least with wood in her mouth, she couldn't.

"Easy, lass," Ian said in a comforting tone. "The doctor will have your leg right and ready very soon."

The physician was a small, thin little man with a bald head, squinty gray eyes and long, nimble fingers. Monsieur Gabeau had introduced the physician as Healer Grimes.

"This is going to hurt, miss." The doctor's voice sounded gentle. "Push my hands away should I cause you more pain than you can stand, and I will stop."

Shannon nodded. With the wood in her mouth, it was impossible for her to reply.

Despite his unattractive physical appearance, Shannon thought the doctor seemed to go out of his way to keep from hurting her. Perhaps he was trustworthy as well.

The physician pressed two slats against her ankle, one on each side, and he wrapped a white cloth around the whole thing. Shannon stiffened and groaned.

"Try to calm yourself, miss. I have almost finished."

The wooden slats would make it difficult for her to walk. However, her ankle hurt too much to walk in any case.

"I think Miss Aimee should stay the night here at my estate," Monsieur Gabeau insisted. "It is clear to me that she is in too much pain to be moved."

"I disagree," Ian retorted. "It would be unseemly for Miss Aimee to spend the night away from her chaperone. We must return her to Gatehaven at once."

Shannon wanted to protest. She didn't want to be under Miss Foster's care any longer. The woman scared her, and never more than when she spoke in a man's voice. But with the wood still in her mouth, she couldn't say a word.

She pressed her tongue against the wood. Then she opened her mouth and pushed the stick with her tongue. The wood shot out. Ian dodged. If he hadn't, it might have landed in his face.

"Shannon!" Ian glared at her. "You could have hurt somebody when you spat out that piece of wood."

"Forgive me. But I would like to stay the night here, Ian. As Monsieur Gabeau said, I am in too much pain to return to Gatehaven tonight."

Ian shook his head. "Your will is as strong as a man's, Shannon Aimee."

"McGregor." The Frenchman motioned for his driver to step forward. "Tell Cook to come and assist Miss Aimee. The young lady will be staying in the blue room tonight."

"Very good, sir." The driver started to walk off.

"Where is the blue bedroom?" Ian reached down as if he expected to carry Shannon somewhere. "I will take Miss Aimee to her bed."

"McGregor will do it, Mr. Colquhoun." Gabeau turned to his driver. "McGregor. Carry Miss Aimee to her room. When she is safely in bed, fetch Cook so she can attend to the needs of this young woman and act as her chaperone while she is here."

McGregor turned and glared at Ian. "Out of my way, Colquhoun." McGregor poked Ian with his left elbow. "A McGregor will handle this task better than a Colquhoun ever could."

The portly carriage driver still glared at Ian; his jaw tightened. McGregor scooped Shannon up into his arms. She thought all his hostility was aimed at Ian. For an instant, she wondered why.

Ian smiled, shrugging his shoulders.

At that moment, she remembered. Ian had said that apparently Mr. McGregor didn't yet know of Ian's Scottish clan roots. Obviously, he knew now. How could she have forgotten that for generations the clan Colquhoun and the clan McGregor were enemies?

+———+———+

Ian followed McGregor into the blue bedroom. The Frenchman limped behind them. He heard the tap, tap of the crippled man's cane.

He'd planned to sneak into the Frenchman's library while the man slept to search for a book on the meaning of words. Now those plans must die; Ian had more important things to do. Once Monsieur's cook arrived and went inside, he would stay the night in the hallway outside, guarding Shannon's door.

The cook finally came into Shannon's bedroom, and Ian and the doctor stepped out into the hallway. However, Monsieur Gabeau stayed in her room, insisting that he wanted to talk to Cook about Shannon's condition before leaving her for the night. After hearing what he heard in the dining room earlier with the boy and the young woman, Ian wasn't about to budge from that hallway until the Frenchman came out.

Monsieur Gabeau had called the physician Healer Grimes. Ian preferred to call him doctor. Ian told him what happened in the dining room without going into much detail.

"I was hoping you would be so good as to pay a visit to the cabin to see how the boy and his mother are doing," Ian whispered. "I will be happy to pay all the costs of their care."

The doctor smiled. "There is no need. I have been looking out for Lela Woodhouse and Stephen for a long time."

"Stephen. Is that the boy's name?"

"Yes. Etienne is Stephen in some foreign language—French, I believe. I could be wrong about that. Regardless, the boy goes by the name of Stephen Woodhouse."

Ian nodded. "I see what you mean."

He glanced down to give himself time to think. The young woman and the boy needed to be rescued before they simply disappeared as others had before them. But what should be done?

"You're wondering what else you can do to help them, are you not, Mr. Colquhoun?"

"Your wit is powerful, doctor. You caught my thoughts without me having to express them. Is there a way to help them leave here forever?"

"Yes." The doctor smiled. "Plans have already been made. Later this day, I will pick up Lela and Stephen and take them to my home in Fairs. My wife is waiting for them now. On the morrow, trusted friends will take them safely to Ireland. They will never have to see the Monsieur Gabeau again."

"Thank you, doctor. Godspeed."

⁕ ⎯⎯◆⎯⎯ ⁕

By midnight, Ian felt his eyes close of their own accord. He opened them. But they closed again. He was seated with his back against the door and his legs stretched out in front of him. He got up and stood. In a standing position, it would be easier to stay awake.

Ian still felt sleepy. He grabbed the handle on the door for support. His eyes closed again.

He heard something—a noise. He squinted into the near darkness but didn't see anybody. He heard a soft thump. Instantly alerted, his hands became fists. He heard another thump on the wooden floor.

Ian's body stiffened. *Is Monsieur Gabeau planning to go into Shannon's room in the dead of night? Surely not. The sounds I heard must have come from elsewhere.*

A shadow crossed in front of a window, blocking its dim light from view.

"Who goes there?" Ian shouted.

"Mr. Colquhoun?"

Ian heard a soft jingling sound like metal against metal.

"Is that you?" the Frenchman asked.

"Indeed."

CHAPTER FOURTEEN

WHAT ARE YOU doing in front of Miss Aimee's door in the middle of the night?" the Frenchman demanded.

"I might ask you the same question," Ian snapped back.

"I was on my way to the kitchen for a spot of tea, and I thought I heard sounds coming from the young lady's room. I came to investigate."

"I heard no such sounds," Ian countered, "other than your footsteps coming here."

The Frenchman chuckled in the darkness. "Then I must be mistaken."

The door bumped against Ian's back. He took a step forward. The door opened a crack.

"What is going on out here in the middle of the night?" the cook demanded. "Poor Miss Aimee is trying to sleep."

"Forgive us for the intrusion." The Frenchman moved into the light coming from the bedroom. "I heard a noise. Mr. Colquhoun and I came to investigate. Do go back to sleep."

"Yes, sir."

The door closed. Ian heard the lock click from the inside.

In that brief instant when the cook stood near the door with a candle in her hand, Ian heard a metallic ping. It was like small pieces of metal no bigger than a door key hitting together—the same sound he'd heard earlier.

Door keys.

Had the Frenchman brought a key to Shannon's room with the

intention of invading her privacy while she slept? Or was his imagination playing games with his mind?

"Miss Aimee is in capable hands," the Frenchman said after a short pause. "Shall we go out back to the kitchen-house, Mr. Colquhoun, and have a cup of tea? I am an expert at warming tea."

"Go if you wish, Monsieur. I plan to stand guard in front of Miss Aimee's door 'till morning comes."

"Do as you will. I am going to go out and have my tea."

Ian sat on the floor with his back against Shannon's door for the rest of the night. He must have drifted off. He awoke the next morning when someone called his name.

"Mr. Colquhoun."

The male voice sounded even louder the second time he heard it. Perhaps the man was getting closer.

Ian looked up. McGregor's gray eyes blazed into his. Some might wonder why the Frenchman's driver disliked him so much. But when Ian learned that the driver's name was McGregor, the reason was clear.

As a Christian, Ian had no hard feelings against either the McGregor or the McFarland clan, but others felt differently about their ancient enemies. Clearly, the Monsieur's carriage driver was one McGregor who hated Colquhouns merely for being Colquhouns.

"I was sent to tell you that Monsieur Gabeau will spend the day at Gatehaven." The carriage driver leaned forward, putting his hand on his legs just above the knees. "He is waiting in the carriage. We plan to leave at once."

Ian nodded. "I am grateful that you told me."

"I was *ordered* to tell you," McGregor corrected hotly. "And don't think I do not know that you are a Colquhoun. I can smell a Colquhoun a mile away."

"We are a long way from Scotland now, sir." Ian released a deep breath of air. "I hope we can become friends."

"Friends?" The stout McGregor straightened to his full height, and standing, he put his arms over his chest. "A Colquhoun will never be a friend of mine."

"If not friends, then maybe the two of us could decide not to be enemies."

"My family have been enemies of the Colquhoun Clan forever." He turned and started to walk off. "That will never change."

"Perhaps it will."

McGregor stopped and looked back. "Perhaps it will what?"

"Change." Ian paused before saying more to let his words sink in. "God willing, we will one day be friends."

"Friends we will never be, Mr. Colquhoun. I can promise you that."

Ian didn't reply.

The Bible said to pray for one's enemies. It was time to pray for the salvation of Monsieur Gabeau's driver as well as the earl and the Frenchman himself. Then he would pray for Shannon and others that he loved.

In a while, Shannon would wake up, and he would go in to see how she fared during the night. Seeing Shannon always encouraged him, even when she wasn't feeling her best.

———◆———

Peter Aimee had never wanted water more than at that moment, and he felt better physically than he had the last time he woke up. His head didn't hurt as much, and his other aches and pains bothered him less than they once had. He sat up and looked around.

His bed was covered with a dark blue cloth edged with fancy stitching that could only had been done by a woman, and flowers in wooden pots had been placed on a shelf under the two windows in the small but tidy bedroom. He breathed in the scent of flowers he couldn't identify, and a sense of warmth and welcoming engulfed him.

Peter had no idea how he got there, but during the short periods when he managed to keep his eyes and ears open, he learned that he was in a cottage and being cared for by strangers. He'd half-heard a woman and a man talking with heavy Scottish accents, and he saw them briefly just before he went back to sleep. The balding man had a big belly and looked much older than the woman. She seemed very capable of doing her household chores and was shapely enough to please any man. However, no woman— no matter how handsome—could compare with Kate Colquhoun.

Clearly, the young Scottish woman had his best interest at heart. However, the uncle indicated that he would like Peter to move on as soon as the physician would allow it. Once when Peter came to himself for a short time, he learned that a physician was looking after him.

And Peter agreed with the uncle. He wanted to leave the cottage at once, but he'd heard the physician say that he must stay in bed a little longer.

"Well, just look at ya." The young woman smiled at him from the doorway. "Awake and sittin' up in bed, you are. Must be feeling better now."

"Yes. And I want to thank you for coming to my rescue, Miss—Miss—"

"Miss Millie McGregor. And who might you be, sir?"

He hesitated because he didn't want to reveal his identity. His sister, Shannon, didn't know he'd followed her to England. To tell who he really was to a perfect stranger was not a good idea.

What should he call himself?

He heard of an author named William Shakespeare. He would be William Spear.

"My name is William Spear," he said.

"Where do you come from, Mr. Spear?"

"The village of Rosslyn."

"Where be that place?"

"In Scotland."

"Scotland? Me parents came from Scotland. But with your dark hair and those brown eyes, I never took ya for a Scot."

"My parents came from France."

"A Frenchy, are ya?" She smiled. "Well. That explains it then."

"I was riding a horse when I hit my head on a branch. I must have fallen off. Would you know what happened to my horse?"

"Sure and I do. My uncle caught your horse. The animal be in our barn outside—watered, fed, and waiting for ya to get better. Your clothes and money bag be there in that chair by ya." She motioned to the only chair in the room. "Can I be helping ya with anything else, sir?"

"Yes. I would like a cup of water."

She whirled around. "I will go and fetch it then, right away now."

Peter was glad she was going for water. He was gladder still that she had left the room. He needed time to think. She was a distraction.

He didn't know why he told her he came from the village of Rosslyn, Scotland. It was another lie—and, of course, a sin. As a Christian, he didn't approve of sin. He needed to repent. But when she asked from where he came, he hadn't wanted to tell the truth. Rosslyn was the first town that came into his mind.

Peter put his legs over the side of the bed and tried to stand. He felt weak, grabbing the nearest bedpost for support. The room turned around and around. He sat back down.

He would sit there awhile, and tonight he would leave.

Millie returned with a large container of water. She handed it to Peter.

"Thank you, miss." He turned up the tin mug and drank down gulp after gulp of water. When the tin was empty, he still felt thirsty. "My thirst is like a giant's. Might I have another?"

"You've been doin' without water for a long while, sir. It's no wonder you were in need of it. But it be too soon to drink more. We shall talk awhile. Then I'll be going out and refilling your cup." She looked away, and the skin on her face turned pink. "Later, I'll bring ya a bucket—a bucket for personal use. Then I will leave you alone for a while. And after that, I'll bring ya another bucket and a cloth so you can clean yourself."

"Could you bring the first bucket right now?" he asked.

She blushed again. "Aye."

"Thank you. And might I ask you more questions?"

"What do ya want to know?"

"Who is the man that sometimes comes into my room with you? And where is he now?"

"You are talking about me uncle, Devlin McGregor. Uncle Devlin be the carriage driver for a very rich man named Etienne Gabeau. My uncle stayed home from work when we first found ya in the woods, sir, and told a lie. He said he was ill when he wasn't to help me care for ya. Still, we must have money in order to live. So he went back to work. Somebody had to. I lost me job."

"Where did you work, miss?"

"At Gatehaven—for the earl—but no more. I worked as a downstairs maid, you see." Millie touched his shoulder as if she was accustomed to doing it. "Now, who be Kate? You called out to her in your sleep many times since ya first came here."

"I have heard tales about the earl and pretty young women. Is that true?" he asked, ignoring her question.

She shook her head and glanced away. "I should not be talking to ya about the earl. Uncle would not like it. I know much too much."

"What do you mean?"

"The earl and the Frenchman be good friends." She looked him in the eye, briefly, and then she looked away. "No, I cannot help ya, sir. My uncle could lose his job as the Frenchman's driver, if I told ya what I know."

"I will tell you about Kate, if you will tell me about the earl. And I promise not to reveal what you say."

"Do ya truly promise?"

"Yes."

CHAPTER FIFTEEN

G OOD ENOUGH THEN, sir." Millie took a deep breath. "I guess if
ya promise not to tell what I say, it should be all right to tell ya
what I know."

Peter smiled, hoping to encourage her to continue.

"The Frenchman's name be Monsieur Etienne Gabeau, and he and the
earl are friends. Uncle never wants them to know that I live here with me
uncle. The earl fancies young women, ya see. I know it be true because—
because—" She looked away again.

"Because he tried to pursue you?" Ian finished for her.

"Aye."

"What else?"

"Me uncle drove a pretty young woman to Gatehaven once as a favor to
the earl. The young woman never showed her sweet face in public again."

"What could have happened to her?"

"I would not be knowing." Millie looked at the floor for a moment. Then
she lifted her head and smiled. "Now tell me about that Kate of yours."

Peter hated to tell another lie. He hadn't found time to repent for the
first one. But he couldn't think of an alternative. And if he told Millie that
Kate was his sweetheart, she might tell someone who would connect him
to Shannon and Ian.

"Kate is—Kate is my sister's name," he said.

"Your sister?" Her warm smile widened. "Well glory be, that sounds
good to me ears. I thought she might be your sweetheart."

Millie McGregor was interested in him as a man. Peter could see it in her smile—in her every gesture—and her earnest desire to please him. She was kind to him, and he would not stay long enough for her interest to turn to love.

He would mount up and ride out as soon as Miss McGregor and her uncle were asleep, and he'd leave money for his keep. He also planned to leave a note, thanking them for their many kindnesses. But he wouldn't tell them how to find him. Better that way.

Later, Peter rode into the village. He would take a room at the inn. Tomorrow he would seek employment and see if he could find Ian.

•——•——•

At dawn, Ian went up to his room to get a pen and paper. A few minutes later, he returned to his post in front of Shannon's door and wrote letters to his parents and to Shannon's. He didn't want to alarm the Aimees any more than necessary until he learned more about what was going on at Gatehaven, and he didn't plan to tell them that Peter was long overdue either. But he would tell them the truth—that their letters to Shannon weren't reaching her. He also intended to suggest that henceforth, they send Shannon's letters to him. He would give them to her, of course.

He'd brought a small leather pouch with him from Scotland. He put his letters and the letter Shannon had written to her parents in the pouch. Later, he hoped to go to the village and mail them.

Ian yawned. Then he stretched his tired limbs and yawned again. He'd had little rest on the previous night and would have liked nothing better than to go up to his room and go to sleep. Instead, he sat down again with his back to Shannon's door and tried to relax.

He'd only been there a moment or two when he felt a big jolt. He jumped. Someone had pushed the door against his back from the inside.

"Open this door at once," he heard the cook demand.

Ian stepped away from the door and stood back against the wall.

"The young lady wishes to break the fast," the cook explained. "I must go out back to the kitchen house and prepare a meal." The door opened a crack. "Please stand further away from the door, sir. The young lady is still in her bedchamber."

"Of course," Ian said. "And tell her that I must go out for a while but will return. Then Miss Aimee and I can talk. Also tell her that Monsieur Gabeau will be gone for the entire day."

"Gone did you say?" the cook asked.

"Yes, ma'am."

The cook stuck her head out the door and frowned at him. "Who told you that the Monsieur would be going away today?"

"His driver—early this morning."

"Why am I the last to know these things?"

"I cannot say, ma'am. But will you please tell Miss Aimee that I am leaving for a while to feed the vicar's dog? But I will return shortly."

"I will tell her." She opened the door all the way. "Now go. I must prepare a meal for the young woman."

Ian found some stale bread and sausages in the kitchen. He ate all the bread and a bit from one of the sausages. He wrapped all that was left of his morning meal in a white cloth he found in the kitchen and set out to feed Buster.

<hr />

Ian had a fondness for dogs and Buster in particular. But now that Gabeau's driver had returned to work after a short absence, McGregor would expect to feed the vicar's dog as part of his daily chores. However, Ian planned to request permission to continue feeding the animal until the vicar returned and hoped the Frenchman would agree to it.

As soon as he finished feeding Buster, Ian took him out for a brisk walk. The air felt cool on Ian's face, and after being set free from his wooden prison, Buster had never been more playful or more eager to please.

Ian threw sticks, and Buster fetched them. He ran through wooded areas and down paths he'd never seen before—the dog at his side.

Not far from Gatehaven, Buster ran ahead and started digging up something from the ground. Whatever the dog found must have been just below the surface. The hole didn't look deep. Ian saw something white. Maybe Buster found a bone.

He went over to see what the dog found so interesting. Before he reached the animal, Buster raced toward Ian, wagging his tail and holding a very large bone in this mouth.

"What have you got there, boy?"

Ian reached out to take the bone from him. Buster raced away as if he thought they were engaged in another game of throw and fetch.

"Come back here, boy. I want to see that bone."

Out of breath and panting, Ian managed to catch up with the dog. He reached out and grabbed hold of the dog's tail, knowing it would take a moment to settle Buster down.

At last, Ian rubbed Buster's head and scratched behind his ears in a way the animal liked. The dog seemed content to stay put. But he refused to open his mouth so Ian could take a look at the bone.

He'd put the cloth with the rest of the sausages in it in the pocket of his jacket. He removed the cloth, took out one of the sausages, and held it just out of Buster's reach.

"If you want this, you must jump for it, boy."

The dog leaped for the sausage. When he did, the bone dropped to the ground. Buster ran off to eat the meat. Ian picked up the bone and studied it.

The bone looked too large to come from a small animal. It must have come from a calf or a colt or—was he imagining things? Or could that be a human bone?

Impossible. Had he lost his senses?

Ian didn't want to contemplate the possibility that the bone might have come from a human. Yet as loathsome as the thought seemed, shallow graves were a reality, and the words *human bones* kept racing through his brain.

Ian wrapped his coat around the bone. It wouldn't do for someone to see the bone until he knew what it was and where it came from.

He went back and marked a tree near where the bone was found. Then he headed back to the vicar's cottage to leave the dog. He hoped to have a conversation with Shannon. But he had no plans to mention the bone.

⁘

Ian hurried upstairs and put his coat with the bone in it under his bed. Then he went down again and knocked at Shannon's door. The plump, middle-aged cook opened the door. Her eyes were red. He wondered if she'd been crying because of what happened to her daughter.

"And what would you be wanting?" she asked.

"I would like to speak to Miss Aimee. Tell her Mr. Colquhoun is here."

"Miss Aimee cannot speak to you now."

"Yes, I can," Shannon shouted from the bed. "I would be delighted to receive Mr. Colquhoun. Tell him to please come in."

"When I worked in London for Mrs. Preston, I was told the ways of the quality—warned that it was disgraceful for a young gentleman to come into a young lady's bedroom." The cook started to shut the door. "Go away."

"Don't go away, Ian," Shannon pleaded. "I can walk a little now." She swung her legs around and sat on the side of the bed. "I will walk to the door." She got up and limped toward him. "Mr. Colquhoun may carry me into the sitting room," she explained to the cook. "We can talk there, can we not? The cook has weepy eyes today, poor lady."

"I disapprove of this," the cook said as if fighting back tears.

"You can join us in the sitting room if you care to do so."

The cook pulled a cloth from the pocket of her apron and wiped her eyes. "I—I"—she sniffed, wiping her eyes again—"I have a house to run. But I will tell you this, young man. I intend to keep a close watch on you. I will come to see what is going on in there when you least expect it—that I promise you. Be forewarned."

With that, the cook turned sharply and headed for the kitchen house out back. Ian's heart went out to the woman as he carried Shannon into the sitting room.

Shannon seemed unaware of the cook's dilemma. If only Ian could let the older woman know that he knew what she was going through while shielding Shannon from the tragedy. Ian placed Shannon on the longest settee he saw, wrapping a gold silk cloth around her.

"Oh, Ian," Shannon said. "You spoil me so."

He gazed at her for a moment and smiled. "You are well worth the trouble, lass." Then he pulled a straight-backed chair close to the settee. "You know that I care little for the earl, but he has a nice library. Have you thought about the topic we discussed in the earl's library?"

Shannon's facial expression had been warm and welcoming since Ian carried her into the parlor. In an instant, the warmth faded, and her forehead wrinkled like it always did when she was displeased.

"If you intend to say unkind things about the earl behind his back, Ian Colquhoun, I will *not* listen." She lifted her chin and looked away.

"I have no time to discuss the earl's faults at the moment, lass. I was about to discuss those words I found in the Bible in the Book of Deuteronomy chapter eighteen."

"Are you saying that you learned their meaning?" she asked.

"Not yet. But if you are willing to sit here in the sitting room while I pay a visit to Monsieur Gabeau's library, I might be able to find some answers. Are you willing?"

"Of course."

"Good." He smiled. "I will just go over and pull back the curtains. That way, you can enjoy a view of the garden while I visit his library."

"How thoughtful of you, Ian. Thank you."

He crossed his eyes and sent her a silly expression. "Nothing is too good for Miss Shannon Aimee."

"You are full of mirth this morning, are you not, Ian? But you could always make me laugh—no matter what dire situation I might be in." She gazed out to the Frenchman's garden. "And the flowers outside that window are beautiful."

"Just keep looking at the garden. I will return shortly."

Ian went right into the library and began searching. He found several books with strange titles that he planned to read later. He took a pen and a sheet of paper from a desk and wrote down the titles. *Other Gods*, he wrote. *The Masters of Babylon*, and finally, *She Gods of Old*.

Clearly Gabeau was a beast, but he certainly had a well-stocked library. What better way to acquaint himself with Etienne Gabeau's interests than to read his books? If only he could find a book on the meaning of words.

He was returning the last of the three volumes when a small book fell from the shelf, landing at his feet. He hadn't noticed the book earlier, and he reached down and picked it up.

Words and Their Meanings.

Ian smiled. This was the book he was hoping to find. He opened the book and looked down. A notation had been written on the title page.

To my friend, Leon Picard—seeker of dark mysteries and a faithful follower of the illuminated one. May you return to Rosslyn soon and visit our group again.

Ian swallowed. Leon Picard? Who was he? Was he one of the Frenchman's evil friends? And why would either of them engage in heathen practices forbidden by the church and the Bible? What were the dark mysteries mentioned in the notation? Were these evil men perhaps wizards? And did they consult with familiar spirits?

Another thought crossed his mind. What if Leon Picard and Etienne Gabeau were one and the same person? It seemed unlikely. Yet why else would the Frenchman own a book dedicated to another man? He thought he knew the answer but didn't wish to dwell on it.

Maybe the earl and his family learned about Rosslyn from Leon Picard instead of the other way around. It sounded logical, considering what he now knew about the Frenchman and the earl. It was all beginning to fit together like an enormous puzzle.

He'd written down a list of words that he found in the Book of Deuteronomy, chapter eighteen, and he planned to search for their meanings. But first he would join Shannon in the sitting room. He wanted to share this new knowledge with her.

Her eyelids were closed. Ian didn't want to wake her, and turned to leave the room. A loose board in the planked floor creaked.

Shannon opened her emerald eyes. "Ian, you're back." She smiled. "How long have you been standing there?"

"Not long." He ambled toward the chair next to the settee she lounged on. "I did not want to wake you."

"I see you are holding a book. Is it the one you went searching for?"

"I think yes. But I have yet to study it." He sat down and placed the book in his lap. "I thought we could do that together."

She sat, placing her feet on the floor. "Come and sit beside me." She patted a spot on the settee. "That way I can hear you better when you read to me."

Ian got up and moved to the settee, trying not to gaze at her. Shannon's beauty always took his breath away and never more than when they sat side-by-side.

He opened the book and fumbled for pages beginning with the letter A. "Abomination," he read. "Hateful, loathsome. Then it says that there are certain acts and practices that the Bible calls abominations, and it names some of them."

"What are they?" she asked.

"It lists certain animals that are not to be eaten or offered as a sacrifice to the Lord because they are considered unclean. And the Bible warns against other unclean practices such as—" He stopped because he couldn't bear to say the words *whore* and *sodomite* in the presence of an innocent young woman.

"Such as what?" she asked.

He felt his cheeks warm. "It wouldn't be prudent to read certain words in front of a young lady. I am sure you understand."

Shannon blushed. "Yes. I understand completely."

"Let us move on to the next word, shall we, lass?"

"Yes."

"Divination," he read. "To foretell the future."

"Is that all it says?' she asked. "Just—to tell the future?"

"There are explanations below that. But I am not sure they are related to the meaning of the word."

"Read them, please."

"Very well." He cleared his throat. "Some attempt to tell the future by reading the lines in one's hand. Some discover possible future events from reading the remains of tealeaves left at the bottom of a cup. Others peer into bowls of water or into balls made of pure crystal in hopes of learning future events. Still others use forked twigs when looking for underground supplies of water." He paused, looking at Shannon. "Why don't people read the Bible to learn the future?" He gazed at the book again. "It says the twigs point downward when water is below ground."

"My chaperone, Miss Foster, has a ball made of crystal."

"Aye. You told me about that."

"Do you think she knows that these practices are an abomination to the Lord?"

"Perhaps not. Though such practices are an abomination according to the Bible, Miss Foster might not know they are wrong if she has never read those scriptures or heard them read to her."

"I cannot recall ever hearing the verses you read to me before," Shannon said. "Yet as soon as Miss Foster took my palm and began to tell things about my future, I knew, somehow, that it was wrong—without being told."

He nodded as if to confirm her statement. "It is the same with me. I often know when something is wrong without being told. I think that is because God directs my path. He directs the paths of all those who love Him and follow Him. The Lord wants us to look to Him for answers—to look to Him for help in time of need. Clearly He does not want us to do as the heathen do and follow outside influences or engage in strange practices." He glanced at her before searching for more answers. "Shall we go on to the next word?"

"Please do."

He flipped to words beginning with the letter C. "Charm," he read. "A charm is an ornament worn or used to avert evil or bring good fortune. And a charmer is one who uses spells for protection and to influence and fascinate others as a witch might do."

"Do you think Miss Foster is a witch?" Shannon asked.

Ian shrugged. "I cannot say. But it is possible—even likely."

"Oh, Ian, that is so sad."

"Aye. But remember, God is always willing to forgive those who truly repent."

"What does it mean to truly repent?" she asked. "I never understood it."

"Our pastor said that to truly repent of one's sins is more than merely saying you are sorry. It means trying never to commit that sin again." He turned to another page. "Necro," he read. "Necro means death—a corpse or a place where the dead are buried. But I do not see the word necromancy—the word actually mentioned in the Bible." He hesitated. "Oh, here it is. Necromancy." He cleared his throat. "Necromancy is divination by means of communication with familiar spirits. Black Magic. Sorcery." He felt his eyes widen. "This is the one I have been looking for."

"What are familiar spirits?" she asked.

"Let me see if I can find the definition."

At last, he smiled. "Here it is." He cleared his throat. "A familiar spirit is a spirit that is close to a witch or a sorcerer, or has an attachment to a particular family. Often, those that conjure a familiar spirit call it 'Master.' They consult familiar spirits when searching for help and guidance, instead of asking the Lord for help in time of need. Such acts are an abomination, according to the Bible."

"*Master*, did you say?"

He nodded. "Yes."

"I think Miss Foster called somebody named Clem her master."

"How awful for Miss Foster. Some people consult familiars to learn things they wouldn't know otherwise. We must pray that Miss Foster repents and becomes a child of God."

He noticed that Shannon's lips turned down and that her shoulders drooped. Either their conversation was upsetting her or her ankle hurt more than she was willing to admit.

"I need to go into the village this morning, lass. Monsieur Gabeau gave me permission to borrow one of his horses whenever I needed to. Why not let me take you back to Gatehaven before I ride into town?"

She shook her head. "I would rather not go back there just yet."

"Your ankle is still paining you then?"

"It is not my ankle. It hardly hurts at all now."

"Then what is the reason, lass?"

"I am not ready to see Miss Foster face-to-face. I doubt I will ever be. She scares me. Perhaps I will stay here until the earl and his family return from London."

Ian didn't think she would be any safer in Leon's home than in the earl's. But he was unsure how to convince her of his conclusions. Even if he could, there was no other place for her to stay.

Leon. When had he started thinking of the Frenchman as Leon instead of Etienne Gabeau? He still had no proof of his conclusions, but somehow he knew that his assumptions were correct. For now, he would keep those conclusions to himself.

"Go on to the village and do the chores you must do there," she suggested after a long pause. "I will be waiting here when you return. Perhaps we can talk again then."

CHAPTER SIXTEEN

✤

WITH THE BOOK he'd borrowed from Leon's library, the letters, his Bible and the bone in a knapsack he brought from
Scotland, he slung the leather pouch over his shoulder and
left Leon's home by way of the door at the rear of the house. Shannon
might be sleeping, and if he left through the main door, he could wake her.

Ian decided not to borrow Leon's horse after all. He didn't want to feel
more obligated to the man than he already was. Instead, he would hike to
the nearby village of Fairs and pay a visit to the physician the Frenchman
called the Healer. He wanted to know how Lela and the boy were doing.
Ian assumed the Frenchman would be furious when he discovered they
were gone. He also hoped to learn more about the bone he found and
whether or not it came from a human. Afterwards, he would see if he
could find a place to post the letters and eat his noon meal.

The sun was high in the sky by the time Ian arrived at the doctor's cottage, only to discover that he wasn't at home. His wife was kind enough
to tell him that Lela and Stephen were safe and on their way to Ireland.
Then she directed him to the nearest inn where he could eat his noon
meal. Ian left the bone and went on his way.

The inn was some distance from the doctor's cottage. Ian set out for
the *Boar and Tongue* at once, dreaming of the beef stew the healer's wife
described. He could almost taste it by the time he reached the entry door
of the inn.

A middle-aged man with a round belly stood behind a desk. His back
was to the door, so apparently, he didn't see Ian when he came inside.

Ian assumed he was the innkeeper, but whoever he was, the man was deep in conversation with a young woman in a blue dress—a dress that was much too small for her portly body. With the innkeeper and the girl preoccupied, Ian had a chance to look around before he made himself known.

Several wooden signs were nailed to the wall near the entry door of the Boar and Tongue. Ian studied them closely. One stated the cost of a room for one night and the cost of food per meal. But the sign that interested him the most was the one near the desk.

It read, *Send Out Your Posts From Here.*

Ian stepped up to the desk and cleared his throat.

The innkeeper turned. His face became almost as red as the silklike ribbons in the young woman's yellow hair.

"Sorry, governor," the man said as if he'd been caught stealing vegetables from a farmer's field. "I did not hear you come in. My hearing ain't the best these days, you see. What can I be doing for you on this fine day? Would you like a room? A good meal?" He smiled at the young woman. "I swear Hitty here is the best little cook in the village, she is."

The girl giggled, pressing out invisible wrinkles from her stained white apron.

"So what can I do for you, sir?" the innkeeper asked again.

"I noticed the sign on the wall there when I first came in," Ian said. "It says you send out letters. Is that true, sir?"

"It is."

Ian pulled the letters from the knapsack. "I have several letters that need to be mailed. Can you send them out for me?"

"The mail coach from London does not come as far as Fairs," the innkeeper said. "But if you be leaving your letters here at me inn and pay me for me trouble, I will send your letters out on the next hired coach to London."

"My letters must go to Scotland."

"All the way to Scotland, you say."

The balding innkeeper had a missing tooth in front, and a sour odor filled the air every time he opened his mouth—a disturbing mixture of garlic and rotten teeth. Ian took a step back.

"You are a Scotsman," the innkeeper insisted. "I thought so as soon as you opened your bloody mouth."

"Can you send my letters to Scotland, sir?" Ian asked.

"That I can do. But I cannot say how long it will take for them letters to get there."

The innkeeper leaned forward, putting both his hands on his desk. Ian wanted to take another step back. Despite the stench, he decided against it. Too many more steps back, and he would be out the door.

"When letters be coming addressed to the townsfolk of Fairs," the innkeeper went on, "they end up here at me inn, they do. Would you be wanting me to post your letters for you, Scotsman?"

"Aye." Ian handed the letters to the innkeeper. Then he placed a coin on the desk near a small wooden box.

The innkeeper put the letters and the coin in the box and shut the lid. "It be peculiar to me—a Scotsman coming here today with letters to send out."

"Why is that?" Ian asked.

"A man staying above them stairs right now be sending letters to Scotland as well. But the man staying here—why he has a French name, he does."

Ian tensed. Was Monsieur Gabeau staying at the inn instead of attending a meeting at Gatehaven? If so, why would he lie? And was he sending letters to Scotland, too? He paused, wondering how to phrase his next question.

"Perhaps I know the man above stairs. Can you give me his name?"

The innkeeper shook his head, biting his thick lower lip the entire time. "I cannot remember his name. But even if I could, I dare not say."

Ian reached inside his knapsack again and pulled out a large coin he'd planted there for such emergencies. He laid the coin on the innkeeper's desk.

The innkeeper's jaw grew slack. His squinty gray eyes focused on the coin.

Ian pushed the coin closer to the innkeeper. "Does this help you remember names?"

The innkeeper sent Ian a knowing smile. "There are always exceptions to me rules. If you put another of them coins on me desk, it would be just about right."

Ian had hidden more coins in his room at Leon's estate, but he'd only brought one more coin with him. To give it up would mean he must go without a noon meal. Still it was worth the cost.

He reached in, pulled out his last coin and dropped it on the desk. The coin spun around and around and finally dropped facedown next to the first coin.

"What is the name of the Frenchman above stairs?" Ian demanded.

The innkeeper opened a large book that lay flat on his desk near the coins. "The truth be that I do not be remembering the Frenchman's name. I cannot read reading, you see." The innkeeper turned the book around so that it faced Ian. "The Frenchman put his mark here." He pointed to the bottom of the page.

Ian looked down and read the name.

Javier Perrine.

Well, at least Etienne Gabeau wasn't staying at the Boar and Tongue.

Footsteps sounded on the wooden stairs. Ian turned to the stairway. Peter Aimee was halfway down and coming straight toward him.

"Peter." Ian moved toward him. "It is good to see you again. I feared the worst and have been praying for your safe return."

A smile that matched Ian's turned Peter's solemn expression to one of great joy. "You thought I was dead, did you?"

"That thought crossed my mind. Did you send letters to Scotland?"

"Of course."

"So did I."

The innkeeper appeared to have a special interest in their conversation. Ian nodded toward the bald-headed man, hoping Peter would realize that the innkeeper was watching them.

"My stomach is making strange noises," Peter said. "I think it is telling me that I must eat my noon meal now or wish I had. Will you join me at a table here at the inn, Ian? We can continue our conversation there."

"I will send Hitty to fetch two meals at once," the innkeeper put in as if he was part of their private conversation.

"Send no food for me, sir," Ian replied. "I will not be eating today. But do send one meal for Mr. Perrine here." He glanced at Peter. "You must eat, Javier. You look even thinner than you did the last time I saw you." Ian followed Peter to a table toward the back. "I will keep you company while you eat."

"Are you sure you will not have some of Hitty's stew?" Peter asked.

"Not today."

Ian sat in a chair across from Peter. As they waited for the meal to arrive, Peter told him all that had happened since they last met.

"Then are you saying that after you were knocked off your horse, you stayed with a young woman and her uncle?" Ian asked.

"Yes. They live in a cottage in the woods not far from Gatehaven, and they were very kind to me."

"I went walking in the woods one day with the vicar's dog, and we came upon a cottage in the woods. From what you told me, I think it might be the very cottage where you stayed. Maybe you were there then. Had I known you might be inside, recovering from your fall, I would have knocked on the door and asked to see you."

"You might have found me sleeping. I slept most of the time the first few days I was there. Were it not for an attractive young woman named Millie, who nursed me back to health, I might not be here today. "

"A young woman by the name of Millie took care of you?"

"Yes. And I will always be grateful to her and her uncle."

"I know a young woman named Millie," Ian said. "She befriended Shannon. Tell me about the uncle."

"His name is McGregor, and he is Monsieur Gabeau's carriage driver and butler. But he pretended to be sick while I was recovering and stayed at home so he could help Millie take care of me. And now, Ian, I am happy to say that I think I can answer your question about Eddie's identity, the boy you went to school with in England. Eddie is the Earl of Northon—all grown up. The earl I visited all but confirmed it."

Ian's stomach growled from lack of food. He coughed several times to mute the sound.

Then he told Peter about the bone he found in the woods and other recent events in his life.

Peter already knew that Shannon was in danger. But he hadn't known that Ian thought Etienne Gabeau was as much of a threat to Shannon's welfare and good name as the earl.

"I have no doubt that you are correct about the earl, Ian. Neither of us trusted him from the beginning. But why do you mistrust this Monsieur Gabeau? What has he done to heat your ire?"

Ian told Peter as much as he knew about the Frenchman, including his suspicions about the man and the strange books he found in the Frenchman's library. When he finished, Peter shook his head.

"Amazing."

Footsteps caused Ian to turn his attention to the front of the inn near the entry door.

The maid, Hitty, hurried toward them, carrying a tray.

"So your meal has arrived," Ian said. "About time, I would say."

"Here you are, sir." Hitty laid a mug and a steaming bowl of stew on the table in front of Peter. "Will there be anything else you would be needing?"

Peter pushed the mug of ale toward Hitty. "Please return this to the kitchen. I would like a cup of water instead."

"I will go and get it, sir."

Ian thought the stew smelled like garlic and well-seasoned meat, and for a moment he was overwhelmed with a desire to have a bowl of stew and a fork and knife to eat it with. His stomach roared inside his belly—an audible reminder that he needed food.

Hitty returned with the water and set it by Peter's bowl.

Ian coughed several times while Peter ate his stew.

At last, Peter put down his fork and glanced at Ian. "Tell me about those words you found in that book you were telling me about—the one that came from Monsieur Gabeau's library. I want to hear more about that."

Ian removed the borrowed book from his knapsack and held it up for Peter to see. "This is the book I was telling you about—the one that contains the meaning of words." He laid the book on the table in front of him. Then he reached inside again and pulled out another book. "This is my Bible. We might need it as well. Our pastor gave it to me as soon as I expressed an interest in becoming a man of the cloth."

Ian placed the Bible beside the other book on the table, and the two young men talked about the meaning of Divination and the other words he and Shannon had discussed. At last he picked up the book on the meaning of words and opened it.

"There were a few words that Shannon and I never discussed. I would like to read their meanings now, if it pleases you to listen."

Peter swallowed a mouthful of stew. "It pleases me."

"Numbers with strange meanings." Ian ran his finger down the page. "Oh, here we are. The day of one's birth is said to influence his or her future." Ian gazed at Peter over the top of the book. "This might be considered part of the abominations mentioned in Deuteronomy chapter eighteen." He put his finger on the page again. "It says here in the Frenchman's book that we can depend on numbers or the stars to direct our way in life, and we *know* that is wrong. Our pastor would say all such talk is an abomination—that we must depend on God alone."

"Yes, he would." Peter put down his knife and fork. "Perhaps we should put away the Frenchman's book for a while lest it spoil my digestion."

Ian smiled. "I agree." He closed the Frenchman's book and let it drop to the table. "Still, there is more I must say."

"More?" Peter shrugged. "What you have already told me this day is beyond comprehension."

"Aye."

"Tell it then while I am still able to hear."

"The earl and his family are away from Gatehaven at the moment."

"Away? Where did they go?" Peter asked.

"London. But they must have known about the meeting and what went on there before they left. Certainly Miss Foster is not bold enough to take on a project like that without getting permission from the earl. Shannon said her chaperone was taking over for the earl after he was forced to leave Gatehaven unexpectedly."

"All this is outrageous," Peter said.

Ian nodded in agreement. "Shannon is reluctant to return to Gatehaven.

I think it is because of Miss Foster's strange behavior. And did I mention that the Frenchman is part of the group attending the spiritual conference at Gatehaven at this very hour? Who knows what other strange events took place after Shannon left the mansion?"

"We must insist that Shannon return to Scotland at once," Peter insisted.

"I agree," Ian replied. "But as you know, it is not easy to make those kinds of suggestions to Shannon. She will not want to leave because she thinks she is in love with the earl."

The door opened.

An elderly little man in a dark suit and hat stepped inside and headed for the innkeeper's desk near the stairway.

The innkeeper reached across his desk in order to shake the stranger's hand. "Well, if it is not Vicar Steen, walking in me door you are. How be your long journey?"

"It went as expected, Hadley. Thank you for asking."

"Is that the vicar you were telling me about?" Peter whispered.

"I think perhaps it is."

"I am tired." The vicar glanced at a vacant table near Ian's chair. "Please have Hitty prepare something for me to eat. She knows what I like. I wish to stay the night here before driving back to the vicarage."

"So *that* is the vicar," Ian whispered to Peter. "I wondered when he would finally return."

"Then you have yet to meet him."

"Aye. When he sits down, I will go over and introduce myself."

The vicar put a small valise on the floor, and his shoulders drooped as he sat down in a chair near Ian's.

"He looks tired all right," Ian said barely above a whisper. "Perhaps I will wait a bit before going over to speak with him—give the vicar a moment to collect his thoughts."

❖———◆———❖

Leon felt a sense of power as he sat at the head of the table where the earl normally sat, presiding over the meeting of fellow spiritualists. As they gorged themselves on huge servings of rich food, he considered what they might be thinking.

They think I have no right to be sitting here. But one day soon the earl will have nothing left to bargain with, and I will own Gatehaven.

He thought of the letter he'd just received and the one he had yet to send. An inn in nearby Fairs called The Boar and Tongue was for sale, and he'd been in recent contact with an underling he knew in France twenty years ago, a former monk by the name of Brother Julian. He hoped to partner with the monk in the purchase of the inn. Brother Julian was an excellent cook and should make the new venture a huge success.

Earlier, he'd sent his driver, McGregor, to fetch the two spies he sent to Scotland before the earl traveled there. Now he would be using their services again.

Leon glanced at the huge clock above the fireplace. His jaw tightened. What was keeping them? They should be here by now.

The butler came in and stood by Leon's chair. "Excuse me, sir. But there are two men waiting outside with your driver. And if I might say, sir, they do not appear to be gentlemen—not at all. Should I tell them to wait or send them on their way?"

"Direct them to the earl's private library. I will join them there."

The butler's jaw dropped. Clearly, Leon's request surprised him. The butler recovered quickly and said, "Very good, sir."

"Very good indeed," Leon said under his breath. Then he excused himself from the table and went out into the hall.

What a joke. The earl would be furious if he knew Leon allowed his driver and two grubby commoners into his precious library.

The earl would be angrier still if he knew Leon used his signet ring to certify a post destined for Scotland—or that Leon also knew where the ring was kept. *Money persuades easily.*

The butler was an easy man to entice. A few more gold coins and he would probably have kept his mouth closed forever.

Leon thought of the letter he planned to send to Rachel Aimee and her husband in Scotland. And how could he forget what he said in the letter to her?

Dear Mr. and Mrs. Aimee, he'd written.

Your daughter, Shannon, is gravelly ill. You must come to Gatehaven in the north of England at once if you ever hope to see her again. Alive.

Regards,

The Earl of Northon.

Leon smiled. He would mail the letter, and then he would see Rachel again—whether she liked it or not.

CHAPTER SEVENTEEN

T HE EARL'S BUTLER stood at attention at the library door, waiting to introduce Leon's three guests. Leon found it amusing that though the butler was probably a poor man's son, he wore the clothes of a gentleman—a fine black suit and tie and a neatly trimmed white wig brimming with powder.

"May I present Mr. Devlin McGregor," the butler said. "Mr. Weedly Jones and Mr. Finn Jones."

The two spies, Weedly and his brother Finn, wore ragged clothes—and dirty ones at that. His driver must have felt superior to them by comparison. And if McGregor felt superior, the butler must have felt like a king. According to his driver, the two young men liked to be called Gabeau's Spies. Perhaps it made them feel important.

Leon noticed when the two ruffians glanced longingly at one of the settees as if they hoped to sit down. He enjoyed upsetting the earl but resolved not to give in to vengeance. He might soon own that good piece of furniture. He had no respect for the earl's belongings but hated to spoil expensive-looking white silk cushions merely to get even. Spite and revenge should only be used when something important was at stake.

Leon stared at Weedly and Finn for a long moment, hoping to frighten them a little—perhaps a lot. From past experience, he knew he was an expert at deflating egos, frightening young women and making them cry. Rachel was the only woman he ever met who refused to be intimidated by his usual tactics.

But she would cry, one day.

"I have an important letter from the earl that I need to have sent to the village of Luss in Scotland," Leon explained to the two brothers. "I want the letter hand-delivered to the person whose name is printed on it, and you both know the location of the farm since you spied for me previously." He glared at Weedly, the older of the two young men. "Is that clear?"

"Yes, governor. But—but—"

"But what?" Leon demanded. "Speak up, boy."

"It took us many days to ride all the way to Scotland and back the first time, sir. And the innkeeper at The Boar and Tongue sends out letters. We know because the innkeeper be our uncle, he is. Why not send your letters by him?"

"Do you think I am so foolish that I do not know that? But the letters the innkeeper sends out go first to London. And from there they would go to Scotland. Letters could be lost in the process, and that would waste time I do not have. You must agree to leave for Scotland tonight—or I will find someone else to do the job." He glared at both of them. "So, what will it be? Will you go to Scotland or must I find someone else?"

Weedly nodded and then Finn did. "We will go."

"Good," Leon said. "I will give my man McGregor the money you will need for your journey, and he will give it to you after he explains exactly what you are to do. You will receive more money when you return and show proof that the letter was received. Without a successful outcome, you will get nothing more. Is that clear?"

"Yes, governor," Weedly said.

"Stop calling me Governor. I am Monsieur Etienne Gabeau, and I expect to be called by that name at all times in the future."

"Yes, Gov—Yes, Mon-sure Gab-bow."

Leon stiffened. If his leg hadn't ached so much, he might have said something more. At last, Leon turned to his driver and said, "McGregor."

"Yes."

"Weedly and Finn are in rags. Go to the guardhouse where the earl's footmen stay and have them fitted with proper attire like you did the last time they went to Scotland. I cannot have them looking like the peasants they actually are. I have a reputation to uphold, as does the earl."

"Very good, sir. I mean Monsieur."

"That's better."

The butler opened the door for the driver and the other two men. All at once, a white cat with long, soft-looking fur crept into the room.

"How did that beast get in here?" Leon demanded.

"I'm sorry, Monsieur." The butler reached down, grabbing the cat with both hands. "The animal belongs to Lady Victoria and normally has the run of the house. I will keep the cat penned for as long as you are here."

"I suggest you do." Leon turned and followed the men out the door, tapping his cane as he went.

He'd always hated animals with no purpose other than as a family pet. But sometimes he pretended otherwise when doing so was to his advantage. Why else would he have asked to care for the vicar's dog during the pastor's absence? It was to his benefit to stay on good terms with the local clergy, if he hoped to one day own Gatehaven.

Ian glanced over at the vicar's table off and on several times. At last, he looked at Peter and said, "I think I will go over to his table now and introduce myself."

Peter nodded as if to give Ian's decision an extra layer of importance. "But please remember that I am Javier Perrine now, not Peter Aimee. For the moment, it might be best if we keep my true identity a secret."

"I quite agree."

Ian got up and stood by the vicar's table. "I am Ian Colquhoun from Scotland." Ian offered the vicar his hand in friendship. "Perhaps the earl wrote and told you that I am to be your new apprentice."

"No, I never heard from the earl. But I heard about you from my French friend from Scotland, Pastor Petit." Mr. Steen stood and shook Ian's hand. "I only wish I could have been here when you arrived." A smile wrinkled the skin around the vicar's thin lips. "My sister became ill, you see, and the dear lady died soon after I arrived at my destination. Of course I stayed on for the funeral."

"May I express my deepest sympathy in your time of sorrow?" Ian said.

"Thank you, sir."

Ian motioned to the table he shared with Peter. "I see that you have not been served yet. Why not join my friend Javier Perrine and me at our table? We would be happy to have you, and it would be a simple thing to have Hitty bring your plate to our table when your food is ready."

The vicar smiled. "Very well, I accept your invitation."

Ian introduced the vicar to Peter and told the vicar that the Earl of Northon invited a young woman from his village by the name of Shannon Aimee and her chaperone to visit him at his estate.

"You were away when I arrived, vicar, and Monsieur Gabeau invited me to stay with him until you returned. So that is where I have been staying ever since then."

However, Ian left out the fact that he had read the letters the vicar wrote to Pastor Petit. He hadn't mentioned the letters to Peter because Pastor Petit had asked that he not share them with anyone until he talked to the vicar first.

The vicar covered a yawn with the palm of his hand. "As much as I am enjoying your company, I must eat quickly and then go up to my room. It has been a long day. I am tired."

"I understand completely, sir. And I want you to know that Monsieur Gabeau speaks well of you. I am sure he would welcome you into his home for the night as he welcomed me."

The vicar had looked as if he was about to fall asleep in his chair. All at once, he seemed to come to himself. "I think not. The Frenchman and I were never close—whatever he might say to the contrary. I couldn't believe my ears when he volunteered to feed my dog."

Never close? Ian had thought they were the best of friends. Was that why the vicar was reluctant to stay the night at Monsieur Gabeau's estate? If this was indeed so, maybe the vicar disliked Etienne Gabeau as much as Ian did.

"Buster is in good health, sir," Ian said. "I've been caring for him myself."

"Thank you, Mr. Colquhoun, I worried about my dog. I've been away from my cottage for a long while, and I hope you do not mind staying at Monsieur Gabeau's estate a bit longer. It could be a day or two before I can have my house in any condition for a guest."

"Of course."

The vicar smiled. "Thank you for being so kind." He glanced down at his plate like Ian did when he was trying to think what to say next. "I will send word to my housekeeper that I have returned from my journey and that it is time for her to get the cottage in proper order once again. Until then, I will be staying here at the inn."

Ian sniffed the air. Did he smell smoke? Hitty rushed toward them from the kitchen, carrying the vicar's food tray. "Come quick. A small fire started in the kitchen." She set the tray on the table. "Cook needs help at once."

"I will go." Peter stood.

Ian got up as well. "Maybe I should go, too."

"Keep your seat," Peter insisted. "If I need more help, Hitty will come and tell you. Please excuse me."

When Peter had gone, Ian noticed that the vicar's eyes looked heavy. The pastor really did look tired as he took in a mouthful of lamb stew.

Ian continued to gaze at the older man. "I know you must be eager to climb the stairs to your room, sir, perhaps take a midday nap after your long journey. But before you retire, there is something I must tell you."

"And what might that be, Mr. Colquhoun?"

Ian glanced around to see if anyone else might be listening. To his relief, all the other tables were empty. They were the only dinner guests left at the inn.

"I have read all the letters you wrote to my minister, Pastor Petit." Ian's voice was barely above a whisper. "I know about the murder of his cousin, Miss Petit, and I gave my word that I would not discuss this matter with anyone but you. It is Pastor Petit's hope that I can help in your quest to find the murderer as well as assist you at the church."

The vicar nodded. "That is my hope as well. Pastor Petit penned a letter to me as soon as he knew for sure that you would be arriving in England, and he told me he gave you the letters."

"There a few things my pastor back in Scotland did not tell you in any of his letters because they occurred since I arrived in England," Ian said. "If you are not too tired, I would like to tell you about them now."

The vicar's smile became a short laugh, and his eyes appeared to come alive with merriment. "I have found that there is only one cure for a lack of sleep, and that is interesting conversation. You have captured my interest. So please, Mr. Colquhoun. Do go on."

Ian had expected to see a measure of surprise in the vicar's eyes as he related all that happened since he left Scotland. But the vicar already knew almost everything Ian told him. In fact, he'd kept notes on the Spiritualist Society for several years.

"Do you know about warfare of the spirit, Mr. Colquhoun?"

"No. What is it?"

"Warfare of the spirit is the casting out of demons or rebuking them in the name of the Lord. Do such actions make you feel uncomfortable? It is biblical, you know. Jesus cast out demons—so did His disciples. Read the Book of Acts."

"I—I know but—"

"But what?"

Ian sat there staring at the vicar because he didn't know what to say. At last he said, "I have been reading in the Book of Deuteronomy chapter eighteen and attempting to discover the meaning of all those new words written there. But I never thought of acting upon them—not really, anyway."

"Perhaps you should." The vicar sent him another smile. "What good are scripture verses that warn us of disasters and tell us what to do to prevent them unless we act upon them?"

"I do try to keep the commandments and do the other things God's requires, but I never thought—"

"You should, and you should also read the Book of Ephesians chapter six and verse eleven."

"Forgive me, I cannot recall that particular verse."

"Put on the whole armor of God, that ye may be able to stand against the wiles of the devil."

"My friend, Miss Aimee, said her father gave her that very scripture in a note he gave her just before she left Scotland."

"Miss Aimee must have a wise father. He must have been washed in the blood of the Lamb—Jesus Christ."

"Yes," Ian said. "Yes, he was. And Miss Aimee asked me how a human would ever be able to put on such a garment. I couldn't say. It would be invisible, wouldn't it?"

The vicar nodded. "To the eye, yes, but perhaps not to the soul and spirit. It takes faith to put on the whole armor of God because you cannot see or touch it in the physical sense."

"Then how can it be done?"

"I cannot say for sure. I can only tell you what I do."

"Please tell me, then. Pastor Petit used almost those exact words back in Luss when he explained how to bind evil spirits in the name of Jesus."

"Another wise man indeed, Mr. Colquhoun, and a dear friend of mine." The vicar cleared his throat. "I put on the whole Armor of God in the order it is given in the Bible," the vicar said. "I think it is important to do things in the proper order."

"Of course."

"Then let us begin." He cleared his throat again. "First, I touch my waist and say in prayer that I am putting on the belt of truth. I touch my chest and say that I am putting on the breastplate of righteousness. I look down at my feet and say that I am putting on the shoes that will allow me to deliver the gospel of peace. I imagine that I am holding a shield and that I am taking the Shield of Faith. I touch my head with both hands and say that I am putting on the Helmet of Salvation. I imagine holding a sword in my right hand—which is the Word of God—and I pray for the Lord's help for myself and for all God's people. Touching one's body is not mentioned with these verses, but it helps keep my mind on God and makes me feel safe."

"How often do you do that—put on the armor of God?"

"I try to do it every morning and especially at night before I go to sleep. But should I forget, I do it when I remember." He chucked softly. "Remember that I forgot."

Ian found himself scrambling for words as well as scripture verses. He'd never heard a preacher with such strength of purpose—such boldness. Where had he learned these skills? Whatever it was, Ian wanted it, too.

"You must share this teaching with Miss Aimee and others."

"Yes, Pastor, I will."

"I have no doubt that you will." The vicar paused before going on.

"Have you ever heard of a pastor by the name of Jonathan Edwards, Mr. Colquhoun?"

"I have not. But you mentioned the man in one of your letters to my pastor."

"Yes, indeed I did. We can all learn much from men like Jonathan Edwards, and I will be telling you more about him in the days and weeks to come. When you return to Scotland, you must share what you have learned with your pastor there. I did not tell him all I wanted to tell in the letters I sent. It will be up to you to inform him of what I dared not say, and since I don't smell smoke anymore, I think it's safe to go up to my room. I have much to do on the morrow."

The vicar had given Ian a lot to think about. In fact, he thought on what they had discussed all the way back to Leon's house. But thinking upon those thoughts and acting upon them were not the same.

+ —————+ +

Shannon was napping on the settee in the parlor when Ian arrived. He wanted to share with her everything the vicar had told him. Instead, he would read the letter that mentioned Jonathan Edwards. If only he could recall which letter he must read. At last, he found it. Ian sat quietly in a chair in the parlor while she napped, and read the letter once again.

Dear Pastor Petit,

Praise the Lord. What a pleasure it is to hear from a man who loves the Lord as I do. You asked how I know so much. But in my personal opinion, humans know little about the God of the Bible. We all have much to learn. Certainly I do. What I know, I learned from scripture reading. As you must know, the Bible is the best teacher of all.

Nevertheless, there are so many things I would love to share with you. If only you could come to England so we could have a long visit.

Did I mention that before I became the vicar here in the village of Fairs I spent time in the colonies? At that time, I heard a sermon given by an elderly clergyman who studied under a man named Jonathan Edwards. Perhaps you have heard of Mr. Edwards. He is not widely known among my peers in the English church. Some would not like what he has to say. Others might consider listening to such a man an outrage. Therefore, you must take care not to repeat the contents of this letter to anyone but your most trusted friends. In some of my future letters, I will try to tell some of the things the preacher said in his sermon. You will be amazed.

Respectfully,

Mr. Steen signed the letter with an unreadable script—perhaps to keep others from knowing his identity if the letter was lost. Ian put away the letter, and while Shannon continued to sleep, he studied the book on the meanings of words.

All at once he heard a knock at the door. McGregor served as the Frenchman's butler as well as his driver, but he was away from the house at the moment. Cook was probably out back in the kitchen house.

Ian got up and opened the door. The physician who cared for Shannon on the previous day stood on the stoop.

"Good day, doctor," Ian said. "It is good to see you again. I stopped by your cottage earlier today. You were not home."

"Yes, Mr. Colquhoun, my wife told me."

"Monsieur Gabeau is not here. But please, do come in."

The physician nodded. "And how is Miss Aimee?"

"She is sleeping at the moment, but feeling much better, I think." Ian motioned toward the settee. "I will wake her, and you can judge for yourself. Then I will fetch Cook, and she will assist you. But first, I left an object in your home when I stopped by. Did you have a chance to look at it?"

"Not yet. My wife had wrapped a cloth around it, and I brought it with me. But I haven't had time to examine it yet." He smiled. "Now I must take another look at the young woman to see how she is doing."

Ian woke Shannon. Then he found Cook and sent her to the parlor to assist the physician when he examined Shannon. He'd wanted to discuss the bone with the doctor at length. Maybe he would get the chance later on.

The physician wrapped a clean cloth around Shannon's ankle. Cook sat in a chair beside her. The doctor spoke to Shannon in whispers. Ian strained to hear but couldn't.

"See, Miss Aimee," the older woman said in a loud voice. "Did I not tell you that your leg was not broken?"

"Yes, ma'am, you did."

"I know your leg still ails you," the doctor said. "But it is much improved."

"Perhaps Miss Aimee and her chaperone would like a quiet moment together." Ian turned to the physician. "Come into the small dining room with me, sir. Let us give the ladies the time they need."

"Yes." The doctor nodded. "That is a fine idea."

Ian led the way to the small dining room. The doctor followed him in, and Ian shut the door.

Ian poured cups of warm tea into two white china cups, and the two men sat down at the table. The doctor's wife had assured Ian that Lela and the boy were safe. Regardless, Ian wanted to inquire as to their well being before mentioning the bone.

"Tell me about Lela and the boy." Ian leaned forward in his chair. "I am eager to hear."

"As my wife told you, they are on their way to Ireland. Cook could lose her job when the Monsieur learns they are gone. And of course, I will never be invited to this estate again."

"As I mentioned, Monsieur Gabeau is gone for the day. It could be several days before he discovers they are gone."

The doctor nodded. "That is my hope."

"Is there anything you can do to protect the cook when that grim outcome comes to pass?"

"Many in the village know everything, and they will gladly hide Cook in their homes, if that becomes necessary."

"Thank you." Ian paused before continuing. "There is something else I would like to discuss with you. It's about the object I left at your house. It's a—it's a bone."

"A bone? Really. I didn't know. What kind of bone would you say that it is?"

"I am hoping you can tell me."

"You mean this?" The physician pulled a wrapped package from his black leather bag and opened it. His eyes appeared to increase in size. He stood and went to the window with the bone in both hands. He turned the object this way and that, studying it from every angle.

"I cannot say what it is until I have had time to examine it further. Where did you get this bone, Mr. Colquhoun?"

"The vicar's dog dug it up in the woods not far from Gatehaven."

"Is that so?" The physician paused and looked down at the bone again. "I suggest you do a little digging of your own. See if you can find more of these bones. And if by chance you do, I should be most interested to see them. I would like to keep this bone. I want to study it in my laboratory."

"Keep it with my blessing. Though I know that at the moment you cannot tell exactly what kind of bone this is with any certainty. Can you tell me what kind of animal it came from?"

"The human kind, I believe."

"What?"

"I think the bone in question is not an animal bone at all. I cannot tell for sure until I have studied it more, but it might be the remains of a human being."

Ian was thinking about the bone and what the physician had said when they returned to the parlor. The cook went out to prepare supper, leaving Shannon in the room with the two men.

The physician stood before her, leaning forward. "I think you should return to Gatehaven as soon as possible, young lady. Will you let me drive you there in my carriage?"

Shannon shook her head.

The doctor might not have known why Shannon refused to take his advice, but her non-verbal response was clear enough to Ian. She didn't want to return to Gatehaven because the earl wasn't there and Miss Foster was.

The physician sent Shannon a stern look. "Monsieur Gabeau's cook has many duties here, Miss Aimee. She must cook and clean for the Monsieur and his other guests and care for your needs besides; therefore, she cannot be a proper chaperone for you. But your chaperone, Miss Foster, has only one task to perform, and that is caring for you."

"I would rather stay here until the earl returns, sir."

The physician shook his head. "I disagree."

"So do I," Ian put in.

Shannon might be safer in Gatehaven with a witch as a chaperone than spend time in the presence of the earl or Monsieur Gabeau.

It took a while, but Shannon finally agreed to return to Gatehaven. The physician drove her back in his carriage. Ian rode along.

Even before the carriage stopped in front of the mansion, it was clear that the conference was still going on. Carriages were parked along the road, and fine horses were hitched to wooden posts.

The physician turned to Ian as if Shannon was invisible. "Perhaps we should not go inside through the main entrance. We might bother those taking part in the meeting. Is there a back entrance?"

"Yes." Ian started off. "Behind the mansion. Follow me."

Ian led the way to the back of the house, hoping nobody noticed when he removed the key from under the mat. Shannon was able to walk a little, but she said that her ankle hurt when she did.

"Let me carry her to her room on the second floor." Ian scooped Shannon up into his arms. "It will be easier that way."

"Put me down, Ian. I can walk."

"Your ankle is weak, Miss Aimee," the physician warned. "If you turned it again, it could break. For the sake of your health, we simply cannot take the chance that you might cause your leg injury to become more serious than it already is."

"Very well, if you insist."

They managed to get Shannon to her room on the second floor without being seen. Ian wanted to stay after the doctor left and visit with Shannon. But it wouldn't be proper for him to do so. Still, he planned to wait in the hallway outside her door until Miss Foster returned.

Ian was standing guard in the hallway outside her bedroom when he noticed that her door wasn't closed all the way. He reached out to shut it.

"Leave the door open a crack," Shannon whispered from inside the bedroom, "so that we can talk."

"Aye. What would you like to talk about?"

"Anything."

Ian thought of the teachings the vicar had given him at the inn. He wasn't certain whether or not he told her that the vicar returned. He would tell her now. He would also tell her what the vicar said about the Armor of God and what Pastor Petit said about binding Satan during prayer time. Somehow he knew that these were things Shannon needed to know in a hurry.

After he'd explained the teachings, Ian wanted to say that her brother was staying at an inn in Fairs and that the earl was every bit as bad as Miss Foster and the Frenchman. But she would not like hearing anything about Peter or anything negative about the earl.

Shannon and Peter had never been close, and it would displease her to learn that her brother followed her to England. If Ian voiced his concerns about the earl, she could slam the door in his face and lock it from the inside.

All at once, he heard footsteps.

"I must go," he whispered through the partly opened door. "Someone is coming."

Ian hurried into the vacant room across the hall from Shannon's but left the door open a crack. Peering out, she saw Miss Foster amble down the hall toward her room.

He couldn't be found on the second floor. He would be expelled from Gatehaven forever. And who would look after Shannon until Peter could take over?

Shannon didn't even know Peter was in England.

Miss Foster went into her room next to Shannon's and shut the door. Ian had no reason to assume she suspected a thing. He slipped down the stairs and out into the night.

The long walk back to Leon's estate would be lonely without Buster nipping at his heels. As Ian strode back down the country road toward the Frenchman's estate, he thought about the danger Shannon was in and all that had happened since he left Scotland. He and Peter needed to put their heads together and come up with a plan to rescue Shannon. If they waited until the earl returned, it might be too late.

It was time to pray.

Ian had almost reached the Frenchman's estate when a carriage pulled up beside him. The door nearest to Ian opened.

"Get in, Mr. Colquhoun."

Ian tensed. It was far from a request; more of a command. He started to ignore it and keep walking. However, this was not the time to ruffle feathers. Monsieur Gabeau was going to be angry enough when he finally realized that Lela, the boy, and perhaps his cook had left him for good. With a deep sense of reluctance, he climbed into the carriage beside Gabeau.

"What were you doing out there after dark?" Leon demanded.

"I believe I mentioned, Monsieur, that I enjoy a brisk walk in the night air."

Leon sniffed with more than a hint of sarcasm. "Foolishness."

*   —◆—   *

Leon wasn't taken in by Ian's flimsy explanation. The young man was up to something, and he intended to find out what. The supper served at the conference that evening wasn't to his liking, and he intended to have Cook fix him a cup of tea and a nice bowl of chicken soup. But when he arrived at his house, the only person he saw was McGregor, his butler/carriage driver.

"Where is Miss Aimee?" the Frenchman shouted to his servant.

"She was not here in the parlor when I arrived, Monsieur, nor is she now."

"That is obvious! Are there no thoughts in your head?" Gabeau glared at McGregor for a moment. "Where is she?"

"It is rather late," Ian put in. "Perhaps she turned in for the night."

"I suppose Cook is with her," Leon said.

"No, Monsieur. She might have been earlier, but when I arrived she was preparing to go home."

"Go home?" Leon's muscles tightened, and his heart became a hard lump in the middle of this chest. "She knows not to go home when I hired her to do a task for me."

"Cook was ill, sir," McGregor said. "Sick to her stomach, she said."

"Well," Leon continued. "Don't just stand there. Go get her. And if she is too sick to come back tonight, bring that daughter of hers."

"Yes, Monsieur." McGregor sent Ian a cold glance and went out the front door.

"I think I will go up to my room now, Monsieur, if that is agreeable to you," Ian said. "It's been a long day. I am tired."

"No wonder with all that walking. But won't you stay and have supper with me before you go up, Mr. Colquhoun?"

"Thank you for the kind invitation, but I have no desire for food at the moment. Just sleep. Perhaps I am a little under the weather as well."

Leon sniffed. "Be gone with you, then. And let us hope that you will be more sociable on the morrow."

＊———＋———＊

Ian was amused by Leon's distress but he tried not to show it. He could only imagine what was going to happen downstairs when the Frenchman learned that Cook, Lela, and the boy had left his estate for good.

Ian lit the lamp as soon as he came in his room. After undressing and climbing into bed, he put on the whole Armor of God for the very first time. He'd been reading the book on the meaning of words for about half an hour when he heard a commotion going on downstairs. Shouting and loud voices filled the air, and what sounded like lamps or dishes crashing to the floor.

Ian couldn't help laughing. Clearly, the Frenchman now knew that Cook, her daughter, and Stephen, Gabeau's son, were no longer under his control. What pieces of furniture would he throw around when he learned that Shannon was back at Gatehaven?

CHAPTER EIGHTEEN

T HE MORNING SUN beamed through the window in Leon's bedroom. Still in bed, he started to reach for his cane when memories of the previous night flooded him with instant rage. His cook, her daughter, and the son he hated had left him forever, and then he discovered that Shannon had returned to Gatehaven. His muscles hardened as if they had turned to stone.

He'd taken a candle and gone into Shannon's room on the previous night, but she was not there. His lips curled upward in a hateful smile. He would find her.

A sudden pain stabbed him in the chest. His breathing became labored, and Leon gulped for air. He tried to call out but couldn't. Nobody would hear him in any case. McGregor would be tending the animals, and nobody else was in the house but Mr. Colquhoun.

"Anger and inner wrath will kill you someday, Monsieur Gabeau," the Healer had said. "If you want these spells of yours to go away, you must force yourself to remain calm."

Calm? He might well be dying. He got up and reached for his cane, and this time, he got up.

Another pain like liquid fire invaded his chest. He staggered to the bed and fell back down.

Where did I put my pills? He thought for a moment. *Oh yes, the table by my bed.*

The pills were inches away. But did he have the strength to reach over and grab them? He needed to try.

It took every bit of strength he had to stretch out his arm and touch the edge of the table with his fingertips. Slowly, he walked his fingers toward the sack with the pills in them. The pain in his chest increased, but he kept on. His finger reached the sack. He attempted to pull it toward him. It came his way for a short distance. Then it slid off the table and fell to the floor with the pills still inside.

Leon opened his mouth to call out. But no words came.

Nobody will find me here. I am doomed.

He felt as alone as he had on the day he fell in the well. Yes, he tripped and fell. Rachel didn't push him. But she might as well have. She ruined his life. Because of her, he would never be the same.

Christians called out to their God at times like this. Maybe he would call on his. Sometimes it worked. But at other times...

Unless he did something, he would soon lose his ability to think. Leon reached down and found the sack. It was almost as if it had been put within his reach on purpose. He slipped his hand inside, grabbed a pill and dropped it in his mouth. He felt as if he was going to faint. But he would not die.

Not this time, at least.

His eyes closed. Sleep tempted him. He wanted it—needed it. But he refused to give in even to his normal bodily desire for rest.

I'm better than that, he told himself.

Leon sat up in bed, moving his legs around until his feet touched the floor. He would sit there awhile and then he would get up.

Shannon was likely in Gatehaven by now. Were it within his power, Leon would go and fetch her at once—bring her back to his estate. However, what he wanted to do was not always what he should do. In this case, logic must reign.

If he hoped to reach his goal, he must plan his moves carefully from this moment on. And nobody must ever know how truly weak he felt at that moment.

✦——✦——✦

The vicar was preparing his sermon for Sunday the next morning when Ian moved from Leon's estate to the vicar's cottage. He gave Ian permission to continue feeding Buster, and he encouraged him to spend the morning as he liked.

"Look around, Mr. Colquhoun. Enjoy yourself. We will have much to discuss after the noon meal."

Ian would have enjoyed a long visit with Shannon or her brother. But he didn't feel welcome at Gatehaven regardless of who was in charge. Peter took a job at The Boar and Tongue in the village of Fairs.

He took Buster out for a stroll in the woods on the chance that he might find more bones. He didn't. Ian was writing a letter to his parents when Mr. Steen called him into his study.

"Please sit down, Mr. Colquhoun. Did you bring your Bible?"

"No, I did not."

"No matter. I have an extra one." He handed Ian an English Bible with a worn brown cover. "Do you own a Bible?"

"Yes, sir."

"Good. Please keep your Bible with you at all times and read it as often as you can. Also, pray in earnest. One never knows when he or she might need a word from the Lord."

Ian nodded. Then he thumbed through his Bible without looking up.

"We've discussed demons and the warfare of the spirit among other things. Is that not correct?"

"Yes, pastor, I believe it is."

"Turn to the Book of Isaiah—chapter fourteen. Read verse twelve."

"Aloud?"

"Of course."

Ian cleared his throat. *"How art thou fallen from heaven, O Lucifer, son of the morning! How art thou cut down to the ground, which didst weaken the nations!"*

"Who is Lucifer?" the pastor asked. "Do you know?"

"Lucifer was a holy angel who fell from grace. Now he is the devil."

"Correct. But why did Lucifer fall from heaven—fall from grace?"

"He weakened the nations."

"Yes. But more than that, he rebelled against God."

"My pastor in Luss said that Lucifer was also called the king of Babylon."

"Correct again. Lucifer was the king of Babylon. But the Lord is the King of Israel."

"And the demons?" Ian asked.

"Demons and fallen angels are Satan's underlings. But believers and holy angels are under God's command." The vicar glanced toward the door. "Now we will walk over to the church, and I will show you how our services must be conducted and your part in it. Pay close attention. Our services are different from what you are accustomed to in the Reformed Church."

Ian wanted the current discussion to continue. He also hoped to learn about warfare of the spirit. His facial expression probably showed his disappointment. Nevertheless, he accompanied the vicar to the church—and listened as he explained the rituals Ian would need to learn in order to perform his duties as the vicar's assistant.

This took several hours. When the teaching finally ended for the day, the vicar turned to Ian and smiled.

"Do not be discouraged, Mr. Colquhoun. We shall discuss the topic you seemed to enjoy again soon. In fact, we will also discuss topics you might find even more interesting."

Ian assisted the vicar for the first time during the service on Sunday morning. Even the young boys who served at the altar seemed to know more than Ian did. He looked around the sanctuary, hoping to see Shannon seated in one of the pews. But nobody from Gatehaven attended services that day.

After the service, Ian changed out of his white robe and hurried to the pastor's cottage. His stomach was making disgusting sounds indicating a need for food by the time he and the vicar finally sat down for their noon meal. Ian was asked to say the blessing.

He couldn't remember the mealtime prayer Mr. Steen had taught him to say. He sent up a prayer from the heart instead. When he finished, he apologized for not remembering.

"There is no need to apologize, Mr. Colquhoun. Prayers from the heart are always better than those that one recites from memory."

Ian couldn't believe his own ears. Had the vicar actually spoken against the kind of prayers that came from a book? He finally concluded that perhaps what the vicar really meant was that there was a place for both.

"You did well today," the vicar added. "When we finish eating, we will go into the sitting room while my cook cleans the dishes, and we will discuss those topics you so enjoy."

Ian's smile was both physical and internal. "Thank you, sir."

The humble meal of roasted calf and vegetables tasted delicious, and Ian intended to thank the cook for preparing it as soon as they finished eating. But his head was so full of thoughts and questions regarding their upcoming discussion, he hoped he wouldn't forget.

At last they went into the sitting room and sat by the fire. The room was larger than Pastor Petit's sitting room, and the shelves held more books. Still, Ian felt a peace there, reminding him of home.

"We are at war, Mr. Colquhoun. Did you know that?"

Ian was stunned. He hadn't heard the news for many days. Still, if England and perhaps Scotland were at war, surely he would have heard.

"Then there is bad news from the colonies?"

"The war I am talking about has nothing to do with England *or* the colonies."

"Then please, Mr. Steen, pray tell where this war is being fought."

"The war I am talking about is taking place here and everywhere else. I am talking about a spiritual war."

Ian nodded. "Oh, I see."

But he was really just beginning to see with spiritual eyes.

"Read from the Book of Revelation—aloud if you please," Pastor Steen ordered, "chapter twelve and verses seven, eight, and nine."

Fortunately, Ian had brought his own Bible this time. He found the Book of Revelation and turned to chapter twelve.

"And there was war in heaven: Michael and his angels fought against the dragon; and the dragon fought and his angels, and prevailed not; neither was their place found any more in heaven…"

Ian remembered Shannon saying that there were carvings of dragons all over Gatehaven, and that the dragon represented Satan. A shudder ran through him. *"And the great dragon was cast out, that old serpent, called the Devil, and Satan, which deceiveth the whole world: he was cast out into the earth, and his angels were cast out with him."*

"That is the war of which I speak. Now, Mr. Colquhoun, read chapter twelve in the Book of Revelation, verse eleven, and learn how to fight this war we find ourselves in."

Ian cleared his throat. *"And they overcame him by the blood of the Lamb, and by the word of their testimony; and they loved not their lives unto the death."*

The vicar smiled. "Perhaps you are wondering what all this means. If so, you are not alone. I also wondered. At times, I still have doubts. But if it could be explained briefly, I think it would be this. We are in a battle against the powers of evil, headed by Satan or the devil or Lucifer or the king of Babylon or by whatever name you call him. And as believers, we have the God-given power to overcome this evil by the blood of the Lamb and by the word of our testimony."

"And am I right in assuming that we might have to give up our lives one day if it is a choice between serving God and keeping the law of man?"

The vicar's nod was slow and perhaps thoughtful. "That would be correct."

"I think I understand what you are saying, Pastor Steen. But how would we apply this to our everyday lives? What would we say? And what must we do?"

"You have asked a very good question. And I can give you but one answer. We must say and do what Jesus said and did while He was on earth. We must resist the devil and he will flee from us as we are told to do in the Book of James—chapter four and verse seven. "

"All these scripture verses at one time are hard for my simple mind to take in at one sitting. Please explain what you mean, sir. I still do not understand."

"If tempted to do something you know is wrong, resist the temptation. Don't act on it. Say no to sin. As long as we have free will to sin or not sin, we can always resist—no matter how strong the urge to sin might be."

The vicar must have known how confused Ian was because he sent him an especially warm and friendly smile. "When the tempter came to Jesus and tried to get him to sin, Jesus told him to go away. Then he quoted a verse from the Bible. True believers must demand that Satan go hence just as Jesus did—but not in our own strength. We must give God the glory for all our accomplishments. Under the Old Covenant, the house of Israel prayed in the name of the Lord. As New Covenant Believers, we must pray in the name of our Lord and Savior, Jesus Christ.

"For many years I went around rebuking Satan at every turn," the vicar explained, "and it is certainly correct to do so according to the Scriptures. Then one day I read in the Bible where it said that God lives in the praises of His people. I finally realized that when I thank and praise the Lord, God is with me as He was with David on the day he defeated the giant, Goliath. The devil, fallen angels, demons, they all back away in the presence of a Holy God."

"Are you saying we should actually speak to Satan and his underlings aloud—rebuke them as Jesus did?"

"Yes, but only in the name of Jesus. The battle is really the Lord's. Never forget the power of prayer, praise, and thanking God for everything in life whether good or bad."

"Good *or* bad? Are you saying we must thank the Lord when things go wrong?"

"Without a doubt."

Ian shrugged his shoulders. "How could any man give thanks to God if he lost his livelihood, his house burned to the ground, or his children died? That would be impossible."

"It's called faith. And with faith, nothing is impossible."

"Faith?"

"Faith is another word for trust, Mr. Colquhoun. It means you choose to believe that the Lord has a plan you are not aware of and that He can and will turn your bad times into blessings. I even have a scripture verse you can recite to the devil at just such a time. I won't quote the entire scripture verse here, but it is found in the Book of Isaiah—chapter 54 and verse 17 (NKJV): 'No weapon formed against you shall prosper.' I like to make it personal and change the word *you* to *me*."

"So?"

"They overcame him by the blood of the Lamb," the vicar said. "But do you know who the *him* in that scripture verse might be, and who the Lamb is?"

"The Lamb is Jesus, the Lamb of God. However, I cannot say the identity of the *him* in that verse."

"Who would believers overcome by the blood of Jesus?" the vicar asked.

"The devil."

"Correct. So now you know the identity of the *him*. Do you not?"

"Clearly, this must be the answer."

"Now," the vicar said. "Let us review what we have learned. The verse you read earlier stated that *they overcame him by the blood of the Lamb, and by the word of their testimony; and they loved not their lives unto the death.* So one might say something like this to Satan, the fallen angels and demons. 'I am a child of the Most High God, and I have been washed in the blood of the Lamb. Therefore, no weapon formed against me will prosper. And I will dwell in the House of the Lord forever.'"

"That is it?" Ian said. "That is all I must say during what you call warfare of the spirit?"

"That is what I sometimes say and one of the things you could say. But don't make it a ritual by always saying the same things in the same way. And don't do anything merely because I do it. I could be wrong. Learn how to live in Christ by reading and studying the Bible. And do not forget the power of prayer, praise, giving thanks, and fasting."

"Fasting. Must I fast as well?"

"Jesus told His disciples that they would fast after He was gone. So fasting must be important."

Ian nodded. "I see what you mean." He glanced down at the Bible in his hands and then looked back at the vicar. "But I must tell you, sir, that except for perhaps my pastor, nobody in *my* church in Scotland would ever do the things you mentioned here today. They sing hymns of praise, of course, but they would never simply praise God aloud as if He was standing right in front of them. And they would never rebuke Satan either."

"Some church members need a better knowledge of the Bible and what God really says in it in order to become doers of the Word and not merely hearers only. Maybe one day you will become a pastor, Mr. Colquhoun, and teach them."

The vicar probably expected Ian to confirm his best wishes—promise that one day soon he would speak to invisible beings as if they were visible, tell them to go away in the name of the Lord and teach others to do the same. Like "Get thee behind me, Satan" and "I rebuke thee in the name of Jesus." But Ian wasn't ready for such a huge step of faith.

Frankly, to suggest such a thing seemed rather bizarre. At the same time, Pastor Steen's lesson caused Ian to want to learn more so that one day he might actually do it.

"Recently, a man I barely knew told me of a dream he had," the vicar continued, "and his dream took place in the future—perhaps at the end of time. According to the Book of Daniel, only God knows the meaning of dreams, and the man didn't tell me whether or not he prayed about the meaning of this dream after he awoke. Before I had the chance to ask him, he stepped away. I never saw him again, but I remember the dream."

The vicar paused and cleared his throat. "He said that in the dream he was in a place where leaders declared what was good and what was bad. He said that sin was based on man's rules, not God's Holy Word. He said God's commandments were outlawed in that those who told others not to break God's laws were called names. Many were put in prison for following the Lord."

"Prison for keeping God's commands?" Ian said. "How could this be?"

The vicar shrugged. "The man who had the dream was confused as well. For example, he said that in the dream it wasn't a sin to kill an unborn child in the womb or soon after it was born. He said that in the dream, such acts were considered lawful and the normal thing to do. However, to warn others *not* to sin was a crime. As I said, in the dream, bad was good and good was bad."

"What a terrible place," Ian said. "What a terrible dream."

"Mr. Colquhoun, there are more terrible dreams, terrible places and terrible acts going on right here in the village of Fairs than I care to think about."

He is talking about Gatehaven, Ian thought.

"But in the Book of John chapter fourteen and verse fifteen," the vicar went on, "Jesus said, 'If ye love me, keep my commandments.' And in the Book of Matthew chapter nineteen and verse seventeen, Jesus said, 'Why callest thou me good? There is none good but one, that is, God: but if thou wilt enter into life, keep the commandments.' What life do you think Jesus was talking about here?"

"Eternal life?"

"Yes, but the Bible also talks about an abundant life that we can have right here on earth. Can you think what a person must do to receive eternal life and an abundant life as well?"

Ian paused to give himself time to think. "The Book of John, chapter three and verse three, stated that we must be born again. Is that what you are talking about?"

"I am indeed talking about that scripture, son. However, we must first seek the Lord with all our hearts, souls, and all that is within us, and we must truly repent of all our sins. It is not enough to merely tell the Lord we are sorry. We must earnestly turn away from the sin and strive to never become ensnared by it again."

Ian's face or mannerisms must have told the vicar that he was tired, slightly confused, and in need of time to digest all that he'd heard. The vicar closed his Bible and placed it on the small table by his chair—exactly as Pastor Petit always did at the end of his sermons.

"This part of our lesson is finished for today," Pastor Steen said. "Next time, we will discuss the signs and wonders mentioned in the Book of Mark. The clergy I met who studied under Jonathan Edwards had a great deal to say about that. And remember, the Bible is never wrong. My personal thoughts and opinions could always be wrong.

"Now, I will ring for my cook and ask her to bring us some tea. Would a cup of tea suit you at this time, Mr. Colquhoun?"

"Yes, I would like a cup of tea and the chance to thank Cook for an excellent noon meal."

Two days later, Ian went out behind the vicar's cottage to feed Buster. He hadn't seen Peter since that day at the inn nor had he seen Shannon.

The vicar had kept him busy learning the ways and rituals of the English church. But he'd also taught him more about the Bible. One of the lessons Ian learned was the importance of being positive every time he spoke—even in jest. If he prayed for a need, he must expect his prayer to be answered, and he must find comfort in that—perhaps thanking the Lord for answering his prayers before the answer came.

"God hates idolatry," the vicar had said, "and according to the Bible, He also dislikes complainers. As believers, we must stop complaining. Thank God for all our blessings."

The minister ended that lesson by promising that as soon as Ian was able to perform his duties at the church correctly, they would discuss topics Ian would find even more interesting. However, on that day the vicar planned to visit in the homes of his flock. Ian had the entire day off.

He'd dug around the spot where the dog found the strange bone several times, hoping to find another one. So far, he was unsuccessful. Maybe he should try again.

Ian opened the pen wide. Buster wagged his tail.

"Come on, boy. It is time for our walk."

This time, Ian planned to stroll all the way to Gatehaven in hopes of seeing Shannon. Ian was eager to see her again, and she'd sent a note via the vicar.

Dear Ian,

I will meet you in the garden behind the kitchen this afternoon at three, if I can get away.

Regards,
Rachel Shannon Aimee

Ian and the dog had almost reached Gatehaven when he saw a carriage drive up. Ian grabbed Buster by the nape of the neck and pulled him in the shadow of a large tree. He watched as the earl and the two women got out and went inside.

So, the earl is back. Ian wondered if Shannon would be told that the earl had returned.

He heard a rustling in the bushes nearby. He froze. Peter stepped out from behind a tree.

"Good day, my friend." Peter smiled. "It is good to see you."

"Peter. It is time you showed your face to me again. How is your job working out?"

"The innkeeper sold the inn. Hitty will likely be fired."

"Fired? Why?"

"Hitty told me in confidence that she knows too much." Peter shook his head. "Strange. Millie, the young girl who nursed me back to health after my fall from the horse, told me the same thing. After Hitty gets off work tonight, I will see if I can convince her to tell me more."

"I would like to speak to both those young women," Ian said. "I know where Millie and her uncle, Devlin McGregor, live." Ian glanced down at the dog. "I think I mentioned that Buster and I came upon it one day when we went for a walk. However, it is unlikely that McGregor would allow a Colquhoun like me to speak with his niece."

Peter shook his head. "You Scots and your clans have always confused me."

Buster put his front feet on Ian's thigh and licked his hand. Peter leaned down, patting Buster on the head. The dog wagged his tail.

"Your dog?" Peter asked.

"His name is Buster, and he belongs to the vicar."

"Buster seems to like you," Peter said. "But that is nothing new. You always had a string of dogs at your heels back home." He paused and looked away.

"I have been thinking a lot about my sister, Ian. If Shannon still refuses to see me, I am going to storm in that mansion and demand that they *make* her see me. I have wasted enough time as it is."

"Demand?" Ian shook his head. "You know Shannon. If you *demand* that she do something, she will likely do just the opposite."

CHAPTER NINETEEN

S HANNON IS MY sister," Peter said, "my flesh and blood. I have no choice but to go after her."

"We should pray. God will find a solution to our problem. We need only to wait on Him."

"That is good enough for you to say. You plan to become a man of the cloth, but what about me? I pray all right, but I am a farmer's son. I hope to have a farm of my own someday."

"You are a follower of the Lord, are you not?"

"Of course. You know I am."

"Then you are blessed. For us, prayer is the answer. And when I pray, like when I pray for rain, I thank God when the answer comes. The Lord will let us know when it is time to rescue Shannon, and He is never late."

"You seem different, Ian, since the vicar arrived and now you're serving as his assistant."

"How am I different?"

"More churched—as my father would say."

"I am no different than the Ian Colquhoun you have always known. I just know more about the Bible and the English church than I did before I arrived."

Peter nodded. But Ian didn't think he seemed convinced.

"Now," Ian said, "tell me what happened at the inn. What did Hitty tell you about the new owner?"

"Not much." Peter straightened and shrugged. "One of The Boar and Tongue's new owners is a former monk from France named Brother

Julian. But I have not heard the name of his partner. Nobody but the monk knows, I suppose. Where is Shannon now?"

Ian swallowed. Pastor Petit's letter had stated that one of the strangers in the village of Cert the night Magdalena Petit was murdered wore the clothes of a monk. Could there be a connection? So many peculiar events had taken place since he arrived in England, Ian wouldn't be surprised at anything he heard or saw.

"Well, Ian. Where is my sister?"

"At the mansion. I was on my way there to meet her in the garden."

"Bring her here, Ian. I have much to tell."

"Do you think she will be willing to come?"

"You have to try."

"Very well, I will see what she says. And promise to stay right here. I will return shortly."

Ian started to walk off. Buster wagged his tail and fell in right behind him.

He stopped and gazed down at the dog. "You stay here, boy, with Peter."

The dog sat down on his haunches and his ears perked up.

"Stay."

The dog didn't move.

"Smart dog." Peter bent down and patted Buster on the head. "The vicar must be proud. Tell him that I like his dog the next time you see him."

"I will try to remember."

◆——◆——◆

Shannon was seated on a stone bench under a tree in the garden behind the house. Ian smiled and sat down beside her. Knowing how she felt about her brother, he needed to prepare Shannon for what was to come before taking her to meet Peter.

"How is your ankle?"

"The pain disappeared. I can walk normally now. And I have good news."

"I have news as well. You tell yours first."

"The earl and his family have returned from London, and he had a note sent up to my room. Oh, Ian, you will never guess what has happened." She leaned against the back of the bench, bubbling with excitement. "I have been invited to dinner in the main dining room tonight. This must mean that the earl plans to announce our engagement." She smiled. "Be happy for me."

"I am happy if you are."

"Oh, I am." Shannon studied Ian for a moment. "I know you have never approved of the earl. That is because you do not really know him yet. Now that will all change. I am sure that you and the earl will become the best of friends."

Ian didn't agree with her assessment of the situation. However, he decided to keep his thoughts to himself.

"Now for my news," he finally said. "Peter is staying at an inn in Fairs called The Boar and Tongue and working there as well, and he is eager to see you. He is waiting for us in the woods this minute."

Shannon's dreamy expression vanished. "Are you saying that my brother is here—in England?"

"Aye."

"Why would he come here?" Her facial muscles tensed. "Is something wrong at home?"

He shook his head. "As far as Peter knows, all is well with your family in Scotland. He came to—to—"

"To spy on me. Is that not right?"

"He did not come to spy," Ian insisted. "Not at all. He came here in case you needed him. Peter is your brother, after all, and he cares about you."

"Peter would never come to England merely because he was concerned for my welfare, Ian, and you know it. He thinks I am a child—Papa's little girl. Mama must have sent him."

"Come to the woods with me and let Peter tell you why he came in his own words."

Shannon stood. "I have no wish to talk to Peter now or ever. I must go inside and prepare for the dinner party tonight."

"Please, lass, go with me to meet your brother even if you can only stay a short while."

She stomped her foot. "No! Tell Peter to go back to Scotland. I have nothing to say to him."

Shannon walked into the kitchen through the back door, and she didn't look back.

◆

Leon had also received a message from the earl. *Come to Gatehaven tonight for the dinner I promised you before I left for London. You will be seated next to Miss Shannon Aimee.*

His plans appeared to be working. Tonight Miss Aimee—soon her beautiful mother.

◆

Shannon pulled the best dress she owned from the box she'd brought from home. She wanted to pinch Ian on the ear for standing up for her brother. At the same time, she hoped that Ian would be attending the dinner too. However, she had no way of knowing for sure.

She held the dress up to the light before putting it on. It was the same gold-colored gown she'd worn to the ball held in Luss, and the earl had seen it twice. The gown would have to do. She had no other that would be suitable for such an occasion.

The dress had a scooped neckline—though not low-cut like some of the dresses she'd seen at balls in Scotland. The silk bodice fit smoothly against her slender waist, and the yards and yards of soft material in the gathered skirt swished and rippled as she moved.

She couldn't afford a wig of any kind, but she planned to have Miss Foster's maid pay special attention to her hair. Perhaps she would braid it and wind it around her head like a sort of crown. Since she didn't own a tiara, spring flowers in gold and yellow would have to do. She wanted to look perfect that evening and nothing like the servant girl the earl's mother first thought her to be.

Shannon's auburn hair hung well below her waist when it wasn't pinned up or braided. In Scotland, she'd often fashioned it into one long braid and tossed the braid across one shoulder in order to get the effect she wanted.

The earl's mother and grandmother could be wearing white wigs and powdering their faces before dinner that night. But the earl had complimented her long hair and fair complexion. If he found her desirable as she normally looked, why should she cover her best features with powder and wigs? However, she would pinch her cheeks before going below stairs to make her face look as fresh and appealing as possible.

At nine o'clock that evening, Shannon stood in the doorway of the large dining room.

The butler announced her. "Miss Rachel Shannon Aimee."

Everyone stood at the table behind their chairs as if waiting for her or someone to arrive. Was she late? Apparently that was the case.

Lady Catherine and her mother, Lady Victoria, and Miss Foster wore powdered wigs. Two other women that she'd never met wore wigs as well, and all the men wore white wigs. Shannon's gold dress clung to her sides while the other women wore panniers under their skirts—to make them look as if they had large hips, she assumed.

Everybody is looking at me. Moisture gathered at the edges of her eyes. *And nobody seems pleased that I am here—including the earl.* Shannon sniffed. *Where is Ian?*

She looked around but didn't see him. Maybe he wasn't invited.

Ian didn't fit in, and she didn't either. She probably looked as if she still belonged in the stable or the maid's quarters. Nevertheless, she would not cry so others would notice—no matter what.

The earl moved around from his place at the head of the table and escorted her to one of two vacant chairs near the middle of the table.

So, she thought, *someone else is late. Maybe it is Ian.*

The earl pulled out a chair in the design of the French upper class and motioned for Shannon to sit down.

Shannon lifted her head and smiled.

He leaned down and whispered in her ear. "You look lovely tonight."

She nodded politely to the earl and looked down at her plate as Miss Foster had taught her to do in these situations. As she settled onto a heavy side chair with its carved back and brocaded cushion, she wondered: Was a dragon carved on the back of her chair like the one on her bed's head-board? She decided not to look. That way, she could at least hope it wasn't there.

"One of the symbols for Satan mentioned in the Bible is the dragon," her father had said.

But the earl wasn't reared by a man who read and studied the Bible daily as her father did. He probably didn't know. Maybe she'd become too obsessed with the meaning of words and with symbols. Perhaps she should think about something else.

Shannon gazed at the elderly woman seated beside her. She wore a black silk dress, and diamonds glittered from her tiara and from the necklace she was wearing. The woman had looked at Shannon for only a moment. Then she turned her back on Shannon in an obvious snub and conversed with the elderly man seated beside her. Shannon wondered why she agreed to come at all.

All at once she sensed that someone had taken the vacant chair beside her. Shannon prayed it was Ian. She turned, and her smile fell away. Etienne Gabeau stared at her.

"Miss Aimee," he said with a heavy French accent. "It is good to see you again. You look lovely tonight."

You look lovely tonight? Shannon blinked. *That was what the earl just said.* And why hadn't she heard the Frenchman when he sat down? He must be as quiet as a kitchen cat about to pounce on an unsuspecting mouse. She had a strange feeling that for tonight, she was the mouse.

He glanced at her torso and smiled in a way she didn't like.

She blushed and reached for her glass. She took a sip of water and tried to pretend it never happened.

Impeccably dressed in a dark suit and a uniquely knotted dark tie, Monsieur Gabeau's air of sophistication and French accent would prob-ably impress any woman despite the obvious limp, but not Shannon. When they first met, he reminded her of her French father, but no more. His disguises were internal and easy to identify now.

She wanted to believe that she'd imagined his ungentlemanly ways and that he was all he claimed to be. Deep down she knew the man was a snake.

Ian might be wrong about the earl. But he was right about the Monsieur.

A waiter in black clothing appeared at her left and offered her a serving of pear slices and bits of apple cut in squares. She scooped up a small serving with a silver spoon and laid it on her plate.

"I like your friend, Mr. Ian Colquhoun." The Frenchman smiled and took a bite of apple. "I understand you both enjoyed the use of my library."

"Yes, thank you."

Shannon put down her fork. Why had Ian stayed with this horrible man—why had she?

Still, Monsieur Gabeau was generous enough to take Ian in until the vicar returned. She could at least show him proper respect for that kindness by keeping up her end of the conversation until the dinner ended.

She forced another smile.

"It was kind of you to invite Mr. Colquhoun to stay in your home until the vicar returned. I understand he is back at his cottage, and Mr. Colquhoun is living with him now."

"Unfortunately. I had hoped Mr. Colquhoun would stay on after the vicar returned. But that was not to be. I would have liked for you to stay on at my estate as well, Miss Aimee."

"What?" She couldn't believe what she'd just heard.

Gabeau laughed softly. "I was joking, of course. I am glad the vicar returned and that you are living at Gatehaven again. I only meant that I enjoyed Mr. Colquhoun's company while he was living with me, and I enjoyed your visit as well. It is lonely living alone in such a large house. It was nice that I had someone to talk to—while it lasted. Have you known him long?"

"Ian Colquhoun is my oldest and dearest friend." She stabbed a slice of pear with her fork. "We grew up together, and Ian is my brother's friend, too."

"Forgive me for staring, Miss Aimee, but you remind me of someone—someone I knew long ago," he said with deep emotion.

"You are talking about the woman in the portrait, are you not?"

"Yes. Old memories flood my mind as I look into your beautiful green eyes."

The Frenchman looked as if he might weep at any moment, and Shannon empathized with his apparent loss. At the same time, he shouldn't have complimented the color of her eyes or said that they were beautiful. She and Gabeau were hardly more than strangers, after all.

"Forgive me. I have displeased you," he said. "I can tell by the look on your face that I have."

He looked so repentant she had to accept his apology even if it wasn't sincere.

"But you look so much like her," he went on. "You saw the portrait at my home. So you know my words are true. Would you like to see the portrait again someday?"

Shannon nodded. "Yes."

It was a lie, of course. She had no wish to see a portrait of the Frenchman's lost love—or whoever she was. But she thought it seemed polite to say that she did. Manners were all-important at an event like this.

"Maybe some day Mr. Colquhoun could drive you out to my estate for another visit," Monsieur Gabeau said. "You and your chaperone, of course. Would you agree to that, Miss Aimee?"

"Perhaps. We must wait and see."

⊹————⊹————⊹

The dinner ended, and the women went into the green room while the men drank whatever such men drank. Shannon had seen and heard enough and wanted to go up to her room. However, she sat down beside Miss Foster and forced a smile. She was getting good at producing smiles at will without giving it a thought. All at once all the women were staring at her. She would have crawled under her chair if that had been an option.

Lady Catherine glared at her. "I understand you met my son in Scotland, Miss Aimee. But I still do not understand why you came to England. I first thought you came to find employment. If not, would you mind explaining why you did come? And if you *are* seeking employment, I cannot see why the earl invited you to our table tonight."

"The earl—" She cleared her throat. "The earl invited me to come to Gatehaven as his guest." Shannon sent Miss Foster a "help me" look. "Is that not true, Miss Foster?"

"The earl hired me to serve as Miss Aimee's chaperone during her stay in England."

"Humph." Lady Catherine shook her head and shrugged. "Chaperone indeed. Since when does a common house maid need a chaperone?"

Shannon bit her lower lip to keep from saying what she really thought and perhaps sounding disrespectful. She hadn't planned to tell the earl's family why she really came to England. She'd wanted them to hear it from the earl. Now she had no choice but to tell the truth.

"I am not a housemaid, Lady Catherine." Shannon lifted her head as if she wore a tiara that outshined all the others. "The earl has asked me to be his wife, and I accepted. I came to Gatehaven to meet his family."

"Wife?" Lady Catherine threw up her hands. "Are you insane? My son is an earl." Her blue eyes bulged as if they were in danger of popping out of her head.

Shannon gripped the arms of her chair and glanced at the earl's grand-mother. Her head shook vigorously, and she had leaned forward to such an extent that her chair tipped forward. Miss Foster jumped up as if to keep the older woman from falling to the floor.

Lady Catherine stood, shaking her forefinger at Shannon. "You are a willful young opportunist, and a wicked one at that. You have no connections—none that I know of. And you are a silly girl, indeed, if you think an earl would marry the likes of you.

"You are no longer welcome in my home, Miss Aimee," Lady Catherine shouted. "Tomorrow, my driver will return you to your home in Scotland without delay." She nodded to Shannon's chaperone. "Miss Foster will serve as your chaperone during the trip, if she chooses to do so. If not, you must make it home without one." Lady Catherine pointed to the door that led into the hallway. "Leave me now, miss. And it is my hope that I will never see you again."

CHAPTER TWENTY

S HANNON'S HEART FELT so heavy inside her chest that she was sure
it weighed a ton. She was insulted in a vicious and unmerciful way
by the earl's mother and grandmother. Did the earl know? Did he
care?

Her throat tightened. The muscles around her mouth contracted as
well. If the floor under her feet had suddenly opened and she'd tumbled
down, down—to her former room in the basement—she wouldn't have
cared. At least in the maid's quarters, she wouldn't have to look at the
haughty, hate-filled expressions on the women's faces.

She gazed at her chaperone, hoping the woman would give her some
sign that she still supported her. Miss Foster sent Shannon a cold glance
and looked away.

Shannon stood. Despite everything that was said, she straightened her
back and lifted her chin a notch. "I don't have to listen to this. If you will
excuse me?" She peered at the earl's mother and his grandmother for a
moment, and then she bobbed her head, forcing her face not to reveal the
pain and humiliation she felt. At last, she left the room.

She raced down the dark corridor with no destination in mind. In
the entry hall, she paused in front of the up stairway she saw on the day
she arrived. She wanted to go down to the basement kitchen and talk to
Millie. The young maid had been kind to Shannon. But Miss Foster had
said that Millie no longer worked as a maid at Gatehaven.

If she went up to her room on the second floor and stayed the night,
she would be shipped back to Scotland in the morning without getting

to tell Ian good-bye, and she needed to see him. She'd never missed Ian more.

What should she do? Papa would say she should pray. Shannon put the palms of her hands together, pressing her forefingers against her lips, and closed her eyes.

She prayed for strength and for guidance, and then she thanked God for hearing her prayer.

I will go up to my room now, she thought. *I will gather a few of my things and leave Gatehaven forever.*

She tiptoed up the stairs.

At the first landing, she noticed several lighted candles in metal bowls with handles. She grabbed the handle of the first one and continued on, praying again as she went. The candle's weak light flickered as she moved. She hoped it wouldn't go out completely.

Three hallways intersected at the head of the stairs. Gatehaven was so huge that for an instant, she couldn't recall which one to take. Then she remembered.

Miss Foster had said that the hall to the right led to the earl's private quarters. The one to the left led to the rooms occupied by the earl's mother and grandmother. To get to her room, she must go straight ahead, walk a short distance, and take the hallway to her left.

Before moving on, Shannon glanced toward the earl's rooms—perhaps secretly hoping to see him one last time. A wide hall seemed to pull her toward it. The walls were made of stone and painted white. Red chair rails the color of blood were nailed, end-to-end, to the walls on both sides of the corridor and at the end of it as well. The rails were placed about three feet from the floor, forming a thin line. Each board looked to be about five inches wide.

About twelve feet from where she stood, the red boards stretched across the corridor from one side of the hall to the other like a kind of barrier; she dared not cross it. A shiver shot down her. Clearly, a kind of red line blocked entry to the earl's bedchamber, a fence that shouldn't be there; and yet, it was.

Was this the red gate the earl and Miss Foster mentioned—the one that gave Gatehaven its name? As her father would say, she needed to pray.

Shannon blinked and looked again. The red barrier had disappeared as if it had never been there. She could still see the red line, but it was nailed to the back wall as it should be and not only a few feet from where she stood.

My eyes deceived me, she thought. *Perhaps my mind as well.*

Did witchcraft and other evil practices have a hand in this? She looked away.

With God's help, she'd faced the red gate and conquered it. She wouldn't go down that hall no matter how much she wanted to see the earl. She would lift her head and move forward.

Still, a feeling of foreboding swept over her as she continued down the dark center hall—again on tiptoes. Before she reached the first turn, she heard footsteps. Shannon pressed her body as close to the wall as she could get it, blew out the candle, and sidestepped to the first turn. Should she take a look around the corner? Or walk on to her room as if she had nothing to fear?

I am hated here and have plenty to fear. But God is with me

Slowly, she peeped around the corner. Shannon gasped. In the dim light coming from lamps stationed at intervals along the walls of the hallway, she swallowed a second gasp.

Men of all ages were lined up in front of a long table that had been set up in the hallway. Dark pieces of cloth were stacked in short piles on the table. Each man grabbed a cloth and walked on. Shannon assumed the men were gathering clean bedding for their rooms.

The last man in line opened his cloth, wrapped it around his shoulders and stuck his arms in the armholes. Shannon held her breath in shocked amazement. Clearly his cloth was a robe, and he pulled the hood down—over his head. At last, he fell in line behind the others.

When the robed men were out of sight, Shannon crept forward. Several grayish robes in neat stacks were left on the table. If she wore one of them, she might be less conspicuous as she continued to her room. Shannon looked both ways down the hall but didn't see anybody. She grabbed a robe and put it on.

Shannon draped the hood over her head, pushing the hood forward as she'd seen the men wear their robes. Looking down, she couldn't see much in the dim light. She was barely able to see the floor under her feet.

The robe was much too long for her and spread out around her feet. A monk or whoever the men were wouldn't hold up the shirt of a robe as a woman might do. She had no choice but to take her chances that she wouldn't trip and move on.

In the hallway in front of her bedroom, she heard a squeaking sound—like someone had opened a door. She whirled around. Something like a rope coiled around her neck, and she reached up in order to pull it off. The loop grew tighter—and tighter. She mouthed the word *help*, but no sound came.

Someone jerked the rope. Shannon coughed.

Though still on her feet, she felt her body being pulled backward. Like a dog on a leash, she had no choice but to take a step back and then another and another.

"Who are you?" a female voice said. "And why is the robe too long for you?"

Shannon tried to loosen the rope so she could answer. It wouldn't budge. But she kept her fingers between the rope and her skin. It felt better that way.

"If I loosen the rope, will you promise not to scream?" the woman said.

Shannon nodded.

A hand touched hers. "Let go of the rope."

Shannon did as she was told. The rope loosened. She breathed in and out deeply. Then she coughed. Someone pulled the robe from her shoulders. She felt it slip to the floor in a pool of rough material. A candle in a metal cup was poked near her face.

"Why, you're a girl," the woman said. "And you look no older than me. Who are you?"

Shannon swallowed. "I—" She coughed again. "I am. I am Miss Sh— Miss Shannon Aimee."

"I thought as much. Maude told us about you one day when she brought us our trays." The woman moved the candle from Shannon's face, placing it near her own. "I mean brought me my tray."

Shannon's jaw hung loose in astonishment. The woman with the candle was probably the young woman with black hair she'd seen standing at a window on the top floor.

"Who are you?" Shannon asked.

"My name is Calleen Winters, it is. Call me Cally."

"But why were you standing at the window? I saw you the day I arrived."

"I saw you, too," the young woman said. "We all did. Follow me, and I'll answer all your questions."

The young woman led the way into a large bedchamber. Light streamed through windows that lined the back wall. Shannon realized that she was in the bedroom across the hall from hers—the one she visited previously with Ian. But something was different. Something had been added since she came in the first time.

The moon highlighted a china vase with a dragon's face etched on it. The dragon's red eyes seemed to watch her as she followed Cally to the French doors. Shannon's skin prickled, and the roots of her hair did, too.

"We can talk out on the porch," Cally said. "It will be cooler there. But we must talk in whispers—can't let them find us here."

Shannon nodded. "I understand. But who are 'them'? The ones in the gray robes?

"Yes. They are very evil. And they will be looking for me—for us."

They sat side by side on the same bench she shared with Ian. Shannon ran her fingertips over a carving on the arm of the bench, wondering if there were more carvings on the back of the bench. If so, did those carving depict two dragons facing each other? And did they have evil-looking eyes?

Shannon had hoped Cally would say more immediately—explain why she was standing at the window on the day Shannon arrived and why she put the rope around her neck. She thought she knew about the rope. Cally might have thought she was one of those strange robed men she called evil. But there were other questions Shannon wanted answered.

At last, Shannon said, "Why were you standing at the window on the day I arrived? I told the earl I saw you, and he said I was imagining things."

"He would say that, he would," Cally said. "I wasn't supposed to be standing at windows where folks can see the likes of me. The girls living on the top floor were told not to let people know we lived at Gatehaven, much less see us standing at windows."

"Are you saying that other girls are up there on that top floor?" Shannon asked.

"I am saying there *were* other girls up there. I was the last, I am."

"What happened to the others?"

Cally shrugged. "I do not know." She hesitated. "I can only guess."

Shannon tensed. "Please, guess. I have to know."

"Very well. But I must warn you. What I am about to say might make you cry—to say the least."

"What do you mean?"

"We are living in an evil place where witches in gray robes—"

"Witches? I don't believe in witches. I don't believe they exist."

"Witches do not want you to believe they exist, my friend. But they do. I think the girls here were used in rituals."

"What kind of rituals?" Shannon asked.

"I do not know, miss. But I know they could only come from the pit of hell. That is what I think—if you care to know."

"What happens in these—these services?" Shannon asked.

Cally shook her head, and then she shrugged. "I cannot say for sure. All I know is that when the service ends, the girls never return to the big room we were kept in. I think they are dead."

The hairs on the back of Shannon's head bristled again. "Murdered?"

"Yes. I was to be next."

"How can you know that?"

"I was the only one left. You see, the girls were taken one-by-one, and always on the night the men put on the gray robes."

Shannon thought of the human bone Ian finally told her he found. Could it be that—? She didn't want to think that the bone was the remains of one of the girls, and she certainly didn't want to mention it to Cally.

"Were these girls your friends?" Shannon asked.

Cally nodded. "There were only three of us on the day you got here. But as I said, I am the only one left. That is why I must escape. It was a miracle that I managed to get this far."

"Oh, Cally! I am *so* glad you did. My father says that God has a hand in all true miracles. But I refused to believe in miracles. Now, I am beginning to."

"I wager when you saw the men in robes tonight you were afraid," Cally said. "Otherwise, you would never have put on that robe."

"It was the only disguise I could think of."

"I can see why you thought putting on a robe was a good idea," Cally said. "But they would have known you weren't one of them as soon as they saw you. They know their own." She paused. "I would enjoy talking with you longer, but we haven't got much time. When the robed men realize I am not in my room on the top floor, they will come looking for me. If we are going to escape from Gatehaven, we must do it now. Do you have any ideas?"

"I was planning to leave anyway. I know of a side entrance on the first floor near the stairway. If we leave that way, we might have a chance."

"Yes," Cally said with excitement. "Let us go at once."

Shannon glanced toward the door leading to the hallway. "I would like to go to my room first. I want to gather a few of my belongings before we leave."

Cally frowned. "Hurry then. As I said, the hooded ones are meeting tonight. And when they send for me and do not find me, they will come looking for me and probably for you as well."

Shannon hurried out the door, stepping over the robe in a heap on the hall floor. "I will not be long," she said over her shoulder. She crossed to her own room on the other side of the hall.

"Miss Aimee."

Shannon stopped before opening the door latch. Nobody said her name quite like the earl did.

"I have missed you, my love." He spread out his arms as if inviting her to step into his embrace.

Shannon melted despite her misgivings. *He still loves me*, she thought.

The earl took her in his arms and held her close. "My poor dear girl. My mother told me what she said to you, and I am so sorry. How can I ever make it up to you?" He kissed her on the forehead. "Do not worry, my love. You will not be sent home. But I will have to move you to another room until I can straighten things out. Do you agree with that?"

"Are you still planning to marry me?" she asked.

"Of course."

For the first time since they left Scotland, the earl sounded like the young man she met and fell in love with, and she loved being in his embrace and feeling cherished again.

"Oh, my lord," she said tenderly. "I knew you would never betray me."

"Never. You must push that thought far from your mind." He touched her chin gently and pulled it closer to his face.

Shannon knew he was going to kiss her. She closed her eyes in anticipation.

Bam.

Shannon opened her eyes. Someone must have hit the earl over the head from behind. He lay on the floor. Bits of white china were all around him.

"My love." Shannon reached out with her arms. "Someone has harmed you."

"I did it." Cally stepped into the light. "I hit him with the china vase."

"Why?"

A cold hardness like metal darts shot from Cally's dark eyes. "He deserved it."

"Deserved it?" Shannon couldn't believe Cally would say such a thing. "How dreadful." Shannon squatted down and wiped away a piece of the shattered china that had landed on the earl's forehead. "You could have killed him."

"He planned to kill me."

"You are wrong about the earl. He would never do such a thing. But his mother hates me. She banished me from Gatehaven. She will think I did this."

"Another reason to leave." Cally grabbed Shannon's arm as if to pull her to her feet.

"But the earl is in need of a physician. We cannot just leave him here."

"They will find him soon enough."

The muscles around Shannon's mouth firmed, and her lips turned down. "But I love him."

"I loved him, too, once. You will get over him."

Shannon glanced toward the door of her room. "I must gather my belongings."

"Forget them." Cally pulled Shannon forward. "Run for the stairs—while we still can!"

CHAPTER TWENTY-ONE

THEY HAD ALMOST reached the down stairwell when Shannon heard rapid footsteps on the wooden floor. She paused. Cally moved ahead of her.

Shannon looked back. "Someone is coming."

"Do not look back," Cally instructed. "Keep going."

Shannon slipped in behind Cally. They headed down the flight of stairs.

"When we get to the first floor," Shannon whispered, "be very quiet. People will be running to and fro there. Someone might see us."

Cally nodded but didn't say anything. But when she'd almost reached the bottom of the stairs, Cally stopped and glanced back at Shannon as if to say, *what must I do now?*

"There is a door directly across the hall from the landing at the bottom of the stairs." Shannon pointed to a paneled door that wasn't completely closed. "See it?"

"Of course."

"If we must, we could hide in there. It's a small room where linen cloths and bedclothes are kept. I know because the door was open on the day I climbed these stairs the first time."

"I do not think we should hide," Cally replied. "We must leave this place. We should keep going and hurry."

Shannon heard footsteps. "In the cloth room," she insisted, "quickly."

Cally didn't move as soon as Shannon expected. Shannon bumped into the back of her. The footfalls were growing louder.

"Go on in," Shannon demanded, "now."

Cally opened the door wider than she needed to. Shannon pushed against her back, and Cally went inside. Shannon followed after her and attempted to close the door.

"Do not close it all the way," Cally whispered.

"Why not?" Puzzled, Shannon left the door open a crack, just as she'd found it. "They might hear us in here if we don't close the door all the way, you know." Shannon touched Cally's shoulder and found that she was trembling. "Why, you are shaking! What is wrong?"

"I cannot—I cannot abide the dark."

"We will be all right in here, Cally. Now move against the back wall and squat down," Shannon whispered. "We are less likely to be seen if someone opens the door." Shannon took Cally's quivering hand and half dragged her to the back wall of the small room.

The footsteps were just outside the door now. Shannon tensed.

"Put your—put your hands over your mouth," Cally whispered softly. "That way, if you want to scream, you can't."

Shannon nodded, hoping Cally took her own advice.

The footsteps moved on down the hall. Shannon hoped that meant she or he would soon be far away. The footsteps stopped abruptly.

What could that mean?

The footsteps became louder again as if someone was returning to the door. Shannon held her breath and hoped Cally was doing the same. All at once the door flung open. Shannon grabbed Cally around the shoulders, praying she wouldn't scream.

A stout woman in a maid's cap and apron stood in the doorway with the light streaming in from the hall behind her. She pulled a cloth from the stack on the shelf to her left, and the entire stack of folded material fell in a heap on the floor.

The woman cursed under her breath.

Shannon held her breath. But Cally stopped shaking. She appeared to relax slightly. Perhaps with the door opened all the way, she didn't feel as threatened by the closeness of the dark room as she had earlier.

The maid took longer to find the cloths than Shannon would have expected. During that brief time while the door was open wide, she glanced at her surroundings. A strange bump on the wall about halfway up reminded her of a small hand latch that might be found on a door. It didn't really look like a door latch. However she was fascinated with the possibility that it might actually be one. Later when the time was right, she intended to investigate that possibility to the fullest.

The maid finished folding and restacking the cloths. She pressed the remaining cloth to her breast and closed the door all the way. Shannon held her breath, praying she wouldn't lock it.

Cally started trembling again—vigorously this time. Her breathing came in gasps.

Shannon touched her shoulder. "What can I do to help?"

Cally hesitated. "Nothing. I must close my eyes and try to sleep. That is the only thing that might help."

Cally had been so brave—even bold—upstairs when she confronted the earl. Now she seemed to have withdrawn into her inner self—afraid of every dark corner—every shadow.

Something must have happened that caused Cally to have such a strong reaction to dark places. But this was not the time to question her about it. All Shannon could do now was hope that after a while Cally would stop shaking.

At last, Cally must have gone to sleep. At least she stopped shaking. Her breathing became less labored. But Shannon was unable to sleep. Each time she felt she might drift off, she heard footfalls again.

All at once Shannon heard loud voices and the sound of shuffling feet.

"The earl was injured," someone shouted. "We need to search the house!"

Shannon shook Cally gently. "Wake up! We need to get out of here."

Cally jerked. "What happened?"

"They must have found the earl."

"What can we do?"

"Sit there a minute. I want to check on something."

Shannon stood. She began to feel around for the bump she saw earlier.

"Wh—What are you doing?" Cally whispered.

"Looking for another way out of here." Shannon found the bump in the darkness. "Maybe I found one."

"What do you mean?"

"I will let you know when I know." She pulled on the bump and heard a slight squeak.

"What was that sound? What did you find?"

"A door. The sound came from the door. Give me your hand and follow me." Shannon reached for Cally's hand in the darkness.

Cally's hand trembled. "I am not going in. It is dark in there."

"It is also dark in here. But if we stay, someone will eventually open the door and find us. But if we go in there, it is possible that nobody will."

Shannon tugged on Cally's hands, but she refused to move. "Come on. We must go."

"I cannot."

"You *must*, Cally."

"No, you go. I want to sit down and close my eyes again."

"Close your eyes, if you want to. But we have to get out of here—now. They could open that door at any moment."

Cally hesitated before saying more. "What do you want me to do?"

"Put your hands on my shoulders. Walk directly behind me. And do not make a sound. I cannot tell how high the door is. So duck just to be safe."

Shannon felt Cally's shaky hands on her shoulders. Carefully, she leaned forward and stepped inside. She hoped they weren't walking into a trap and took another step.

"Are you through the door?" Shannon asked.

"I am not sure."

"I do not know how high the ceiling is," Shannon explained, "but it is time to find out. Stand up straight, and watch your head."

Shannon stretched to her full five feet and four inches. She hadn't bumped her head.

"Stay exactly where you are, Cally. I am going to go back and close that door."

"Please do not leave me here in the dark alone," Cally protested.

"I will only be gone a minute."

Shannon felt around in the darkness in hopes of finding a wall of some kind. She took a step. A board squeaked. She reached out and felt something hard. Her fingers explored rough stones, placed side by side along the right wall. Shannon inched to the door and finally found the open space they must have walked through earlier. She reached out for the door and found it. However, finding the bump, if there was one, on her side of the door might not be easy in total darkness. She couldn't pull the door closed all the way without something to hold on to, and there didn't appear to be a knob of any kind on their side of the door.

No matter.

She would leave it open a crack, and they would move on.

"I think I found something." Cally's voice sounded stronger somehow. "A railing. Yes, I feel a railing."

"Are there steps going down?" Shannon asked.

"Give me a moment, and I will see." Cally grew silent. "Yes, there are steps going down—one, two. Two steps and then a hallway."

"What a miracle," Shannon said. "My father would say that the Lord is leading us home. I am beginning to believe it."

"This time," Cally said, "you put your hands on my shoulders, Shannon."

"Does this mean that you are not afraid of the dark anymore?"

"It means that I am about to escape from Gatehaven with my eyes wide open."

The hall ended at yet another strange door. They didn't hear anything. Still, Shannon wondered if they should open it. Or what they might find if they did.

Shannon moved ahead of Cally and pressed her shoulder against the door. It opened, and a weak light filled the crack between the door and the door's frame. Best of all, she heard no squeak or any other sound.

"I have my eyes closed again," Cally whispered. "What do you see?"

"I thought you said you were keeping them open. No matter. Anyway, I see light."

"Light," Cally said aloud.

"Shush," Shannon warned. "We must speak in whispers."

Shannon went through the door and found herself in a long hall. Lighted candles on wooden stands were attached to the walls at intervals. She looked to her left and to her right but didn't see anybody.

"Come on out," Shannon said. "I think I know where we are."

"Then tell me. Where are we?"

"In the hall that leads to the door. Take your shoes off, and follow me. If I am correct, we should soon be out of Gatehaven forever."

They removed their shoes and tiptoed to the very end of the hall where the door was located. A candle on a stand was nailed over the door as if to light their way.

Shannon reached for the latch. The door wouldn't budge. "It is locked," Shannon said. "The door is locked."

"What can we do?"

"Find the key." Shannon got down on her hands and knees and felt around on the floor. "Since a key is hidden on the other side of the door, perhaps there is one on this side, too."

Noises came from the up stairway. "Come on," someone shouted. "Maybe they are below stairs."

Shannon heard footsteps, a lot of them, on the stairway nearby. Frantic, she searched for the key in earnest but was unable to find it.

Maybe we should go back and hide where we were earlier again.

Cally put something hard and cold in her hand. "Is this the key?" she whispered.

"Yes. It must be. Thank you." Shannon put the key in the lock and turned the latch. The door opened without so much as a tiny squeak. "Come on, and hurry."

They raced out. Cool fresh air welcomed them.

"You go on," Shannon instructed. "I must lock the door."

"I will wait for you," Cally said. "But for you, I would still be locked inside."

Shannon locked the door. As soon as she put the key under the mat, she heard voices—perhaps as close as the other side of the solid wooden door.

She started running.

Shannon and Cally raced to the shadows of the trees and kept running. Shannon was panting by the time she decided it would be all right to stop. Still panting, she found a log and sat down on it. Cally sat down beside her.

"Why are you so afraid of the dark?" Shannon blurted out without thinking.

Cally didn't reply.

In hindsight, Shannon knew she shouldn't have been so blunt. "Never mind," she said. "I had no right to ask."

"Yes, you have the right to ask, you do. You earned it. And sometime soon I will tell you everything you want to know. But for now, I want to just sit here and get to know what it is like to be truly free again."

She must have been a prisoner on the fourth floor, Shannon thought. *Maybe they also locked her in a dark room.*

But she didn't actually share any of those thoughts verbally.

The first glow of morning would soon be rising in the east, and if they hoped to reach the vicar's cottage before daybreak, they would need to start out again.

"Soon those at Gatehaven will stop looking for us inside," Shannon explained. "They will search for us on the grounds around the mansion and beyond. I have a childhood friend by the name of Ian Colquhoun who is staying at a vicar's cottage nearby. I have never visited the cottage. I know it will be difficult to find in the dark. But we have to try." Shannon stood. "If you have rested enough, I guess we should go now."

"Yes," Cally said. "Your friend sounds like the perfect one to help us."

"Then let us set out for the vicar's cottage at once.

+ —+— +

At dawn, Ian set out for Gatehaven with the vicar's dog at his heels. He didn't know what happened at the dinner party in the main dining room on the previous night or whether Shannon was in even more danger. However, he knew the Frenchman attended that dinner, and that alone put her in peril. He hoped to persuade Shannon to change her mind and meet with her brother in the hope that Peter could convince her to leave Gatehaven this very day, if possible.

Buster barked and ran ahead. The dog seemed especially frisky. Perhaps the cool morning air contributed to the animal's sense of excitement. Ian would have to run to catch up with him.

"Slow down, boy," Ian urged. "The morning is young, and we are not in great haste."

Buster raced on, circled Ian a few times, and ran ahead again.

Ian laughed, glad that the vicar's dog seemed to enjoy their outing. But his thoughts kept returning to Shannon. He sensed that she might be in greater danger than ever before.

Ian sat down on a log while Buster dug a hole in the damp ground. It must have rained during the night, making the soil ripe for exploration. He shook his head. Buster sure did like digging for bones.

Ian thought of the bone Buster had found in those very woods—a human bone, according to the physician. He got up and moved toward the animal. Maybe he should check to see what Buster found so interesting.

Ian leaned forward. He saw something white in the hole but couldn't tell what it was.

"Find yourself another bone, boy?"

More soil was pushed aside. Ian thought he saw two bones—if that was what they were.

"Stand back, boy. And let me have a try."

The dog growled, showing his fangs.

Ian kept a leather choker around the dog's neck now when they went walking in the woods. He pulled out a coil of rope attached to his belt and unwound it. A small hook was fashioned at one end. He held the coil of rope in his right hand. Quickly, he put it behind him and moved slowly toward Buster.

The dog's lips still curved in a snarl. Ian thought the animal looked as if he was ready to pounce at any moment—especially if his precious bone was threatened. Ian carried a bit of dried meat in the pouch he'd slung over her shoulder. He removed the meat and offered it to the dog.

"Here, boy. I have something for you."

Ian crept closer, forcing his voice to sound as soft and non-threatening as possible. This time, he didn't want Buster to jump for the meat, nor did he want to throw it near the dog. Buster would eat the meat from his hand or not at all.

He knelt down. The meat lay temptingly across his open palm. Ian inched closer.

"Want it, boy?" His voice sounded softer still. "Well, if you do, you are going to have to eat it out of my hand."

The animal's ears perked up, and he wagged his tail. He barked and leaped toward him playfully.

Normally, Ian would have petted the animal's head, but his right hand was occupied with the rope. "Good boy."

While Buster gobbled a bite of the meat, Ian's fingers found the hook at the end of the rope. He slowly brought his right hand around and fastened the hook to the leather collar around the animal's throat. It was done so slowly and carefully, Buster didn't appear to notice that he was captured.

Buster ate the last of the meat and licked Ian's hand. Ian returned the favor by patting Buster on the head.

"I am going to have to tie you up for a while, boy, and then we will go walking in the woods some more."

Ian tied Buster to a branch of the nearest tree. Then he went back to the hole and started digging. He didn't have a shovel. But he found a stick that worked almost as well in moving around damp soil. On his hands and knees, he laid the stick beside him and starting digging with eager fingers.

The bone felt soft to the touch—softer than a bone should. Why? Frantic, he dug faster. Ian stiffened. It wasn't a bone at all. It was a partly decomposed human hand.

The word *murder* screamed in his ears.

CHAPTER TWENTY-TWO

IAN REMOVED MORE of the dirt from the grave. A shoulder encased in purple material stared back at him. It could only belong to a woman.

He was digging out double handfuls of dirt and faster than he would ever have thought possible. He saw long strands of gold-colored hair mixed with dirt. Ian trembled. He'd uncovered a woman's head. A rope was still tied around her neck.

Ian froze. He'd seen enough.

He scrambled to pour dirt back on the decomposed body. Buster howled to be loosened from the prison of the tree, but Ian tried not to notice. Why was it taking longer to fill the hole than it had to uncover the body?

At last he finished.

It wasn't the best job he had ever done at covering a hole with dirt, but it would have to do. He wanted to return Buster to his pen and report what he believed was a crime of murder.

He took his knife and marked an M on the tree where he'd tied Buster. If he'd had time to consider, he might have come up with a more unique marking. But he was in a hurry. He wanted to be away from the wretched place as soon as possible.

Ian untied the dog from the tree but didn't remove the leash. He wasn't in the mood for chasing after Buster. The leash would keep that from happening.

"Come on, boy. Let's go home."

He wouldn't be paying Shannon a visit at Gatehaven now. He would return Buster to his pen, tell the vicar what he knew and set out for the village. Doctor Grimes would know what to do. Ian knew better than to tell Etienne Gabeau or the earl what he'd found.

The physician once told him that he knew a man in London that he could trust, and that if Ian ever found any clear evidence of a possible murder, he would gladly contact his friend in London and ask him to take care of the matter. He believed that time had finally come.

Shannon and Cally had been walking in the forest that surrounded Gatehaven for some time. Now that day replaced the darkness, Shannon realized they were lost.

"I am not familiar with these woods, Cally. I have not a guess where the vicar's cottage might be located."

"Look!" Cally pointed to a puff of smoke above the line of trees. "Smoke. Could it be coming from the chimney of a house?"

"Yes, it could. Let us find out for ourselves. Hurry."

The ground under their feet had been damp but not muddy. All at once, walking became difficult. Muddy soil stuck to the bottoms of Shannon's shoes, and she was forced to go around puddles of water. Obviously, it had rained during the night—probably before they left the mansion.

The birth of the morning turned the sky overhead to gold. They raced on to the cottage in the distance. But would Ian be waiting there?

"That must be the place I was telling you about," Shannon said. "Hurry, we are almost there."

Shannon hated to knock on the door at such an early hour and looking as she did.

"Let us remove our shoes and leave them by the stoop before I knock at the door," Shannon suggested. "We would not want to bring mud into the vicar's cottage."

Cally nodded. "We certainly would not."

The two young women took off their shoes, lined them up beside the stoop, and Shannon reached for the heavy metal knock-hammer on a chain and that was attached to the doorframe. She gripped the hammer and hit the door with it. When nobody came to the door, she hit it again.

"I am coming," a female voice said from the other side of the door.

Someone opened the door but only a crack. "What do you want at such an early hour?" the woman said.

"I am looking for the vicar's cottage," Shannon said. "Am I in the right place?"

"Miss Aimee." Millie opened the door all the way. "What a blessing to see ya again. Welcome to me home. I mean our home."

"Millie? It is good to see you, too. But what are you doing here?"

Millie chuckled softly. "I live here. And as you can see, this be not the vicar's cottage. It belongs to me uncle. But please come inside and bring your friend with ya."

Shannon introduced Cally to Millie, and then they sat on a comfortable settee while Millie served them cups of hot tea and bread with marmalade.

"It has been a long time since I've had marmalade, I wager," Cally said. "It tastes like fresh fruit. Thank you for your kindness."

"Yes, Millie," Shannon put in. "Thank you."

Shannon explained their predicament without being too specific. She knew Millie no longer worked as a maid at Gatehaven, but she didn't really know how Millie felt about the earl or Monsieur Gabeau and didn't want to put Millie and her uncle in danger. Perhaps they should go as soon as they finished their tea and cakes.

"This cake is wonderful." Cally smiled. "As I said, it has been a long time since I ate anything this good, it has."

Shannon tensed, trying to hold in a secret frown. She and Cally still hadn't discussed what went on at Gatehaven on the top floor, but clearly, food that made Cally smile was never on the menu.

"It makes me happy to hear your kind words about me cakes," Millie said, "and I wish ya both could stay here with us forever. But Uncle is at work now. And after hearing what ya told me, I think our cottage and the vicar's would be the first places the earl and the Frenchman would go lookin' for you."

"We should go," Shannon said.

"No. You must stay. Me uncle rode his horse to Monsieur Gabeau's estate early this mornin'," Millie went on. "He works for Monsieur Gabeau as his carriage driver. I do not know how long Uncle will be away from the house. He could return in time for dinner. Or he could stay away until late this night. But when the Monsieur has no need of his services, he returns home within the hour.

"My bonnie father and me uncle be born in Scotland," Millie continued. "McGregors all, we are. And my uncle took me in after me parents died. Miss Aimee said that she hoped to find her friend, Ian Colquhoun, and my uncle mentioned this man. He also mentioned you, Miss Aimee. I have no hard feeling against those from other clans—not in the least. But me uncle hates all Colquhouns, especially Ian Colquhoun. He might have a poor regard for you as well, Miss Aimee. He knows that you and Mr. Colquhoun be friends."

Shannon rose from her chair. "Cally and I really must leave this time." She motioned for Cally to stand as well. "I will not allow you to be put in low regard by your uncle on our behalf."

"Wait!" Millie gestured with the palms of both hands as if she wanted to halt. "I have a plan—a wee plan for your escape that might work."

Shannon shook her head. "That is out of the question. We cannot put you in still more danger."

"Sit back down and hear me plan. Then decide."

Shannon returned to her chair. Then Cally did.

"I think I know of another location where ya both might be safe." She smiled. "A fortnight ago, maybe less, my uncle and I found an injured young man in the woods." Her smile widened. "A very *handsome* young man."

Shannon and Cally laughed. Then Millie joined in.

"He'd hit his head on something. He suffered from the long sleep when we found him. One day he woke up. I think him most charming, and he spoke like a Frenchy. But he left me care sooner than he should have. I was told that a gentleman that sounds like him now works at The Boar and Tongue in the village of Fairs. If he be the young man I cared for, I would be delighted to have a reason to see him again."

"What is the young man's name?" Shannon said.

"William Spear. His name does not sound French, does it?"

Shannon shook her head. "It does not. I'm asking because I heard that my brother Peter Aimee followed me to England."

"So the young man I met cannot be your brother."

"No," Shannon agreed. "He cannot."

"Nevertheless," Millie continued, "we must set out for The Boar and Tongue at once. Uncle knew I needed to go to the village this morning to purchase flour from the mill, and he left his cart and his other horse behind. We shall prepare the horse and cart for travel and drive into the village. But we must be quiet. Wouldn't want to cause me uncle or anyone to become suspicious now."

———◆———

Shannon and Cally lay on the bed of the cart. Millie covered them with a large piece of tent material. Then Millie drove them to The Boar and Tongue where the young man she knew as William Spear now worked.

After hearing Millie go on and on about the handsome Mr. Spear with the French accent, Shannon thought Millie was half in love with the man. She was eager to see him face-to-face and learn if he was truly as strikingly good to look at as Millie said he was.

The cart stopped. Shannon felt a jerk. She didn't move and tried not to breathe. Perhaps they had arrived in the village of Fairs. Were they in front of the mill? Or perhaps The Boar and Tongue?

"Wait here, now, and do not move," Millie whispered. "I shall go inside the inn to find Mr. Spear. I will return when I can."

Peter Aimee was standing at a window on the first floor of The Boar and Tongue when Millie pulled her horse and cart to a stop some distance from the front door of the inn. She went around and straightened things in the back of the cart. Then she strode toward the inn's entry door.

His new boss, a man they called Brother Julian, had stepped out. Peter was expected to greet any new guests who came in. If only he could recall the name he'd used while staying at Millie's cottage.

He moved around to the back of the main desk and waited for the front door to open. He had thought Miss Millie McGregor had a fondness for him when he recovered from his fall at her cottage, and she was a kind and gentle person. He must not encourage that fondness in any way.

Millie opened the door, all smiles. "Oh, Mr. Spear. I was hoping to find you here."

Oh yes, he thought. *That was my name. William Spear.*

"It is good to see you, too, Miss McGregor. What brings you to The Boar and Tongue on this fine day?"

Her forehead wrinkled, and he thought she looked troubled all at once. She looked to her left and to her right as if she was surveying the entire inn.

"May we speak in private?" she asked.

"Of course." He nodded toward a table in the back of the eating area. "Follow me."

They sat at a small table near the back door of the establishment.

"Now, what would you like to talk about, miss?"

"Do ya promise not to repeat anything I will be sayin'?" she whispered.

He nodded. This sounded interesting.

"Do go on," he said.

Millie told him all that had transpired since the two young women knocked at her door earlier in the day.

"And who are these young women?" he said. "Do you know their names?"

"Aye. One be called Cally. The other—Miss Shannon Aimee. Perhaps you have heard of Miss Aimee. She came to Gatehaven as the earl's special guest some days ago."

Peter was so astonished he couldn't speak for a moment. "Did you say Miss *Shannon* Aimee?"

"Aye. Do you know her?"

"Indeed I do."

Peter had no choice but to tell Millie McGregor who he really was now, and he felt slightly embarrassed doing it. He didn't make a habit of telling lies. Now that he'd been caught, he had no choice but to admit it.

Peter leaned back in his chair, resting his hands on his knees, and shook his head. "I have a confession to make, Miss McGregor."

"Confession?"

He nodded and leaned forward in his chair. "I am not who I said I was."

"Then you lied to me Christian heart?"

"I am afraid so."

"But why?"

He took in a deep breath and released it slowly. "I have no excuse. You were kind to me. Yet I lied to you. Forgive me. You see, I didn't want anyone here to know my true identity. My real name is Peter Aimee, and Miss Shannon Aimee is my sister."

"Your sister?"

"Yes. Where is Shannon now?"

"In the back of me cart with the other girl. I came here today to ask for your help. We must hide them. They could be in great danger now."

"I realize that." Peter stood. "And we have no time to waste. We must bring them into the inn and hide them at once. Brother Julian could return at any moment."

Peter and Millie hurried out the entry door of The Boar and Tongue.

"Shannon will not be pleased to see me," Peter said. "It might be best if you did the explaining and most of the talking. I would rather not have a confrontation with my sister now. As I mentioned, Brother Julian could return at any moment, and I want Shannon and the other young woman safely hidden in the attic of this inn before he gets back."

Peter saw anger boiling in Shannon's eyes before anybody said a word.

"Peter," Shannon demanded. "What are doing here?"

He forced a halfhearted grin. "I will let Millie tell you." However, he hardly listened to Millie's explanation. He was too busy surveying the woods nearby for Brother Julian, a portly little man who claimed to once have been a French monk.

Shannon's facial expression had softened a little by the time Millie stopped talking. Still, she kept looking away each time Peter tried to make eye contact with her.

"I plan to hide both of you in the attic here at the inn," Peter said at last. "But you must promise to be very quiet. The attic's wooden floor is just above the ceiling on the second floor of The Boar and Tongue. When the inn's guests turn in for the night, they are likely to hear any sounds coming from above. They are also likely to complain to the innkeeper, Brother Julian, if they hear anything."

Shannon's nod had a defiant edge to it. "I understand," she said.

Peter thought that she was still angry. His conclusion was confirmed when she refused to look him in the eye.

＋——＋——＋

As Shannon followed Peter up the stairs to the attic, she glanced back at Millie and smiled.

"Thank you, Millie, for all you have done for Cally and me. I shall never forget you."

"Me either, miss," Cally said.

For Shannon, saying goodbye to Millie would not be easy because she knew she might never see her again. Millie planned to go to the mill and some other places after she left the inn as if nothing unusual happened that day. Peter had said he would ride to the vicar's cottage at once to inform Ian of Shannon's current location and tell him all that had happened since the dinner party on the previous night.

Peter and Millie spent a few moments in the attic, visiting with Shannon and Cally. As soon as they went below stairs, Shannon decided to search the attic for possible hiding places. If someone happened to hear them moving around in the attic, Shannon wanted to know exactly where they would hide.

The attic contained two big rooms with a wall and a door between them. They found no beds, but did find stacks of old quilts that would do well enough. Shannon remembered the secret door she found in the mansion that led to a hidden hallway. Perhaps she would search the walls in both attic rooms. Who can say what she might find?

She paused in front of the wall to the right of the stairway, pressing both hands directly to the rough wooden panels in hopes of finding a hidden door.

"What are you doing?" Cally whispered.

"Looking for another hidden door. We might need a place to hide."

"I will look as well."

After searching for almost an hour, Shannon felt a lump on the back wall of the second room behind some large wooden boxes. The room was some distance from the stairway; so if the lump was a door latch, the door couldn't be in a safer place.

Shannon pushed the lump. It inched to one side.

"Cally, come here." She opened the little door all the way. "I think I found a place to hide."

Shannon ducked under the short door and went into a dark and narrow crawl space that lined the back wall.

"Come on in, Cally," Shannon said.

Cally shook her head, and her shoulders were shaking.

"Please, Cally. I promise to leave the door open a crack."

Cally didn't move.

"If I leave the door all the way open, will you come inside?"

Cally nodded, but she was still shaking. She hesitated a moment and, leaning forward, she climbed inside.

Shannon held her knees in order to fit in the narrow space, and warm, cozy memories filled her mind. She remembered childhood picnics in Scotland where she sat on a blanket in just that way and listened as her father told of his childhood in France, and she remembered games she and Peter played as children—where hiding in dark places was commonplace.

She looked over at Cally, trembling in front of the opened door, and her heart went out to her. Cally's memories of small and dark places were nothing like her own. She longed to talk—find out why her new friend was so frightened. Perhaps it was time to just sit there and say nothing.

"If we just sit here with the little door open and try not to move, there would be no need to talk—unless you really want to do so," Shannon said. "Of course if we did talk, it must be in whispers. But whispers can be fun, if we make it a game."

"I understand why you want me in here, Miss Aimee." Cally's once strong voice sounded shaky and unsure. "But penned inside—penned inside a dark room is not a game I care to play."

"Maybe if you tell me why you feel as you do, it might make sitting here easier."

I said I would not try to get her to talk, Shannon thought, *and I have gone and done it.*

Cally didn't move or say a word.

"You do not have to tell me anything," Shannon said. "But we might need to hide again at a moment's notice." She pressed her back against the wall, hoping Cally would relax and do the same. "If we sit here now with the door open, it might make sitting in the dark with the door closed easier, if it should ever come to that."

"I know."

"Well then?"

Shannon heard the sound of Cally's heavy breathing. She patted her quivering hand.

"I was born in London, I was," Cally said softly, "and we were very poor. In my eighteenth year, I went to work at an inn near my home—bringing food and drink to those eating at tables and such. One day a handsome young gentleman came into the inn and took a special notice of me. He kept looking at me all evening and finally invited me to have supper with him at the inn that very night. The innkeeper said it was all right. The handsome stranger told me that he was the Earl of Northon and that I was the most beautiful girl he had ever seen."

Shannon tensed. The earl had told her exactly the same thing.

"The earl came back to the inn on the very next night," Cally went on, "and he came again the night after that—and the night after that. He brought me gifts—flowers at first. One day he gave me a lovely pearl necklace. Such a gift was more than I had ever hoped for. I have never felt so blessed. He asked if he could drive me home after I finished work that night, and I said yes." Cally grew silent for a moment. "I should never have gotten in the carriage with him."

Shannon leaned toward her. "What happened?"

Cally looked away. There was another long pause. Shannon didn't think Cally was going to reply at all.

At last, Cally said, "The earl didn't take me to my home as he'd promised. He took me—he took me to another inn and—and."

CHAPTER TWENTY-THREE

C ALLY DIDN'T SPEAK or move for what seemed to Shannon like
a long time. "I cannot tell you the terrible things that happened
that night."

"I would not expect you to," Shannon replied.

"If the earl ever loved me as he said he did, that love had turned to hate
by the next morning. He tied me up, and we set out for Gatehaven. It took
another day and—and another night to get there."

"Oh, Cally, I wish I had been there to comfort you."

"As soon as we arrived, I was taken to the top floor and thrown inside
a room with other girls—maybe ten or so. They told me that what happened to me happened to all of them—on their trips to Gatehaven."

Shannon reached out and touched Cally trembling shoulder. "It must
have been awful."

"It was." Cally sniffed. "I soon learned that if I didn't do exactly as I was
told, I was put in a dark room without food or water."

"None at all?"

"None. Once I stayed for almost three days. But that was not the worst
of it."

"There is more?"

"Much more. On nights when the moon was full—and on other nights,
too—one of the girls would be taken out, and she never came back. I was
told that one of the girls managed to escape on the very night another
girl was taken out. She found a room on the top floor—a big room. She
peeked inside for only a moment. But she saw enough to last the rest of
her life."

"What did she see?"

"Everybody wore robes like the one you were wearing when I first saw you. The girl that was taken out lay on an altar, tied and unclothed. A man in a robe stood over her, holding a knife. The girl who managed to escape the room we were kept in turned and ran.

"She tried to find the stairs, but could not. She heard someone coming and ran back inside the room where the other girls were, hoping the robed ones never knew she left. All the girls were determined to leave after that. But none managed to escape. And they were taken away—one by one. The last girl to go came from London, too. She had long golden hair. But one night she was taken. I am the only one left."

"Oh, Cally, I am so sorry you had to go through such tragedies. You must be very brave."

"Not brave. Tough. I had to be. And I will overcome my fear of the dark. I must. You will see. It is the only choice we have."

"Yes," Shannon whispered. "I fear it is." She paused as thoughts filled her head. "Cally, I made a mistake, and now I'm feeling guilty. I truly thought the earl loved me. Now, I know he never did. My pastor would call my mistake the Spirit of Error, and there is a Bible scripture that I keep thinking about. I would like to recite it aloud. Do you mind?"

"Not at all. Please, recite it. Maybe it will help."

"And I will give unto thee the keys to the kingdom of heaven: and whosoever thou shalt bind on earth shall be bound in heaven: and whosoever thou shalt loose on earth shall be loosed in heaven."

"But what does it mean?" Cally asked.

"I do not understand it well myself yet. I can only tell you what my pastor said it meant to him with regard to the Spirit of Error. He said to ask the Lord in prayer to bind the Spirit of Error in heaven as we bind it on earth and to loose the Spirit of Love and Power and a Sound Mind in the name of Jesus."

A gray rat on spindly legs raced across the floor in front of them.

Startled, Shannon jerked. "Are not rats the wickedest of animals? Frankly, I hate the little beasts."

"I do not like them either, Miss Shannon. But if I had a choice between holding a rat in my lap and hiding in a dark place, I would take the rat."

Shannon shook her head. "There we disagree. I would take the darkness every single time because God's light shines—even in darkness."

◆——◆——◆

Leon had his driver park his carriage near the front entrance of The Boar and Tongue. He was about to go inside when he noticed Brother Julian approaching from the opposite direction.

"Hello there, monk." Leon laughed mockingly as the round little man in the brown robe started toward him. "I see you went out for a bit of fresh air."

"I went to the woods to relieve myself, and you know it. Then I went for a walk. What brings you here today?"

"I came to discuss our business partnership and a few other things. Have you forgotten that I have the controlling interest in the inn here?"

"You will not allow me to forget."

"I am proud of you, Julian. You were once afraid of the shadow you made on a sunny day. But now you appear to have developed the ability to stand up like a man. Shall we go above stairs to one of the rooms and discuss business matters there?"

"The rooms are full today," Brother Julian said. "And I have no wish to talk our kind of business where others might hear. I will fill mugs of ale, and we can go up in the attic to talk. Nobody is likely to hear us there."

Leon laughed. "Did you say ale? My, you really have changed. I never knew you to be a drinking man. And you a man of the cloth."

"I have not been a *real* monk since I left France."

"I am absolutely void of all speech at the moment. Are you saying that now you are a partaker of spirits as well?"

"Until recently, we had not seen each other in over twenty years," Brother Julian pointed out. "As you say, I have changed. Now, do you want to stand on this stoop talking all day? Or do you want to pour some ale and go up to the attic?"

"I say ale and the attic." Leon motioned for the monk to lead the way. "Carry on."

Brother Julian opened the door and motioned for Leon to go in first. As Leon waited for the monk to follow him inside, he looked around. A portly old woman polished one of the eating tables with what looked like a damp cloth, but nobody stood behind the desk.

"Who stands behind the desk to greet the customers when you are doing your business in the woods, Monk? I own more than half of this establishment, and I have a right to know."

"I am as surprised as you," the monk said. "My new assistant was here when I left. I will go and speak with Maybell—see if I can learn where he might be."

The monk walked over and began talking to the old woman wiping the table. Leon tried to hear what was being said, but apparently they conversed in whispers. At last, the monk looked back at Leon and moved toward him.

"What did you discover?" Leon asked.

"My assistant must have left after I did. Maybell said he sat at one of the tables for a short while, talking to a young woman, and then the two of them went outside in front of the inn. She didn't know what happened after that. She went up the stairs to clean the rooms there.

"But she said that Cook said he came into the kitchen, talking with that French accent of his, and said that he had to leave for a short while and that it was very important. He promised to return as soon as possible."

"You mentioned a French accent," Leon said. "I have been looking for a young man by the name of Peter Aimee. He would likely have a French accent as well. Was that the man's name?"

The monk shook his head. "It was not."

"Get someone to stand behind this desk while we are in the attic," Leon demanded.

"All right." Brother Julian gazed at the old woman again. "Maybell."

She turned. "Yes, sir."

"Go into the kitchen and take over as my cook for a while. I want you to tell Cook I want him out here minding my front desk until I am able to mind it myself. Tell him I will be above stairs talking with my friend, Monsieur Gabeau."

"At once, sir," the old woman said.

＊ ───＋── ＊

Shannon and Cally continued to sit in the semi-darkness without saying much. Shannon had no idea what Cally might be thinking, but the last shred of trust and love she had for the earl had gone out of her. What had once been love was torn from her heart.

But I must not hate, she thought. *Papa said it was wrong, and so did Ian. Ian.* How she missed him. Would she ever see him again?

"I want you to close the door all the way now," Cally whispered. "I am ready."

"Are you sure?"

"Yes."

"Perhaps we should pray first." Shannon forced a smile that Cally probably wouldn't be able to see. "My papa is a praying man."

"Yes, pray. I would like that."

Shannon prayed for their safety in the name of Jesus, and then she reached out in search of the lump on the door. At last, she found it.

"Are you sure you want me to shut it all the way?"

"Please, all the way."

"Very well."

Shannon shut the little door. Semi-darkness turned to ebony. She couldn't see her hand in front of her face.

"Cally, are you all right?"

"Not yet—but I will be. It takes time would be my guess."

"Let me count to one hundred silently, and then I will open it. Is that all right with you?"

"Fifty would be better." Cally gave a weak chuckle. "But go right ahead."

Shannon counted to one hundred as fast as she could. The total darkness and closeness of the tiny room was beginning to bother her as well. She reached for the lump.

Sounds came from outside the door. Shannon froze. She heard shuffling feet on the wooden stairway and men's voices, and they were growing louder.

"Someone is coming," she whispered.

"I—I know."

If God was listening, Shannon hoped He had a plan because she had no idea what to do.

+ ——+—— +

Leon's breath came in gasps and sweat dampened his brow by the time he'd climbed the first flights of stairs to the attic, and fire filled the veins in his crippled leg instead of blood. He realized he needed to stop and rest before going on.

Rachel, he thought, putting down his mug of ale. *This is all her fault.*

Leon slumped against the wall by the stairway. He pulled the portrait of Rachel from inside his jacket and gazed at it.

"After all these years, you are still obsessed with that woman," Brother Julian said. "You need to forget her. There are plenty of women who would favor a man as rich as you."

The monk had no idea what he was talking about, and his foolish conclusions didn't even deserve a reply. Leon continued to study the portrait as if he was alone on the narrow stairway.

Rachel disappeared from his life after she married Shannon's witless father, but twenty-five years ago he'd thought he found her. It was the day he entered the English village of Cert. Rachel had lied and said her real name was Magdalena Petit, and he learned that a woman by that name lived in Cert.

He knocked on a door that day, expecting to see Rachel. A woman much older and less attractive than Rachel stood in the doorway, claiming to be Magdalena Petit.

So he killed her.

Leon killed her for having Rachel's name and not being Rachel, and he'd never killed a woman until that day. But after the first time, killing women became as easy as spreading butter on bread with a dull knife.

He finally glanced at Brother Julian a few steps ahead. The monk was Leon's senior by at least ten years. Yet Julian continued to march up those stairs a few steps ahead of him and wasn't panting at all, and he was sipping ale from a mug.

"Wait." Leon gripped the railing. "I must stop and catch what little of my breath is left."

The monk stopped and turned around. "Are you sure you can go on, Monsieur?" he asked in French. "We can always have our meeting on another day."

"No. We must go on. Give me a moment, and I shall climb those stairs as if I was twenty again—crippled leg and all."

Leon grimaced. He counted to ten and stepped to the next level. Now his chest hurt as well as his leg. Panting, he counted to twenty and slowly climbed once again.

Brother Julian stood at the top of the stairs. He'd also put down his mug, and his chubby hands were on his enormous hips. He offered Leon his right hand.

"May I give you a help up, Monsieur?"

Leon motioned his hand away. "That will not be necessary."

True, Leon needed assistance. Still, he did have his pride. He straightened his stooped shoulders as best he could and limped forward. To do otherwise would prove he'd given in to the suggestions of a man of lesser birth, and Leon couldn't tolerate such an outcome.

He saw a chair near the stairway. It had a straight back, no arms, and it looked terribly uncomfortable to a man in Leon's condition, but he sat down on it anyway. Another uncomfortable looking chair faced it, and the monk took that one.

A door led to a second room in the attic. Leon gazed through the open doorway. Wooden boxes were stacked against the back wall. He saw a bundle of what looked like hay in one corner and little else. He turned to the monk, pressing his head back against the hard planks of the chair.

"Is my inn making money?" Leon asked the monk.

"Yes, Leon. New people are staying at The Boar and Tongue almost every day."

"Leon? You called me by my real name."

"So I did, Monsieur. Most regretful indeed."

"You must remember that I am Monsieur Etienne Gabeau now," Leon said, "not Leon Picard." Leon flinched as the pains in his back and chest increased. "This chair is most uncomfortable. Perhaps we should have discussed our business on the stoop out front instead of coming up to this attic."

Leon heard a noise. He glanced toward the door leading to the other room. "Did you hear that?" he asked.

"Rats. They are everywhere up here. I need to set some traps."

Shannon stiffened, afraid to breathe or move. Etienne Gabeau wasn't the Frenchman's real name. It was Leon—Leon— She tried to remember his last name but couldn't.

Nevertheless, she was able to hear everything else the men said, and it wasn't rats they heard. She'd hit her arm against the wall accidentally in an attempt to find a comfortable sitting position. She thanked God that they thought the sound came from a rat or perhaps several.

"You might recall that I came to England over twenty years ago in search of a certain woman," Leon said. "Her name was Rachel Aimee."

Rachel. Shannon froze. *He is talking about my mother.*

"I remember her well," the monk finally said. "I also remember how beautiful she was and how you fancied her."

Shannon remembered that the Frenchman said the portrait of the woman reminded him of Shannon. Small wonder. The portrait was really of her mother, Rachel Aimee. Leon Whatever-his-name-was must be insane to have kept her mother's portrait at his side all those years.

"And you sent the earl to Scotland to bring her here so you could have her and then kill her," the monk said. "Is that not true?'

"Of course. But the earl brought her daughter, Shannon, by mistake."

Shannon's stomach knotted. She feared that at any moment she might lose the morning meal Millie had served them.

The earl had never loved her. That fact had never been clearer. He brought her to England for evil purposes. If he'd brought her mother instead as the Monsieur had wanted, her mother could be dead by now. She could scarcely breathe.

At last, Leon said, "I might add that my traps are better than those one might set for a mouse or a rat. And I understand the son, Peter, is already here. Soon the entire Aimee family will be, and I shall have my revenge."

"Am I right in saying, Monsieur, that you sent the young men we spoke of earlier to Scotland to bring Rachel's entire family here?"

"Yes, including that husband of hers and the new baby. When all are safely trapped, I will have my way. And then I will be free of Rachel Aimee forever."

Shannon put both her hands over her mouth to keep from screaming. She was also shaking. Cally must have noticed. Cally found Shannon's hand in the darkness and gave it a quick squeeze.

Shannon squeezed back and tried to stop shaking. She couldn't. Had these new revelations affected Cally as adversely as they were affecting her? Earlier, when she hadn't heard Cally speak or so much as move for a long time, she'd thought that perhaps the darkness had induced a case of the vapors, and Cally was unable to think—only sleep. Cally's firm hand-squeeze confirmed that she was well enough. Despite everything that was going on around them, that simple act encouraged Shannon.

"We had planned to make a sacrifice to the god of forces last night," Leon declared. "But I asked them to omit that part of the meeting at Gatehaven since I would not be able to attend. Therefore, we shall sacrifice a young woman tonight. Pretty girl, too, according to the earl. He said her name was Cally."

Shannon grabbed Cally's hand and squeezed it as tightly as she could.

"After Cally, we shall sacrifice Miss Shannon Aimee and then, perhaps, her whole family. Now would that not be a feast? Care to join us, monk?"

"I believe not," Brother Julian said. "I might have rejected my vows as a monk and rejected every other law of God; but I will not go as far as you. Even I have my limits."

"Come tonight or not. As long as our—our partnership continues as it has so far, I have no complaint."

Shannon sucked in her breath. She'd already done it at least a hundred times or more. Her hands were over her mouth again, and if the men didn't leave soon, she was sure she would explode.

Her elbow bumped the door of the enclosure. Thump. The door opened a crack. A thin line of light blinded her for a moment.

"I heard that noise again," Leon said, "only louder. I think we should go in that other room and see what is there. If it is a rat, it must be bigger than a cat."

"It could be a cat," the monk said. "Lucifer has been missing since yesterday."

"You have a cat named Lucifer?"

"What else would I name a cat?"

Leon laughed. "Perhaps you should come to the meeting tonight after all."

Shannon jerked, causing another sound. Leon's words and satanic laughter hit her like the blast of a pistol.

"That was no rat I just heard." Leon reached for his cane and rose a few inches. He fell back down. "I do not think it was a cat either. Help me up. We should go and investigate."

Shannon bit her lower lip to keep from shouting out in protest. Then she shut her eyes—tight. She needed to pray as she'd never prayed before.

She could hear footfalls coming closer and another sound—step, tap, step. She'd heard that noise before, and it was probably coming from the Frenchman's cane. Would he beat her with his cane? Or hit her over the head with it?

"See what is under that stack of hay," Leon demanded.

There was a brief pause, and then the monk said, "I see nothing, Monsieur."

"What are in those boxes?"

"Supplies for the inn, but the boxes are small. Nobody could be hiding in them."

"What is behind them?" Leon asked.

"The wall."

"I want to see what is behind those boxes."

Shannon heard a step-tap-step. It sounded much closer. She pressed her hands to her mouth so hard her teeth scraped against them. She could only hope that Cally was doing the same thing.

If Leon saw the crack, he would know to look for a door. Shannon tensed. If that happened, they were doomed.

CHAPTER TWENTY-FOUR

S HANNON HEARD SCAMPERING sounds like tiny feet. Was it a mouse—a rat—or something worse? *Bang!* Shannon jumped. She was sure Cally must have jumped too. The sound had a metallic ring to it—as if something made of metal had crashed to the floor. What was happening on the other side of that little door?

"Catch that rat," Leon shouted. "Before it gets away."

The monk laughed. "I will catch it soon enough. At least now you know what caused the sounds you heard."

"I expected the animal to be bigger. But it certainly upset that little pail it was perched on easy enough."

Shannon heard another step-tap.

"I do not like rats, monk. I would like to leave here now. And I want all the rats removed from this inn before we meet here again."

Shannon kept her hand over her mouth long after the men apparently left the attic. When she could no longer hear their footsteps on the stairway below, she reached out and opened the short door a little wider.

◆———◆———◆

Ian left his room on the second floor of the vicar's home and went downstairs. Pastor Steen drove to a nearby farm to visit a member of his congregation who was ill. While he was away, Ian planned to go to the physician's home to report a murder. The vicar agreed that he should.

But even if he hadn't, Ian would have reported the crime anyway.

He came to England to rescue Shannon from an evil earl and to solve the twenty-five-year-old murder of a Frenchwoman by the name of Magdalena Petit who happened to be Pastor Petit's cousin, and he hadn't reached either of those goals. But at least he could tell what he knew about the body he and Buster found in the woods.

Ian heard the sound of hoofbeats outside the vicar's cottage. A rider had driven up on a brown-colored horse, but he hadn't seen the man's face yet.

With the vicar away, it was up to Ian to answer the pastor's door if someone knocked, even if it meant delaying his journey into the village. He hurried toward the entry door. He'd almost reached it when he heard a knock.

Ian opened the door. Peter Aimee stood before him. Ian was glad to see his friend again and welcomed Peter with a smile. But the tight expression around Peter's mouth indicated that things were not as they should be.

"Gather a few things and come," Peter ordered. "Shannon is in danger. We all are. We must leave for Scotland at once."

"I—I cannot just leave without saying good-bye to the vicar. He has been kind to me."

"Write him a note, and leave it where he will find it," Peter suggested. "But do not say too much. Monsieur Gabeau and perhaps the earl might take possession of your letter."

Ian was so taken by surprise, he couldn't reply for a moment. No matter what Peter said to the contrary, he would not leave England without first reporting the body he found in the woods.

"Where is your room?" Peter asked.

"Above stairs. First door to the right. Why?"

"I am going up to gather your things. I trust you will have the letter completed by the time I return."

"I trust you will have my belongings gathered by the time I finish the letter."

Peter grinned. "I will return shortly."

Ian went to the desk in the sitting room by the window and sat down. The vicar had given him permission to use his pen, ink, and papers whenever he liked. Still, he felt a wave of guilt for using that privilege in such a way.

Dear Vicar,

I appreciate your kindness and all you have done for me, and I especially thank you for the excellent teachings you have provided since
you returned to your parish church. I dislike leaving without saying
good-bye. However, I have just received a bit of news that makes
staying longer impossible. I must set out for Scotland at once. I will

write a long letter and mail it to you as soon as possible after I get home.

Your servant,
    Ian Colquhoun

Ian was standing in the doorway when Peter flew down the stairs, and he hoped he looked as if he had been standing there a long time.

"What kept you?" Ian asked, forcing a serious expression.

"Your dirty clothes. You should try washing them sometime."

"Aye. And you should work a little faster."

"You have a point. So, saddle your horse. We must be on our way."

Ian shook his head. "I cannot take the horse I have been riding. It does not belong to me. I must leave it here."

"Then we shall ride double on my horse," Peter said.

"Double?" Ian laughed despite the deep trouble they were in. "As we did when we were boys?"

Yes." Peter laughed too then. "As we did when we were boys."

After all that had gone on earlier that day, it felt good to laugh again. However, Ian knew that he must tell Peter about the woman's body he had found in the woods and that he thought she was murdered. Could these murders be related to the death of his pastor's cousin somehow?

As soon as they arrived in the village of Fairs, Ian asked that Peter stop his horse so he could get off.

"I must pay a visit to the local physician and tell him what I know. As I mentioned earlier, I think the young woman was murdered. Her death must be reported."

"Of course. Meet me in the woods outside The Boar and Tongue as soon as you can. Shannon and her friend will be waiting with me there."

"Aye. I should not be long."

+ —+— +

Peter put his horse in the barn near the inn. Though he was an employee at the inn, he stood in the underbrush near the door of the inn for a moment before going inside, to see what he could see. Plenty of unusual events had occurred that day. If the monk found Shannon and Cally while he was away, he needed to find a way to rescue them. He would also need to map out in advance every step he would take until they left England

A fine carriage pulled up in front of The Boar and Tongue. An expensive-looking brown gelding was tied to the back of it.

Peter squinted in hopes of seeing who was inside. A footman stepped down from a narrow standing perch at the back of the carriage and went around to the door of the carriage. He wore a green uniform similar to the ones Peter saw at the estate owned by the Earl of Willowbrook.

Could it be that the old gentleman who once rescued his parents had come to Fairs to rescue him and his sister? Nonsense; he couldn't know the danger they were in. Still, if the person inside the sitting place of the carriage was the elderly earl, he couldn't have arrived at a more advantageous time.

The door opened. A much younger man stepped out. He wore dark clothing in the stylish design of the English upper class. Peter returned to a shadowy spot behind a clump of bushes.

"'Tis been a while since I visited Gatehaven," the man said to the footman. "I need directions. Tell the innkeeper that I am looking for Mr. Peter Aimee and a Miss Aimee."

"Very good, sir."

Still in the shadows, Peter moved closer to the carriage. Should he go forward and make himself known—or wait a little longer? Fear didn't cause him to hesitate; caution did.

Peter moved out from under the trees. "My lord, I could not help but hear what you said to your man, and I would be glad to direct you to Gatehaven."

The gentleman turned and smiled.

Peter was taken back. The quality didn't often show acts of friendship to an underling like himself. Who was this man?

"I am Lord Wilburn, and I appreciate your offer of help."

Lord Wilburn. Wasn't that the name the Earl of Willowbrook used when referring to his son?

"I am Mr. Peter Aimee, my lord, at your service."

"How fortunate." The gentleman's smile became a short chuckle. "You and your sister are the ones I came here to see. And to think, I found you as soon as I arrived. God is certainly with us this day. Come inside the inn and share a meal with me. We have much to discuss."

"I would be delighted to do so. But alas, I cannot. I promised to meet a friend in the woods near the inn. He should arrive soon, and I must be here when he does."

The footman came out of the inn and stood before Lord Wilburn. "I was given directions to Gatehaven, my lord, but the caretaker is away. Nobody has heard of Mr. or Miss Aimee."

"Thank you, Higgs," Lord Wilburn said to the footman. "My friend is waiting for a friend to arrive. Keep a watch out for him, and tell us when he arrives. My friend and I are going inside, if he is willing. Are you?"

"Yes." Peter grinned. "I accept your kind offer. Much has occurred since we arrived in England, and I look forward to speaking with you about it."

Peter noticed that the cook was standing behind the desk instead of back in the kitchen working. And where was Brother Julian? Peter needed to find out. Lord Wilburn motioned toward a table near the back of the eating area with a clear view of the entry door.

"I am employed here at The Boar and Tongue," Peter explained. "I must speak to the cook before I sit down."

Lord Wilburn nodded. "Of course." He moved toward the table.

Peter stopped to talk to the cook, learning that not long before he and Lord Wilburn came in, Brother Julian and a Monsieur Gabeau left in a carriage to attend some kind of meeting, and Cook didn't know when they might return.

Shannon and her friend must still be in the attic. Would Peter be able to rescue them before the Frenchman and the monk returned? He would need to explain the situation to the English lord with haste.

Peter crossed the floor to Lord Wilburn's table, moving his chair slightly in order to have a clear view of the entry door before sitting down. He wanted to know the instant Ian came inside.

As they drank cups of hot tea, Peter told Lord Wilburn all that had happened since he and Shannon and Ian arrived in England. Was Lord Wilburn as kind and trustworthy as his father, the Earl of Willowbrook, appeared to be? Would Lord Wilburn help them as his father had once helped Peter's parents?

The entry door opened. Ian Colquhoun stepped inside.

"Is that the friend you were telling me about?" Lord Wilburn asked.

"Yes. That is Mr. Ian Colquhoun of Luss, Scotland."

+——+——+

Ian had heard of the Earl of Willowbrook and his son, Lord Wilburn, from Peter and also from Pastor Steen. The vicar had said that the Earl of Willowbrook heard of Magdalena's murder soon after she died. Later, he shared that news with his son, Lord Wilburn.

The earl's son was the gentleman who told the vicar about Magdalena's death years after the murder. And here Ian was, sharing a table with him and looking at the man face-to-face. He'd hoped to meet with the earl and Lord Wilburn before he left England in order to discuss Magdalena's death as he promised Pastor Petit he would do. But with Shannon and her friend in danger, this was not the time to pay the Earl of Willowbrook a visit.

Ian looked up and found Lord Wilburn watching him. He realized he'd allowed his mind to drift a bit. Embarrassed, he forced a smile and sat down at the table.

Lord Wilburn returned his smile. "I have a plan in mind," he said. "I want you to have full use of my carriage on your journey back to Scotland as well as my horses and my footmen."

Peter shook his head. "That is impossible. We would never impose on your kindness to that extent."

"I insist," Lord Wilburn said. "I have brought along a spare horse, and he is tied to the back of my carriage. I will ride back to my estate on the horse I brought with me. After you are safely home, my footmen will drive my carriage back to England and return it to me."

"But, my lord, I—."

"This is the way it must be. You see, my carriage, horses, and all I own belongs to the Lord. I am merely using these things until Jesus, the rightful owner, returns." Lord Wilburn turned to Peter. "If I were the one in need, would you not do as much for me?"

"Of course."

"Then it is settled." The British lord rose from the table. "Mr. Aimee, while you go to the attic to gather your sister and her friend, the Scotsman and I will prepare the carriage. By the time you return, my footman should be ready to set out for Scotland. And may God go with you."

"May God go with you as well, my lord," Peter replied.

"Aye," Ian nodded. "It is a pleasure to meet you, my lord. And I will pray for you and your family for the rest of my days."

"Godspeed. And I shall pray for you as well, Mr. Colquhoun," Lord Wilburn said. "In fact, I will pray for all of you. But now we must make haste."

"Yes," Peter agreed. "The monk and Monsieur Gabeau could return at any moment."

* —◆— *

Shannon stumbled climbing into Lord Wilburn's carriage, and turned the same ankle she injured previously.

"Oh, my."

If Ian hadn't caught her, she might have fallen all the way to the ground.

His smile and kind nature warmed her as he gently lifted her into the carriage, and for an instant, all pain was blocked from her mind. Then her ankle began to swell. The pain returned in earnest, as well as thoughts— memories of all the horrible things the Frenchman said in that attic.

"The physician from Fairs warned you, Shannon, that your ankle would be weak for some time after you hurt it the first time," Ian reminded her. "If you try to walk, the injury could become serious. You could lose the use of your leg entirely. Therefore, one of us will carry you until all the pain disappears."

"We must tell the driver to hurry," Shannon said. "The Frenchman sent men ahead to bring the rest of my family to England in order to kill them."

For Shannon, the next few hours were a blur as they rode along. She thought of Ian, but she also kept thinking about what the Frenchman said. Were they being followed?

At last, she whispered to Cally. "I think someone is following us."

"As do I," Cally replied.

"I heard that," Peter put in. "But there is no reason for you to worry. The earl and Etienne Gabeau would likely expect us to be traveling in a cart pulled by an ailing horse." He laughed. "But they would not expect to find us riding in a fine carriage such as this. And with footmen in green uniforms fulfilling our every wish, I think we are truly safe."

"I hope you are right, Peter," Shannon said. "But Cally and I learned quite by accident that the Frenchman's name is *not* Etienne Gabeau."

"Not Etienne Gabeau?" Peter's face had astonishment written all over it. "Whatever can you mean, sister?"

"The Frenchman's real name is Leon Picard," Ian put in. "That name was written in a book in the Frenchman's library. I saw it with my own eyes. I've thought for some days that the Frenchman's real name was Leon Picard but kept those thoughts to myself. Now we have proof that my conclusions were entirely correct."

"The time I spent searching for information on the earl and the Frenchman was a waste of time." Wrinkles formed on Peter's forehead. "I should have been looking for Leon Picard."

"If you have new information on any of those names," Ian said, "share it with us now."

"I have no knowledge of Leon Picard. But while working at the inn, I met a man who once lived in Rosslyn. He was on his way to London and stopped at the inn for the night. I had the opportunity to talk with him as he ate his supper, and after giving him a few coins, he told me things I will never forget." Peter stopped for a moment and shook his head as if he hesitated to say more. "According to the traveler, some of the members of the Spiritualist Society here in Fairs are also members of the Spiritualist Society of Rosslyn, Scotland. And somehow, they are connected to a group of men who lived in France long ago—a group called the Knights Templar. Some think these knights later came to Scotland and are associated with a chapel in Rosslyn."

"Did you say Knights Templar?" Ian asked. "I read about them in a book in Monsieur Gabeau's—I mean in Leon Picard's library. Evidently, these men committed heresies—crimes so evil some were burned at the stake. However, the pages telling of their crimes were ripped from the book. So I was unable to learn the details of these crimes I so wished to know."

Peter shrugged. "Who can say whether or not the story is true." He glanced down at his hands. "Some say the Knights went to Jerusalem during the Crusades and did some digging there. They uncovered *something*—something important. They must have found gold because they came home rich men. But they also exposed a secret of some kind."

"What was it, Peter?" Ian demanded. "Tell us."

"Nobody knows. But the traveler said that some in the group at Rosslyn say that the Knights found a human head that was cut off from its body. It could be a skull or an actual head that was preserved in some way. Others say it was a crystal skull and not human at all. But whether crystal skull or preserved head, the thing was evil." He shook his head again. "I dare not say more."

"Please," Ian insisted. "Tell us all you know."

"The traveler said that the skull or head was able to—was able to speak—tell the Knights things they would not know otherwise, and that the knights worshipped the evil thing."

"Enough!" Shannon shivered, putting her hands over her ears. "Stop such talk at once. Otherwise, I am sure I will be sick."

Peter and Ian promised to say no more, also assuring her that they had nothing to worry about. Perhaps the stories were merely myths. But Shannon saw the look in her brother's eyes when he told that tale, and she felt sure that Peter believed every word of it.

"If it was true," Ian put in, "to worship such a relic or anything but God alone is idolatry. Let us hope it is merely a fable."

Nevertheless, Ian and Peter looked back down the road they were traveling on when they thought Shannon wasn't watching. Maybe those stories about the earl and the Frenchman with regard to the doings at Rosslyn were truer than Peter and Ian were willing to admit.

"Peter and I decided not to stay at inns or eat our meals there until we are far, far from Gatehaven," Ian said. "Later, we will stop near a lake and go fishing."

"Fishing?" Shannon repeated. "Whatever for?"

"Food, lass. Our fish supper will be cooked over an open fire. Lord Wilburn told of lakes and streams that hold an abundance of fish. He also informed me that he kept poles for fishing and hooks under the seats of this carriage for just such outings."

Shannon was forced to sit alone in the carriage while Peter, Cally, Ian and all but the carriage driver went fishing in a nearby stream.

A few minutes later, the driver said that he wanted to take a short walk in the woods, leaving Shannon alone in the carriage.

She pressed her body against the seat's wooden back. Her ankle didn't hurt as much as it had earlier. She closed her eyes.

Shannon heard a noise—like horse's hooves—close by. She turned and looked toward the sound. A lone rider approached, and her all alone inside the carriage. Trembling, she searched for a weapon but didn't see anything.

The rider dismounted.

Shannon stiffened. She still hadn't seen his face. She leaned forward and focused her attention on her hurting ankle.

"Good day," she heard the earl say.

Shannon froze. The earl found her. Nobody could rescue her this time.

The earl tied his horse to a bush near the carriage, blocking the animal from view.

CHAPTER TWENTY-FIVE

MADAM," THE EARL said. "Is it possible that you saw two young women and two men on the road today?"

Anger swelled within her. *If I had, I would not tell you.*

But if she hoped to survive, she must become like an actress on a stage. She must pretend that her feelings for the earl had not changed. She lifted her head and looked at the earl face-to-face.

"Miss Aimee?" the earl said with a look of surprise.

She nodded. "Yes."

"My love," he said. "You cannot know how glad I am to find you."

"And I you," she lied.

"You must have been frightened when someone hit me over the head. No wonder you ran away. But what are you doing in a carriage like this—and all alone, too?"

"Alas, my wicked brother and Ian Colquhoun forced me into this carriage and are driving me back to Scotland."

"And against your will," he concluded. "My poor darling. Where are they now?"

"In the woods—fishing if you can believe it."

"Fishing. And they left you here all alone?"

She sniffed for a better effect. "Yes."

"Have no fear, my inspiration. I am here now." He opened the carriage door on her side. Then he motioned for her to move in order to make room for him.

She lifted her leg and groaned as she inched to the other side of the seat. Once settled, she groaned one more time but even louder.

"My dear, are you in pain?"

"Yes. I have injured my ankle again." She bit her lower lip so he would think the pain was greater than it actually was.

"I shall take you back to Gatehaven and notify your physician at once."

"You are always so thoughtful and kind, my lord. But will we ever marry?"

"Of course. We shall marry as soon as we arrive in Gatehaven—whether my mother likes it or not. "

Shannon knew his words of love were all lies. Nevertheless, she looked up at him with the eyes of an innocent schoolgirl and smiled in hopes of keeping him off guard.

"If only we could go back to Gatehaven," she finally said. "But that might not be the best way to—"

"To what?" he asked.

"As I said, I have hurt my ankle again and must be seen by a physician before we ride on. This cannot wait. My physician from Fairs said that my ankle would be weak for some time to come, and if I injured it again, I could become a cripple."

"A cripple?"

"Yes." She sniffed again.

"I will not allow that to happen, dear one."

"Do you remember that on our way to Gatehaven, we stayed the night at an inn in the village of Petre?"

"I do recall that, yes."

"Before we left, the Innkeeper told that he had a brother who was a physician. Petre is not far from here. But Gatehaven is half a day's ride. If I rode on with you, I would tire quickly. The pain in my leg would force us to stop and rest often. Worst of all, my brother and Ian Colquhoun would catch up with us, and they have footmen with them that could be armed."

"Then what would you suggest we do, my love?"

"Go to Petre now, and wait for me at the inn. When we arrive, I will have my ankle seen by the physician and prepare to spend the night."

"And then?" he said.

"I will knock on your door tonight when everyone else is asleep. And we will ride away together."

"How will you knock on my door tonight?" he asked. "You said you were unable to walk."

"I will crawl to your door on my hands and knees if I have to."

He laughed. "You still love me that much?"

She gazed up at him and forced a tender expression. "You know I do."

"Then give me a kiss," he said, "and I will go."

Shannon had no wish to see the earl again much less kiss his lying lips. But in order for her plan to work, she had no choice but to kiss him.

•——————•

Ian was not comfortable leaving Shannon alone in the carriage even though the driver stood watch. He left the others fishing and set out for the carriage to make sure she was all right. He had heard her tell her brother that she hated the Earl of Northon, now that she knew him to be an evil man, and she'd seemed much more interested in Ian as a possible suitor since she left Gatehaven. This had given him a reason to hope.

Now as he stood in the bushes nearby, he heard voices. The driver was nowhere to be seen. Yet someone was inside that carriage with Shannon. Ian's jaw tightened. Had the driver lost his wits? Was he inside that carriage treating Shannon in unseemly ways?

His hands became fists.

Ian wanted to open that carriage door and punch the intruder again and again. But he could have a gun. If Ian opened that door, he could kill Shannon. Better to sneak a look through the window first and learn the situation before putting her in even more danger.

He crept closer to the carriage. The voices he'd heard earlier vanished. He tensed. Had the intruder already killed Shannon?

Ian cast his eyes inside the carriage. A man held Shannon close, kissing her again and again. Ian stiffened. The intruder wasn't the driver. He wore the stylish clothes of an English gentleman. Ian drew back his arm. He wouldn't open that door and hit the man in the face.

The kisses ended. The couple drew apart slightly.

"I love you my little turtle dove," Ian heard the Earl of Northon say.

"And I you," Shannon replied.

Ian's heart knotted. He stepped back––out of view.

He felt as if all love and emotion were drained from his body. Only his love for God remained. His hopes—his dreams of a future with Shannon—were gone forever. He'd played the fool for too long. Now he would give up the chase—let Shannon go.

He tried to swallow a lump that had formed in his throat. Shannon would never be his wife. It still seemed hard to believe. After all that had happened, she still loved the earl.

Hidden among the trees and bushes, Ian waited until the earl rode away and the driver was once again perched on the top of the carriage. Then he went back and joined the others at the fishing hole, pretending that life was never better.

But all he could think about was one thing. He would never trust Shannon again.

When Shannon could no longer see the earl on his black gelding, she released a deep sigh. He'd kissed her one more time before he left, and the nasty taste of it still lingered in her mouth. She leaned her head out the window of the carriage and spat. It didn't help. She still felt dirty.

Shannon longed to be held in Ian's arms—to tell him that she loved him—that she had always loved him. She wanted *his* love—not the earl's. She wished to drive away from this dreadful place. What was keeping Ian and the rest of the fishing party?

They soon arrived. Ian hardly seemed to notice her. She would have expected him to walk over to the carriage and stick his head inside—see how she had faired while he was away. Instead, he helped her brother gather wood, and they built a fire in an opening near the carriage.

When they finished eating, Ian, Peter, and Cally climbed back inside the carriage. Ian sat as far from Shannon as he possibly could. Then they rode away.

Shannon tried to explain what happened while they were fishing. But Ian didn't appear to be listening.

"Now we must avoid all inns until we cross over into Scotland," Peter said. "We will fish or kill animals for our food. The women will sleep in the carriage at night. The rest of us will sleep on the grounds outside." He glanced at Ian. "Is that all right with you, Mr. Colquhoun?"

Ian nodded without expression. "Whatever you decide is all right with me."

During the journey home, Shannon heard Peter announce that he and Kate planned to marry soon after he arrived. Apparently, Peter hoped she would agree to marry him aboard the ship—the ship that would carry them to the colonies.

After he finished speaking, Shannon spent time thinking about the colonies and wondering. Her parents would expect her to go to the colonies with them now, and after all that had happened, the thought of going sounded better somehow. She also wondered why Ian seemed so cold toward her. If only she could tell him how she really felt about him. But he was so distant—as if an invisible door separated them now.

She thought of the portrait the Frenchman showed her of the young woman who looked very much like Shannon. But maybe it looked even more like her mother at a young age.

These and other thoughts rolled about in her mind during the long journey to Scotland. She wondered what the earl must have thought when she and her party never showed up at the inn. But her main concern was whether they would arrive in Luss in time to save her parents and baby brother. If she'd done as her father asked, she would never have traveled to England in the first place.

But mostly, she thought of Ian, wishing he knew how much she loved him. She was not opposed to telling him face-to-face exactly how she felt. But he didn't appear interested in hearing anything she had to say.

＊—＋—＊

Two days after Shannon and Cally left for Scotland, Leon heard a knock at his door.

"Answer the door," he yelled to Sally, the new cook his driver found for him in the village of Fairs.

She didn't reply.

That defective old woman was probably in the kitchen house, cooking his noon meal. And his driver was in the carriage house. He frowned and reached for his cane. It was bad enough that the latest meeting of the Spiritualist Society fell flat. But now he could not depend on his servants when he really needed them. The muscles around his mouth tightened as he hobbled to the door and opened it.

The Earl of Northon stood before him, and he wasn't smiling. "May I come in?"

Leon Picard frowned. "Come in then. And I have to say that I am quite put out with you, my lord. Why did you miss the recent meeting of the Spiritualist Society? My word, it was held at Gatehaven. You could at least have climbed up to the fourth floor and explained why we had no sacrifice. One of our members had each of us cut a finger so the ceremony would not be a total loss, but that did little good I am afraid."

"I dislike hearing stories like that, Frenchman—even in private. It is unsettling to say the least."

"When did such news start bothering you, my lord? You've always relished such tales."

"People can change, you know." The earl walked inside and slumped down onto Leon's favorite chair by the fireplace. "The young woman, Miss Aimee, and Cally, another of our girls, escaped. That is why we had no sacrifice. I went after them and managed to speak with Miss Aimee."

"Did you bring her back?"

"Unfortunately, I did not." The earl leaned forward in his chair and appeared to be looking at a speck of something on the floor. "She betrayed me."

"Betrayed you? Then you must go after both young women at once and bring them back." Leon lifted one dark brow. "If you expect me to destroy your gambling debt, you will go at once."

"That will not be necessary." The earl sent Leon a hard look. "I just received word that the young woman I courted in London has accepted my proposal of marriage. She is very rich."

"Congratulations."

"Therefore, I have no need for you to pay my gambling debts any longer. I shall be coming into a great deal of money soon. And I am told that my betrothed and her family are very religious. She and her father will not like to learn of our meetings on the top floor of the mansion or what goes on there. So from this day forth, I am no longer a member of the society. There will be no more meetings at Gatehaven nor will young girls be held captive there against their will. If such meetings continue, they must be held elsewhere." The earl stood and walked to the door. "Good day, Monsieur. I hope these new revelations will not cause you undo difficulties. But in any case, I must ask you not to visit my home again. The young lady's father would not be pleased to learn that we were once friends." The earl grabbed his hat and umbrella from the table by the door.

Leon stared at his back until the earl went out and slammed the door behind him.

Of course Leon was disappointed that he no longer had a hold on the earl's life. At the same time, he was glad to see that the earl finally stood up and acted like a man. He'd always hated weakness, including his own.

Leon limped back to his chair and sat down. Without the earl's backing, he could be in trouble with the law. Perhaps it was time for him to relocate.

A mental picture of Rachel's beautiful face came into his mind. The edges of Leon's lips turned up in a smile. He could move to Scotland if he wished. Or he could sail for the colonies. The earl had said that Shannon and her family hoped to move to Charles Towne.

His spies informed him that the wife he abandoned years ago and his son, Leon Picard II, had moved to Charles Towne. The boy would be a man now. Perhaps he still lived there.

If not Scotland, he would go to the colonies. Yes, that was exactly what he would do. But not before he paid the earl back for walking away.

He would write a letter to a high official he knew with the government in London, and as Etienne Gabeau, he would say he had a change of heart. He would tell all he knew about the Spiritualist Society and about the doings on the fourth floor. However, he would wait until he reached Plymouth before mailing the letter. Then Etienne Gabeau would become Leon Picard once again.

The earl expected to be free of Leon's hold on him after he wed the rich young woman from London. However, Leon had no intentions of selling his rights to the earl's debts to the girl's father or anyone else. Someday, he would own Gatehaven as he'd always planned.

That afternoon Leon had his driver take him to The Boar and Tongue in order to speak to his business partner. If anybody knew what the people of the village were saying and perhaps thinking, it was Brother Julian. He'd hoped that during the meeting the monk would remove any worries he might have about the law. Unfortunately, speaking with him only increased Leon's decision to leave the country as soon as he was able.

Apparently, to reside in England any longer might not be a sane decision. If the law intended to round up all members of the Spiritualist Society merely because a few poorly connected young women were missing, he would be wise to leave England as soon as possible. He must sell all his holdings as well. And he intended to pay out a fine sum of money to stop those idle tongues from wagging until he was safely out of the country.

⁘ ——◆—— ⁘

The sun was low some weeks later when Shannon, Ian, Cally, and Peter arrived in the village of Luss. Exhausted, all Shannon could think about was getting to the farm to see if her family was all right, and Peter wished to do the same. Yet she also knew that Peter was eager to see his beloved Kate.

Ian might feel obligated to escort them to the farm as well, but she knew his heart would not be in it. He should go to his own home now.

"Peter," she said, "I know you want to know if our family is all right. But I also know you want to see Kate as soon as possible. Why don't you and Ian go now? Cally and I will be safe with the earl's footmen and a driver at our sides. If our parents are in any danger, I promise to let you know at once."

"Are you sure?" Peter asked.

"Positive."

"Well, I guess I'll go then."

Ian walked off with Peter without really saying good-bye. Then he turned and looked at Shannon. His expression was as cold as the loch in winter.

⁘ ——◆—— ⁘

Peter waited in the shadows while Ian went inside his family home for a reunion with his parents and sisters. Ian had promised to tell Kate that Peter would be waiting for her at the loch. But he'd expected her to spend time with her brother first. Instead, she ran out of the house and headed straight for the loch. She'd promised to meet him there before he left. But Peter couldn't wait that long; he wanted to hold her now and tell her how much he loved her.

"Kate, wait." He raced across the grass. "I am here."

"Peter?"

"How I have missed you, Kate. But I am home now. I will never leave you again."

His kiss was filled with promise. "I can wait no longer. I want us to marry as soon as possible."

"As do I."

He squeezed her hand. "I wanted to go down to the loch—dreamed of sitting beside you on our log and looking out at the cold blue beyond the water's edge. But this is not the time. My parents and baby brother could be in danger. I wish to go to your house now and tell your parents our good news. Then we must hurry to my family to see if they are all right."

+ —•— +

The carriage pulled to a stop at the farm's front gate, but it was too wide to go through the narrow opening. Two footmen walked Shannon and Cally to the farmhouse door, then waited to see if they were needed. Shannon hurried inside. Her parents were packing things in boxes.

Shannon released a sign of relief. Her parents were all right. "Mama, Papa. I am home."

At first, her parents didn't move. Then they looked at each other for a moment as if they were frozen in time.

"Oh, Javier. Our daughter is home."

Shannon was touched by the deep emotion she heard in her mother's voice. She glanced back to the footmen. "Looks like my family is all right. You may go now, and thank you for all your help. And please thank the earl and his son for us as well."

The footmen nodded. Then Mama rushed toward her, followed by Papa. They hugged Shannon until she could scarcely breathe, but for Shannon, it was a good feeling.

"Oh Shannon." Her mother wiped a tear from her eye. "After we got that letter from the earl, we feared you might be dead. We were preparing to leave for England at once."

"What letter?"

"This one." Her mother pulled a letter from the pocket of her dress covering. "It was written some time ago but must have been delayed. It just arrived today."

"May I read it, please?"

"Of course." Mrs. Aimee handed the letter to Shannon.

Your daughter, Shannon, is gravely ill. You must come to Gatehaven in the north of England at once, if you hope to see her again. Alive.

One glance convinced Shannon it was *not* written by the earl.

"The earl never wrote this letter, Mama. I know the way he forms his letters." She turned the letter over. "Whoever wrote it used the earl's seal. But the earl did not write it. This document was forged."

"Forged?" Her mother's green eyes widened, and she slanted her head to one side. "But why?"

"His purpose was evil." Shannon looked away. "Let us not discuss that now."

"Very well." Mrs. Aimee frowned. "But where is Peter? Did he not come with you?"

"He came. But he went home with Ian to see Kate."

Her mother smiled. "That explains it. Peter would want to see Kate before seeing anyone else."

Kate Colquhoun was Shannon's best friend. She was happy for her. But would Shannon ever walk down a church aisle with Ian?

Topics needed to be discussed. Questions required answers. It would take time to get it all out. She glanced at Cally, standing just inside the entry door.

"I have much to tell you, Mama and Papa." Shannon grabbed Cally's hand and pulled her forward. "But first, I would like you to meet my friend, Cally Winters. Cally is from London, England. She helped me escape from a dangerous situation. I would like her to stay with us until she can find other arrangements."

"Of course she may stay—for as long as she likes. We are glad to have her." Shannon's mother embraced Cally as if she were a member of the family.

Her father shook Cally's slender hand.

Cally bobbed a bow. "I am glad to meet all of you, I'm sure."

"Come and sit by the fire," Mrs. Aimee said. "And we shall see if we can make some sense of all this."

Shannon listened as her mother told how she and her father fled France to escape from an evil man by the name of Leon Picard, a man who wished them harm merely because her mother refused his advances. Peter had told Shannon that story previously, but until that moment, she'd never heard it in her mother's words. To hear the name *Leon Picard* come out of her mother's mouth brought back all that happened at Gatehaven—every hour—every evil moment.

Shannon felt weak. She'd never had a fainting spell. But she was afraid she might be about to have her first.

CHAPTER TWENTY-SIX

HER MOTHER'S FACE grew pale. "Are you all right, Shannon?"
Shannon managed a slow nod. "I will be."
She was feeling better. The weak spell was almost gone.

"I know this is not the time to ask questions, but you looked strange when I said Leon Picard's name. Did you meet him in England? Tell me, Shannon, if you did."

"Yes, I met him."

Mama's face contorted. She glared at Papa. "This was all your fault, Javier. I warned you not to let her go. But you said it was safe for any of us to go to England now. You knew the danger Shannon would be under. Yet you let her go."

"You were right, Rachel. I was wrong. I should never have let Shannon go to England. But instead of fighting, we should give thanks. The Lord provided Shannon and Miss Winters a means of escape."

Her mother sat there in her chair for a moment without saying anything. Her mouth quivered. Her eyes were moist with tears.

Shannon got up and stood at her side. "I am all right, Mama—really I am." She patted her mother's shoulder. "I had some narrow escapes, but nothing truly bad occurred."

"Things happened to me when I was your age, Shannon," her mother said. "Things that could have destroyed the good name of this family. Your father and I went to England but Leon followed us there. If a kindly earl hadn't helped us escape to Scotland, I might have been ravished, killed, or both."

"And the son of that British earl helped us escape, Mama," Shannon said. "He even gave us the use of his fancy carriage, horses, and footmen to assure our safe journey home. The nobleman's name is Lord Wilburn, and Peter and I will be eternally thankful that the Lord sent him to us."

"Oh, Shannon." Her mother's voice broke with emotion. "I never wanted that for you. Tongues will wag. They always do."

"My reputation was not destroyed, Mama. God knows I am innocent. And who but us can say what truly happened in England?"

Shannon's father crossed the room, lifting her mother in his arms. "Fear not, my love."

"But Javier, Leon Picard could have followed Shannon to Luss. We could all be in danger."

"Dear, sweet Rachel, have you forgotten? We dwell in the secret place of the Most High."

Shannon blushed as her father kissed her mother on the lips. She glanced at Cally and found her smiling.

"My father kissed my mother like that when I was a child," Cally whispered. "It warms my heart to see it again."

As the evening progressed, Shannon learned that her parents had originally intended to take a ship to the colonies as soon as Shannon returned. Now that she had, there was no reason to delay. They invited Cally to make the trip with them, but she declined. Cally chose to return to her parents and younger brothers in England.

The door opened. Peter and Kate came in—holding hands. Shannon had hoped that Ian would be with them. He wasn't. Her parents embraced Peter and told him how glad they were to see him, and they welcomed Kate into their home. At first Shannon stepped back and let her parents greet Kate and their son. But Kate was Shannon's best friend.

At last, she went over and hugged Kate as if she was already her sister. If only Ian were with them. He was ever on her mind. Shannon took Kate's hand and took her over to meet Cally.

For a while, everybody stood around talking. Then they returned to the sitting area. The women sat on chairs or benches. The two men stood with their backs to the fireplace.

Peter grinned at Kate. "Miss Colquhoun has some news she wishes to share."

Kate glanced at the floor. Her cheeks turned rosy pink. "I thought you were going to do this, Peter."

"And prevent you from the opportunity? Never."

"Please, this is your family. You do it."

"Very well then." He went over and took hold of both Kate's hands, pulling her to her feet. "Miss Colquhoun has agreed to become my wife."

He put his arm around her. "We plan to marry aboard the ship bound for the colonies."

Mrs. Aimee burst from her chair, warmly showering her love and best regards on their coming marriage. Shannon was happy for Peter and Kate. At the same time, she was sad—wishing that she and Ian were announcing their engagement as well.

Shannon held in what she wanted to say all evening.

At last, she turned to Kate and said, "Is Ian going on the ship with us? He said once that he might."

"No. My brother will be staying here in Scotland. He said it was where he belonged."

The next morning, Ian visited his pastor's office in a small room off the sanctuary.

Pastor Petit looked up. He smiled when Ian came in the door. "Mr. Colquhoun." The elderly gentleman got up from his chair and hobbled across the room. "I heard you had returned from your journey and hoped you would stop by." He offered his hand in friendship. "Please, sit down."

Ian shook his pastor's hand, settling onto the chair in front of his oak desk. How would he tell Pastor Petit that he failed in his mission to solve Magdalena's murder—how would he put that fact into words?

Ian gazed at the spotless floor. "I have much to tell you, sir."

"I am eager to hear it."

Ian swallowed something that felt like a lump lodged in his throat. "Many evil people live in and around Gatehaven. But I was unable to discover who killed your cousin, Miss Petit."

"Did you ask the Lord to help you in your quest?"

"Yes, sir, many times."

"Then you must wait on the Lord. He *will* answer—in His good time—not ours." The minister smiled as he got up from his chair. "I will fix us some tea. As we drink it, you can tell me all that occurred while you were away."

Two days later, Shannon, her parents, her baby brother, her grandmother, Peter, and Ian's sister, Kate, gathered at the edge of town, preparing to leave. Ian had kissed his sister good-bye at their home earlier that morning but hadn't bid Shannon farewell as he so wanted to do. The travelers would caravan in wooden carts to the ship that would carry them to the colonies.

Ian stood in the shadows by the ruins of an ancient fortress, watching as Shannon and her family drove away—perhaps never to return. All at

once she looked back. His heart skipped a beat. Was she looking for Ian?
Or was she hoping the earl followed her to Scotland?

At last, the carts and those inside them disappeared. All that remained
was the chill of a late summer morning and the Scottish countryside.

+ —— + —— +

Shannon's father drove one of the two carts with her mother in the seat
beside him. Peter drove the second cart filled with most of their belongings, and Kate sat beside him. Shannon sat beside Grandma Aimee in the
back of the first cart, holding the baby, and trying not to dwell on the fact
that she and Grandma were squeezed between two wooden barrels with
a third heavy barrel at their backs.

She'd reminded her father that if they hit a big bump or made a sudden
stop, Shannon and the baby could be crushed to death. But he had
explained that they had nothing to fear. Had she forgotten that they were
in the secret place of the Most High? Shannon was beginning to believe
it. The cart had already hit several bumps and made several sudden stops.
Yet nothing bad happened.

From then on, Shannon tried to keep her mouth closed. With the
wind howling all around the open cart, her thoughts drifted elsewhere.
Her parents might not have heard her anyway, and Grandma Aimee had
a serious hearing problem. She wouldn't have heard. Besides, Grandma
liked to converse in French, and Shannon was never fluent in that language.

In the late evenings, they stopped to camp for the night. Peter and
Kate held hands as they sat around the campfire—so full of hope and
excitement. Shannon could see it in their eyes every time they looked at
each other. They knew she missed Ian, but she didn't want to spoil their
joy by putting the depths of her despair into words.

One night her father turned to Kate and said, "From Plymouth, we
will sail to the colony in Charles Towne. My brother Henri and his wife
live there."

How many times had Papa said those same words since they left Luss?
When he repeated them yet again, Shannon chuckled for perhaps the first
time since Ian had stopped talking to her.

For Shannon, laughter became a sort of door that opened her heart
and mind to the conversations going on around her and the needs and
wishes of others. Despair and bitterness had filled her mind for too long.
She couldn't let that happen again.

"My family, the Colquhouns, have roots in the Carolinas, too," Kate
finally said. "But some of them have changed the spelling of the name to
Calhoun. Still, they are Scots and Colquhouns no matter how they spell
their names. I hope to meet my distant Scottish relatives when we arrive
in the colonies."

———◆———

Leon Picard arrived in Plymouth long before Shannon and her family did. A ship, the *Carolina*, was scheduled to sail for Charles Towne in a few days, but he wasn't sure the Aimee family would reach Plymouth in time. Therefore, he'd held off paying his fee until he knew they had arrived.

He'd sold his holdings in England, including The Boar and Tongue, for less than they were worth, but he still had proof that he held the controlling interest in Gatehaven—the result of the earl's gambling debts. Someday he would cash in on that debt.

On his first night in town, Leon had his driver stop in front of The Lion's Cub Inn.

"I am going inside, McGregor, for a meal and a bed for the night. When you have finished seeing to my animals, you may join me. Your supper and a room will be waiting for you."

Leon got out of the carriage, went inside and ordered a room. The inn was crowded, and Leon was unable to find a vacant table.

He was about to go up to his room when someone said, "Mate. Want to sit at *my* table?"

Leon turned to the voice he heard. "Is someone talking to me?" He felt a little dizzy and grabbed hold of the back of a chair for support.

"That would be me, mate."

A sailor motioned for Leon to sit down. He had a stocky build, a bald head and bloodshot eyes. "Sit if you will in the empty chair beside me."

Leon nodded and sat down. "Thank you, sir."

The sailor peered at Leon over a mug of ale. "Are you from France? I do not take to Frenchmen, and you sound like one to me."

Leon leaned across the small table and offered the sailor his hand. He'd sent a note to the vicar as he promised and mailed the letter telling all the earl's secrets, and he could safely tell his real name now.

"I'm Leon Picard. I was born in France. But I've lived most of my life in England. Who are you, sir?"

"I ain't no gentleman such as yourself—I can tell you that. But me name be Deaver Simpson—at your service." He took Leon's hand and shook it. "What would you be doing in Plymouth? If you are looking for a ship, I'm the one to see." He pointed to his chest with his thumb. The muscles in his forearms bulged.

"Are you familiar with passenger ships going to the colonies?"

"I am." He pushed out his chest. "The captain and me be like this." He crossed his fingers, holding them up so Leon could see them. "What would you be wanting to know?"

"I know a ship is going to Charles Towne soon. But I want to surprise my relatives. If I book passage now, they will know. My surprise will be ruined. Can you tell me how I can book passage without anybody else knowing about it?"

The sailor looked down briefly and shook his head. "I do not know, mate. Information like *that* can be expensive."

Leon handed the sailor a gold coin. "Will this cover the cost?"

"For now."

"I would also like to have special permission to stay in a cabin with the ship's officers during the voyage," Leon said. "Can you arrange it? I'm willing to pay extra for that."

"I cannot say, mate. A request like that would take at least two more gold coins—if not more."

"If you expect to get more than I have already given you, you must provide me with the information I need. Until then, you will receive nothing more from me." Leon leaned back in his chair, crossing his hands over his middle. "When can you have it for me?"

"I will see the captain at dawn, mate. I can have the information by Friday."

Leon nodded. "Meet me at one of the tables here on Friday about this same time. And do not call me mate. I am Monsieur Picard to you. Now, let us see if we can get something to eat. I am in need of food. How about you?"

"Me cup is empty. I would rather have more ale."

Two days later, Leon paid for his passage to Charles Towne without waiting to see if the Aimees had arrived, and he gave his sailor friend three gold coins for making it possible for him to stay in the officers' quarters. It wouldn't be wise to stay with the other passengers during the journey and perhaps be seen by the Aimees. He needed to leave England while he still could. If the Aimee family missed the ship, he would catch up with them once they arrived in the colonies.

Ordinarily, he would have paid the sailor less or nothing at all for help such as this. But Leon would need a loyal friend while aboard the ship. Good friends were often expensive items to purchase, and Deaver Simpson had signed on as a sailor on the *Carolina*.

⁘

Ian paid another visit to Pastor Petit's office. As he was leaving, he noticed a woman in the church graveyard. She stood in the shadows, and he was unable to recognize her. As he approached, she seemed distressed to see him. She started running down the road toward the center of town. Curious, Ian followed her.

It started to rain—a sprinkle first, then a downpour. He ran for cover and saw the woman standing on the stoop in front of the baker's shop.

She turned and stared at him, and he suddenly realized that she was none other than Miss Foster, Shannon's former chaperone.

The small overhang over the door of the bakery was keeping her partially dry. She looked at him a moment longer and dashed out into the rain again.

"Wait." Ian opened his umbrella and raced after her. "Miss Foster, please wait."

The race continued to the end of the row of shops and houses. She darted into a rundown shed and shut the door.

Ian slowly opened it. She cringed and slumped forward—crossing her arms over her chest like a kind of shield.

"Please do not be frightened, Miss Foster. I mean you no harm. Why did you run away?"

He could see that she was shaking, and she still hadn't said a word.

"You are trembling. You must be cold." He removed his jacket, putting it around her shoulders. "There." He'd tried to make his voice as gentle and non-threatening as possible. "That should warm you up in the twinkling of an eye."

A rickety old bench had been shoved in one corner of the shed with stacks of hay all around it. She was seated on the bench. He sat down beside her.

"Are you feeling better now?"

She refused to look at him.

"This bench appears to be the only sitting box in the shed. Hope it's all right, me sitting here."

She nodded, and Ian sat down. He hoped to make her feel comfortable enough to tell what was bothering her. They had never been close, but they were never enemies either. Her strange reaction to his mere presence caused him to want to learn her secret all the more.

"Are you staying in the earl's hunting lodge?"

She nodded for the third time.

Her nonverbal responses to his questions would not do. He would have to find a way to get her to talk to him.

"The rain has stopped, Miss Foster, and I have an umbrella. Will you allow me to escort you to the nearest inn before the rain comes again?"

She nodded instead of making a reply, but at least he was making progress. He led her to The Lion Heart across the street. They went inside and sat at a table. Now she would have to talk.

"Would you like a cup of tea?"

She didn't reply for a moment. "Yes. I would."

Ian smiled internally. Miss Foster actually said something. He felt as if he'd won a kind of victory. He would wait until their tea was served before speaking again.

At last, he asked, "How is the earl?"

"I promised not to talk to anyone about the earl."

Ian took a sip of tea. "Did something happen at Gatehaven after I left?"

She didn't reply.

"Please, Miss Foster, talk to me. If you do not, innocent people could die. Would you want something like that on your soul?"

She opened her mouth as if she planned to speak. Then she closed her lips again and shook her head.

"You liked Miss Aimee once. I know you did. I beg you, please tell me what you know."

She hesitated. "If I tell you what I know, will you promise never to tell that I told?"

"Of course. Have you forgotten that I am a man of the cloth—or soon will be?"

She paused for a moment as if perhaps she was making her decision. He wished he knew what she was thinking.

"Very well then." Miss Foster took a sip of tea and then another. "While the earl was in London the last time, he became engaged to a young woman from a wealthy family." She set down her cup, which rattled against the cup holder. Warm tea sloshed over the side of the cup and onto the table. She pulled a white napkin from her lap and wiped up the spill. "Before his engagement was announced publicly, her father discovered—" She trembled again. "He accused the earl, the Frenchman, and the rest of us of being—of being murderers."

Ian expected that news to come out but not so soon. He tried not to let the surprise he felt show in his face.

"He said that bodies were found in the woods," she went on, "and we were responsible. I was a member of the Spiritualist Society, but I never killed anyone. None of the ladies did. You must believe me." She sent Ian what he perceived as a pleading look.

He nodded slowly but made no reply.

"After the earl was arrested, I came here to Luss with the earl's mother and grandmother. We are staying at the hunting lodge. If you repeat what I just told you, we could be arrested, too, and we are innocent. But I cannot say what went on when the men put on robes and went up on the top floor of Gatehaven."

"Was Leon—was Etienne Gabeau arrested as well?"

"No, he got away before the authorities could catch him."

"Where did he go?"

"I cannot say for certain." Miss Foster picked up her cup and tipped it to her lips again. "But I overheard the earl tell his mother once that if the Frenchman ever left his estate in England, he would be in pursuit of a woman named Rachel. He said that as much as Monsieur Gabeau hated her, he would likely chase after her for the rest of his life."

Ian squirmed in his chair, unable to put the many thoughts forming in his head into words that would be understandable. "Who would know where he went?"

She shrugged. "Millie McGregor might know." She removed Ian's jacket and placed it in the chair next to her. "Millie helped us escape to Scotland. She said her uncle was driving Etienne Gabeau somewhere. However, she had no idea of their destination."

"Did Millie say anything else?"

"Her uncle expected to be gone for a long time. In fact, the Frenchman might never return, or her uncle either. Then her uncle asked if she'd ever heard of a place called Charles Towne."

Ian got up from the table. "Thank you, Miss Foster, you helped much."

He put his jacket back on, paid for the tea, and left, leaving Miss Foster alone at the table. He had to warn Shannon and her family of the danger they were in. He would pack a few things, mount his horse, and set out for Plymouth within the hour.

Shannon's family would be traveling in carts bearing heavy loads and pulled by strong horses known for their endurance. Also, they would need to drive slowly and make many stops along the way because of the baby. He should be able to overtake them—if he found the path they took. Otherwise, he would be waiting when they arrived in Plymouth.

But Leon Picard might be waiting, too.

CHAPTER TWENTY-SEVEN

I AN ARRIVED IN Plymouth after days of riding, camping at night and riding again. However, on especially damp and chilly nights in late summer, he stayed at inns where he ate meals that were well prepared and slept under warm blankets in fairly comfortable beds. Tired from the long journey, he planned to spend that night at an inn in town. A good meal and a warm bed were just what he needed.

He'd hoped to overtake Shannon and her family along the way, but by the time he reached the outskirts of Plymouth, he knew that was not going to happen. A brisk wind moaned all around him, but he continued on, searching for a place to stay. He'd almost given up hope when he noticed lights just ahead.

As he grew closer, he realized it was an inn with lanterns hanging from its eves. He squinted to read the name of the establishment through a heavy mist. *The Anchor*, he read.

A light rain trickled down. Shivering from the dampness and the cold, he kicked his horse with the heels of his boots until the animal's trot was replaced by a fast gallop.

At the inn, he stabled his horse in the barn out back and went inside. The odor of stew cooking filled his nostrils, making him all the hungrier. His senses came alive with all kinds of pleasing sensations—food, warmth. He pictured a bowl of meat with vegetables all around it and could almost taste it. But as soon as he sat down at one of the tables, he felt someone watching him.

Ian looked around the room but didn't see anyone or anything that aroused his suspicion. Stew and warm tea were set before him, but as he ate his meal the feeling of being watched never left him. He happened to look up. A flabby, overweight, older man opened the entry door of the inn and went out. He never saw his face, but there was something about him that reminded him of—of McGregor, Leon's driver. The man he saw could be him.

He finished eating and went above stairs to turn in for the evening. But as he climbed into bed, he couldn't dispel McGregor from his thoughts and the fact that he was watching Ian without making himself known.

It was a damp and chilly night. Leon Picard was seated at a table in front of the inn's huge fireplace. He'd visited with Deaver Simpson for almost an hour, eating and drinking with the sailor—his new employee. Now it was time for Mr. Simpson to go.

He'd given McGregor a few hours off so Leon could meet with Deaver Simpson in private. But McGregor would be arriving within the hour. It wouldn't be wise for the three of them to be seen together.

Leon leaned across the table in the hope that nobody but the sailor would hear what he planned to say. "Mr. Simpson, you better go now. My driver could return at any moment."

"I will be on me way then, mate."

Leon sent him a thunderous frown.

The sailor's laugh had a nervous edge to it. "I mean Monsieur Picard."

"Do not laugh at me, Simpson, or you will be sorry."

"Yes, sir."

"Now go."

Leon watched the sailor leave the inn. Then he continued eating.

He didn't want McGregor to know about the sailor just yet.

McGregor had worked as Leon's driver at his estate in England for years, and Leon actually liked him. But he had no wish to take McGregor with him to Charles Towne. He couldn't allow him to return to Fairs. McGregor knew too much and was an honest man at heart. It would be easy for the authorities back in Fairs to convince McGregor to testify against Leon.

Perhaps it wouldn't matter. Leon would be living in the colonies across an ocean from England and the village of Fairs, and using a different name. Still, who can say that he might not be arrested? He couldn't afford to take that chance.

Simpson agreed to take McGregor's life for a handsome fee. Leon had only to tell him when and where.

Earlier that evening, Leon had McGregor follow two carts as they rolled slowly into town. He'd kept his carriage at a distance so Rachel

and Shannon Aimee and the rest of their party wouldn't notice him. Leon
wanted to know exactly where they would be staying until they sailed for
Charles Towne, and he'd learned that the Aimees were staying at The
Ship's Crew, an inn closer to the docks than the inn where Leon now
resided.

Leon told Deaver Simpson to stay at the inn where the Aimees were
staying in order to keep a close watch on them. He also told Simpson to
wear regular clothes. He didn't want Simpson to be identified as a sailor.

The entry door opened and McGregor came inside. He smiled when he
saw Leon seated at a table alone, hurrying to join him.

"I have news for you tonight, Monsieur."

"Really?" Leon stuck his fork into a slice of beef. "And what might that
be?" He lifted the fork to his mouth and chewed slowly.

"Ian Colquhoun has arrived in Plymouth."

"What?" Leon stood on shaky legs. The white cloth he'd placed on his
lap fell to the floor.

"Colquhoun is staying at The Anchor Inn. I know. I saw him there."

Leon grabbed the back of his chair for support. "I will not allow this
Scotsman to destroy all I have worked for." He gripped the handle of his
cane. "Good night, Mr. McGregor. I am going above stairs now. I will
need time to decide what to do next."

◆—◆—◆

Shannon was tired from their long journey and eager to climb into bed.
But first she must break bread with her family in the big eating room.
Afterward, she would need to help her mother with the baby and get her
grandmother settled for the night before she could afford the luxury of
sleep.

On the morrow, they would sign on to the *Carolina*. A few days after
that, they would leave England and Scotland forever.

And she would never see Ian again.

If not for that fact, she might actually enjoy the thought of such an
adventure.

The eating room was filled with people, mostly rowdy sailors. Shannon's
chair faced the entry door, so she was able to see who went in and out.

A muscular man with a bald head came in and looked around. He
appeared to be searching for someone. All at once he fixed his gaze on
Shannon from across the room. She knew she'd never seen him previously.
He seemed overly interested in her.

"Mama." Shannon poked her mother's arm with her elbow. "That man
over there is staring at us."

Rachel Aimee followed her daughter's gaze. "The one with the bald
head?"

"Yes."

Her mother smiled. "You must get used to men looking at you, Shannon. You are a very beautiful young lady."

Still, the man was unsettling. He continued to stare at Shannon the entire time they were in the eating room. Shannon was glad when they all finished eating, and they went above stairs to their rooms. She would be sharing a room with Kate until Kate became her sister-in-law, and she looked forward to talking in whispers with her. Perhaps Kate would tell her something about Ian that Shannon never knew.

Ian was not able to discover where Shannon and her family were staying. But it really didn't matter. He would be seeing them when they boarded the ship.

On the morning they were to set out to sea, Ian got up early. He was dressed and preparing to go down to break the fast when he heard a knock at his door.

He opened the door without thinking. A muscular man with a bald head burst inside, holding some sort of weapon. It all happened so fast, Ian didn't have time to think. He saw the man lift his arm to hit Ian with something. Darkness covered him.

Ian awoke as moonlight shimmered into the damp and darkened room. Had he slept all day? And why was he on the floor? He touched his head. It hurt, and he felt a lump.

He got up and staggered to the door.

At the head of the stairs, he looked down, trying to remember what happened. The world was spinning around and around. He grabbed the railings to keep from falling and crept down the stairs on shaky legs— slow and easy like an old man would.

"What happened to you?" the innkeeper asked.

Ian shrugged. "I cannot say. But I must get to the docks right away. I am sailing to Charles Towne on the *Carolina*."

"The *Carolina*, did you say?"

"Aye."

"Well, you are too late. The *Carolina* would be out in the channel by now."

Ian didn't feel well enough to venture out, but he was thirsty. He sat down and ordered water and a small meal. The innkeeper sat at Ian's table as if he was an honored guest.

What made that big bump on your head, squire?" The innkeeper chuckled softly. "Did you walk into a door?"

"Someone came into my room and hit me."

"Hit you? Not at my inn."

"It is true. I heard a knock on my door soon after I dressed to go down to the docks. I opened the door, and a man with no hair hit me over the head with something hard—like a big stick. I slept all day after the blow. I awoke only a few minutes ago. Did you see any strangers come in the inn today?"

"Strangers come here to and fro every day. Some have bald heads. But I saw no man come in the inn carrying a weapon like the one you described. Only those staying here are allowed above the stairs. He must have sneaked in the inn and up the stairs while I was out or busy in the kitchen."

As soon as Ian finished eating and drinking, he went back to his room and then to bed. He'd missed the ship anyway. In the morning, he would go to the dock to see if he could sign onto another ship bound for Charles Towne. The *Carolina* couldn't be the only ship in the harbor.

Ian felt much better the next morning and set out for the docks on foot. A walk might do him good. The innkeeper had said that he would not have far to go, and he wanted to sign onto another ship as soon as one became available. But having arrived at night, he was unfamiliar with the city of Plymouth. He took a wrong turn.

Ian found himself on a dark and narrow street where the scent of garbage hung stronger in the air than anywhere else he'd been so far. Rotten food and clutter littered the roadway and was stacked against the outer walls of houses and shops. Rats darted in and out between the layers of stench.

He considered turning around and taking another route, but he couldn't guess which way to go. Just ahead the body of a man lay in the middle of the street. Ian felt nauseous. He would have to step over the man to get around the mess. At least the body hadn't bloated yet, meaning the death was quite recent.

Ian held his nose and kept walking. He would walk around the body as best he could, but would have to step over the man's outstretched arm. He'd planned to keep looking straight ahead. But at the last instant, he looked down. The man lay with his face to one side. Someone had whacked him on the head, too, and his eyes were still open. Could it be that he was still alive?

Ian turned him over on his back. The man moaned. All at once, Ian realized that the man was someone he knew.

"McGregor? Are you all right?"

Leon's driver moaned again.

McGregor was a big Scot. He probably weighed a great deal. It would be difficult to get him down the street to a safe place without help, and he didn't want to drag him anywhere.

"Just rest now, my friend. I am going for help. I will return as soon as I can."

McGregor didn't moan this time. Ian thought he'd gone back to sleep. But at least he was alive.

A little further on, Ian found a man with a horse and an empty cart. He paid the man to help load McGregor into the back of the cart and drive him to the inn where Ian was staying. Then the innkeeper helped them take McGregor up the stairs to Ian's room. They laid him on the bed, and the innkeeper promised to send for a physician.

The physician said that McGregor's injuries were more serious than Ian's. He must stay in bed for many days if he hoped to recover. Under the direction of the physician, Ian tended to McGregor's needs all that day.

While the big man slept, Ian wrote to McGregor's niece, Millie, and told her what happened, promising to write her again later on. That night, he slept on the floor at the foot of McGregor's bed.

The next day, while a maid at the inn stood watch by McGregor's side, Ian went to the docks. The next boat bound for Charles Towne was scheduled to leave in two weeks, and it was a cargo ship. If Ian wanted to go to Charles Towne that month, he would need to sign on as a sailor aboard the cargo ship.

For the next three days McGregor never truly came to himself. But they did manage to rouse him enough to get him to drink water and take a little soup. Ian spent time praying—for McGregor, and especially for Shannon and the Aimees. If Leon Picard hired someone to kill Ian and McGregor, what would he do to Shannon and her family? And what would McGregor say when he finally realized that his sworn enemy, a Colquhoun, was the one who helped nurse him back to health?

For some Scots, the animosity among the clans was real and deep. Unexplained hatred had gone on for generations, and apparently McGregor was one of those Scots that hated with no logical reason for it.

Yes, clan pride and ancient hatred was real. But while some people hated even members of their own families, Scottish clan members had an unconditional love and respect for members of their own clans and their spouses.

Ian's father once said, "You must never turn away from members of your own family, lad, or from members of your own clan—no matter what they do. You must love their spouses, too. Anyone who has the good sense to marry into our clan deserves to be respected and honored forever."

Ian had meditated on his father's words, and the Lord seemed to say that his father's thoughts were true. But Ian should go one step farther. Ian should love and show respect to everyone regardless of who they were or where they came from.

Still, he had no idea what to say to McGregor when the man truly came to himself and started speaking again.

Three days later, while Ian gathered dirty clothes that were scattered around the room, someone kicked him from behind. He fell forward, landing on his knees. He spun around.

"What are you doing here, Colquhoun?"

Ian smiled. "So, you are finally awake. Welcome back."

"You did not answer my question."

"I found you in the street—half dead. I brought you to this inn and have been nursing you back to health. You are in my room."

McGregor's forehead wrinkled, and he glanced around the room. "How long have I been here?"

"Four days."

"Why would you nurse me back to health? I am a McGregor."

"The second commandment tells us to love our neighbors as ourselves. You were one of my neighbors while I was staying with the Frenchman. Were you not?"

"I am a McGregor. You are a Colquhoun. Our clans have been enemies for generations. Why would you help me?"

"As I read the second commandment, it applies to both clans alike."

"You must have another reason for helping me. What is it?"

"I like to please God. And I would like to go to heaven when I die. I cannot think of better reasons. Can you?"

"I suppose I am in your debt then."

"You owe me nothing, and I am glad you are feeling better. Do you know who might have hit you on the head?"

"At first, I thought you were the one, Mr. Colquhoun. But the man had a bald head."

"A bald-headed man attacked me as well. Do you know who he might be?"

McGregor shrugged. "I never saw him in my life until he came at me. I was sitting in the Frenchman's carriage waiting to take him to the docks. I thought the bald-headed man came over to ask for directions. I didn't see the big stick until it was too late."

"I found you on a dirty street—not in a carriage. Do you know how you got there?"

"No, I do not."

"You can disagree with me if you wish." Ian went over and straightened the covers on McGregor's bed. "But I think Leon Picard hired someone to kill us both. Sure and it could be that the bald-headed man didn't want to actually kill us but merely wound us instead."

"Who is Leon Picard?" McGregor asked.

"You know him as Etienne Gabeau. They are one and the same man."

McGregor shook his head. "You are wrong, Colquhoun. The Frenchman would never harm me. I worked for him for years."

"I disagree. And when you are feeling better, I will tell you why I feel as I do."

✦——✦——✦

Leon stood on the *Carolina's* main deck behind several tall sailors as the ship's captain joined Peter Aimee and Kate Colquhoun in holy matrimony. The sails popped and fluttered in a chilling early September breeze. The air tasted like salt. On tiptoes, Leon thought the bride looked lovely in a long white dress and a veil that covered her long hair. But he hadn't come to the ceremony to witness a marriage. He came to see Shannon's mother, Rachel Aimee. Clearly, she was out of his line of vision, so far.

Leon squeezed between two sailors. "Out of my way."

One of the sailors grabbed Leon around the neck and held him with muscled arms. "Who do you think you are, a king or something?"

Leon could scarcely breathe. He felt everyone looking at him—everyone but the bride and groom. They were gazing at each other.

"Let him go," someone whispered.

So, Leon thought. *The bald-headed sailor came to my rescue.*

"The man is well dressed, mates." The sailor's voice had a ring of authority. "If he is someone important, we could all get a beating."

The tall man with the muscled arms released him. Leon rubbed his neck as he hurried back to the officers' quarters where he was staying. He'd hoped to capture Rachel or her daughter unaware during the long voyage—perhaps steal a kiss, or more. Now he would stay in his quarters as much as possible during the remainder of the trip to Charles Towne. The less time he spent on deck, the less chance someone would have to identify him.

He would capture Rachel in Charles Towne, and when she least expected it.

CHAPTER TWENTY-EIGHT

✦

I AN HIRED ON as a sailor on a cargo ship headed for Charles Towne. However, before he signed the contract, he made it clear that he was only taking the one run. As soon as they docked in Charles Towne, he would be out of the ship's navy and a private citizen again.

His fellow sailors seemed surprised that the captain would accept such an arrangement. But the captain had explained that with several men out with a strange fever, he would hire any man who fit into a uniform.

Ian and the other crewmembers boarded a cargo vessel called *The Quest*. The ship was destined to bear them from Plymouth to Charles Towne and the shores of the Carolinas. They set out in the first good wind, delaying their departure for several days, and finally left port on a breeze favorable enough to carry them out of the channel. However, while still in the channel, Ian thought all was lost. An unexpected storm stranded them on the rocks for three more days, and waves rose on the deck. All their clothes and bedding were soaked, and Ian feared he might be swept over the side of the ship at any moment.

But under the care of God, another fair wind provided them with a second chance. They were able to sail out of the channel and into the open sea.

The journey was uneventful after that.

Nevertheless, life aboard ship meant little food, cold and sometimes wet days working on deck and sleepless nights in the belly of the ship with smelly men who snored constantly. Ian worked every bit as hard as the other men; however, their years on the high seas made it possible for them to produce more work than Ian and in the same amount of time.

Ian was glad when someone saw land, and they entered the waters that edged Charles Towne. But Shannon and her family had arrived almost a month before Ian did. If Leon Picard managed to board the same ship that the Aimee family had, it might already be too late to save them.

At last, they arrived in Charles Towne. Ian could hardly wait to have a decent meal and change into regular clothes. But the first thing he actually did after stepping off the boat was find a place to stay. After that, he planned to search for Shannon's uncle, Henri Aimee. Ian felt sure that Shannon and her family would be staying with him.

At the inn where he would be staying, Ian asked the innkeeper if he knew a Henri Aimee. He did not. However, he directed Ian to the French Protestant Church nearby.

"Somebody there is likely to know him."

Ian left the inn and turned left as the innkeeper suggested.

Head down, Ian trudged into the wind. He looked to his right and to his left. Then he opened the door of the church and went inside.

At first, he thought the sanctuary was empty. As he moved forward, he saw a man bent over as if picking up something from the floor. He assumed the man was the pastor.

Ian cleared his throat.

The man turned and smiled. "Hello." He held up a coin so Ian could see. "I was picking up a coin I dropped." He moved toward Ian. "Forgive me for not introducing myself sooner." He stretched out his hand in friendship. "My name is Jeremiah D'Span—the pastor here."

"Hello, pastor." Ian relaxed. The man was a friendly person. "My name is Ian Colquhoun." He shook the pastor's hand.

"How can I help you this afternoon, Mr. Colquhoun."

"Right now, I am looking for a place to hide."

Pastor D'Span stared at Ian for a moment and then laughed. "My word."

"I was joking, sir. Actually I'm looking for someone."

The pastor focused his squinty eyes on Ian. "And who might that be?"

"Henri Aimee and his young wife. Do you know them?"

"Maybe." The pastor motioned for Ian to come forward. "Follow me." He pointed to a door on the back wall behind the podium. "My office is right through that door."

Ian fell in behind the minister and went into the pastor's office. Pastor D'Span shut the door.

"Now, sit down, young man, and tell me why you're looking for Henri Aimee. Do you owe him money, or is it the other way around?"

"Neither. We came from the same village in Scotland. I saw the sign out front stating that this was a French Protestant Church. I thought they might be members here." Ian forced a smile in the hope that it would conceal his internal concerns for Shannon and her family.

"I have been a pastor long enough to know trouble when I see it. So what is troubling you, young man? I truly want to help."

Ian released a deep breath. "Almost a month ago, a ship carrying Henri Aimee's brother and his family arrived in Charles Towne. The Aimee family would be staying with Henri until they found a place of their own, and I am concerned for their safety. According to what I have heard, a Frenchman by the name of Leon Picard intends to kill every single one of them. I am especially worried about a young woman with long auburn hair by the name of Shannon Aimee. Do you know of these people and if they are safe."

The pastor shrugged. "In all honesty, I do not. Henri Aimee and his wife are regular members of this church, but about a month ago they stopped coming as frequently. I had planned to pay a visit to their home this very week. Perhaps they are afraid to go out if this Mr. Picard is determined to kill them."

Ian tensed. *Or has already killed them.*

Pastor D'Span put his hands on the desk. "If you are looking for a place to hide so the Frenchman won't find you, I can suggest a place. Many Huguenots and others pay a visit to Bonneau Ferry Plantation soon after they arrive here. It is an estate not far from Charles Towne and owned by Huguenots. You might be able to find shelter there. But I am fairly new to Charles Towne. I have only a general knowledge of the location of Henri Aimee's home. Still, I have no reason to think you will not be able to find it easy enough. "

The pastor studied Ian for a moment without saying anything. "I believe you said your name was Colquhoun."

"Yes."

"The name reminds me of the name Calhoun. We have several Calhouns in our congregation here."

"That is not surprising. As I understand it, some Colquhouns living in the colonies changed the spelling of the name to Calhoun."

"We no longer call ourselves colonists, Mr. Colquhoun. We are a country now. And the Calhouns living here might well be related to you. If true, I have some bad news to report." The edges of the pastor's mouth turned down. "You might not have heard, but some members of the Calhoun family were killed some years ago in a massacre."

"A massacre? How horrible. What kind of massacre?"

"A Cherokee Indian massacre. I was told it was bad, but I have no details. It happened here in the Carolinas in a place called Long Cane. A member of our congregation said that his grandfather told him about it when he was a child."

Ian didn't say more, and for a moment, neither did the pastor.

"I only have a general idea of the location of Henri Aimee's farm," the pastor added. "But I will be glad to draw you a map. It won't be perfect, but it might help you get started in the right direction."

The pastor took pen and ink and drew a rather rough sketch of the entire area. As he said, it wasn't perfect. But it would have to do.

◆———◆

Leon Picard had planned to have his bald-headed sailor friend do harm to the Aimee family on the day they arrived in Charles Towne. The sailor was only scheduled to be in port a few days and then he planned to set out to sea once again. But Leon's plans had not worked out as he had hoped.

Leon became ill with a fever while still on the ship. As soon as they docked, he was taken to the home of a local physician and told to stay there for at least a week. During that week, pains in Leon's chest became more severe. He was required to stay even longer.

He never heard from the sailor while living in the physician's home and was not able to find him since then. For all Leon knew, Simpson might have sailed away weeks ago.

Now that Leon was finally released and living at a local inn in Charles Towne, he was feeling a little better but not as well as he pretended.

The inn was located near the ocean. At sunset, Leon walked down to the beach to see if the waves were as spectacular as the innkeeper said they were. All at once he heard two young men speaking French. It pleased him to hear his native tongue spoken so freely in the colonies and stopped to listen.

"What kind of a Huguenot are you?" the first man asked.

"A good one, I hope."

"Maybe yes. Maybe no. But remember, the Lord is watching. And you haven't attended services at our church in a long time."

The muscles in Leon's throat contracted. He hadn't expected the two young men to be French Protestants, and he still hated Huguenots as much as ever. But for his own purposes, he would pretend to be one of them.

"I could not help but notice that you are speaking French," Leon said in that language and moved toward them. "I am a stranger here and seeking directions to the home of a friend, Henri Aimee. Perhaps you know him."

"I know him," the first man said. "He and his wife go to our church."

"Then would you be so good as to direct me to his home, please? I am eager to see him."

Leon listened to the young man's direction. When he finished, Leon had hoped to ask them to help him back to the inn. He wasn't feeling as well as he had when he left. But when he turned to make that request, he saw them walking away.

"Come back! I need your help."

They kept walking.

CHAPTER TWENTY-NINE

T HE WIND AND the sound of waves lapping against the shore
seemed unusually loud. Perhaps the two young men hadn't heard
his call for help.

Leon could come to only one conclusion. If he hoped to return to the
inn before morning when others would see his distress, he would have to
make it back alone.

Alone.

Leon had always been there. What a comfort it would be to have
someone to lean on—especially now when he was ailing.

Long ago, after he fell in the well, Rachel had looked down at him,
promising to help. But she lied. Instead of throwing him a rope, she told
him about Jesus—of all things.

Leon dug his cane into the sand and took one step. His leg hurt. His
chest hurt even more. He took another step.

Who needs Jesus? Who needs anyone? *I can make it to the inn on my
own.*

Leon rubbed his left arm, hoping that the aching would go away. He
took a deep breath and then another step. If he hoped to hire a carriage
that would take him to Henri's farm, he must somehow make it back to
the inn. He couldn't give up his quest now when he was so close.

A large log stood in his path—a piece of driftwood, no doubt. Should
he go around it? But that would require needless extra steps. He stepped
over it. But he didn't step high enough. He stumbled and fell on the wet
ground.

As he lay there, listening to the sound of the sea and feeling a salty breeze on his face, he heard Rachel's words again in the valley of his mind.

"I will pray for you," she'd said.

"No," Leon had shouted back. "Don't pray for me. Save me!"

"Your salvation is exactly what I'm hoping for."

Salvation. What nonsense.

Perhaps if he lay there until he was feeling better, his health would improve. Waves lapped against the shore, and he heard the chirping sounds of strange birds overhead.

There was really no rush. The Aimees probably planned to stay with Henri Aimee for at least another month—perhaps longer. He had plenty of time to do what he planned to do. But his weakened and sickly body told him otherwise. Perhaps it was now or never.

Leon strained with all his might, forcing crippled muscles to work and forcing Rachel's words about Jesus to vanish from his mind. He grabbed the log he'd tripped on with one hand and his cane with the other, inching his torso up on the log. The bark's sharp edges bruised his side. Yet he kept on—dragging his body up and over until the seat of his pants brushed the end of the log. He pushed again and again until his entire body lay on the log.

If he sat up straight, he would be sitting on it. But if he failed, he could fall back on the wet ground, and he wasn't sure he had the strength to try again.

Should he pray? Rachel and perhaps Shannon would say that he should.

"Prayer is a sign of weakness," his father once said.

He put his cane directly in front of him and put both hands upon it—one hand over the other. With all of his weight pressing against the wooden cane, it sank deep into the sand. He spread his legs and forced his body forward. His wobbly legs could barely carry the weight, inching further apart. If he didn't get up at once, his legs would give away. He would fall back on the ground or over the log—perhaps with two broken legs to add to his misery.

He leaned forward, shifting the weight from his hands to his legs. Suddenly he was standing, but his legs were spreading apart even more. He forced them to come together and it worked. He released another deep breath. Now all he had to do was walk back to the inn as if he was a well man instead of a crippled one.

Depend on your own strength.

Was that not what the Spiritualist Society had always said?

He took a step forward and then another. He wasn't strolling back to the inn at a brisk pace as a young man might. But he was getting there, and that was all that really mattered.

A carriage was parked in front of the inn. Its driver sat on top of it. Leon hobbled to the carriage and looked up at the driver.

"I am in need of a carriage and someone to drive it. May I rent your carriage for the rest of the night and into the morrow?"

"Yes, sir. For the right price, my carriage is yours for as long as you have need of it."

——◆——

Shannon only pretended to listen as her family gathered in the sitting room, discussing old times back in Scotland. She'd heard all the stories a hundred times or more, and if she heard someone mention Ian's name one more time, she knew she would burst out crying.

When nobody was watching, Shannon crept to the entry door and went out. Fresh country air mixed with sea breezes would surely cure her weepy mood.

Yet her thoughts of Ian continued as she moved toward the beach.

Ian was a man of God, and she'd once rejected him and his kind of life in favor of money, excitement, and a lavish lifestyle. She'd considered marriage to someone like Ian out of the question—unless she was willing to settle for a rather boring existence as a preacher's wife.

Her mother had settled and was gloriously happy, and though her father was a man of little means, she adored him. However, after the Earl of Northon came into her life, settling for what she once called *second best* was not an option—at least for Shannon.

Why had she ever thought the earl loved her? Why had she ever thought she loved him?

Ian was always the only man she could truly trust and depend on. Why had it taken her so long to realize that those qualities were a part of true love? What she would give to go back to the day Ian warned her that the earl was dangerous.

Shannon shook her head. She mustn't look back. Her father told her to go forward, and she would.

Where was the silly girl who dreamed of marrying a prince who lived in a mansion? She felt as if she'd aged twenty years since she stepped in that carriage bound for Gatehaven in the north of England. Despite everything that happened, she'd grown as a person—or maybe it was because of it. Deep inside she wondered. Had she gone through all that happened in England in order to become a better woman?

She smiled. That sounded like something Peter would say.

Peter. How good to have Peter as a friend now as well as a brother.

But Papa.

Guilt threatened to strangle her. She was reared by good Christian parents. They had loved her and always had her best interest at heart. Yet she had criticized them behind their backs. She'd called Papa a bore, and she hadn't liked to hear him call her Rachel Shannon instead of merely Shannon. But Rachel Shannon Aimee was her Christian name. The family Bible had confirmed that fact.

And Mama. She'd had unkind thoughts about her, too, insisting that Mama was an overprotective mother. But all the while, Mama was merely looking out for Shannon's welfare. They would be her friends now as well as her parents, and Papa could call her Rachel Shannon whenever he wanted.

Now that she was a true believer, she would make Ian a proper wife—a proper preacher's wife. But it was too late. Yet she now had the strength to move on.

Shannon considered every member of her family a friend now. What was most amazing was that God was becoming her best friend.

She stood at the edge of the water, looking out at waves she could hear better than she could see in the dim light of late evening. She glanced back toward the house.

The sea was an endless place, and Ian was on the other side of it. Tears that had been welling in her eyes rolled down both cheeks. She would never see him again.

— ◆ —

Ian stood in the shadows, watching Shannon. The wind flattened her dress against her body, making her slender form almost visible by moonlight. Should he go up and speak to her—let his presence be known? It could break the spell. She could turn him away.

He scarcely hoped she might change her mind and love him. His jaw firmed. Shannon loved the earl. He sent up a quick prayer all the same.

"Shannon, it's me, Ian."

Shannon turned. "Ian?" She gazed at him for a long moment, squinting as if she couldn't quite believe her eyes. "Is it really you?"

"Aye. May I come and join you?"

Slowly, the expression of doubt and sheer astonishment so clear in her face melted into a smile filled with promise and tender warmth. "Yes. Oh, yes. Please, come." She stretched out her arms to him as if she was welcoming home a dear relative.

He hurried to her side and took her in his arms. It didn't matter that she could never love him as he loved her. He never wanted to let her go.

"Oh, Ian, I wanted it to be you. I prayed that you would come, and now you are here."

He couldn't believe his ears. Could it be that she changed her mind— that she loved him?

She wrapped her arms around him and lifted her head as if she expected him to kiss her. "I love you, Ian. I always have. It just took me a while to realize it."

"Oh, lass. You cannot know how long I have waited to hear you say those words."

"Does this mean that despite everything, you love me, too?"

"Yes my love, I love you now. And I will love you for the rest of my life."

Ian had never kissed her once in all the years he'd known her, but oh, how he wanted to. He lowered his head.

There were first times for all things—even kissing the one you love. And this was their time, at last.

◆——◆——◆

Leon's carriage driver knew exactly where Henri lived. He'd been to his farm several times, delivering guests to and from a Bible class Henri held in his home. The driver was even invited inside once and attended one of the classes.

As the driver described the interior of the farmhouse, Leon touched the pistol he'd hidden under his coat. Before they saw lights coming from the farmhouse, Leon had a good mental picture of the layout of the two-story home and just how he would break inside.

"Stop here," Leon instructed. "Today is Henri's birthday. I wouldn't want to spoil my surprise by having you pull to a stop in front of the house. Just park over behind that barn until I return."

The driver did as he was told. Leon limped toward the house. He climbed in a back window and crept up the stairs. The driver had told him that Henri's bedroom was on the first floor. He assumed that his guests would be living above stairs.

At the head of the stairs he saw three doors. He had no idea which one to go in first. One room probably held Rachel, her husband, and perhaps the baby. The second would be Shannon's room, and if the grandmother was with them, she was probably sharing a room with Shannon. Peter and his new wife would be in the third room.

If all Leon wanted to do was kill people, he would go in the first room he saw and start shooting. But he wanted Rachel and Shannon. So he hesitated to open any of the doors. A squeaky latch would ruin everything.

He felt something furry rub against his leg. Leon gasped. In the light coming from a lamp near a window, he saw a cat push against one of the doors and go in. The door didn't squeak and wasn't locked. He followed the cat inside.

CHAPTER THIRTY

THE LIGHT IN the room was poor. Two people slept in a large bed. Leon looked around as best he could to see if he could find a crib or another person. He didn't see anyone. This must be Peter's room—Peter and his wife.

It would be easy to kill Peter while he slept. But that was only part of his plan. He tiptoed out into the hall again. Then he sat down in a dark corner to think.

Leon sucked in his breath as one of the other doors opened. A woman went out and headed for the stairway. He got up and moved forward slowly. Perhaps she planned to go out back to relieve herself. He would grab her before she reached the stairs.

He crept up behind her and slapped a hand over her mouth. With his other hand, he put the pistol to her head.

"Do not make a sound or I will kill you. Understand?"

She nodded.

"Now, we are going down those stairs. Be quiet, if you want to live."

Was she Rachel or Shannon or Peter's wife? He still didn't know.

At the bottom of the stairs, he heard footsteps on the wooden porch outside.

"Someone is coming! Do not even breathe."

His hand was still over the woman's mouth as Leon pulled her into a dark sitting room that his driver described as just off the entry. He heard the door open. Then he heard a man and woman talking in whispers.

He noticed a cord that was used to tie back one of the curtains. He wanted to rip it loose from the window and tie her hands with it. But with one hand over her mouth and the other holding the gun, he didn't have that option.

"I hate to wake my parents at this hour, Ian," the woman said.

"You must, lass. Leon Picard could be here at any moment."

That was Shannon's voice I heard. So maybe he had Rachel at last. Leon stepped out in the open with the pistol at her head.

"Mama!" Shannon shouted.

Leon glared at Ian and Shannon. "Do not go above stairs, Shannon, if you want to see your mother take another breath. You either, Mr. Colquhoun."

Shannon turned and faced Leon, standing tall and as straight as an arrow.

"You would never kill my mother, Monsieur, not until you had your way with her. And I do not think you have—yet."

Leon's lips trembled. He loosened his grip on the gun. Ian kicked it out of his hand. The pistol fell on the floor near the door.

Ian and Leon scrambled for it. A fight ensued. The two men rolled around on the floor, punching each other. Leon heard sounds—bedroom doors opening above stairs.

In that instant, Ian grabbed the gun, pointing it at Leon.

"What is all that noise I hear down there?" Javier Aimee, Shannon's father, stood at the top of the stairs. "Rachel, are you all right?"

"I am fine," she said barely above a whisper.

"Go upstairs to bed, Rachel" Javier hurried down the stairs. "It's not safe down there."

"I will not," Rachel declared, still standing alone by the door.

Henri, in a robe and cap and followed by his wife, rushed out of the downstairs bedroom. "What is all this about?"

Ian glanced at Henri. Leon knocked the gun out of his hand. The gun tumbled to the floor.

Shannon grabbed the pistol and pointed it at Leon. "Your quest has ended, Leon Picard. You lost."

Ian and Rachel stood beside Shannon. Leon lay on the floor.

"Did you kill Magdalena Petit?" Ian demanded. "I *have* to know."

Leon hesitated. "Yes, I killed her."

Rachel glared down at him. "Why? What did Magdalena ever do to you?"

"She was a Huguenot. I hate Jews and Huguenots. But that was not my real reason." Leon covered a cough with his hand.

"What was it then?" Rachel crouched on the floor and leaned over Leon

Picard. "Why did you kill an innocent woman? Why did you kill all those people? Why?"

"I was searching for you, Rachel. I wanted you. I always have. And you said—" He seemed to be having a hard time breathing. "You once told me that your name was Magdalena Petit. I had to know if you were living under that name."

"You killed someone because of a name? The name Magdalena Petit came from a book I read once," Rachel said. "I lied when I said my name was Magdalena. I never knew a real person that went by that name."

Leon gasped for air. "When I finally found her, I discovered that she was not you. So I—so I killed her." Leon grabbed his chest. "She was the first woman I ever—I ever killed."

Leon's face contorted. "Pills! I must have my pills." He clutched the front of his shirt. "They are—"

Crouched on the floor, Rachel leaned over Leon. "Where are your pills, Leon?"

He sent her a weak smile. "You called me Leon. Nobody has—" He grimaced. "Nobody has called me by that name in a very long time."

"Yes, yes." Rachel looked around. "But where are your pills?"

"In the—in the pocket inside my—my jacket."

Shannon knelt on the other side of Leon Picard while her mother found the sack of pills. "Are these what you are looking for?"

"Yes." Leon tensed as if the pain was unbearable. "Put one in my—my mouth."

Rachel reached in and got one of the pills.

"Do not give it to him, Rachel," Henri shouted. "Let him die."

"I cannot let someone die when I have the power to help him live. The authorities will take care of him. Open your mouth."

He did. She dropped in a pill.

"You will go to hell, unless you repent." Shannon said. "Do you repent, Mr. Picard?"

He looked at her for a long moment. His eyes slowly closed.

Rachel put her hand on his chest. "We have done all we could. Leon Picard has stopped breathing. I think he is dead."

Shannon looked at her mother. "Do you think he repented?"

Her mother shrugged. "Only God knows."

There was a knock at the door. Before anyone could open it, the door opened and a man stepped inside.

"Forgive me for intruding," the man said, "but I drove a Frenchman here some time ago, and I heard shouting. Can I be of help?"

"You are the carriage driver from town, are you not?" Henri said.

"I am."

"Then you can help us get the Frenchman into town. He had pains in his chest, and now he is dead."

"I have known the Frenchman for over twenty years," Shannon's father said. "I will ride into town with his body."

Ian and the other men loaded Leon's body onto the carriage. Then Ian went and stood with the women. When the lights from the carriage were no longer visible, he put one arm around Shannon and the other around her mother.

"This might not be the best time to mention this, Mrs. Aimee, but Shannon and I want to get married. I will ask for her hand as soon as her father returns."

"Well it is about time," her mother said. "Welcome to the family, Ian. And how do you like the colonies so far?"

He reached over and kissed the top of Shannon's head. "If you are asking whether I like this new country so far, the answer is yes. I think I am going to like it here—very well."

Shannon was sure that the day Ian asked her to marry him was the best day of her life. Obviously, marriage to the man she loved brought joy now and would in the future. But there was another reason why this day would be forever special.

She'd been in and around the church and Christians all her life, but when she saw her mother reach out in love to the one man who had hurt her the most, Shannon knew at last that God's Word was truth. They really were living under the shadow of the Almighty.

EPILOGUE

Five years later

Early on a summer morning, Shannon and Ian took their two children and Peter and Kate's two on a picnic at a beach near Charles Towne. Ian took out his boat to do a little fishing, and Shannon minded the four children. She'd put their infant son, Pete, on a quilt spread on the ground while the older children waded in the water nearby.

All at once a toddler with big brown eyes and dark, curly hair walked right up to the quilt and stood there, staring at the baby. No adults were in sight as far as Shannon could tell.

"Baby." The little boy smiled, pointing to Pete on the blanket.

"Yes, he is a very tiny baby, is he not?" Shannon looked around for the child's parents, but was unable to see them. "Do not stand too close," she warned, "or you might wake him up."

A dark-haired young man with an olive complexion and a young woman with gold-colored hair raced out from behind a small shed. They appeared to be searching for someone. Shannon thought they looked frantic.

"Lee," they shouted against a soft breeze. "Come back here."

Shannon motioned toward the toddler. "Is this who you are looking for?"

"Yes!" the woman called back.

The mother and father hurried forward.

The woman scooped up the little boy in her arms and held him close.

"Thank you. We thought Lee was standing right beside us. But then I looked back, and he was gone."

"I know what you mean." Shannon motioned to their daughter, Rachel, wading in the water, and to Peter's twin boys. "Not long before you came, I could not find Pierre, one of my brother's twins. He was hiding in that very shed." Shannon shrugged. "Forgive me for not introducing myself sooner. I am Mrs. Colquhoun. My husband, Mr. Ian Colquhoun, is off in his boat, fishing. But I expect him to return very soon."

Shannon offered the woman her hand, and she shook it.

"I am Mrs. Picard," the woman said, "and this is my husband, Mr. Picard."

Stunned, Shannon froze for a moment. "Did you say Picard?"

"Yes, my husband is Mr. *Leon* Picard. Our son, Lee, is named for him."

It must be a coincidence. The Leon Picard Shannon knew couldn't be related to these fine people.

"You seemed surprised by our name," Mrs. Picard said. "It's French. Do you know someone by that name?"

Shannon didn't want to reply. "I spent some time in England a few years ago, and I met a man there named Leon Picard. But he was much older than either of you."

"This truly is ironic," Mr. Picard said. "I was born in Paris, France, but my father went to England before I was born. We lost track of him after that and assumed he died there. Then only a few weeks ago, I met a woman from England—a Mrs. Woodhouse—and she said her son, Stephen Woodhouse, was also related to my father.

"When I was two," he went on, "my mother and I moved to the colonies and lived in Charles Towne for a short while. Then we moved north. My mother is dead now, but I moved my wife and child back to Charles Towne a few weeks ago." He smiled. "We noticed you and your husband at church last Sunday morning."

"You attend the French Protestant church?"

"Yes. You see, we are Huguenots."

Puzzled and in deep thought, Shannon shook her head. The Leon Picard who stood before her looked a great deal like a younger version of the man who had done her such harm. Could it be that *this* Leon Picard and little Lee were the son and grandson of the man who had haunted her family until the day he died?

After they married, Ian finally told Shannon about Lela and Stephen Woodhouse and that he thought Stephen was Leon's out-of-wedlock son. Had Lela and Stephen arrived in the colonies as well? It seemed impossible, and yet…

Shannon never saw anything but evil in the eyes of the older Leon

Picard, but the younger man's eyes were clear. When *this* Leon Picard looked at his wife and child, Shannon saw nothing but love and tenderness. She knew there was good in him no matter who his father might have been.

She thought of the portrait of her mother that Ian found at the inn where Leon was staying when he died. Peter had commissioned an artist to paint duplicates so Peter and Shannon as well as their mother would have copies of the painting.

But if this man was truly the Frenchman's son, he and Stephen were the rightful owners of the original portrait as well as the money and other personal items they found in Leon's room at the inn. In a way, Shannon hated to part with the original since it was a painting of her mother. Yet she knew she would never want to hang it on a wall or even look at it because it brought back too many unpleasant memories. If Mama agreed, Shannon would give the original portrait to Stephen or to Mr. Picard as soon as their identities were confirmed.

Shannon was writing a journal to pass on to her descendants, detailing all that happened to her at Gatehaven as well as what went on before and afterward. Perhaps she would also tell Leon Picard's son part of the story that went with the painting—but certainly not all. It would be cruel to tell him all that she knew about his father.

Shannon glanced out at the sea. Ian was rowing his boat toward the shore. She would see his smiling face in a matter of minutes. "That is my husband you see coming." She looked back at the man and his wife.

Leon Picard smiled. "My wife and I are eager to meet him."

She'd already shaken the woman's hand, but at first, she was reluctant to shake the man's. At last, she offered him her hand in friendship, and he shook Shannon's hand.

"I know that God has put us together," Shannon said with a kind of glory. "My husband is the assistant pastor at the French church under Pastor D'Span. And I know the four of us will become great friends as well as brothers and sisters in the Lord."

They had come full circle. And the scripture verse that says, "Love your enemies," had never seemed more relevant.

God is good.

ABOUT THE AUTHOR

MOLLY NOBLE BULL, Christian novelist, is a native Texan and a graduate of Texas A&M University at Kingsville, Texas. She grew up on a sixty-thousand-acre cattle ranch, and married Charlie Bull, her college sweetheart. Charlie encouraged Molly to write about faraway places, and she did just that.

Her first two novels, *For Always* and *The Rogue's Daughter*, were published by Zondervan, and later reprinted as Promise Romances from Guideposts. She also sold novels to Love Inspired and Tsaba House. Her novel *Sanctuary* won the 2008 Gayle Wilson Award of Excellence in the inspirational category, and tied for first place in the 2008 Winter Rose contest, also in the inspirational category.

Molly struggled with dyslexia as a child, and still struggles. But with God's help, she continues to be a victorious overcomer in Christ. She and four other Christian authors with learning disabilities collaborated in writing *The Overcomers: Christian Authors Who Conquered Learning Disabilities*, a nonfiction work published by Westbow Press.

Molly has always been interested in genealogy, and when she learned that one branch of her family came from Luss, Scotland, and another branch included French Huguenots, she felt compelled to write about her ancestors. Thus, her latest novel, *Gatehaven*, was born. *Gatehaven* won the 2013 Creation House Fiction Writing Contest and is scheduled to release in 2014.

Molly and Charlie have three grown sons and six grandchildren, and reside in Kingsville, Texas.

CONTACT THE AUTHOR

To learn more about Molly and her books, please visit her website at www.mollynoblebull.com.